# Warwickshire County Council

This item is to be returned or renewed before the latest date above. It may be borrowed for a further period if not in demand. **To renew your books:**

- **Phone the 24/7 Renewal Line 01926 499273 or**
- **Visit www.warwickshire.gov.uk/libraries**

**Discover ● Imagine● Learn ● *with libraries***

**Warwickshire**
County Council

Working for
Warwickshire

# FINDING HOME

Also by Roisin McAuley

*Meeting Point*
*Singing Bird*

# FINDING HOME

## Roisin McAuley

sphere

SPHERE

First published in Great Britain in 2009 by Sphere

Copyright © Roisin McAuley 2009

The moral right of the author has been asserted.

A CIP catalogue record for this book
is available from the British Library.

Extract from 'I'm Gonna Sit Right Down And Write Myself A Letter'
(Music by Fred E Ahlert, Words by Joseph Young)
Reproduced by kind permission of Moncur Street Music Ltd,
Hornall Brothers Music Ltd & Memory Lane Music Ltd.
International Copyright Secured
All Rights Reserved

Extract from 'Ballad to Traditional Refrain' reproduced by
kind permission of the author, Maurice Craig

'Delay' by Elizabeth Jennings from *Poems* (Fantasy Press, 1953) reproduced by
kind permission of David Higham Associates

'Christmas in Envelopes' by U.A. Fanthorpe, taken from *Christmas Poems* by
U.A. Fanthorpe (Peterloo and Enitharmon, 2002)

HB ISBN 978-1-84744-038-9
C ISBN 978-1-84744-037-2

Typeset in Bembo by Palimpsest Book Production Limited,
Grangemouth, Stirlingshire
Printed and bound in Great Britain by Clays Ltd, St Ives plc

Papers used by Sphere are natural, renewable and recyclable
products made from wood grown in sustainable forests and certified
in accordance with the rules of the Forest Stewardship Council.

*For Richard*

# Acknowledgements

My thanks to Joanna Beresford at 2DTV and Robert Cooper and Kate Triggs of Great Meadow Productions for sharing their knowledge of the film industry; and to my good friend Pamela Watts for her support and encouragement throughout the writing of this book.

# 1

# Louise

Winter reveals.

That late November afternoon, through the bare trees and hedges that line the lanes of Oxfordshire, I saw – flickering past me like frames from a silent film, muted grey and brown – houses, barns, bleached fields, a wood, a steep roof and tall, crooked chimneys straining to the sky.

'Stop,' I said. 'Go back a bit. I thought I saw something.'

Rebecca reversed the car and parked in a gateway.

The wood had been cleared of undergrowth. It looked as though it had been swept. Naked trees rose unsteadily from a carpet of copper leaves. The sun cast an amber glow on their trunks and branches. What had flashed past me like a film was now a single frame, a sepia photograph.

'Is this what they call a spinney?' The word felt foreign in my mouth. I had come across it in books. Had never heard it used in Ireland.

'Don't ask me,' Rebecca said. 'I'm a townie. As in Shepherd's Bush. No shepherds, no sheep, no bushes, no trees. I haven't the faintest idea what a spinney is.'

'There are trees on Shepherd's Bush Green,' I said.

'You're too literal, Louise.'

'I'm just keen on detail.'

We got out of the car and walked back down the road until

we saw again, through the trees, the roof and decorated chimneys of what was surely an Elizabethan manor.

Rebecca stared at the timber and brick gable end, the narrow, mullioned window, just visible at the far side of the wood, beyond the brown furrows of a ploughed field, about a quarter of a mile from us.

'Well spotted, Louise.' She looked around. 'It's in a valley. There must be a way down to it.'

We had taken a side road to see more of the countryside on our way back to London, having spent a disappointing two days hunting for a sixteenth-century house in which to shoot the most ambitious film of Rebecca's career. 'This is my breakthrough,' she had announced when she hired me. 'The chance I've been waiting for. This production could put me in the premier league. You too, Louise.'

By that time, most of the production money had been secured. The big names that reassured the backers were negotiating their contracts. A production designer was working on the sets.

There wasn't a final screenplay. One of the backers, an American distribution company, had reservations about the third draft of the script. This wasn't unusual. Rebecca wasn't bothered. She was more worried about finding a location.

She had intended to use a Tudor house in Cheshire. In the time it had taken to get agreement from the film council to finance the first draft of the script, the actress who was to play the lead, and whose name had persuaded the other backers to put up the rest of the money, became pregnant and had twins. They were now ten months old. The actress wanted her contract to guarantee that she could get home to London every day after filming. Rebecca had to find a location within easy travelling distance, or provide a plane. A trawl of several location companies had thrown up nothing suitable. The actress had suggested a couple of houses in the Chilterns. I had gone with Rebecca to see them. One had no space for parking. The other was Queen Anne, the wrong period.

'Cross your fingers,' said Rebecca.

She turned into a single-track road that skirted the wood and twisted down into the valley. After about half a mile it bottomed out and turned left. We passed a sawmill, a row of cottages beside a pond, then a farmhouse, with outbuildings and wooden barns and a sign for free-range eggs.

Sheep grazed in parkland on one side of the road. On the other, a sloping field of stubble glowed pale gold in the thin rays of the sun. A man in a tweed jacket and breeches leaned against a tree in the middle of the field. He had a black-and-white spaniel at his feet and a shotgun under his arm. A yellow scarf flopped around his neck.

A painting flashed into my head. Tree, cornfield, clouds in the sky, a man with a dog and a gun.

'He reminds me of one of those landowners painted by Reynolds or Gainsborough,' I said. 'Complacent. Gazing on his acres. The master of all he surveys. Like that Gainsborough in the National Gallery, *Mr and Mrs Andrews*.'

Rebecca slowed down. 'I see what you mean.' She glanced sideways again before accelerating. 'I don't see any Mrs Andrews.'

'If he's free you can have him,' I said.

'Gone off men?'

'English landlords aren't popular where I grew up,' I said drily.

A crumbling wall of brick and flint now ran along the left-hand side of the road. Ahead of us, in the angle of a bend, crumbling gateposts stood like full stops on two lines of trees. A hand-painted wooden sign swung from the wrought iron arch that curled between the posts. 'Wooldene Hall Herb Farm and Garden Centre. Plants. Compost. Christmas trees. Holly. Mistletoe.'

Rebecca steered the car through the open gates. The avenue rose slightly, then dipped and curved around a low hill. The gable and chimneys came into view again behind a high wall. The road turned and widened to run between the wall and a stable block, which had been converted to a shop and garden centre. It looked closed. Christmas trees were lined up in the yard, like a miniature forest. We parked opposite a wooden door set into the wall. A plaque on the door was inscribed, 'House'.

We peered at the date chiselled into the stone lintel: 1498.

'Five hundred years old,' said Rebecca. 'I wonder what kind of condition it's in.'

There was nobody about. She pushed the door. It swung open. 'Wow,' she said. 'It's perfect.'

The brick and flint façade blushed; the mullioned windows glinted in the setting sun. The house and its tall chimneys stood out with perfect clarity, as though framed by the air around them.

The garden in front of the house was divided by narrow brick paths that criss-crossed to make squares and rectangles of flowerbeds and tiny lawns lined with low, boxwood hedges. Beyond the geometry of the formal garden, a plain lawn blended seamlessly into a field where black cattle congregated around a trough beside a towering, leafless tree.

I lived in London. I spent my leisure time in the cinemas, theatres, museums, art galleries, bars and restaurants. The city was my toy box and my springboard to adventures elsewhere. For the first time in my life I was free to visit Paris, Rome, Amsterdam on weekends and holidays. Sometimes I went back home to Belfast. Occasionally I visited friends in Brighton, Manchester and Glasgow, glimpsing the countryside from the window of a train as I hurtled from city to city.

I had never seen a house look so settled in the landscape, as though it had grown up naturally like the trees in the walled orchard, the fat sculpted hedges, the grass in the fields beyond. As my brain absorbed this timeless picture of tranquillity, I realised I had been living in London with no real sense of inhabiting England. I felt I was now encountering it, like a foreigner, for the first time.

'There's a telephone number on the shop sign. I'll ring the owner.' Rebecca tapped the number into her mobile. 'Bugger. No signal.' She dropped the phone into her bag and took out a camera. 'I'll take a few photographs.'

A fragment of poetry came into my head. It seemed to sum up a kind of English certainty and a sense of place.

'"With ruffs about their necks, their portion sure,"' I said out loud.

Rebecca stopped clicking. 'What?'

'It's a line from a poem by Louis MacNeice.'

She looked blankly at me.

'I was thinking about the distance between here and where I grew up,' I said. 'It's a far cry from Ardoyne.'

'It's not Shepherd's Bush either,' said Rebecca. And she resumed capturing what I had already decided was the essence of England.

I closed my eyes and pictured the narrow streets of red brick houses in North Belfast. The back alleys and the front gardens, five feet square and hardly qualifying for the name. Flax Street Mill and Holy Cross Monastery marking the boundaries of the parish that had been my secure, happy world until I was fourteen years old.

My dad was a taxi driver. He had learned to drive in the Royal Army Service Corps in 1941. Thirty years later, when we had come to view British squaddies as an unwelcome frightening presence in our streets, I asked Dad why he had joined the British army.

'Was it because of Hitler, Daddy?' We had been studying the Second World War at school.

'Daughter dear, God only knows.' Dad thought for a moment. 'It was better than being a barman in the Midland Hotel. It made me feel more of a grown man. I wanted to see what war was like. To see a bit of the world.' He sighed. 'Maybe some of the men out there joined up for the same reasons.' He was silent again. 'The Brits only fought one good war,' he added softly. 'And I was in it.' His voice hardened. 'You make sure and work hard to pass your exams and get a decent job, my girl. You can't eat a flag. And you can't eat a gun.'

Mum was a hairdresser. She met Dad at a dance in the Floral Hall in 1947. She was twenty-one and going out with a steward on the Larne–Stranraer ferry, the Princess Victoria. He died when she sank in the great storm of 1953.

'Imagine. If I'd married him I would have been widowed before I was thirty,' Mum said when she told us about him.

I remember Dad winked at us. 'I'll make sure I outlive you, Kathleen.'

'Don't be too sure,' Mum said, laughing.

Mum wanted us to be middle class. Not that she ever uttered the words, but I knew that was what she meant when she said the same things as Dad. Work hard. Get a good job. Save money. Buy a house.

I knew she dreamed about living in the kind of big house advertised in magazines like *Vogue* and *Country Living*. 'Fine country property on six acres. Garden and paddock. Grade II listed.' The magazines were bought for the customers at the salon. Mum took them home to read when they were out of date.

She read books as well. Romantic novels, mostly, from the library. When I was born she wanted to call me Daisy after the heroine of a book she enjoyed while she was pregnant. 'That's no name for a Catholic child,' roared the parish priest. 'If you want something fancy, call her Louise.'

My baptism was over before anybody could voice even a feeble protest. Granny agreed with Father Doyle. She thought Daisy was a Protestant kind of name.

I found the story both funny and unsettling. I wondered if it explained my sense of uncertainty about everything. My younger brother, Michael, said that was fanciful. He said I felt insecure because we had been forced to move house so often.

Wooldene Hall looked a safe kind of house. The kind of house my mother dreamed about. Secure and self-assured. It was a house a Daisy would live in.

# 2

# Diana

Winter makes me want to hibernate. I snuggle into the bedclothes like a burrowing animal. I sleep longer and more deeply. But I wakened early on my birthday.

I pushed my head out of the tunnel of blankets and said out loud, 'Today is my birthday. Happy birthday to me.'

The words felt satisfying and I felt wonderfully alert. I lay waiting for familiar objects to take shape in the darkness, musing about the dinner party the night before. Celery soup, winter salad, pheasant with Calvados. I had found a bottle in the back of the drinks cupboard. I bought a whole Wigmore cheese – the most expensive item – and made a sort of pre-Christmas pudding with odds and ends of dried fruit and the rest of the Calvados. We had a similar sort of pudding at school, minus the Calvados of course. We called it Lucky Dip.

I did the entire meal for three pounds a head and felt terrifically relieved that we could still afford to entertain. Not that my brother seemed to care. He was becoming less sociable.

'You hardly ever go into town these days,' I had remarked to him a few weeks previously.

Henry didn't look up from the newspaper. 'Can't park in Henley. Reading is full of rubbish. Streets covered in spat-out chewing gum. Disgusting. Can't park in Oxford, *and* it's full of rubbish. Jenny spent most of my money in Marlow. Can't walk down the street there without thinking about her. Rather stay here, thank you very much,' said with a lip smack on the last consonants.

'It's my birthday on Monday,' I had said. 'I'd like to invite one or two people to dinner on Sunday night, I think.'

Henry put down the newspaper. 'Thank God for something to celebrate.'

He went over to the old house and brought back a bottle of port. 'Good excuse to open this. Taylor's. Your birth year. We ought to drink it. Past its best if we leave it too long.'

Like me, I said silently to myself.

'Gosh, that's frightfully good,' Ronnie Bolton had said when he tasted it. His brown, piggy eyes shone with pleasure. 'Best port I've ever tasted.'

Henry was gratified. 'My father liked port. Liked wine too. There's a lot of interesting stuff in the cellar.'

I made a mental note to get the wines valued. Henry needed every penny to pay for the roof.

Ronnie blew me a kiss across the table. 'Happy birthday, Diana. I won't ask what age you are.'

Susan Reynolds, who was always trying to find out, raised a dark eyebrow and said, 'But younger than you, Henry?'

'Nowadays, yes,' said Henry. He was becoming more sardonic every day.

Ronnie said, with mock gloom, 'I used to have three older sisters. Over the years they've all got younger than me.'

I tried not to glare at Henry.

'You don't look your age, Ronnie,' I said lightly. 'So that's all right then.' And I changed the subject.

We played bridge after dinner. Susan partnered Henry. 'We play awfully well together,' she said. I began to think she had her eye on him.

The idea now roused me out of bed. I got dressed, went to the kitchen, let Paddy out, and took the vegetable peelings and coffee grounds from the night before to the compost bin. I tripped over the spade that Tomasz had left propped up against the bungalow wall and only just managed to stop the plastic basin from spilling its contents over the back step.

I hopped around on one foot, rubbing my shin and cursing Tomasz and his recent absent-mindedness. A girl, of course. He had shown me her photograph.

'Her name is Anna. From Posnan.' His smile was a mixture of greediness and awe.

I thought how nice it would be to make men smile like that again, and how one never quite gives up hope.

Catherine telephoned as I was making breakfast.

'Happy birthday, Mummy darling.'

'Lovely to hear your voice,' I said. 'Did you stay up late to call me?'

'We had friends to dinner. I've just finished clearing up. It's nearly midnight here.'

'How are the children?'

'Sound asleep, thank heavens. They're going to telephone you in the morning. About six in the evening, your time. You're closed on Mondays, aren't you? What are you going to do with your day?'

'Plant tulips. Visit Aunt Lucy,' I said.

'Oh, give yourself a day off, Mummy,' Catherine said. She had that bossy tone in her voice. 'Lucy won't remember whether you came to see her or not.'

'She loves having visitors.'

'She didn't recognise me when I went to see her in the summer.'

'She hadn't seen you for two years.'

'You take on too much, Mummy.'

Catherine had taken to scolding me. She was horrified when I said I was moving in with Henry.

'You're utterly insane. You know he's useless around the house. You'll end up doing absolutely everything for him.'

'It will be cheaper for both of us. He's on his own. I'm on my own. We get on terribly well. I've got a nice little business going now with the garden centre. It's much easier than driving over from Amersham every day.'

'When the business gets too much for you, you'll be stuck there.'

9

That was another thing that irritated me. Catherine talked as though I was decrepit. She was always banging on about planning for old age.

'We get along,' I said. 'Henry's tidy.'

'Only because he was in the army. He's not organised in any other way. I'll see what Carl thinks.'

When Carl pronounced in his calm Californian way, 'I think your mother's right, honey. It makes sense,' Catherine was mollified. 'But you have to make Henry help around the house,' she said. 'He can't afford a cleaner. The old house just eats up money.'

She asked me what I had got for my birthday.

'Henry gave me a sketch of you and Carl and the children in the orchard. He must have done it when you were here in the summer. Susan gave me a bottle of gin with a card saying "Better than botox. Paralyses more muscles."'

Catherine has a hearty laugh. I wished I heard it more often.

'Have a wonderful day, Mummy. Don't go charging off to see Lucy. Give yourself a rest.'

'Why are grown-up daughters more bossy than grown-up sons?' I said to Henry when he came into the kitchen. 'Peter isn't bossy, is he?'

'If you ask me, he's not bossy enough,' Henry said. 'He lets Christine run his life.'

'Don't you like her?'

'Not much. She's got no sparkle. She's all wrong for him. At least Jenny had a bit of sparkle.'

Most of it round her neck and paid for by Henry, I thought to myself.

'His mother couldn't let a day pass without spending money. Now he's engaged to a woman who wouldn't spend Christmas.' Henry gave a short laugh. 'Peter is thirty-five. I suppose he knows what he's doing.'

'Catherine will be forty next year,' I said. 'I can't believe I have a daughter who's nearly forty.'

Where does time go? I asked myself. One moment I am a teenager. I blink, and I'm sixty-two.

# 3

# Louise

I stood in the doorway to the garden, watching Rebecca move around the lawn, framing shots, pausing to push her hair behind her ear in a familiar gesture. She had hardly changed in fourteen years. Dark and dainty. I still felt all legs and freckles next to her.

We met in Belfast in the early eighties. I had just got a job with an independent production company making a children's series for the BBC. I had been living at home in West Belfast with Mum, Dad and Michael. In those days, you could never be sure of getting back there easily after dark. Besides, I was twenty-six and anxious to begin life outside the comforting cocoon of the family.

I rented a flat near the university. It was not much more than a mile, as the helicopters flew, from the treeless streets, crescents and culs-de-sac of Andersonstown to the leafy avenues of South Belfast, but it was like living in a parallel universe, entered through checkpoints and security barriers that lifted in the morning, fell with the night and closed off the troubled areas of the city like a cordon sanitaire.

I advertised on the BBC noticeboard for someone to share the flat. Rebecca was on attachment to the drama department and needed somewhere to stay. We liked each other straight away. We seemed to fill the gaps in each other's personalities. I was anxious and attentive to detail. Rebecca was confident and always saw the big picture.

When things were going swimmingly for Rebecca she rode the wave. She felt success would follow success. I was nervous when things were going well for me. A little voice fed doomy clichés into my brain. 'Pride comes before a fall'; 'Don't count your chickens;' 'Many a slip'. I was afraid to banish the gloomy whisperer. I felt a sense of foreboding was a price I had to pay for the granting of my wishes.

Our backgrounds were similar. Both our fathers were taxi drivers. Our mothers wanted us to have careers. To succeed. Our parents had left school aged fourteen. Rebecca and I were grammar school girls. We had gone to university. We had aspirations. We were on our way. But Rebecca had an audacity I lacked.

She pushed me into applying for a unit manager's job I didn't think I'd get.

'You're intelligent, organised, hard-working. The job's ideal for you.' She had coached me and made me borrow from the bank to buy a well-cut suit for the interview. 'Stop worrying. It's an investment.'

She supervised my shopping. 'You have a great sense of colour in everything else, so why do you wear beige? Stop trying to vanish into the background. You can't; you're tall, you have flaming red hair. Make the most of it. Be dramatic. Wear deep pink, violet, midnight blue. Wear high heels.'

'I'll tower over them like a shipyard crane.'

'Good,' said Rebecca.

Under her tutelage, I became braver at work. I spoke up in meetings. I argued for changes I knew would make the unit more efficient. I began to enjoy being assertive.

Rebecca tried to make me more self-assured in my dealings with men.

'I'm afraid Louise isn't here at the moment. Can I take a message?' Waving me away. 'I think she's been asked to the theatre tonight.' Putting down the telephone. 'Don't let him think he can ask you out on Saturday morning for Saturday night. Have some faith in yourself. He'll give you more notice the next time he calls.'

We had promised to keep in touch when she went back to London and so we did, for a while. I flew over to spend a weekend with her. She spent a week with me in Donegal. But my mother was descending deeper into depression and it became harder for me to get away. Rebecca and I telephoned each other a few times and exchanged Christmas cards. Then she moved to New York. About a year later I got an invitation to her wedding. I couldn't go. Gradually, we lost contact.

I had been living in London for two years when I picked up a copy of the *Evening Standard* and saw a photograph of Rebecca. It was more like half a photograph, for she was almost out of shot, turning away from the camera, on the edge of a group of BAFTA award winners. Her surname in the caption was Hood, not Morrison, but I recognised her straightaway. She had the same sweep of straight dark hair to her shoulders, and held herself in a posture I remembered; energy coiled inside her, ready to spring into action.

I looked her up on the Internet and found her company website, Telekineticproductions.com. I sent her an email. She telephoned the next day. As soon as she heard me say I was now a line producer, she offered me a job.

'I'm developing an Elizabethan murder mystery based on the Amy Robsart story. I've got Teddy Hammond working on the third draft.'

I knew the name. He'd adapted *The Watsons*, an unfinished novel by Jane Austen, for Granada. He'd won a BAFTA.

'I'm half lined-up for something else.' It was half-true. The film industry is a-twitter with birds in bushes. I had just finished a picture and was beginning to wonder which of several new projects would take off and fly. There were a couple of low-budget films being planned by producers I had worked for before and who had got in touch. Still, a bird in the hand . . . and this was a bigger production.

'I've got development money to pay you.' Rebecca sounded confident.

That clinched it. I accepted her offer.

'Hire one, fire one,' Rebecca laughed. 'I've just sacked a useless production assistant. But there's a queue of wannabes ready to work for nothing to get into the business. It's harder to find a good director.'

'Jacky McQuitty has just directed *Treasure Island* for the BBC. We ran into each other last week.'

'Jacky McQuitty? That's a good thought. It'll be like old times.'

'Nice to be in touch again,' I said.

'You should have come to London a long time ago, Louise.'

'I'm here now.'

And then we began our catching up.

'Things went wrong for me in New York,' Rebecca told me. 'It was full of single women and all men were fair game. Including my husband. After a while, Sam didn't even try to keep his affairs secret. I came back to London after the divorce. What about you?'

'Still single,' I said.

'I'm seeing a lawyer,' Rebecca said. 'A barrister, actually. I met him through the lawyer who's negotiating the contracts on this film. His name's Robert. My boyfriend, I mean. Robert Thompson.'

I could tell he was important from the way she said his name.

'What about you, Louise? Are you seeing anybody?'

'Not at the moment.'

'So, still looking?'

'Where there is life there is hope,' I said.

I was smiling to myself, recalling this conversation, thinking how nice it was to be working with Rebecca, and wondering if I should organise a Christmas party with Jacky and some other friends from the old days, when a well-bred voice behind me said, 'Can I help you?'

I swung round and saw an imposing blonde woman with a look of cold surprise on her big-boned face and a three-pronged stainless steel garden fork in her hand. She looked like a statue of Britannia.

Rebecca hurried to my side. 'There was no one in the shop. We're looking for the owner of the house.'

'May I ask why?' There was a hint of sharpness under the drawl.

14

'We need a Tudor house for a film that's due to start shooting in the spring.' Rebecca proffered her business card. 'I'm Rebecca Hood. Telekinetic Productions. This is my colleague, Louise O'Neill.'

Britannia studied the card. Her face relaxed. 'I'm Diana Wiseman. How do you do.'

We shook hands.

'You'd better come into the house.'

We stood back, expecting her to step through the doorway. Instead, she turned on her heel and led us further up the road, past a field of polythene tunnels and a well-tended vegetable garden.

The road swung right. On the bend stood a steep-roofed wooden barn. Behind it crouched a conventional, suburban brick bungalow with a lawn and flowerbeds to the front, a garage to the side and window boxes of winter pansies. Its incongruity, in otherwise ancient surroundings, was concealed by the black immensity of the barn.

'The big house is far too expensive to heat in the winter, I'm afraid. This is much cosier,' said Britannia. 'We rent the house for parties and weddings. We've never had a film company before.' Her eyes danced. 'This is rather exciting.'

She propped the garden fork beside a companion spade in the back porch and ushered us into a long room divided by a table. On one side were an ancient leather sofa and armchair, and a wood-burning stove. On the other was the kitchen.

'Please sit down.' She glanced at the clock. Half-past three. 'Will you take tea?'

'Thank you, Mrs Wiseman,' I said.

'Do please call me Diana.' Her tone was friendly now. Her smile warm. She began to fill a kettle at the sink.

Rebecca glanced at the dog hairs on the sofa. I glanced at Diana. She had her back to us. I brushed the cushions with the back of my hand and winked at Rebecca. We sat down.

Diana unhooked mugs from a dresser. 'What's your film about?'

'It's a remake of *Kenilworth*,' said Rebecca.

'Walter Scott? I saw it on television. Black and white. Must have been ages ago.'

'Forty years,' Rebecca said. 'Forty-one to be precise. 1957. You must have been very young when you saw it.'

Diana looked pleased at the compliment.

'It's a good story,' said Rebecca. 'Historical films are in vogue at the moment.'

'Who's going to be in it?'

'Caroline Cross and William Bowman.'

'Golly,' said Diana. 'You want to film them here?'

'Possibly. If the timing is right. The house might be suitable for a Josephine Tey series we're planning as well.'

'Good Lord,' said Diana. 'I used to adore her books.' She pulled a chair out from the table and sat down. 'This is all jolly surprising.'

I heard footsteps and a scurrying sound in the porch. The kitchen door opened. A black-and-white spaniel dashed in, followed by a man with a yellow scarf around his neck, a shotgun in one hand and a dead rabbit in the other. It was the man I'd seen earlier, leaning against the tree. He held the rabbit up by its hind legs.

'Dinner,' he announced.

# 4

# Diana

I thought at first they were teenagers, in their blue jeans, short jackets and high-heeled boots. When they turned around to answer me, I saw they had older, more knowledgeable features and were probably in their late thirties.

When they explained their interest in the Hall, I felt a surge of excitement and all the time I was chatting and making tea I was thinking they had appeared out of nowhere like the answer to a prayer.

'What we need is a miracle,' Henry had said sombrely when he opened the letter from the surveyor. 'It's worse than I thought. Even if I doubled my commissions it wouldn't come near this.'

'You've got your Christmas exhibition in December. That sold well last year.'

'Not enough to cover a tenth of it.' He showed me the estimate.

He had a strained look around the eyes. He had worn that look all the time his divorce was going through and for about a year afterwards. Then he became himself again, painted in his studio most days, seemed happy and productive. Until the roof fell in.

We didn't notice it at first, because it was behind the chimney on the north-west gable. In fact, Henry and I didn't notice it at all. It was brought to our attention by Bob Fingleton who rents the fields beyond the orchard. He was harvesting a crop of fodder maize at the beginning of October when he saw a few loose slates and alerted us.

We went over to the house immediately. There was a damp patch on the ceiling of the drawing room in the west wing. We galloped upstairs to the long gallery and saw the plaster coming away from the ceiling and a pool of water on the floor near the fireplace. It had been raining for three days, so the water had been seeping through the floor all that time.

We went up through the attics into the roof space. We couldn't find a hole in the roof, but when Henry shone his torch on the timbers we saw water glistening on the wood.

The surveyor was a lugubrious man with pale grey eyes and the unlikely name of Blossom. Henry asked him to go over the whole house. 'Might as well get all the bad news at once.'

We followed him around like anxious puppies. A light had gone in the cellar. I went upstairs to fetch a light bulb from the store cupboard in the kitchen. When I descended once more into the gloom, Mr Blossom was holding the torch and Henry was removing bottles from a wine-rack to allow closer inspection of the cellar wall. I helped him remove the last half-dozen bottles of port.

'We ought to drink these,' Henry said.

We pulled the empty rack away from the wall and saw it had obscured the opening to another cellar.

I handed the torch to Henry. 'We haven't been down here in ages. I don't remember this bit.'

'Me neither.' He shone the torch through the archway. His hand found a light switch. 'Good Lord.'

The naked bulb hanging from the ceiling lit a room, about ten feet square, stacked with wooden boxes. Henry put on his reading glasses and peered at the black lettering on a box at eye level.

'Clos Saint Hune Grand Reserve 1945. Good Heavens. These have been here since the end of the war.'

Henry and Mr Blossom began unstacking the boxes and dragging them away from the wall, reciting a litany of the labels.

'Domaine Schlumberger Grand Cru Kitterlé 1945.'

'Chateau Lafite Rothschild 1945.'

'Coutet Cuvée Madame 1943.'

'Chateau Lafleur Pomerol 1945.'

I imagined my father steering an army truck through the vineyards he had helped to liberate, smiling his terrific smile, clapping shoulders, shaking hands, clinking glasses in celebration, loading boxes of wine into the back of the vehicle, waving goodbye, driving away in a cloud of dust.

'There's one here from 1949,' Henry said. 'And another from 1950.'

'He must have brought those back when he took Mummy to France after the war. You mightn't remember, Henry. You were only about five.'

I supposed Daddy had laid them down, planning to drink them, not knowing he was going to die three years later. I suddenly felt tremendously tired and sat down on one of the boxes.

'I hope you're a wine drinker,' said Mr Blossom. 'There must be forty dozen bottles here. I'm more of a beer man myself, though I like a nice Australian Shiraz.'

'These wines are ancient,' Henry said. 'Probably past their best. I don't think Mummy drank much wine. Not after Daddy died.'

Mr Blossom ran his hand down the wall and smelt it. 'You don't seem to have dry rot down here, anyway.'

'That's good news,' I said.

'Of course it could be elsewhere,' said Mr Blossom.

His report confirmed dry rot in three of the oak panels near the fireplace in the gallery and wet rot in the roof timbers. A quarter of them needed to be replaced. A section of the drawing room ceiling would have to be replaced as well. We would need to put up scaffolding, which would add to the expense. We would need to do the work within the next twelve months.

Henry went to his studio in the barn, although the light had seeped from the sky and he hated painting in artificial light. He stayed there most of the evening. When he came back to the house he had that taut look again. I let him mope for two days.

Then I made him sit down with me and go over all of his, and my, expenditure.

'I know the Hall was left to you, Henry. But it was my home too. If you had to sell it, a little bit of me would go with it. I want to help.'

We made a plan. We would live on my income. I had been thinking of hiring more staff for the garden centre. Instead, I would manage with Tomasz. We were coming into the quiet period. It wouldn't get busy again until a couple of weeks before Christmas. There were always students looking for work in the holidays. I would take on a couple of them for the Christmas rush.

We would be as self-sufficient as we could. Henry would get the smallest loan possible to pay for the roof, and use his income – his army pension and what he made from his paintings – to cover the interest on the loan and as much of the capital sum as possible.

'Wait for the estimate. It might not be as bad as you think,' I said.

It was worse.

I had some money in a savings account I'd kept while I was married. It was money Granny had left me, plus my income from part-time gardening. Geoffrey had called it my running away fund.

'I have a small nest egg,' I said to Henry.

'You do enough already. It's my responsibility.'

'I don't want to see the house sold. Let me help.'

'Buy a lottery ticket,' Henry said.


I had no idea how much a film company might pay for the use of the Hall, but I thought we could ask for at least three times the weekly rental rate. Then I wondered if the film company would fix the roof. That would really be a miracle. Then I worried they would reject the Hall as a location because it terribly needed repairs, although that wouldn't be obvious unless they were doing close-ups of the roof and chimneys. All these thoughts were bouncing around in my brain when Henry came in with Paddy and a dead rabbit, and I started wondering how I would cook the rabbit and hoping Rebecca and Louise, now being assaulted by Paddy on the sofa, weren't vegetarians or frightfully against blood sports, or dog-haters. I wanted Henry to be especially charming to them but he barely paid attention as I tried to introduce everybody with Paddy barking like crazy, the rabbit stretched out on the table like a votive offering, Henry hunting in the drawer for a knife, and my thoughts whizzing around like vegetables in a food processor.

# 5

# Louise

I thought Rebecca was going to vomit when Henry cut the head off the rabbit. She went white under her tan and put her hand over her mouth.

Henry tossed the rabbit's head into a basin. The inky smell of blood filled the room.

Diana wrinkled her nose. 'Do you have to do that in here, Henry?'

'It's cold outside. It's easier on the table.'

He's doing it deliberately, I thought. It's a wind-up. He has marked us down as a couple of townies. Probably vegetarians as well. I bet he went on that pro-hunting march. He looked up and caught my eye.

'Disapprove of shooting, do you?'

'It depends what end of the gun I'm on.' I wasn't going to be wound up. Besides, he had the kind of clipped, commanding voice that brought out the rebel in me.

'That's an awful lot of bother,' I said airily. 'I get mine from the butcher.'

It was a lie. I had never bought or cooked a rabbit. But I had caught his attention. He looked intently at me. A half-smile quivered on his lips.

'Like rabbit, do you?'

'It's not my favourite meat. But at least it's cheap.'

'Quite so,' Henry said.

Immediately I sensed I had said something wrong. The half-smile vanished. He resumed peeling back the fur as though taking off a glove. The belly and forelegs of the dead animal glistened darkly pink. Henry lifted the knife to cut into the flesh. Rebecca gulped.

'Louise and Rebecca are interested in renting the Hall for a film,' Diana said, hurriedly. 'Starring Caroline Cross and William Bowman.'

Henry put the knife down. 'Well, well.' The half-smile returned. 'No more rabbit.'

'We haven't talked about money,' said Diana.

'Then let's talk about it now.' Henry swept the carcass and skin into the basin and carried it outside.

Arrogant and obsessed with money, I decided.

'The house costs a lot to maintain, I'm afraid,' Diana said, with an embarrassed smile. 'But we're rather attached to it. Our family has lived here for five hundred years.'

'We can't talk about money until we decide if it's suitable,' said Rebecca. The colour had returned to her cheeks. 'We won't know that until we have a look around.' She glanced out the window. The sky was slate grey. A low flame ran along the horizon. 'It's too dark to do that now. Louise will have to come back. I'd like the director to see it as well. Will that be all right?' Rebecca looked to Diana.

Diana looked at Henry, who had come back into the kitchen.

'Fine with me,' he said. 'The sooner we know, the better.' He cleared his throat. 'Can you give me any idea of the sort of money involved? Always supposing Wooldene is the kind of thing you're looking for.'

His tone was bright, but there was tension in the set of his shoulders and a dark, unreadable expression in his eyes.

'It depends on the number of days,' Rebecca said. 'And whether we're filming interiors or exteriors, or both.'

'What's the daily rate?'

Rebecca sighed. 'It varies. It's negotiable. I can't say any more than that until we've had a proper look around, and I know roughly how many days we'll need it.'

'Look, I need some idea, otherwise we will all be wasting our time.'

I thought about all the time wasted on films that never got made. I wondered if this production would be one of them.

Rebecca looked at me. 'Louise?'

I read the message in her eyes. Relax. Stop worrying. Sound confident.

'Six weeks,' I said. 'Maybe more.'

'How much a day?'

'I don't necessarily work it out like that.'

'Well I necessarily do,' said Henry.

Diana put a hand on his arm, but he wasn't letting go of the bone.

'You must have some idea,' he said. 'Unless you haven't done this before.'

'Every location is different,' I said. 'We need to do a proper recce.'

'When can you do the recce?'

'I'll call you in the next few days.'

'Whenever suits,' he said stiffly.

Diana walked with us to the car, exchanging platitudes about the weather and how Christmas seemed to start earlier every year. The chimneys of the old house were hardly visible against the darkening sky.

A pheasant scuttled across the headlights as I drove back through the gates. I braked hard. The pheasant disappeared into the dark.

'"Nature, red in tooth and claw." We nearly had a dead pheasant as well as a dead rabbit.'

'Yuk.' Rebecca shuddered. 'I'm surprised it didn't bother you.'

'It's guns I hate. I don't like guns in kitchens.'

Memory hit me like a wave. I felt again the tightness in my chest when I heard the banging on the front door, saw the Saracen armoured car squatting outside like a fat malevolent animal, Mum crying, Rebecca wide-eyed with horror and fascination as the police pushed past us into the scullery to pull apart the shelves, smash the backs of the cupboards, soldiers holding Dad and Michael at gunpoint against the kitchen wall.

'You'll find no guns here,' my father shouted in a frenzy of mortification. He was trying to hold up his trousers with one hand because they were falling off him. They weren't his trousers. He had got the wrong pair back from the dry-cleaners. He had been laughing about it only a few minutes earlier. 'Now I know why them dry-cleaners are so cheap. They're bloody useless. They've sent back the wrong things. Michael is going mad upstairs because he's no clean jacket to meet this new girl of his.'

I remembered the tramp of boots upstairs and the sound of floorboards being torn up. I remembered shivering in the damp air that crept into the house, past the bulky soldiers in the back-yard. I remembered thinking they must have got the wrong address.

I couldn't believe it when they took Dad and Michael away and kept them for a week in Castlereagh detention centre. Dad had his fatal heart attack a week after he was released.

Rebecca snapped me out of the past by touching me on the arm. 'You're gripping that wheel as though you're going to strangle it.'

'Sorry. I was thinking about the first time you came to our house.'

'Will I ever forget it?' Rebecca began to mimic my accent. 'Never worry, you said. It looks worse on television. Our wee crescent is quiet. There's never any trouble at all. You might not even see a foot patrol.' She laughed. 'One minute we're having tea and sandwiches and the next minute the army is all over the place and your mother is having hysterics.'

'It was no joke.' My fingers tightened again on the wheel. I felt the old anger rise in me and burn my throat. 'I blame that raid for pushing Michael into the IRA. For Dad's heart attack. I blame it for everything.'

'I'm sorry,' said Rebecca. 'I didn't mean to be insensitive.'

'Many's the one has a worse tale to tell,' I said shortly. 'People died. Were crippled for life. Had relatives and friends shot dead or blown to smithereens. I was spared that. But Mum's never been the same since Dad died.'

'You should have left, Louise. Got out.'

'How could I?' I tried to stop my voice rising. Rebecca had touched a nerve. 'Mum was sick and depressed. Who else was going to look after her?'

Not Michael, serving ten years for possession of a gun and membership of the IRA. What else could I do but stay at home? My older sister, Noreen, was married and living in Dublin. She told her three children and her middle-class Dublin friends that Michael was in America. She came up to Belfast twice a year to see Mum. Once a year she went to visit Michael in Long Kesh.

'Louise is a career woman,' I heard her say on the telephone to her Dublin friends.

I hated the expression. It seemed to un-gender me and set me apart from the world of husbands and children.

'How come you don't describe yourself as a career woman, Noreen?' I said. 'You have a job.'

'It's not the be-all and end-all to me,' she said.

My younger sister, Rosemary, was working illegally in Boston. She couldn't come back to Belfast because she wouldn't be able to re-enter the United States. Just before Michael got out of prison, she won a green card in a visa lottery for illegal immigrants. She came home and stayed long enough to get married to the boyfriend to whom she had been writing for four years.

'Seamus and I are going to start a family when we get back to Boston,' she said. 'I'm thirty-six. I can't leave it too late. You should get a move on too, Louise.'

It was her wedding day. I didn't say a word.

Six months later, and a week before my fortieth birthday, Michael was released on licence. For once, the timing was right. That same week I was offered, and accepted, a job in London.

Now I said to Rebecca, 'Amn't I here now?' I tried to sound light, but my voice was tight.

My mobile phone rang.

Rebecca answered it for me. 'Louise's phone. She can't speak to you now. She's driving. Oh. Hello, Michael.' Pause. 'I'll ask her for you.'

'Don't tell me,' I said. 'Mum can't find her tablets. Tell him to look in her washbag.'

'And he says someone called Pauline Murphy telephoned your mum looking for you.'

'Pauline Murphy?' I didn't know anyone of that name. 'Probably someone looking for a job,' I said. 'Tell Michael to give her the office number if she calls again. If this film gets the green light we'll be hiring more people.' I took one hand from the wheel to cross my fingers.

Rebecca stowed the phone in the glove compartment. 'Michael sounds in good spirits.'

'He's doing well now.' My face relaxed into a smile. 'Funny how things turn out. He was always mitching off school. He dropped out of Queen's. He wouldn't have got a degree if he hadn't gone to prison. All that time to study. And the tutors were good.'

Rebecca twisted uncomfortably in her seat. 'I don't like to think about prison.'

'Neither do I,' I said sharply.

But Rebecca had reminded me of the one good thing that had come out of it all. My anger drained away. 'Michael likes teaching. The job suits him,' I said. 'Marriage suits him too. He looks well on it.'

'He was a good-looking teenager.' Rebecca paused. I sensed her studying me. 'I thought the bunny-killer back there was rather a dish.'

'He's not my type.'

'He's tall enough for you.'

'He sounded too interested in money.'

'You were quite combative with him.'

'It's in my DNA. The rebel in me rears up when I hear that accent.'

'If we use the Hall for filming, you'll see a lot of him.'

'I'll see a lot of his wife as well.'

I knew what lay down that road. Furtive, thrilling weekends and afternoons. Hurried phone calls. Tears. Lies. Excuses. And at the end of it all, a bad conscience. The film business is full of people having affairs. I had been one of them. I had arrived in London like a fugitive, emotionally exhausted, ready to lean on the first shoulder that presented itself. The shoulder in question belonged to a married television executive.

Even when that first affair ended in tears, as I had known it would, I accepted every invitation with a heart full of hope. After a series of short, disappointing liaisons, the small voice in my head stopped whispering, Maybe you'll meet someone tonight.

'What you want,' said Rebecca shrewdly, 'is a man you can bring home to your mum.'

'Don't be ridiculous. I'm forty-one. I have more chance of being knocked down by a bus.' But the small voice inside me had started up again, was whispering, Go on, admit it, Rebecca's right, wouldn't it be lovely to bring an eligible man home to Mum? It would bring some cheer into her life. I could imagine the fuss, the relief on her face, a smile even. She had stopped asking whom I was seeing. I was mostly seeing nobody. I knew she wanted me to meet someone and settle down. My being single was something else to reproach herself for.

'If you hadn't stayed here. If you'd left Belfast earlier maybe you'd have met someone. If only I hadn't got sick . . .'

If only Dad hadn't died. If only Mum hadn't been so depressed she could hardly bring herself to leave the house. If only I had been able to take the job in London that was offered to me a week before Michael was arrested in a house on the Whiterock road with an ArmaLite rifle and ammunition, a black balaclava and four ounces of Semtex plastic explosive.

Now I said to Rebecca, 'I've got used to being single. I like my work. I like my flat. I like my friends.'

'Just as I thought,' said Rebecca. 'Still looking.'

# 6

# Diana

When I got back to the bungalow after walking with Louise and Rebecca to their car, Henry took two glasses from the dresser. 'Might as well finish the port.'

I cut the rabbit meat into smaller pieces and sprinkled flour and mustard on a plate. Henry pushed a glass across the table to me.

'What a turn up. Six weeks. Maybe more. We might get enough to pay for the roof.' He tried to sound off-hand but I sensed his excitement.

I shook salt and pepper over the rabbit pieces, rolled them in the flour and put them in a pot to brown. 'We don't know how much they'll pay. We don't even know if they're going to use it. Better not get our hopes up until then.'

'Which one of them is coming back? I didn't get the names properly. Paddy was making too much of a racket.'

'You're jolly lucky you didn't send them screaming from the room. Sometimes you go too far, Henry. I thought the little one, Rebecca, was going to faint.'

'"Nature, red in tooth and claw," eh? Bit too much for her. Probably a vegetarian.'

'Definitely the boss,' I said. 'You might have blown it, Henry.'

'She got her colour back,' he said. 'What's the redhead called? She had a bit more sparkle.'

'Louise.'

'Mmnn. Sort of bold and hesitant at the same time. Don't give me that look, Diana. She's not my type.'

'I'm not giving you a look. I'm merely wondering what part of Ireland she's from.'

'The black North,' said Henry. 'I recognised the accent.' He grimaced. 'I had my fill of Northern Ireland.' His face darkened. '*Un beau pays, mal habité.*'

Henry had never talked to me about his time in Ireland. I didn't see him much during his army years. I was married to Geoffrey. We seemed to spend a lot of time moving house. And I had Catherine, of course.

We saw Henry when he was home on leave, but it seemed the last thing he wanted to talk about was his deployment in Ulster. It didn't help that Jenny put her hands over her ears every time the subject was raised and chanted, 'boring, boring'.

I worried about him, naturally, and said so. Henry had muttered something about being involved in back-room stuff, 'Desk job mostly. Hardly ever out on patrol.' Even so, I was relieved when he left the army and decided to use the money Mummy left him to go to art college. It was what he should have done in the first place. I remember being surprised when he chose Sandhurst after Oxford.

'Why are you joining the army?' I had asked him one afternoon, not long after he had announced his decision.

He didn't reply for a moment. Then he said gruffly, 'Some part of every man wishes he had been a soldier. Becoming a man and all that. We think we can change the world.'

'Henry's such a romantic,' I had remarked to Geoffrey.

'He'll not get on in the city, then,' Geoffrey had grunted in reply.

Now Henry was staring into his wine glass as though it contained the past.

'We went in to help,' he said. 'The Catholics welcomed us with cups of tea. But it wasn't long before they were calling us fucking Brit bastards and shooting us in the back. The Protestants hated the Catholics. I've never seen hatred like it. But they were our friends and the Catholics were our enemies.'

He sighed. 'Our co-religionists, and they came to mean the enemy.'

I waited for him to go on.

'We trained to fight the enemy,' he said. 'There's more than one way to fight a war. And you can't make an omelette without breaking eggs.' He drained his glass and set it abruptly on the table. 'Fight fire with fire. Sometimes it's the only way.'

I stopped chopping celery and put the knife down.

'I've never really been clear about what you did over there,' I said quietly. 'What exactly did you do, Henry?'

'Intelligence,' he said. 'Vital in any war. Not really supposed to talk about it. Don't want to talk about it.'

He had that closed look again. I passed him an onion to chop and changed the subject. 'Rather exciting to think of sitting in a cinema and seeing the Hall on the big screen.'

Henry smiled. 'For the first time in months, I feel a smidgeon of hope. We might be able to hang on to the old place after all.' I wasn't sure if his moist eyes were entirely the fault of the onion.

'Please God,' I said. 'Please God.'

I crushed a few sage leaves and added them to the pot with the onions and celery. I poured in a splash of cider and put the pot in the oven. Then we sat in peaceful silence for a while. I could hear Paddy whimpering in his dreams in front of the fire. I thought about how much the old house meant to Henry and me, and to our Aunt Lucy. We had all grown up at Wooldene. It was part of all our childhoods.

I thought back to my visit to Aunt Lucy earlier in the day.

She had been waiting in a wheelchair by the door when I arrived at The Lindens. She was wearing her tweed coat and a faux fur hat. Sunitra must have helped her get ready, I thought. She always picked out something smart for Lucy to wear.

I bent down to kiss her. 'How are you today?'

'Today goes slow, but time goes fast,' she said.

I drove her to a country park and wheeled her along a tarmac path by the river. Lucy leaned forward, pushed her face out to the wind, and moved her hands as though stroking the air.

These places are all stuffy and overheated, I thought, when

I wheeled her back into The Lindens. They're noisy as well. The television is always on. A blur of sound, interrupted by riffs of electronic music and applause. The staff raise their voices, so that the increasingly deaf can hear them. The deaf yell back.

I steered the wheelchair across the lounge. Ugly, inelegant word, I thought to myself. It's inappropriate too. The elderly don't lounge. They sit stiffly in long-backed chairs with armrests. It was an ugly, inelegant room as well. Bright and soulless at the same time. Overheated, but with no warmth.

Lucy's usual chair was in the big bay window, thirty feet from the squawking television, thank God. As we drew near, a bellowed conversation started up somewhere behind me.

'Johnny's not at school, Mother. He's sixty-five.'

'Don't be ridiculous. I haven't got a son who's sixty-five.'

A tall, broad-shouldered man in a tweed overcoat caught my eye and grinned. His mother said, in a piercing whisper, 'At least I'm not as bad as she is. I know what day it is and who the prime minister is.'

'Mr Chamberlain,' Lucy said suddenly. 'He was the prime minister. "Out of this nettle, danger, we pluck this flower, safety." Shakespeare. *Henry the Fourth.*'

Lucy's short-term memory was getting worse, but she could recite reams of poetry and significant dates in history.

I put my foot on the brake and parked the wheelchair. 'What year was that, Lucy?'

'1940,' Lucy said. 'The year I had the baby.'

I was too surprised to speak. I fumbled with her seatbelt and found myself asking, 'What was the baby's name?'

She stared fiercely out the window and gripped the hat on her lap. 'I called him Edward.'

I sank on to Lucy's chair, dumbfounded.

'That's my —' she hesitated, 'thing I sit in.'

'I need to get you out of the wheelchair, and get your coat off.' I leaned across to undo the buttons and knocked Lucy's hat to the floor.

The man in the tweed coat leaned down and picked it up. He handed the hat to Lucy with a smile.

'Thank you,' she said. 'I just need to get out of this –' She cocked her elbow at him. 'Please. Need to sit.'

Before I had got to my feet, he had lifted Lucy from the wheelchair. She was so light, she seemed to float up.

'Thank you.' She smiled at him. 'Have we met before?'

'Finnegan. John Finnegan. This is my mother, Agnes Finnegan.' There was a slight burr in his voice. Kent? Sussex?

'Of course I know Agnes.' Lucy gave her a nod of recognition. 'It's nice to have visitors. This is . . .' another hesitation. I saw a flash of panic in her eyes.

'Diana Wiseman. I'm Miss Wintour's niece.'

I shook hands distractedly. I had not expected Lucy to remember my birthday, but this was the first time she had not remembered my name.

'I've heard Lucy talk about you,' said Mrs Finnegan. 'I see you here. At least once a week. Sometimes more.' She nodded approvingly.

'Sometimes less, I'm afraid, when I'm busy.'

'It must be a drive of near enough thirty miles.'

'It doesn't take long in the car.'

'John lives in London. That's a good distance too.' She smiled up at him.

'An hour on the motorway.' He squeezed her hand. 'I wish I could come more often.'

'He wanted me to move in with him, didn't you, John? But I said no. You have a business to run. Besides, that house of yours is all stairs. I thought it was better to move here. It's only down the road from where we used to live.' She looked away for a moment. 'His dad and I spent most of our married life near here.'

'Dad died five years ago,' John said.

I murmured my regret. There was a pause. Lucy's eyes were closed. I could tell from her breathing that she had fallen asleep. I wondered what baby she had been talking about.

'We started off in Hastings,' Mrs Finnegan said. 'The business took off in the seventies when everybody started drinking wine. We moved the business to London and bought a house out here.'

I dragged my attention away from Lucy. 'You were in the wine business, Mrs Finnegan?'

'Agnes, call me Agnes,' she said in a friendly way. 'Finnegan's Fine Wines. John's in charge now.' She smiled affectionately at him.

'Do you specialise in particular wines?'

'Wines that age well,' he said. 'I like things that get better as they get older.' There was extra warmth in his smile.

I found myself grinning back at him like a lunatic.

Lucy woke up with a start. 'Where is he?' She sounded alarmed.

I crouched beside her and held her hands in mine. 'Who, Lucy? Who are you talking about?'

'I'm not supposed to tell,' she said.

John Finnegan said, in an embarrassed tone, 'I'd better be going.' He gave his mother a kiss. 'See you on Thursday.'

She rose stiffly. 'I'll walk to the car with you. I could do with the exercise.'

John Finnegan shook hands with Lucy, then me. He had a firm handshake and I thought he held my hand a fraction longer than necessary. 'Perhaps I'll see you when you're next visiting?'

Lucy had fallen asleep again. I sat beside her for a while, going over what she had said. 'The year I had the baby.'

Lucy had never married. As far as I knew, she had never had a baby. 1940. I was born in November 1936. In 1940 I would have been living in the old house with my parents. Grandpa and Granny were living in the west wing. Lucy must have been living with them. Daddy would have been twenty-nine or thirty. Had he joined up by then? He was away for most of the war. Lucy too. She was six years younger than Daddy. Could she have had a baby without him knowing anything about it?

I leaned over and whispered, 'Lucy? Are you awake?'

She didn't stir. She looked like a dormouse. Her hat lying in her lap like a great, furry paw.

Henry summoned me back to the present. 'Penny for them, Diana. You're miles away.'

'I was thinking about Lucy. She forgot my name today. She's never done that before.'

'Is she upset about losing her memory?'

'Hard to know. She covers up well. But there was something else bothering her, Henry. Has Lucy ever mentioned a baby to you?'

'We don't talk much when I visit. Paddy jumps up on her lap. She fusses over him. He loves it. I really think one should be allowed dogs in those places.' He gazed fondly at Paddy.

'It's the first time I've seen Lucy distressed,' I said. 'The baby died, I think.'

'Perhaps it was someone else's baby?'

'There was something in the way she said it.' I repeated Lucy's words. '1940. The year I had the baby.'

'Good Lord.' Henry sat up.

'She sounded awfully miserable, Henry. She was locked into the past. Then she said she wasn't supposed to talk about it.'

'Poor Lucy,' Henry said softly. 'She used to drive up and take me out from school. Send me postal orders. There ought to be a feminine equivalent of avuncular.'

'We could ask Daphne,' I said. 'We owe her a visit.'

'I don't think Daphne knows any Latin.'

'Ask her about Lucy, you idiot.' Then I saw he was teasing me. I laughed. I didn't mind. It was a sign of good spirits.

'Where's all Lucy's stuff?' he asked.

'She doesn't have a lot,' I said. 'She sold her furniture when she sold the cottage. She couldn't take much to The Lindens. A small escritoire that Daddy gave her, I think. It was in the Hall originally. A few photograph albums. A vase. Two of your paintings, Henry. A watercolour of Wooldene and a portrait of Granny. And an engraving of Saint Nicholas Owen and Edward Oldcorne.'

Nicholas Owen and Edward Oldcorne were English Catholic martyrs. Nicholas Owen died under torture. Edward Oldcorne was hanged, drawn and quartered.

'I know the engraving you mean,' Henry said. 'Torture on the rack. Artist's grisly imaginings, of course. Still, doesn't bear thinking about.' He shuddered. 'Not a cheery scene to have hanging on one's wall.'

'Lucy said it was an injunction against complaining. It reminded her how easy her life was. Granny gave it to her.' I had a sudden thought. 'Do you suppose it was because Lucy had a baby and Granny made her give it up for adoption?'

'You'll have to ask Lucy.' Henry thought for a moment. 'There might be something in her will.'

'I don't remember seeing anything,' I said. 'I had a look when Lucy was selling the cottage, in case there were things that had to be kept because she'd bequeathed them to someone. She was beginning to be forgetful even then. It wasn't a long document. She hasn't much to leave. The money from the sale of the cottage is paying for The Lindens.'

'Not much left for us, then.'

'Henry!'

He looked ashamed. 'I love her too.' He inhaled deeply through his nostrils. 'You are a wonderful cook, Diana. The rabbit smells divine. But sometimes I yearn for a bloody great steak.' He topped up our glasses.

'I met a wine merchant at The Lindens today,' I said casually. 'Runs quite a big company, I think. He was visiting his mother. Have you thought about getting someone to value the wine we found in the cellar?'

'I've got a chap I was at school with. He's coming next week. Simon Duff Pemberton. Otherwise known as Plum.'

'Good.' I felt a ripple of disappointment.

'A second opinion would be no bad thing, I suppose,' said Henry. 'Might raise the price a bit.'

'I could ask him, next time I see him, if you like.'

'Good idea.'

I felt suddenly keyed up at the thought of seeing John Finnegan again. Had I imagined the flash of interest in his eyes? An utterly unexpected birthday present.

# 7

# Louise

The film business floats on a sea of promises. Nobody signs until everybody signs. A single backer can hold everything up. Until all the promises are on paper, signed and countersigned, and the money is in the bank, a production is like a boat, idling at anchor, with only a skeleton crew.

As one of the skeleton crew, I spent most days with a telephone in one hand and my contacts book in the other, 'checking availability'. Not actually booking people or ordering equipment, just trying to get them on board without committing Rebecca to spending money.

The ear that wasn't stuck to the telephone was a receiver for updates on finance as Rebecca tried to persuade half a dozen smaller backers to invest more in exchange for a bigger share of the profits.

She had wheedled fifty thousand pounds out of one of Robert's friends. 'A venture capitalist,' she told me. 'Rich as Croesus. Loves the idea of being a movie angel, but he drives a hard bargain. There'll be nothing left for us at this rate.'

The office of Telekinetic Productions was on the second floor of a former warehouse behind Borough market. It was a long open-plan room with a concrete floor and a boxed-off corner for a sink, a cupboard and a small fridge. Two portable gas heaters and a two-bar electric fire took the chill out of the damp air. Four desks and a sofa stood against an interior wall. High windows ran along the opposite wall, overlooking an entrance to the market. Background shouting, banging and crashing of crates, gave a sense of breeziness and bustle, but was not loud enough to disturb.

At the end of the week I came into the office to find Rebecca glowering at an email. I could tell, from the way she was drumming her fingers on the desk, that the last backer, an American distribution company, hadn't come through.

'They want a modern twist. Whatever that is.'

'They're just flexing their financial muscles.' I tried to ignore the knot of anxiety in my stomach.

'I find the perfect location and five days later this happens.'

'Sure you know what they're like, these companies. Don't worry yourself. Teddy and Jacky will be here at eleven. They'll have a few ideas.'

'Teddy is tearing his hair out. He's done four rewrites already. Jacky is dropping hints about directing something else.'

'He hasn't got anything else,' I said, winking at Chloe, the newly hired, nervous-looking production assistant who was hovering beside us. She had black-and-pink striped hair, thin shoulders and a dishevelled air. She wanted to get into the film business and so was working for next to nothing. I hoped she was more efficient than she looked. Rebecca wasn't patient with slow learners.

'Mr McQuitty dropped off a CD,' Chloe said, 'along with a note of the pieces that might be suitable for the soundtrack. I could make you some coffee. You could listen to them before he arrives.'

She checked the CD against Jacky's note, wrote a label, fixed it to the box and slid the disc into the player on Rebecca's desk.

Now the office vibrated with music from the man-sized speakers at either end. Ebullient, quivering strings bounded from note to note, bringing to my mind an image of fields and woods and a billowing sky.

Rebecca stopped drumming with her fingers. 'Might do for the opening sequence when Amy is galloping with the hunt.' She looked thoughtful.

Chloe answered the unspoken question. 'Elgar. *Introduction and Allegro* for strings. He died in 1934. We need to clear copyright.'

'Find out how much. Might be worth it,' said Rebecca. She turned the music down and stared again at the screen.

I could hear Teddy Hammond and Jacky McQuitty arguing as they came up the stairs. Their voices, loud with conviction, echoed in the stone stairway.

'Drama has rules,' Teddy was saying as he came through the door. 'Remember Chekhov? If a gun is hanging on the wall in the first act, it must go off in the third.'

'Film rules are different.' Jacky was louder, even more exasperated, jigging about on the balls of his feet.

'Not that different. The audience has the same expectations.'

'The script is too wordy,' said Jacky.

'It just needs a polish. Anyway, everyone is happy with it now.'

'Hold it right there.' Rebecca pressed the stop button on the CD player and held up her hand like a policeman. 'Not everyone is happy with it.' She looked grim as she quoted from the screen, 'We expect to begin distribution in 2000. While we are still, in principle, willing to commit the agreed sum to the budget, we feel the story lacks the modern twist that would make it more relevant to a twenty-first-century audience.'

'What the fuck does that mean?' said Teddy.

'It means we don't get four hundred thousand pounds. It means the film doesn't go ahead. It means we tear up your script and start again.' Rebecca's voice was even but the edge of her mouth trembled.

'It was a great pitch,' Jacky said. 'Low budget. High concept. Sex, frocks and royalty.' He swung his head sideways and jabbed the air like a boxer.

I tried not to think about my mortgage and my overdraft.

Teddy swung his head sideways as though banging it against a wall.

Chloe said, 'I'll make more coffee.'

I went back to my desk and began looking for ways to save

four hundred thousand pounds from the budget. When I broke my concentration to stretch my legs by walking to the window and looking out over the muffled commotion of the market, I could hear the script conference, punctuated with agonised shouts and groans, at the far side of the office.

Chloe perched on my desk during a break in the discussion. 'They keep looking at me as though they want me to contribute,' she said. 'It's nice. Nobody asked my opinion about anything in my last job. But I don't know enough about the story. We didn't do that period of history at school. I haven't read *Kenilworth*. I haven't read Mr Hammond's script yet. I don't know who the characters are.'

'Robert Dudley is the Earl of Leicester,' I began. 'He's the favourite of Queen Elizabeth the first. You know who she is?'

Chloe nodded. 'Good Queen Bess. The Virgin Queen.'

'She's in love with Leicester. He would like to marry her. But he's already married to Amy Robsart.'

I was aware that Jacky and Teddy had moved to stand by the window and were listening to my résumé of the plot.

'Amy lives in the country while Leicester stays up at court in London,' I continued. 'Then, one evening she's found dead at the bottom of a flight of stairs, with her neck broken.'

Chloe shuddered. 'Poor thing.'

'You see?' Teddy waved his long arms. 'Amy has the sympathy of the audience.'

'That depends on how you write her character,' said Jacky. 'Nobody knows what really happened to her. Which is why you can make anything happen.'

'As long as it satisfies some idiot distributor,' said Teddy.

'Who might know a thing or two about what pleases audiences.' Rebecca had moved across the room to join us.

'But not a lot about the rules of drama,' Teddy said sourly.

Chloe's eyes sparkled. 'What are the rules?'

'Classic storytelling rules,' said Teddy. 'Old as Aristotle. First act: introduce your characters, the main plot and subplots. Second act: build the plots to a climax. Third act: resolve everything.' He paused. 'Then there are the Hollywood rules. Create a character who wants something and stop him getting it for two and a half hours. Throw in three car chases and four explosions.' He rolled his eyes and put his hand to his mouth in a mock yawn.

'So Robert Dudley, Earl of Leicester,' Chloe glanced at me to check she had got the name and title right. I nodded. 'He wants to marry the queen and his wife is the obstacle in his way?' I nodded again. 'So he's a sort of anti-hero?'

'Not in my screenplay,' said Teddy. 'I have a proper hero. Tressilian, a childhood friend of Amy who tries to protect her. Invented by Walter Scott. He didn't pay much attention to historical accuracy but he knew how to tell a good story.'

'You tell a good story as well, Teddy,' said Rebecca. 'It just needs a modern twist for the Americans.'

Teddy bared his teeth at her.

'What happens to Tressilian?' asked Chloe.

'He dies of a broken heart.'

'He can't do that in Hollywood,' said Jacky. 'They'd prefer he was a serial killer.'

'Who kills Amy?' asked Chloe.

'Leicester's steward, Varney. He's ambitious. He wants his boss to marry the queen.'

'Walter Scott made that up as well,' murmured Teddy.

'A modern twist?' Chloe's eyes narrowed in concentration. 'What if . . .' She gave a little shrug, as though disowning what she was about to say. 'What if you turn it all on its head? Leicester loves his wife. He's torn between the two women. Amy and the queen. The villain is Tressilian, Amy's childhood lover. He's become her stalker.'

'Good God,' said Teddy. 'The child's a genius.'

He seized Chloe by the shoulders and kissed her on both cheeks.

Jacky was nodding and smiling. 'A stalker. That's not bad. I like it.' He looked at Rebecca. 'You don't like it?'

'Yes. It's a good idea.'

'You don't look like you like it.'

Rebecca wet her lips with a tiny movement of her tongue.

'No. It's great. I was thinking about something else.' She gave a little shake. 'Fine. We'll go with it. The Americans will love it. Full steam ahead.' She hoisted her jacket from the back of the door and sailed off to a meeting at Channel 4.

# 8

# Louise

There was a sense of anticlimax, as though Rebecca had taken all the energy in the room with her. Jacky opened a drawer in his desk and took out a bottle of whiskey. 'We could all do with a splash of this in our coffee.'

We stood at the window clutching our mugs, looking down into the street.

'I'm putting an ad in the personal column of the *London Review of Books*.' Jacky waved a notebook in the air. 'Will you all have a listen and tell me what you think of this?' A pause for throat clearing. 'Film director – brackets, forty-nine – would like to meet lover of classic cinema, theatre, opera, books, food and fine wines.'

Chloe said, 'You need to be more specific. Which opera, what books?'

'All right.' Jacky began crossing out and rewriting. 'Would like to meet lover of Bach, Sheridan, Sean O'Casey and the films of Jean Renoir.'

'What do you really want, Jacky?' I asked.

'"The deep peace of the double bed after the hurly-burly of the chaise longue."'

'Clever,' said Chloe.

'Not original,' said Teddy. 'A quote from Mrs Patrick Campbell, I think. And a bit fey?'

Jacky gave a little skip and raised his mug in a mock toast.

'Three cheers for fey.' He studied the revisions. 'How's this? Director – brackets, forty-nine – would like to meet . . . et cetera, et cetera . . . and have fun.'

'Not bad,' Chloe said. 'If I was a man, I'd respond to that.'

'I wish you were, Ducky. You and I could have a lot of fun.' Jacky winked at me.

'You're a terrible flirt, Jacky,' I said.

'On the contrary, I'm an excellent flirt.' He stored the notebook in his jacket pocket. 'I could give you lessons.'

I had learned a lot from Jacky. He had introduced me to poetry, 'not just a pleasure but food for the brain'; fine wines, 'the better the wine, the less you drink: better for your health and cheaper in the long run'; and baroque music, 'the perfect combination of beauty, precision and wit. Just like me,' said with a dazzling smile. He was eight years older than me and treated me like a younger sister.

We first met each other at a party in Belfast when I was a student. It was a hot night in June, just after final exams. There was a lot of drink and dope and head clutching, interspersed with wild and exuberant dancing. I lost my boyfriend in the melee and found him in a bedroom with a pile of coats and a blonde girl I vaguely recognised from the politics department, even though she had no clothes on. I stumbled into the street and into the middle of a magnificent row between Jacky and his then partner. I sat on a windowsill, sobbing, but gradually became distracted from my misery by Jacky's orotund insults delivered in mellifluous tones to a blond boy in a brocade waistcoat who swung his fists wildly and yelled, 'Fuck you too!' before running off down the street in tears. Jacky raised his arms to the sky and made a noise somewhere between a groan and a sigh before becoming aware of me watching him.

'Well, my Venus in blue jeans, it looks like we've both been dumped.' He crouched to scan my face. 'I can't resist a crying beauty.'

I pointed at the glimmer of brocade in the distance. 'You seem to be resisting that one.'

'A stickler for accuracy, I see. That's no bad thing. I can't mend Billy's tears so I might as well try to mend yours.' His sudden smile was like sunshine after rain.

We walked to his flat a few streets away. 'Welcome to Heartbreak Hotel,' he said, deliberately droll. We sat, alternately talking and listening to his selection of 'music to cry to'. Sometime before dawn he played Purcell's *Dido and Aeneas*. It was the first time I had heard the sad, descending semi-tones of Dido's lament, 'Remember me, but ah! forget my fate'.

When the final chorus died away, Jacky said, 'If your heart was broken you'd sing like that.' He gently lifted the record from the turntable and held it between his fingers. 'In the opera, Dido builds a funeral pyre and throws herself on it as Aeneas sails into the sunset. But I'm not going to immolate myself over a boy. And neither are you.'

Then he played Paul Simon singing 'Fifty Ways to Leave Your Lover' and we danced and laughed until the sun came up. It was a great way to begin a friendship.

Jacky worked for Ulster Television. He moved to Glasgow, then to London. We never lost touch. We always saw each other when he came back to Northern Ireland to visit his mother. In the first few years of Mum's depression, it was Jacky I telephoned when I felt sucked dry by her misery and neediness. He understood. He had kept me sane. He was the first person I contacted when I moved to London.

A sudden bang and rattle drew our eyes to a man dressed as Santa Claus unloading Christmas trees from a lorry in the street below.

'Bloody Christmas,' said Jacky, suddenly morose. '"Frosty the fucking Snowman" and "White Christmas" all day long.'

'Are you going home for Christmas?' I asked.

'Mammy expects it.'

'Where's home?' asked Chloe.

'London,' said Jacky. 'But Louise means Belfast. She hasn't been in London long enough to call it home. Isn't that right, Louise?'

'Where's home for you, Chloe?' I asked.

'I'll give you a clue. My second name is McPherson.'

'You don't sound Scottish,' I said, surprised.

'Chloe's one of those posh Scottish girls with an English accent,' said Jacky. 'Fettes?'

Chloe laughed. 'Loretto.'

I was alternately astonished and amused by Jacky's ability to decipher social codes and rituals. It was like speaking a parallel language.

'It's quite amusing to learn,' he said when I first remarked on it.

'That's a very English turn of phrase, Jacky. You've gone native.'

'And where do you think that phrase comes from?' had been his retort.

He had taken me to a couple of smart London parties where nearly everybody had a nickname and they had all been at school with each other. The kind of party someone called Daisy might go to, I thought. But I wasn't a delicate Daisy. I was lanky Louise. I had felt uncomfortable and out of place.

'All yahs, and waugh-waughs and haw-haws,' I muttered to Jacky in the taxi on the way home.

'They can't help how they speak. You've met lots of people in the film industry who talk like that. What about Jonny whatshisname. He's a Lord, isn't he?'

'He's bohemian. They're in a class of their own.'

Jacky had overcome my reluctance and dragged me to a charity ball. 'It's for a good cause.'

'Why don't I just write a cheque?'

'Don't be like that.'

'Like what?'

'Like a disapproving Cinderella.'

'I wasn't born sophisticated,' I said.

'Nobody's born sophisticated. We aspire to sophistication.'

'I want to stay who I am, Jacky.'

'Do you think I'm a different person?'

'You sound different.'

'I've been in England nearly half my life,' Jacky said. 'I've lost my accent. That doesn't mean I've lost my soul. I know who I am and where I come from.'

'Do you know where you're going?'

'Half the fun in life is not knowing where you're going. I just wish there was someone with me on the road.'

I had glimpsed the loneliness beneath the wit and wisdom playfully dispensed.

Now Jacky was smiling, splashing more whiskey into our mugs. 'Where's home for you, Teddy?' he asked.

Teddy shrugged. 'I don't have a particular spot I call home.'

'"Home is where the heart is,"' Jacky sang out. 'Where's your heart?'

'Not on my sleeve,' Teddy muttered.

There was an awkward pause. Chloe broke the silence. 'Rebecca says the man who owns the manor is a bit of a dish. Might do for you, Louise.'

'Not handsome enough to tempt me.'

'Handsome has never tempted you,' Jacky said.

'Are you saying all my boyfriends have been ugly?'

'You've always been attracted to brains. That's why you like me. And Chloe.'

'I'm glad you think I've got brains,' Chloe said. 'My boyfriend thinks I'm stupid.'

'Why do you stay with him then?' asked Teddy.

'Because he's handsome enough to tempt me.' Chloe curtsied.

Teddy laughed. The awkwardness passed.

We went back to our desks in a mood of cheerful optimism.

# 9

# Diana

I found myself hoping John Finnegan would be visiting his mother when I arrived at The Lindens on my next visit to Aunt Lucy. I looked around the car park, wondering what kind of car he drove. He was the kind of man who would drive something splendidly solid and comfortable. A Mercedes? A BMW? Then I felt foolish. One smile and you're anybody's, I said crossly to myself. Stop behaving like a teenager. You're a grandmother for heaven's sake. John Finnegan is probably married and even if he isn't he won't be looking for a middle-aged woman. And anyway, middle-aged is an utterly ridiculous term for a woman of sixty-two because how many people live to be one hundred and twenty?

I was still scolding myself as I walked towards my reflection in the glass door of The Lindens. As always, there was a moment between one heartbeat and the next when I didn't recognise myself. A moment in which I am forever eighteen, before the present reasserts itself and I know I am the angular figure smiling wryly back at me.

The matron, Morag Hamilton, a pleasant, dark-haired Scottish woman, was hovering in the lobby.

'Can I have a wee word?'

She closed her office door behind me, indicated a chair, and seated herself behind the desk.

'Have you noticed a change in your auntie?'

'Her memory is getting worse,' I said unhappily.

'Aye, you'll have noticed that. We had the doctor to her on Tuesday. We've taken blood samples. Sometimes these wee lapses are down to vitamin deficiencies. We did a few other wee tests as well. Name ten animals. Who's the prime minister, that kind of thing.' She paused.

'You think she has Alzheimer's?'

'You can never be sure what's causing memory loss. The doctor thinks she's been having transient, ischaemic attacks this while back.' She checked my expression to see if I understood.

'Mini-strokes,' I said. 'She's been having mini-strokes. And you think she has Alzheimer's as well?'

Morag nodded. 'Maybe so. But no need to worry yourself just now.'

How could I not worry?

'We're keeping an eye on her blood pressure,' Morag continued calmly. 'We're reviewing her assessment. She may need more nursing care, a bit more of a hand with some things.' Her voice dropped. 'More expensive, I'm afraid.' Another pause.

By now I was expecting what she said next, but it still came as a shock.

'We don't think Lucy is competent to sign cheques any longer.'

'She gave me enduring power of attorney when she made the decision to come here,' I said.

'Sensible woman,' said Morag.

'Not any more.' I started to laugh but my eyes filled with tears. I found a tissue in my handbag and blew my nose. All comedy is tragedy, I thought to myself. And death is the great punchline waiting for us all.

'You have to laugh sometimes.' Morag's smile was all sympathy. 'They get funny notions. Lucy was talking about limbo dancing. Now where did that come from? Your auntie wasn't a dancer, was she?'

'She was a hospital almoner,' I said. 'I imagine she had to deal with Alzheimer's. Do you think she knows she has it?'

'She's never down in the mouth. Always a smile and a thank you.' Morag stood up and looked out of the window. 'The weather's no been holding up. It looks like rain. I don't advise taking her out today. She has a wee bit of a cough.'

I thought about asking if Lucy had talked to any of the staff about a baby, but dismissed the idea. It was a private matter. I would bring it up only if I failed to find out more from Lucy.

I found Lucy in the lounge. Sunitra was giving her some liquid medicine in a plastic cup.

I looked around. Agnes was not in her usual chair. Apart from Sunitra, there was no one within ten yards of us.

'Hairdressing today,' said Sunitra. 'But not good for Lucy to have wet hair now.'

The television blinked and burbled at a low volume in the corner but the room was otherwise quiet. Sunitra gave a little wave of farewell and wheeled the medicine trolley away.

'They're frightfully nice here,' Lucy said. 'The staff are pleasant and the food is quite good. But I will be glad when I go home.'

I listened with a sinking heart as she chatted placidly on.

'I'm just here until they finish the . . . until they finish the thing that makes the . . . where I live . . . bigger. Then I am going home.' There was a defiant note in her voice.

I pulled my chair closer, took her hands in mine and positioned myself to look directly into her eyes. 'Do you know who I am, Lucy?'

She blinked. Her eyes focused. 'Of course,' she said. 'You're Diana. It's very good of you to come and see me.'

'Lucy,' I began. 'I came to see you last week. You were talking about a baby. Whose baby was that?'

Lucy lowered her voice to a whisper. 'My baby. Edward. I named him Edward.'

'What happened to Edward?' I was whispering too.

'I promised not to tell.'

'It's all right to tell me, Lucy. What happened to him?'

Lucy closed her eyes. The muscles in her face tightened in concentration. 'I know my . . . it's not right. I'm trying . . . where . . .' She coughed and opened her eyes. They were sad and

50

unfocused now. She shook her head and her voice was little more than a breath. 'Somewhere.'

The door of the lounge opened and a procession of newly coiffed white and silver heads bobbed across the room. Lucy squeezed my hand and nodded towards her Zimmer. It was a signal she wanted to go to the lavatory. I helped her to her feet and watched her inch across the room, inclining her head in a greeting to the returning residents.

Agnes Finnegan brought up the rear. I had not realised she was so tall. Almost as tall as her son, I thought.

'Good afternoon. Not so good for a drive, however.' She nodded towards the rain-streaked window.

I returned her smile. 'We're not going out today. Lucy has a cold.'

Agnes settled into her chair. 'Always cheerful, Lucy. Never complains. Not like some.'

She had a sensible, friendly air. She saw more of Lucy than I did. I decided she was discreet.

'Does Lucy talk much to you?'

'Yes. We have nice chats,' said Agnes.

'Does she make sense?'

'Her memory isn't so good,' Agnes said carefully. 'But I usually work out what she's talking about.'

'Matron said she was talking about limbo dancing.'

'Limbo dancing?' Agnes looked incredulous. 'Nonsense.' She snorted. 'Nobody knows anything these days. They're all pagans. Limbo dancing?' She gestured impatiently. 'Rubbish. Lucy was talking about limbo.' She gave each syllable its full weight. Lim-bo.

I stared at her.

'She's a Catholic, isn't she? Same as me. Father Dominic pops in to visit us both. I heard her ask him about limbo. I don't know why, but it was on her mind. She asked me as well. Asked me what I thought it was like.'

A long-forgotten phrase from a childhood catechism came to mind. A place or state of natural happiness, free from suffering and pain . . . I couldn't remember any more.

'When I started nursing,' said Agnes, 'I was told by the nuns always to baptise a baby that was in danger of death. So they wouldn't go to limbo.' She frowned in concentration before reciting, in a low voice, 'A place or state of natural happiness, free from suffering and pain but without a share in the eternal life God promises to those who die in grace.'

'You have a good memory,' I said softly.

'I have great recall for things I learned years ago. But sometimes I can't remember what I did yesterday. Mind you, there's not much to remember. Every day is the same. The food's not bad, I'll say that. I couldn't stay somewhere they didn't know how to cook. Your aunt is the same. They make a nice light sponge here.' She sighed. 'There's no mention of limbo these days. I don't think they learn about it any more. Father Dominic said it wasn't in the new catechism.'

'I think limbo has been left in a kind of . . . limbo,' I said.

'No bad thing,' said Agnes. 'I never liked to think about poor souls kept in some sort of heavenly waiting room. A happy enough place, we were told. But it made me think of waiting rooms in railway stations. All brown linoleum and cigarette smoke.' She shook her head. 'Hard to know what we're supposed to believe in. I don't think people believe in hell any more either.'

The light above the lavatory was still red. 'Has Lucy ever talked about a baby?' I said quickly.

'Not to me.' Agnes gave me a sharp look. 'Did you want me to say something to her?'

Her directness threw me.

'I don't know,' I said. 'Perhaps if she mentions it?'

Agnes dipped her head in assent. 'I'll let you know.'

'Is your son coming to visit you today?' The words were out before I could stop them.

'It's my daughter's turn today.'

Out of the corner of my eye I saw the red light turn to green. Lucy emerged and began her slow journey back across the room. I thought how small she had become, as though her bones were shrinking with her memory. I thought how awfully small my disappointments were in comparison.

'It's just that I wanted to ask him about wine,' I said, grateful for the ready explanation. 'My brother inherited some old wines. He wants to have them valued. I wondered . . .' I gave a little shrug.

'If John would be interested?' Agnes looked past my shoulder. 'What do you think, Lydia?'

A petite blonde with short feathery hair materialised beside me.

'Diana has some wines she wants valued,' Agnes said, presenting her cheek to be kissed. I stood up to shake hands, praying I didn't look discomfited.

'I'm sure John would be delighted,' Lydia said affably. 'I'll ask him to call you.' She took a Filofax from her handbag.

'Lydia works in the business as well,' Agnes said.

'Perhaps you might . . .' I began, confused.

'John's the one you want,' Lydia said, pen poised. 'He's the expert. What's your telephone number?'

Lucy was more than halfway across the room. I saw that her skirt was caught up at the front, saw her follow my gaze and become aware of it, saw her shuffle gamely on. She will be much more embarrassed if I go over now and adjust her dress, I thought. What is my embarrassment to hers? I recited my telephone number and waited for Lucy to reach me.

Agnes and Lydia busied themselves in conversation while I tugged Lucy's petticoat from her tights and straightened her skirt.

She leaned stoically on her Zimmer. 'I'm back to front and upside down,' she said. Her eyes closed when she sat down. The muscles of her face were taut under her pale, powdery skin. 'Can you please find my . . . I know what it is . . . I can't remember what it's called . . . that thing you gave me . . . listening.'

The portable CD player was in the soft red handbag at Lucy's feet, a splash of colour on the dull beige carpet. She always had an eye for colour. I clipped the black spongy headphones over her ears, checked there was a disc in the player and clicked the switch.

After about a minute, Lucy opened her eyes. 'Thank you, dear.' She took off the headphones and handed them to me. I put them on. My head was filled by the entire string section of an orchestra soaring and swooping around a line of melody so sweet it lifted and filled my spirits like a gust of wind.

'Vaughan Williams,' I said. '"Variations on a theme by Thomas Tallis."'

'It makes me think of home,' Lucy said. 'In the fields . . . Nicky and me . . . apples . . .' Her eyes closed again. I replaced the headphones on her ears.

I knew she wasn't remembering her cottage near Checkendon. The music had summoned the landscape of her childhood in Wooldene. I didn't want to disturb her peace by asking questions.

# 10

# Diana

Two days later I left Tomasz in charge of the shop and set off for Northamptonshire with Henry to visit my father's cousin, Daphne, the repository of all the family history. She could explain how someone was related to someone else to the smallest drop of consanguinity.

We don't visit her nearly enough, I thought guiltily, as she led us through the draughty, marble-tiled hall and into the drawing room.

She had laid a table in the great bay window, overlooking the pale winter lawn and the dank green shrubbery beyond. A soup tureen and two covered casserole dishes rested on an electric hotplate on a side-table.

'I don't use the dining room any more. There are hardly any of my friends left to entertain. I only heat this room and my bedroom.'

Daphne's seal point Siamese cats, Damson and Peach, reclined against each other in a basket in front of a glowing coal fire. The ancient cast-iron radiators seemed to shudder with exertion. The impression was one of warmth and faded cosiness, but I noticed Daphne was wearing two cardigans to ward off the draughts seeping through cracks in the window frame.

She carefully ladled soup into our bowls from the tureen.

'Winter vegetable. Made by a sweet New Zealand lady who comes in three days a week to do my shopping and cooking.

She puts it all in the freezer. She works for the agency for a few months and gets enough money to pay for a nice holiday in Europe. So enterprising, don't you think?'

'Nice to be able to stay in one's own home,' said Henry.

'At least while I have my marbles,' Daphne said. 'Which is more than can be said for poor Lucy. George drove me down to visit her in that place. I had to remind her who I was.'

There was a hint of pride as well as pity in her voice. Underlying her blithe complaints about aching joints and the indignity of using a stairlift, was a sense of satisfaction in holding on to her wits.

'I'm ninety, dear. Older than Lucy. I can't walk very far. Otherwise can't complain.'

Her hands were mottled purple, brown and red, the skin so thin and transparent that every bone and vein was visible. Her eyes had shrunk. They looked lidless but alert, like the eyes of a bird. An eagle, I decided. A scrawny white-headed eagle, surveying the landscape of her life.

Daphne had been a widow for nearly forty years. Her sons, my second cousins, worked in the city and lived in London. They had never succumbed to the allure of country living. Tommy was fond of saying airily, in invisible inverted commas, '"There is nothing good to be had in the country, or if there is, they will not let you have it."' He attributed the quote to Hazlitt.

'My grandchildren love London,' Daphne said. 'Although one can't really call them children any more. Hugo is thirty-two and Harriet is thirty. Neither of them shows the slightest intention of getting married. When I was their age I had George and Tommy.'

'I'm surprised Lucy never married,' I said, plunging in. 'So pretty, so much fun.'

'Three times a bridesmaid, never a bride. Do they still say that?' The question was rhetorical. 'No one seems to get married or have bridesmaids these days. I don't know what's wrong with the young. They don't want to settle down. I was married when I was twenty-two. Lucy was one of my bridesmaids. She was a bridesmaid when Nicky married your mother. I was a maid of honour. Then she was a bridesmaid for one of her friends. I can't remember her name. She was at Woldingham with her. Three times a bridesmaid, never a bride, I said to Lucy at the time. She didn't seem to care. She had plenty of young men dancing attendance on her.'

'Anyone in particular?' I asked.

'It's all so long ago,' Daphne said. 'But there was one chap I remember. Nigel Farndale. I met him two or three times. Good looking. His father was a baronet. But,' she grimaced, 'parents didn't approve. Timing was wrong. I don't suppose it would matter much these days, but it did then.'

'He wasn't a Catholic? Granny and Grandpa saw him off?'

'Not at all. They liked him. He had money and prospects. He was going to inherit a title. He told Lucy he was prepared to bring their children up as Catholics,' Daphne said. 'The trouble was, his father wouldn't have Lucy. Bloody papist, he said. Not having my grandchildren brought up papists. Bloody big row, according to Lucy. Nigel stuck to his guns at first. Then there was the double whatsit with Grandpa and Uncle George.' She gestured impatiently. 'What's the word everyone uses these days?'

'Double whammy,' said Henry. 'Double whammy with estate duty.'

My grandfather and great-grandfather had died within two years of each other. Half the estate, or what was left of it, went to the Treasury.

'No money for Lucy,' said Daphne. 'Not just a papist but a pauper as well. Not so enticing. He broke it off.'

'Poor Lucy,' I said. 'She had just lost her father.'

'He married a girl with a face like a frog and oodles of money. Nigel, I mean. Saw his death in the paper sometime last year.'

We sat in silence for a moment. I thought how our family had once owned most of the land for miles around Wooldene. At least half of it had been sold to pay the recusancy fines imposed because my ancestors didn't attend the new Anglican services and stayed staunchly Roman Catholic. The fine was twenty pounds a month. More than two thousand pounds in today's money. My great-grandfather had gambled away some of the remainder before further disobliging the family by dying inconveniently close to his son.

'Lucy may have been happier not being married,' Henry said.

'How is Jenny?' Daphne asked. She knew about Henry's divorce and undoubtedly disapproved, but I absolved her of malice. The question was the automatic opening to a long series of answers and responses that was the family litany. Before Daphne brought out the cheese and biscuits, we would be up to date with relatives and their friends, and friends and their relatives. Including people we had heard about but not actually met. Daphne was bound to ask about Jenny. Not only had she met her, she had been to school with Jenny's grandmother. They were still in touch, Daphne said.

'I gather Jenny is living in Fulham. I expect she likes being near the shops again.'

'We don't have much communication,' Henry said, in an even tone. 'Peter tells me she likes her flat.'

'And how is Peter? Any sign of him getting married?'

'Unfortunately, yes,' said Henry.

Daphne gave him a beaky look but decided not to pursue the enquiry. She rose stiffly from the table and slowly led the way across the room to the sofa and armchairs by the fire. The cats stared lazily at us for a moment, yawned, and went back to sleep. Henry slumped into an armchair.

Daphne moved on to Catherine and Carl and my grandchildren, diligently asking about Carl's work, the children's progress at school, 'How are their grades? Isn't that what the Americans say?', my garden business, 'And how is your little enterprise going?', gradually working her way towards the outer circle of our acquaintance.

Henry tried to look interested and gamely recounted what he knew about the captain of industry whose portrait he had just been commissioned to paint and who would now join the currency of Daphne's conversation. She would find a way of mentioning his name in conversation in order to add, 'My cousin is painting his portrait, you know.'

'I must tell Golly Hunter,' Daphne said. 'Her grandson is an artist. He's having a show in Brighton. Apparently he's famous. He doesn't paint. He does things called installations.'

'Henry is having a show in London the week before Christmas,' I said, in a sudden urge to trump the unknown Golly Hunter.

'Golly's nephew was in the army with you, Henry,' said Daphne. 'Hector Hargreaves. He's married to a cousin of Vanessa.'

I thought I remembered him from one of George and Vanessa's parties. 'Side-swept hair? Estate agent? Is that Hector, Henry?'

Henry was fidgeting, looking at his watch, disinclined to gossip any more. The conversation had drifted a long way from Lucy. I dragged it back.

'You said George drove you to see Lucy?'

'I don't drive much these days, dear. Only to Mass on Sundays. I don't drive after dark. Or when it's icy. Or raining.' She stretched her mouth in a smile, but there was more stoicism than humour in it. She nodded towards the window and the waning light. 'One is pretty much marooned here in winter.'

I felt another stab of guilt, mixed with compassion and melancholy. An almost dizzy sense of time racing and my own future facing me on a faded chintz sofa. I began to calculate if I could fit in another visit to Daphne before Christmas. Probably not.

'I'll come again in the New Year,' I said.

One of the cats detached itself from its companion and sprang gracefully on to Daphne's lap.

'That would be nice, dear.' She stroked the cat tenderly. 'Now, you were asking me about Lucy?'

'I wondered when you had last seen her.'

Daphne frowned in concentration. 'It must have been the summer. I remember it was still bright when we got back and George stayed the night because it was too late to drive home to London.'

'Did Lucy tell you she'd had a baby?'

The cat yowled and jumped on to the floor. Daphne looked startled.

'The last time I went to see Lucy she told me she'd had a

baby in 1940. I thought at first she was talking nonsense. Then I wasn't so sure. Do you think it could be true?'

Daphne put her head to one side and considered my question. There was a gleam of excitement in her eyes.

'I always wondered,' she said.

'Bingo,' said Henry.

We waited for Daphne to begin.

'It must have been February or March 1940,' she said slowly. 'Tommy was a baby. We were living in Northumberland. It was frightfully cold. Your grandmother telephoned and asked if she could drive up to see me because she had a special favour to ask. She sounded decidedly put out. I said, Of course, and what was the problem? And she said she would discuss it when she saw me. I asked how everyone was. She said everyone was fine. She asked about the children. Then she said something to the effect that Lucy needed to know how demanding a baby was, even with a nanny and a husband.' She paused. 'Virginia never came. She sent me a woolly hat she had knitted for Tommy with a note saying she didn't need a favour after all. It was a rather pretty hat. Pale blue.'

'You think Granny wanted you to keep a pregnant Lucy secluded in the north,' said Henry.

'Theo thought there was something up. He said Lucy had gone a bit wild after that chap jilted her. There was some rumour about a Polish officer she met in London. Then we heard Lucy had gone to Ireland to stay with her old nanny. We thought that was rather odd. She'd been working with evacuees. Why would she abandon war-work and go to Ireland?'

'Safer?' I suggested. 'Everybody was expecting the Germans to invade.'

'Nonsense. No member of the family ever ran away from a fight. Especially the women. I remember your mother drilling the farmhands. Had the Germans occupied us, she would have led the resistance. I remember her saying so.'

'How long did Lucy stay in Ireland?'

'Ages,' said Daphne. 'At least six months, if not longer. When she came back she started driving ambulances in London. I didn't see her again until the end of the war. When you were born, Henry, we went down to visit.'

We sat in silence for a moment.

'Daddy never said anything about Lucy going to Ireland or having a baby. Not to me. Not to Henry.'

'I don't suppose your father knew. I should think he was fighting in France by then. Virginia might not even have told your grandfather. She might have told your mother, I suppose.' She paused. 'Of course this is all speculation.' Her eyes glittered again. 'But isn't it all terrifically interesting? I wish I could remember the name of the Irish nanny. I remember Virginia saying she'd done quite well for herself: she married a doctor.'

'Daddy used to talk about her. She went back to Ireland to get married.' Her name was hovering on the edge of my memory. 'Her name will come to me,' I said. 'Her maiden name. I don't know her married name, or where she lived. Have you any idea, Daphne? Do you know where Lucy went to in Ireland?'

Daphne shook her head. 'It's such a long time ago, dear. The child, if there was a child, would be nearly sixty now.'

'He died,' I said. 'Lucy said he died. She was going to call him Edward.'

Daphne was silent for a moment. Then she made the sign of the cross. 'Poor Lucy.' She sat brooding in her chair.

I searched my brain for the name of my father's Irish nanny. I tried going through the letters of the alphabet. I tried picturing Daddy telling me a story. I went through all the Irish names I could think of. Brigid. Kathleen. Deirdre. Maeve. Siobhan. The name was like a shiny apple dangling on a tree, always just out of reach.

'Sometimes I despair about my memory,' I said to Henry on the way home. 'I go into my bedroom to look for something and can't remember what I'm looking for. I have to write everything down. I'm getting like Lucy.' I felt suddenly old and fretful.

'I bought a tin of flake-white and a tube of sap green the other day,' said Henry. 'I don't know where I put them.'

'It's no fun getting older.'

'Beats the alternative.'

My laughter must have dislodged the apple in the tree. 'Peggy O'Rourke. Her name was Peggy O'Rourke.' I leaned back and closed my eyes in relief.

# 11

# Louise

It got dark earlier each day, which seemed to match the mood in the office as we waited to hear if the script had finally been approved. Rebecca was alternately morose and agitated. Jacky was subdued. By the end of the week, Chloe was openly fretting.

'Is there any point in doing a recce? Is this film going to get made? Have you had to wait this long before?'

'Longer.' I tried to ignore the fluttering in my own ribcage. 'This is par for the course.'

We were the only two left in the office. Rebecca and Jacky had gone to meet two of our backers. Teddy had called in to ask if the distributor had been in touch, and slunk out again when the answer was no.

I dispatched Chloe to do her Christmas shopping and made a few more calls before deciding I might as well do some shopping myself.

I was walking from the tube to my flat, totting up what I had spent, calculating how much I had left in my dwindling bank account, when my mobile rang. It was Rebecca. Her voice was hoarse and strained.

'Where are you?'

'I left early. I'm nearly home.' I had my keys in my hand and was crossing the road towards the Victorian terraced house in which I had the first-floor flat. I had used my share of the profits from my last film to take out what suddenly felt like a sickeningly large mortgage.

'I'm in the pub at the bottom of the road. I'll leave now.' She rang off.

Two minutes later she was in the hallway.

'What's wrong, Rebecca?' Even in the gloom of a forty-watt light bulb, I could see she was white-faced and shivering.

'I thought I saw Barry Shaw.'

My immediate gut reaction was relief that the backers were still on board. I ushered Rebecca upstairs, unlocked the door of my flat, switched on the lights and steered her into the kitchen.

'He was in the Marks and Spencer at Marble Arch,' said Rebecca. 'I ran outside and jumped into a taxi. I didn't want to go home.'

'I'll make tea. Or do you want something stronger?'

'I couldn't think where else to go.'

'What about Robert? I don't mean you're not welcome here. Of course you are. I just mean he'd know what to do. He's a lawyer.'

She shook her head in an angry, dismissive way.

'He's in Hong Kong, remember? Anyway, he doesn't know about Barry and I don't have the energy to explain it all on the phone.'

'Are you sure it was Barry?'

She shook her head, wearily this time.

'No. Yes. I didn't stand and stare. I just wanted to get away from him.'

Barry Shaw. I hadn't thought about him for years.

He was an actor Rebecca met at a party in our flat in Belfast. I knew him slightly. He had been at school with my cousins. He had dark good looks and a kind of nervous intensity. Rebecca gave him a small part in a radio play she was producing.

For the next month or so he seemed to be around all the time. I was working late. They were usually in bed when I got back. I hardly ever saw Rebecca on her own. Then I went on holiday, followed by a week's filming in Wicklow, so I hadn't seen Rebecca for about three weeks when I got back to the flat one summer evening to find Barry throwing stones at the windows.

'She won't let me in,' he said.

'She's probably not there.'

'She's there,' he said. 'I saw her go in.'

I should have been struck by the oddity of that remark, but I was tired. I unlocked the front door and led the way across the hall. Rebecca appeared in the doorway of our flat at the top of the stairs and called down to me.

'Hi, Louise. There's a problem with the edit. I'm going back to work.'

'I'll drive you,' Barry said.

'No need.'

A horn tooted. Rebecca ran down the stairs shouting, 'Wait. I'm here.' She jumped into the minicab that had just pulled up at the kerb. It accelerated away. Rebecca didn't look back.

Barry said in a mournful tone, 'We've had a bit of a row. Can I come in?'

I made some coffee and listened for hours to Barry talking about himself and Rebecca. They were soulmates. They were meant for each other. He had known it immediately. She knew it as well but was resisting. She worked too hard. She needed to relax. He could help her. Only he could give her the support she needed.

'She's perfect for me. She can make me happy.'

I was trying not to yawn.

'I came round last night with a bunch of flowers but she wasn't in then either.'

'I'm sure you'll sort it out, Barry.'

The telephone rang. I went out to the landing to answer it.

'Don't say my name,' Rebecca said. 'Pretend it's someone else. Is he there?'

'That's a shame,' I said loudly into the phone. 'When do you think you'll be finished?'

'Thanks, Louise. Can you get rid of him?'

'It always takes longer than you think.'

65

'I'm in the BBC Club. Call me when he's gone.'

Barry was hovering in the doorway of the kitchen. He seemed to know it was Rebecca. 'Tell her I'll go down to the Club and wait for her.'

'There's somebody here going down to the club,' I said quickly into the phone. 'I'll get him to drop it off at the front desk on his way.'

'Bugger,' said Rebecca. 'I'll have to go to the Europa and phone you from there.' She rang off.

I found that day's film schedule in my bag. I put it in an envelope, wrote a cameraman's name on it and handed it to Barry.

'Can you drop that off at the BBC front desk on your way round to the club? He needs it for tomorrow.'

'I thought you were talking to Rebecca.' He looked annoyed.

I'm not good at outright lies. 'Rebecca often goes to the Club when she finishes work,' I said.

When I heard the outside door slam, I went to the window and watched Barry drive off. Then I had Rebecca paged at the Europa Hotel.

When she got back to the flat she looked flushed and upset.

'Have you two had a row?' I said.

'That would be too easy. I just can't shake him off.'

'He's been here for hours, telling me how wonderful you are. He said he'd been round yesterday with flowers for you.'

'He can stuff his flowers.'

'You must have had a row.'

'There's no row.'

'I thought you were keen on him.'

'He's weird.'

'He's in love with you.'

'He's in love with himself.'

'What's happened?'

'Nothing's happened. I just don't want him in my life.' Her voice rose. 'And he can't get the message into his stupid, thick head.'

The telephone rang.

'Don't answer it!' She became hysterical. 'He's been telephoning night and day. He leaves messages all the time. Look.' Her hand shook as she pointed at the winking red light on the answering machine. 'He's leaving a message. You can listen to it. I can't bear to.'

But it was only Jacky McQuitty wondering if I wanted to see a film on Sunday.

Rebecca took the telephone off the hook, and removed the battery from the doorbell. I thought she was being overdramatic, but didn't say anything. We opened a bottle of wine and sat talking until the early hours.

'We all want somebody,' Rebecca said. 'You, me, everybody wants someone to share their life with, to come first with. I thought Barry could be that person. He was so eager and attentive. He was interested in me. He wanted to know everything about me. It was nice for a couple of weeks. Then I just wanted some time to myself.' Her voice rose. 'But he was always there. I felt suffocated. Then I came back one lunchtime to collect a script and found him going through my things, reading my letters. We had a row. I said maybe we should see a bit less of each other. That's when the telephone calls began.' She shuddered. 'He's bonkers, Louise.'

If I didn't believe her, the next week was enough to convince me. There were at least three messages from Barry every day. Rebecca went into her room and shut the door while I listened to him alternately cajoling and threatening suicide. The telephone rang in the middle of the night. I couldn't stop myself answering. When I heard Barry's voice I hung up. The second night I let it ring and lay worrying in case something had happened to my parents, or Michael, or my sisters, and thinking I couldn't find out because whomever I telephoned would be equally worried by a call before dawn. We unplugged the telephone before going to bed. Barry began ringing the doorbell instead.

I saw energy and confidence drain out of Rebecca. She trembled with exhaustion. After two weeks of disrupted sleep, I went with her to the police. An equally tired-looking sergeant took notes, looked back over them and said, 'As far as I can see, this fella hasn't committed a crime.'

'He's pestering me night and day. Can you speak to him? Stop him pestering me.' Rebecca was close to tears.

He sighed. 'Not much we can do, love. Unless he does something criminal. He hasn't hit you or anything?'

'I'm frightened he'll do something.'

'There's many's a one in this town frightened of the people in the next street doing something. If making people frightened was a crime, half of Belfast would be locked up.' The sergeant sighed, more deeply this time. 'If I were you, love, I'd see if you can sort this out between you.' He looked at me. 'Or maybe your friend can have a wee word with him.'

'I'll try,' I said. 'But he's as odd as two left feet. I don't think he'll listen. He doesn't understand the word no.'

The sergeant laughed. 'That makes him odd, all right. No is the only word most people round here understand.' He jerked his head towards the window. Through the bars and the grey film of grime I could just make out the graffiti on the wall beside the police station. Ulster Says No.

Rebecca went home to London for the weekend. On the three nights she was away the telephone was mostly silent and the doorbell didn't ring. I picked her up at the airport and we stopped briefly at the flat before going to work. There was a menacing bunch of carnations on the doorstep.

'Bastard,' said Rebecca. 'He's not going to ruin my life.' She sounded calm and determined. The weekend at home had done her good, I thought.

That evening she listened dispassionately while I played back the inevitable message from Barry.

'If Dad was around he'd deal with him.' Rebecca's parents had just retired to Spain. She paused. 'Could you get Michael to do something?'

'What do you mean, do something?'

'Come on, Louise. Warn him off.'

'Michael's in prison,' I said.

'You visit him. Dad thought you could ask him to do something.'

'Like what?'

'Come on, Louise. Get some of his friends to teach Barry a lesson. Everybody knows how the IRA deals with petty criminals.'

'For God's sake, Rebecca. You're not asking me to have Barry kneecapped? Even if I could do it, I wouldn't. I don't believe in rough justice. Anyway, Barry's a lunatic, not a criminal.'

'And if he did something criminal?'

'Then I'd call the police.'

Rebecca's expression was a mixture of disbelief and exasperation. 'You said if you had something stolen you'd have a better chance of getting it back if you reported it to the Provos.'

'That's only if I was living at home. The police don't come into our area unless they're with the army.'

'So you'd report it to the Provos?'

I sighed. 'I wouldn't. Because I wouldn't want them to beat up some pathetic wee thief with hurley sticks, or put a bullet in his knees.'

'I'd like to put a bullet in Barry's knees.' Her smile had no humour in it.

'No, you don't. But I know how you feel. That would definitely put a stop to his gallop.'

We both started laughing in a kind of weak hysteria. Afterwards, we unplugged the telephone and the doorbell as though it was a natural part of our domestic routine.

'I could go back to London,' Rebecca said. 'I've thought about it. But I'm only two months into this new contract. I need at least six months under my belt before I can move.'

I hugged her. 'I was worried he would drive you away.'

'I won't let him ruin my life,' she said. 'He can ruin his own.'

Two weeks later Barry was arrested and charged with the theft of a necklace and earrings from our flat. They were a distinctive matching set of garnets and amethysts in gold filigree. Rebecca had inherited them from her grandmother. She kept them in a cream leather case in her bedside table and wore them frequently. They suited her dark hair and brown eyes.

A pawnbroker on the Crumlin road recognised the necklace and earrings from the description circulated by the police. Detectives were waiting when Barry returned to the pawnshop.

He broke the nose of the sergeant who arrested him. His finger-prints were all over the necklace. He was charged with burglary and assault. He got three years.

Rebecca didn't even need to go to court.

Now Rebecca sat drumming her fingers on the kitchen table, looking frightened and angry.

'I don't see how he could trace you,' I said. 'I tried to find you when I first came over to London. And didn't succeed.'

'How hard did you try?' Rebecca said peevishly.

'I went to the last address I had. Nobody knew you there. The last telephone number I had for you was ringing unobtainable. You didn't come up on a search engine under Morrison.'

She dropped her head into her hands. 'Sorry, Louise. I kept my married name because of that creep. I knew it would make me harder to trace. I avoided photographs.' She lifted her head. 'I bet it was that fucking photo you saw in the *Standard* that did it.'

'You could go to the police.'

'And tell them I thought I saw someone in Marks and Spencer? Don't be ridiculous.'

'Do you think it was an accident bumping into him like that?'

Rebecca jumped up from the table. 'Do you think he was following me?'

'No. No,' I cried. 'Sit down. It was probably coincidence. You never saw him near the office, or near your flat, did you?'

She shook her head and slumped on to the chair again.

'You could be imagining all this, you know.' I had a sudden thought. 'You've been reading the new script. I bet it was all that stuff about the stalker that put this into your head.'

'You think so?' There was a hint of hope in her voice.

'Did it make you think about him?'

She sat up. 'I thought about him straight away.'

'Were you thinking about him in Marks and Spencer?'

She nodded.

'You see? Auto-suggestion. I tell you what, forget tea. I'll pour you a glass of wine and make us something to eat.'

I took half a dozen eggs out of the fridge. 'Omelette and a glass of wine?' I pushed a bottle of red wine and a corkscrew towards Rebecca. 'You know where the glasses are.'

'Could you ask your brother if he knows where Barry is?'

I cracked the eggs into a bowl. 'Sure why would Michael know?'

'They were in prison at the same time, weren't they?'

'Michael was a political prisoner. He was in Long Kesh,' I said shortly. 'Barry would have been in Crumlin with the other criminals. Or Meghaberry.' I wiped some mushrooms, chopped them, and threw them into a saucepan.

'But he'd know who to ask, wouldn't he? Don't they keep an eye on things?'

'For someone who is apolitical, by her own account, you put a lot of faith in the IRA, Rebecca.'

'I put a lot of faith in my friends,' she said. 'My only loyalty is to my friends. And to myself.'

I added a knob of butter and a splash of olive oil to the saucepan. 'I'll give Michael a ring,' I said. 'You watch the mushrooms.'

'Barry Shaw?' said Michael. 'That head-the-ball? I haven't heard tell of him in years. Why do you want to know about him?'

'Rebecca thought she saw him in London. He stalked her years ago. You remember? She's worried he might be over here now.'

'I'll ask around,' said Michael. 'I found Mum's tablets. They were in her washbag, like you said. Will you make an appointment to see Doctor Gormley about her when you're over?'

'You could go and see him yourself.'

'You're better at that kind of thing, Louise. Do you want to speak to Mum?'

I felt suddenly weary. 'I'll give her a ring tomorrow.'

I went back into the kitchen. Rebecca was poking dubiously at the mushrooms. Her colour had returned.

Michael telephoned an hour later.

'Skippy McAlinden saw Barry Shaw in Falls Park last month. He said he had a job with the council. He's living with some woman on the Whiterock road. He said he had a small part in the Christmas pantomime at the Opera House.'

'Hold on,' I said. 'I want you to repeat this to Rebecca.' I handed her the telephone. She listened. I saw the tension leave her face. She smiled.

'You see? All in the mind,' I said.

I was wakened in the middle of the night by a drunken argument in the street. A man roared, 'You slept with him, you slag. A friend told me.'

A woman shrieked back, 'Your friend's a liar.'

A memory flashed into my head. Coming face to face with Barry's mother about a month after the trial. I had walked into a dentist's waiting room. Mrs Shaw was leafing through a magazine. She looked up. The magazine fell to the floor. I opened my mouth to say something, anything, but she spoke first.

'Your friend's a liar,' she said. 'My Barry never stole anything in his life.'

I remembered the defiant way she spoke, despite her white face and the tremble in her shoulders. Poor Mrs Shaw. She was the same age as Mum I supposed. I wondered if Barry still lived with her. I couldn't help feeling sorry for them both.

# 12

# Diana

The Christmas rush began suddenly. One day it was quiet. The next day it seemed as though all the mothers for miles around had decided to drop in after driving their children to school. Tomasz was cutting trees almost as fast as they went out of the shop. By mid-morning I had sold all but three of the Christmas wreaths, a dozen sets of outdoor lights, two-dozen sets of indoor tree lights and four-dozen boxes of crackers. And although part of me mourned the days when we decorated the tree on Christmas Eve and Christmas was about Midnight Mass and a sense of wonder, and not about shopping, I felt a thrill of triumph every time I shut the till after a sale.

Fortunately, I had taken on an athletic-looking student called Amanda, who rowed for one of the women's colleges and consequently had no trouble heaving six-foot trees into the backs of Range Rovers, lifting heavy pots and hauling a trailer full of mistletoe from the orchard.

I thought we could probably manage, so I told the job applicant who turned up mid-afternoon that I wasn't planning to employ anyone else.

'The job centre said you had seasonal work.'

'I'm frightfully sorry, but I've just taken somebody on, I'm afraid.'

'I'm good with plants.' He had some kind of West Country accent. 'Got a bit of experience. I came all this way on a bicycle,' he said fretfully.

'I'm sorry,' I repeated, tentatively mumbling, 'Mr . . . ?' and wishing for the umpteenth time that our lovely English language had a polite formula for addressing strangers. One can't use Sir or Madam without sounding satirical or ridiculous.

'Smith. My name's Bill Smith.'

He pushed a fringe of black hair back from his forehead. He had well-defined eyebrows. His pale blue eyes were narrowed and anxious. 'I heard you might be having a film company here. You'll need help getting the place ready.'

He had the air of a man fallen on hard times. I felt sorry for him. Tomasz might need some help with the trees, I thought. If the film went ahead we would need to get the grounds into shape.

'If things stay busy, I might need somebody for the week before Christmas,' I said hesitantly. 'You could telephone. It would save you cycling here again.'

'Nothing better to do,' he said despondently.

I gave him my business card. 'In case you don't feel like cycling.'

My good deed for the day.

There was a run on angels and I had to send Henry to the wholesalers for some more, which meant he was away when Plum Duff Pemberton arrived to value the wines. I gave him a cup of tea, took him over to the house, and left him in the cellar.

'I'll have to abandon you here, I'm afraid. Henry should be back in an hour. Might you be finished before then?'

'Not likely.' He looked around him with astonishment. 'I had no idea you had so many cases.'

I left him reciting the labels into a Dictaphone of some kind and went back to the bungalow to prepare lunch for everybody. Muntjac ravioli I had made the night before for Plum and Henry, celery soup and ham sandwiches to take over to the shop for Tomasz, Amanda and me. I couldn't afford to stop for lunch when we were this busy.

There was a lull about half-past three. I went back to the bungalow to make sure Henry had remembered to offer Plum some of the apple pie in the pantry.

The pie had been demolished, along with a Stilton and a bottle of wine from the cellar. Henry was flushed and cheerful.

'Plum says some of the wines are rather good. He's going to check the prices and get back to me.'

'Your brother claims to be not much of a wine man,' Plum said. 'Likes drinking the stuff. Ha. Don't we all?' He swirled the wine around in his glass. 'This is not bad. Not bad at all. What about you, Diana?'

'I'm not very knowledgeable, I'm afraid. Daddy was interested and I've often thought of taking a wine course. I've never had the time.'

'So neither of you have much idea of what you've got down there?'

'Not really,' Henry said.

'You didn't think of looking the wines up on the Internet?'

'I'm afraid we're not hooked up on that,' Henry said. 'We advertise the Hall through an agency that's on the Internet, but we're not actually on the thingy ourselves. My son tells me I ought to have a website to advertise my paintings.'

'I hope I'll be able to come to your opening,' Plum said. 'Sell a lot at these things, do you?'

'Hoping to,' said Henry.

'I'll get Mandy to type this lot up,' said Plum, tapping his Dictaphone. 'Might have an estimate for you by next week.'

'Have you any idea how much the wine is worth?' Henry asked diffidently.

Plum pursed his lips. 'Hard to say.' He studied the floor for a moment, tapping his chin with his fingers. 'Two grand?'

'Two thousand!'

'Maybe, at the absolute outside, two and a half.'

'Golly,' I said.

'Of course, some of them might be past their best. I might have to revise downwards. But two grand won't be far off the mark. I might even be able to take them off your hands before the New Year,' said Plum. 'Fingers crossed and all that. Here's hoping.' He drained his glass and stood up. 'Thank you for lunch.

Delicious ravioli, Diana. Wish I had a woman who could cook like that. Must crack on. Be in touch.'

He roared off in a silver Aston Martin. Henry and I stood watching the red tail lights disappear into the dusk.

'There must be money in the wine trade,' Henry said.

'Two thousand pounds. Gosh. Are you going to get a second opinion?'

'The chap you met at The Lindens?' Henry's eyebrow made a question mark. 'Could do, I suppose. But Plum seemed to know his stuff.'

'Yes.'

'You'd like me to ask your chap whatshisname?'

'John Finnegan. He's not my chap.'

Henry contemplated me. 'You fancy him, Diana.'

'Don't be ridiculous.'

'Hah,' said Henry. 'You don't fool me. You rather like him. And why not, Sis? Where there is life there is hope, eh?'

'He's probably married. Bound to be, I should think.'

'Ah,' said Henry. He managed to fill the syllable with commiseration.

'He may not know much about fine wines.'

'Perhaps I should give him a bell? Second opinion and all that? Yes. Let's do that.'

'I don't know the number. I don't have his card,' I said in a tight voice.

Henry squeezed my arm. 'I'm lonely too,' he said softly, unexpectedly.

It must have been the wine.


At six o'clock I shut the shop and walked back to the bungalow. The kitchen was filled with the sound of gentle snoring. In the flickering light from the stove I could make out Henry asleep on the sofa, Paddy asleep in his basket. They didn't stir when I switched on the light over the cooker and the lamp on the dresser. I heated the last of the soup and baked myself a potato in the microwave. When I finished eating and pushed my chair back from the table, Paddy ambled over to me and nuzzled my leg.

'Want a walk, Paddy?' I whispered.

There was a half-moon and the sky was clear and filled with stars. My eyes were soon accustomed to the dark. Paddy trotted beside me up the lane. The air was cold and damp. The wood was a black shape at the side of the road. The sheep in the upper meadow were like pale statues. An empty trailer stood aslant in a gateway. The only sounds were Paddy's panting and the soft scrunch of my wellingtons on gravel.

Silent night, holy night. Christmas is coming and the geese are getting fat. Please put a penny in the poor man's hat. *Adeste Fideles, laeti triumphantes*, my favourite Christmas carol. Henry sang it solo as a boy soprano.

I wondered if the film would get made, if Henry would get the money for the roof. I thought about his sudden admission of loneliness.

How long had he been separated from Jenny? When did it start to go wrong for him? Probably when he was sent to Belize. When the cat's away the mice will play.

But Henry had been more like the mouse in that relationship. Jenny toyed with him. Why had she chosen Henry out of a battalion of suitors, all frightfully keen on her?

She saw his softness. The child inside.

I remembered one Christmas Eve, running all around the house, hunting for Henry. I must have been thirteen or fourteen. Henry would have been five. I found him in the oratory on his knees, eyes shut, rosebud mouth working rapidly in silent prayer.

'Tea time, Henry. Before we dress the tree.'

'I've nearly finished a pair of bootees.'

His mouth worked faster for another minute. I was mystified. Then he heaved a sigh, opened his eyes and stood up. 'I was knitting clothes for baby Jesus. To keep him warm.'

Mummy's aunt, who was a nun, had told him prayers kept baby Jesus warm in his crib. Praying was like knitting. Even at that age, Henry was keen on detail. He had demanded to know exactly how many prayers, and of what kind, made up a line of knitting. She had invented for him a pattern of Hail Marys and Our Fathers. Henry had knitted an entire layette.

Daddy was soft too. Mummy was much steelier. Daddy said, 'He'll get his heart broken a few times, I expect.' Mummy said, 'I shouldn't say this but I hope he doesn't become a priest, and I hope you don't become a nun, Diana. I'd like to be surrounded by grandchildren in my old age.' She got her grandchildren, I reflected, even if surrounded was hardly the right participle.

I missed Catherine, and Freddy and Grizelda. Sad not to see them growing up. California seemed awfully far away. Did they even see the same stars in the sky?

Of course I wasn't lonely in the ordinary sense. Catherine telephoned at least once a week. I had friends. I had company all day at work and at home in the evening. When Henry was in the studio, Paddy was slumbering in front of the stove or following me happily about the house. I wasn't unwanted or unloved. But the world went two by two, like Noah's ark. I missed the feeling of coming first in someone's life. Carl and the children came first with Catherine now. That was the way it should be. Catherine still came first in my life. She had been equal first with Geoffrey.

For a long time after Geoffrey died, I would wake and shift my body sideways in the bed, expecting to come up against the radiant heat of his body, finding cold space instead.

I remembered the first morning I woke up and knew I was alone. It was summer. The room was filled with golden light and I could hear birdsong. Then I thought about Geoffrey. It was like tugging on something that had drifted away. All the dead, loved people in my life – Mummy, Daddy, Geoffrey, Granny, my cousin Robert, Uncle George – were like balloons, I thought. All of them tethered to me by invisible strings, floating higher and higher into the infinite sky, until I was hardly aware of them.

For a long time I had felt a jolt in my heart when I heard Geoffrey in Freddy's sneeze, saw him in Catherine's quick tilt of the head, heard 'Under the Bridges of Paris' on the radio, saw my wedding date in the calendar, or the date of Geoffrey's death. When had that changed? How had it happened that I was aware of the balloon from time to time, but no longer felt the jerk of the string?

Maybe we all ended up in some kind of eternal limbo. Neither heaven nor hell. Millions of balloons, distantly tethered to earth, floating about in the universe like stars. I was almost dizzy thinking about it.

'The radiance of that star that leans on me
Was shining years ago. The light that now
Glitters up there my eyes may never see . . .'

Where had I read that? On a tube train. Yes, a poster in a tube train. The District and Circle line from Paddington to Sloane Square, on my way to the Chelsea Flower Show. Strap hanging. Crushed against a rhinoceros of a man in a leather jacket. The smell of new leather and old sweat. My eyes scanning the advertisements. Haemorrhoid cream. Don't need to read that. This is better. Poems on the Underground. What a wonderful idea. The train rocking, gathering speed. Ten stops. Time to memorise. I like the way poetry sums up how I'm feeling sometimes. Thoughts I can't put into words.

Shakespeare was good at that. I was good at English at school. I could have gone to university instead of the convent in Freibourg and Miss Hudson's secretarial college. I remembered lots of Shakespeare. 'Bare ruined choirs, where late the sweet birds sang.' Shakespeare was a Catholic. Sister Mary Mercedes told us the evidence was there. Nobody would accept it. England was a Protestant nation so England's national poet had to be a Protestant. But his father was a recusant. His mother's family kept a Catholic priest disguised as a gardener. Edward Arden was hanged, drawn and quartered. Unimaginable. There was a Catholic history too. Just as English. More so, even. We're part of it, Henry and I. Our ancestors suffered for the faith. Died for their beliefs. Unimaginable. Who would die for their faith these days?

What did I believe? Did I believe Geoffrey and I and everyone I loved would be united in heaven? Did I believe the words of the creed I recited every Sunday? The resurrection of the body and life everlasting, amen. One would think faith got stronger as one grew older and closer to death, but it seemed to be weaker. Nothing seemed as certain as it had been when I was young.

And if there was a heaven, was Geoffrey there? He had been a good man. Short-tempered sometimes, especially when I questioned his judgement. 'Our money's as safe as it would be in the bank. The returns are terrific. It's an honour, Diana, to be a name at Lloyd's.'

What was better, to be a widow with mostly happy memories or be divorced, like Henry, remembering only disappointment and betrayal? To live happily with someone until they died or to live unhappily with someone until they ran off with a fellow officer who just happened to be an old school friend? Henry had been heartbroken.

He still kept his wedding photograph in a silver frame. I saw it on the chest of drawers when I hoovered his room. Henry heart-swellingly handsome in his dress uniform, Jenny all blonde fragility in clouds of tulle as they smiled beneath an arch of swords.

I thought how much I would like Henry to meet someone and be happy again. How things change! When I was in my teens and twenties I understood that marriage was for life. 'Till death do us part'. To divorce and re-marry was to leave the Church, be barred from Holy Communion. I would have been as shocked by divorce as Mummy was. 'Living in sin,' she said tartly when she heard one of her school friends had divorced and re-married. But I wanted Henry to re-marry and be happy. Sin seemed harder to define these days. I had asked our parish priest for guidance on what constituted a mortal sin. 'Grave matter, full knowledge, clear consent of the will,' he replied. 'And what is grave matter?' I asked. 'Murder,' he said. It seemed to me his answer provided a lot of leeway.

What if Henry married again?

'What would happen to me, Paddy?' I said out loud. 'What would I do? Where would I call home?'

A picture of John Finnegan came into my head. No. Don't

think that. Don't dare to hope. He is not a knight in shining armour. He cares for his mother, as I care for Lucy. We have that in common. That's all. Be realistic, Diana. Stop dreaming.

Paddy was looking up at me. I realised I had stopped walking. I breathed in a lungful of night air and looked around. We were above the woods. The pale ribbon of lane ran back towards the black outline of the Hall. An owl hooted, hoo-hoo-hoo. My gaze shifted automatically to the yew tree in the walled garden. Centuries older than the house. I needed to prune the black-currants. And the climbing roses on the wall. Move the lewesias into the greenhouse. So much to do.

A light went on in the bungalow. Henry must have woken up. Maybe he would move into the big house again. If the film happened and he sold enough paintings and was able to repair the roof.

Jenny had insisted on living there, swathed in layers of cash-mere and running up huge heating bills. Henry had borrowed from the bank, using the house as collateral, to pay her a lump sum. Thank heavens he wasn't paying her alimony.

If he moved back into the Hall I could rent the bungalow from him. Or I could move back to my house in Amersham, but the rent was a big part of my income and I would have to drive over to Wooldene every day.

Maybe the new wife I envisaged for Henry wouldn't want my business on her doorstep. But they were my fields. Daddy gave them to me when I married Geoffrey. 'Not much of a dowry, I'm afraid,' he had said. 'You can rent them out. There'll always be a demand for land.'

Most of the fields for miles around were in set-aside now. I remembered them thick with cauliflower, golden with corn. At least my fields still sprouted cabbages and parsnips as well as Christmas trees, and returned a small profit.

Paddy nudged the back of my knees. I walked on towards the end of the lane and the gate lodge.

'Maybe I could rent the gate lodge,' I said to Paddy, thinking at the same time that too many of my private thoughts were addressed to a dog. A super dog. But a dog, nonetheless.

Through the window I could see Tomasz sitting forward in an armchair, staring at tiny red and white figures on a bright green background. He had a can of beer in one hand, a fork in the other and a plate on his knee. I watched him spear a sausage and steer it to his mouth. His eyes never left the screen. I wondered if he was lonely without his Anna.

# 13

# Diana

The prospect of two thousand pounds for Daddy's wine lifted Henry's spirits. He whistled as he walked over to his studio in the barn. He talked about having the Hall ready to rent out for the millennium: 'It's only thirteen months away. A lot of places are booked up already.'

By the end of the week, pessimism had set in again. 'Drop in the ocean, two thousand pounds. And those women aren't going to come back, they've found somewhere else for their film.' I could almost see the cloud of gloom surrounding him as he trudged over to the studio.

When Louise O'Neill finally telephoned on Friday afternoon, I felt like cheering.

I carried a cup of tea and a buttered scone through the dusk to the barn. Henry was standing in a pool of yellow lamplight, cleaning his paint brush, sweeping it backwards and forwards on a bar of soap, working up a lather in the palm of his hand, rinsing the hairs in a plastic basin. He became aware of me and looked up.

'The film company telephoned. They're coming on Monday.'

Henry threw back his head and tossed the brush into the air. The metal ferrule twinkled as the brush turned over and over before he caught it and twirled it like a tiny baton.

'Praise be,' he shouted. His shoulders relaxed. He smiled. 'You've been very good to me, Diana. I've been a bit of a grump recently.'

'I thought they'd never ring,' I said.

'Me too.'

Three of them bowled up mid-morning on Monday. The tall redhead, Louise; a younger, bright-as-a-button assistant, with pink hair and a matching mouth; the director, a man about Henry's age, with grey-blond Dylan Thomas curls.

I memorised their names as we took them through the grounds and the gardens. It was a cold, bright morning. The grass was crunchy underfoot and frost sparkled on the paths. We led them through the knot garden, into the orchard and out into the park. Jacky, the blond director, stood for what seemed like ages looking at the house. The windows winked back at him.

'Crane,' he said. 'OK for overhead.' Louise nodded. The girl with the pink hair, Chloe, took notes.

We took them further up the lane and through the wood to the back fields. I explained how the lane ran round the perimeter of the estate and they could drive into it from the other road. 'Nobody uses it much.'

'Plenty of space for shooting,' said Jacky.

'Only a few rabbits, I'm afraid,' said Henry. 'Wood pigeon. Shot a muntjac last winter.'

'I hope that's an animal,' murmured Louise. She exchanged a smile with Jacky.

'Enough room for the key crew vehicles and the main generator,' she called out. 'And six Portaloos.' She smiled at me. 'I have to think about the important things.'

On the way back to the house she stopped and surveyed the great height of the barn. 'That might do for the art department. Or make-up and wardrobe. Could we have a look, please?'

Henry was terribly shy about letting people see his work in progress, but he hardly hesitated. 'Of course. I use it as a studio so you'll have to forgive the frightful mess, I'm afraid.'

The barn was stacked with canvases stretched on light wooden frames, waiting to be collected. It was freezing. We hunched into our coats. A cold light fell through the big window in the roof on to the easel. I saw that Henry had gone back to work on my portrait, felt immediately shy myself, and hung back.

'I have an exhibition coming up,' Henry said, in an offhand manner. He was far too modest about his work. 'Just getting a few things ready. Finishing this thing off. Oil and collage.'

I recognised myself with a kind of wonder. He had painted me standing on a patch of grass, spade in hand, wearing a brown apron and a straw hat, surrounded by a collage of seed packets and pages torn from gardening magazines and catalogues. I was looking straight back at the admiring cluster around the canvas as though asking myself, Who are these people in my garden?

'That's great,' said Jacky. 'I love the way you've worked earth into the oils. Love the collage.'

'It's a perfect likeness,' said Louise, shifting her gaze from the canvas to me, then back to the canvas. 'Have you done a lot of paintings of your wife?'

'And do you still beat her?' I heard Jacky whisper to Louise.

Henry heard him too. He was momentarily startled. Then he said in his driest tone, 'Diana is my sister, actually.'

Louise went pink and said, 'Oh, God. Sorry.'

'Don't apologise,' I called out to her. 'I'm terrifically flattered. Henry's lots younger than me.'

Everybody laughed. Louise looked abashed.

'Come to the opening,' I said. Henry was anxious to get a good crowd, but I knew he would be too diffident to ask them himself. 'It's in London on Thursday. Six to eight. A little gallery in Fitzrovia.' I had put some invitations in my pocket. Now I distributed them. 'Lovely if you could all come.'

I could tell Henry was pleased. He became quite chatty and answered questions about why he liked portraiture and how long he needed people to sit for him and why he would have more landscapes than portraits in the exhibition.

'Easier to sell is the simple answer, I'm afraid. The portraits are there in the hope that someone will commission me to do one.'

By the time we ushered our little group back through the garden and into the Great Hall, Henry was relaxed and fluent.

'The family made its money in wool. We ran sheep on three thousand acres around here. A long time ago, I'm afraid.'

I had cleaned the windows, polished the furniture and silver, lit a fire in the inglenook, and burned scented candles to sweeten the air. The Hall seemed to glow. My heart swelled with pride.

'The beam above the fireplace has a date carved into it. 1510,' said Henry. 'The date on the fireback is earlier, 1498.'

'Big enough to roast a ram,' said Louise. 'Or a hundred rabbits.'

Henry gave her a sharp look. Her expression was innocent. His mouth twitched in a smile. He threw open the door to the winter parlour.

'Most-used room in the house, apart from the bedrooms.'

I was pleased I had lit a fire here as well. The silver candlesticks on the polished oak table reflected the flames and drew the eyes away from the faded chintz on the sofa and chairs, the threadbare rugs and the worn brocade of the curtains.

'The far door leads through to the kitchen.'

My parents had put in a new kitchen before they gave up and built the bungalow. How old-fashioned all that stainless steel and Formica now looked, I thought.

'Plenty of power points,' said Louise, nodding her head. 'This could be the production office.'

Henry led the party up the back stairs. For the first time in ages he seemed happy and engaged, and at his most charming.

'The Long Gallery,' he announced, with the sweep of an arm in a mock bow. 'Sixty feet long. Original windows. Two working fireplaces.'

'Tracking shot. Dolly,' said Jacky. The girl with the pink hair took more notes.

'I thought her name was Chloe,' I whispered to Louise.

'It is,' she whispered back. 'Dolly is the thing we move the camera on.'

Jacky whistled. 'Linenfold panelling. Original?'

'Some of it was refurbished in the middle of the last century,' said Henry. 'Otherwise the house is pretty much as it was in the sixteenth century. Couldn't afford to do much to it.'

'Collapse of the wool trade?'

'Catholics,' said Henry. 'Half the estate was sold to pay recusancy fines. Then it was confiscated by Cromwell. We petitioned Charles the second and got it back in 1662. But then there was the double land tax.'

Louise looked surprised. She seemed on the point of saying something but checked herself.

'Are there any secret hiding places behind all that panelling?' asked Jacky. 'A priest hole?'

'We looked,' said Henry. 'There's a family tradition that Saint Nicholas Owen stayed here. He built most of the hides in England, I think. There was some publicity about a hide discovered in a house somewhere in the fifties. My grandfather got a bee in his bonnet about there being a hide here. He reckoned it was closed up before the Cromwellians came. He and my father searched everywhere: roof, cellars, chimneys. Didn't find a thing, I'm afraid.'

Louise said, 'This is the most beautiful house I've ever seen. I hope we're going to be able to use it.'

'I hope so too,' said Henry, smiling at her.

He led them to the oriel window at the east end of the gallery. 'From here you can see the spire of the church an ancestor built in the fourteenth century. The Wintours are still buried in the crypt, even though it's no longer a Catholic church. We lost it in the Reformation. There's an inscription on a flagstone at the entrance. 'We thank God for ever more, 'twas Wintour's sheep that laid the floor, and raised the roof and built the tower, in glorious tribute to His power.'

I caught Henry's eye as I joined in the general laughter. I knew we were both thinking, Please God we'll be able to say this lot paid for the roof.

I said a silent prayer. Please Lord, don't let us be disappointed.

Louise walked to a casement window on the north side of the gallery. 'We could run a cable through that,' she said to me. 'Does it open?'

'Yes.' I lifted the catch to demonstrate.

Louise glanced out the window. I saw her eye caught by the

circle of poppies and the white marble cross under the yew tree in the walled garden.

'A family grave,' I said quickly. 'My father's older brother.'

I saw her puzzlement.

'He shot himself just after the First World War,' I said. 'He couldn't be buried in consecrated ground. We think of him as a war casualty. He was only nineteen. We lay a wreath on Remembrance Day.'

Louise stepped back from the window. 'War's horrible,' she said quietly.

Jacky shut one eye and curled his hand around the other to make a telescope. He turned his head slowly, like the beam on a lighthouse. The others waited for him to speak.

'I'd like to lighten the walls. Repaint above the panelling.'

He took his hand away from his eye and looked up at the ceiling. 'And put in a false ceiling.'

'No problem,' said Henry.

'Cool. We can get a few blondes up there.'

'Good Lord,' said Henry.

'Lighting,' said Louise. 'Blondes are two-thousand-watt lamps.' A shaft of pale sunlight caught her hair and turned it into flame.

'How many watts is a redhead?' said Henry.

'Eight hundred,' said Jacky. 'Not half as bright as blondes.' He ran his hand through his curls and winked at me and then at Louise.

I wondered if he was her boyfriend, although that was another ridiculous word, I thought to myself. Susan talked about her boyfriends when she meant men in their fifties and sixties. What would I call a man I got involved with? I had a sudden memory of John Finnegan's smile and allowed my thoughts to drift pleasantly for a few moments before steering them back to what Henry was saying about the paintings.

'All ancestors. German and Dutch artists. Nobody famous, I'm afraid. Rather a lot of nuns.'

'We'd have to remove some of them,' said Jacky. 'If that's OK with you. Wrong period. I'll get some mocked up.'

We showed them the bedrooms in the east and west wings

leading from the gallery and then descended the great stairs to the hall.

'You think you might use the old place?' Henry sounded casual but he had put his hands together in a steeple of prayer.

Louise glanced at Jacky. 'What do you think?'

'How much stuff can I move?'

'Move what you like,' said Henry.

'That's it, then,' said Louise. 'We'll send a letter with a formal offer.'

I nearly cried with relief. I glanced at Henry. He was looking uncomfortable.

'There is one thing I ought to mention.' He cleared his throat. 'The roof's not sound.'

I held my breath.

Louise looked at him appraisingly. 'Is it likely to fall in while we're filming?'

'No,' said Henry with the voice of a clear conscience.

'In that case,' said Louise, 'we'd like to go into pre-production after Christmas.' She paused. 'We're ninety per cent there.'

I felt a quiver of unease. 'Ninety per cent? When will you be sure?'

'We all want it to happen,' said Louise. 'But this is a funny business. Sometimes you don't know if a film's going to go ahead or not until the last minute.'

Henry groaned.

'I'll get back to you when we know how many weeks we need here,' said Louise. 'We might want to use it in pre-production as well.'

Henry brightened. 'You mean you might use it even if the film doesn't go ahead.'

'No,' said Louise. 'Pre-production doesn't start until we know we're going ahead.'

'What do you call all this scouting,' said Henry, 'if it's not pre-production?'

'The triumph of hope over experience,' said Louise.

# 14

## Louise

By midweek we still hadn't heard back from the American distributors. There wasn't much any of us could do until we got the green light. I drafted a letter for Henry Wintour proposing a fee of ten thousand pounds a week during filming and five thousand pounds a week for use of the Hall during pre-production. A deposit of ten thousand pounds would be paid when we were greenlit. Half the balance when filming started, the rest when the shoot was finished. If it ever starts, I thought to myself.

It was one of those paralysing afternoons when Rebecca and I were staying late for an evening conference call with the backers who were still on board. I put on my coat.

'Come on, let's go for a walk on the Southbank. Get some fresh air,' I said to Rebecca. 'We haven't been out of here all day.'

A damp wind blew from the west, urging the Thames ever faster towards the sea. The sky was a dark grey, tinged with the orange glow from a million streetlights. White Christmas lights were strung like beads between the lampposts. We stood for a while watching their reflections bouncing on the oily waters. A riverboat, lit from prow to stern and packed with Christmas revellers, motored past us upstream, pleating the water in its wake. Rebecca seemed lost in thought.

There was a squawk and flurry behind us. I looked around. Three pigeons were fighting over a scattering of crisps. I had the impression of someone disappearing down the side of a building.

Rebecca came out of her reverie. 'What was that?'

'Somebody dropped a packet of crisps,' I said. 'Pigeons are landing like vultures.'

I didn't tell her about my sudden goosebumpy feeling that someone had been watching us. Rebecca had enough on her mind.

I steered her towards the lights of a café further along the Southbank. We sat at an outside table close to a tall gas heater that promised, but did not deliver, warmth. I pulled my coat more tightly around me and ordered mulled wine. Rebecca had retreated into her thoughts again and seemed oblivious to the cold.

'I'm sick with worry,' she said eventually. 'The consortium only put up ten per cent on condition we have an American distributor.'

'Do they know about the problem?'

'You know it's impossible to keep things quiet in this business.'

'Have they said they'll pull out?'

'Not yet.' Her mouth twisted. A teardrop ran down her cheek. 'I've fought hard for this, Louise. Everything I've done in the last fifteen years. Fifteen years.' She dispatched the teardrop with an angry swipe. 'I've worked my socks off.'

'You're nearly there, Rebecca.'

'Stop being so bloody cheerful,' she snapped. 'You don't know what it's like, pandering to idiots. "Yes, Mr so-and-so. No, Mr so-and-so,"' she mimicked. 'I've schmoozed with creeps and wheedled like a beggar. I've pitched to two-year-olds who know fuck-all. I've grovelled to the little shits. This is my big chance, Louise. I don't want to lose it.' Tears glittered in her eyes.

I leaned across the table and squeezed her hand. 'You're freezing.'

'I've had to be cold inside as well,' she said. 'I've sacrificed my soul for this. I've given up marriage, children. I didn't let anything, anybody stand in my way.'

A waiter placed two steaming glass mugs on the table. 'That'll warm your cockles, ladies.'

I inhaled the clove and cinnamon smell, warmed my hands around the glass, and waited for Rebecca to continue.

'I'm not surprised Sam had affairs. I worked too hard. I was never there. When we broke up, I worked even harder. I didn't think I would meet anybody else.'

'But Robert came along.' I smiled at her.

She smiled shakily back. 'He's like me, you know. A worker. Always wanted to succeed. He loves me being in the film business. He's been with me all the way on this. He's put money into it. We both have. It's our baby.' The storm had passed, but her voice was tight with anxiety. 'I'm worried what will happen if I fail. He's younger than me, you know.'

I had met Robert briefly when he dropped into the office to collect Rebecca and whisk her off to a reception in the Inner Temple. He seemed quick-witted and assertive, with a hint of theatricality that probably made him effective in court. He had waited while Rebecca concluded a brisk negotiation with one of the backers. He had gazed on her with pride and fondness.

'She really doesn't need me at all,' he whispered to me. 'Terrifyingly competent, really.'

Now Rebecca looked nervy and vulnerable. She turned the glass around in her hands and stared at it, as though trying to conjure a genie out of the steam.

'I've seen the way Robert looks at you,' I said. 'He adores you. Age has nothing to do with it. Not getting a film off the ground isn't failure, Rebecca. Happens all the time. Robert has seen enough of the business to know how risky it is. He won't think you've failed.'

Rebecca raised her head and looked at the night sky. 'This was my dream, Louise. I used to imagine being a film producer. Every Saturday I'd go with my friends to the Odeon in Shepherd's Bush. They'd all be dreaming about being film stars – Elizabeth Taylor, Audrey Hepburn. I dreamed about being a producer. I didn't even know what a producer did. I just knew they were the ones that made things happen.'

I felt pleased Rebecca was confiding in me. When your friend becomes your boss, the relationship is redefined. An almost imperceptible distance is established. The relationship shifts slightly. Now I felt it was settling on its old foundations again. I sipped the hot, sweet wine, and waited for Rebecca to continue.

'Three, nearly four years' work,' she said. 'I started putting this together three and a half years ago.' She leaned across the table. 'I heard a whisper the other day there's another Elizabethan drama in development. Good Queen Bess is the next big thing. I want to get my film off the ground first.' She banged the table with her fist.

'That's better,' I said. 'Get that fighting spirit into you.'

We drained our glasses.

'Right,' said Rebecca. 'Let's get back to work.'

# 15

# Louise

The next day, Chloe printed out an email, kissed it and placed it in front of Rebecca. 'They like the new plot twist,' she said.

Teddy, who had put on his coat to leave, sank to his knees and threw his arms out. 'Hallelujah!'

The atmosphere brightened.

'Well done, Teddy.' Rebecca scanned the document. 'One caveat. They want a more upbeat ending.'

'Upbeat ending?' Teddy sprang to his feet. 'What the fuck do they mean by that? Amy is pushed down the stairs and breaks her neck. Leicester can't marry the queen. Nobody wins. That's the whole point.'

'That's the whole *problem*. They want a winner. They want the murderer caught.'

'This is not an Elizabethan crime story,' cried Teddy. He looked distraught. 'I've turned my hero into a villain. But I'm not creating some fucking Elizabethan Kojak to catch him.'

He snatched the document from Rebecca. His eyes devoured the page. 'Arc of the story.' He groaned. 'Conflict.' A snort of angry laughter. 'Negative to positive.' He ripped the paper in two. 'Fucking accountants who've been on some one-day seminar about storytelling. What the fuck do they know?'

Teddy picked up an empty mug from his desk and hurled it across the room. It caught the side of Jacky's head. Jacky fell back in his chair, clutching his ear. The mug bounced on the floor and shattered.

There was a silence.

'Omigod.' Teddy rushed over to apologise.

'Calm down, everybody,' said Rebecca. 'Let's go back to basics. Whose story is this? Who are we rooting for?'

Teddy called out, 'Amy. Poor, sweet, loving, vulnerable Amy.' Each adjective was accompanied by an awkward pat on Jacky's head, as though feeling for a bump. 'Amy as played magnificently by the nation's favourite two-hanky actress.'

'Betrayed by her husband, stalked by her former lover,' said Chloe, stooping to pick up the pieces.

'A loser,' said Jacky. 'That's the problem. We need to shift the focus.'

A voice in the telephone held to my other ear announced the person I had been waiting to speak to. I automatically shut out the rest of the discussion. When I replaced the receiver, Teddy was swinging his arm as though hitting balls with a tennis racquet. Jacky was pretending to return them. Rebecca and Chloe were spectators.

'The Earl of Leicester is the hero, the focus. He's attractive, ambitious, clever. I've made him likeable,' said Teddy.

'We need to root for him instead of Amy.' Jacky returned a ball across the invisible net. 'Leicester is bold and buccaneering and led by his dick. He had to marry Amy to get her into bed. But he's also in love with the queen. It's not ambition. He really truly loves her. Didn't you tell me she kept his last letter until she died? That's so romantic.'

'Leicester is torn between the two women,' said Teddy. 'Then Amy is killed by Tressilian, her former-lover-turned-stalker.' He reached for a smash.

'Make sure the talent is OK with the changes,' said Jacky. 'I don't want any dramas on the set. The guy playing Tressilian?'

'It's his big break,' said Rebecca. 'He'd chop his legs off and play an Elizabethan dwarf to get an American release.'

'Caroline Cross?'

'She's got the same number of lines. Same number of scenes,' said Chloe.

'And the nicest frocks.' Jacky dispatched an invisible ball to the end of the room. He folded his arms and rocked on his feet. 'Let's talk upbeat.'

'How about a big scene between Leicester and the queen,' said Rebecca.

Teddy stood still, eyes closed. He held his hands out, palms down, as though about to conduct an orchestra. His eyes flashed open. We waited for him to speak.

'Leicester comes to see the queen after Amy dies,' Teddy began. 'He admits he was secretly married to Amy. He tells the queen he married when he was young, before he came to court and met her again. They were childhood sweethearts, you know.'

Jacky rocked faster on his feet. 'They're in the queen's bedchamber. The scene is fizzing with sex. I like it.'

'Big close-ups. Heaving bosoms. Lots of scope for actors to emote,' said Teddy. 'They love that.'

'It's still not a happy ending,' said Rebecca.

'They didn't say happy. They said upbeat,' said Teddy.

'Can you give them a big upbeat moment? Something humungous. Dramatic,' said Rebecca. 'Something to remind the queen that nothing, absolutely nothing, is as important to her as Britain.'

'England,' I called out automatically. 'Not Britain. England. Britain is later.'

'Whatever.' Rebecca waved her hand impatiently. 'Nothing is as important to her as England. It's more important than love, than sex. We can see it in her face, in her eyes.' She broke off. 'Has Caroline signed a contract? We might need a bigger name.'

'Nobody has signed a contract yet,' I said.

But Rebecca's imagination was back in the queen's bedchamber. 'Someone knocks on the door. Some kind of flunkey.'

'An ambassador?' suggested Chloe.

'Yeah. An ambassador,' said Jacky. 'With amazing news. He

announces a great victory.' Jacky threw another imaginary ball in the air and smashed it into the far corner of the room. 'The defeat of the Armada!'

There was a silence.

Teddy said, 'The Armada was 1588. Leicester died the same year. The romance with the queen was thirty years earlier. Amy Robsart died in 1560.'

'Who cares? It's a great story.'

Chloe said tentatively, 'Will the audience not notice?'

'Nah,' said Rebecca.

'They only learn about the Second World War in school these days,' said Jacky. 'We're not history teachers. We're entertainers. We're not trying for accuracy. We're trying for truth.'

Chloe persisted, 'Doesn't truth depend on accuracy?'

'We're talking emotional truth here,' said Jacky.

'We're talking another rewrite,' Teddy collapsed on to a chair.

Rebecca held up a thumb and forefinger a millimetre apart. 'We are as close as this. We could be in pre-production next month.'

'We could all get paid,' said Jacky.

'I'm trying to think of a single project I've been involved in that actually made money,' said Teddy. 'I should go back to writing soaps.'

'I could get someone else to do the rewrite,' said Rebecca.

'I'm going to Morocco for Christmas,' said Teddy. 'I'm going to lie on the beach at Essouira and drink mint tea and not think about Elizabethan bloody England for ten whole days.'

'Can you liaise with Jacky on the rewrite before you go?' Rebecca hoisted her jacket from the back of a chair. 'Must dash. Meeting Robert at Heathrow. See you.' A wave. The door banged, and she was gone.

Teddy opened his laptop and sat staring at the screen. His hands curled into fists. Chloe busied herself making tea.

Jacky said, 'I'm off as well. I've had three replies to my ad in the *London Review of Books*. I'm meeting the first one in fifteen minutes.'

'Why don't you just go to pubs and parties and get drunk like the rest of us? Isn't that how most people go about it,' Teddy muttered.

'Speak for yourself.' Jacky was equally tart.

Chloe handed me a mug of tea. 'We should go to the opening of Henry Wintour's exhibition.'

'I'm exhausted,' I said. 'Too much tennis.'

'You might meet someone.'

'Why do you think I want to meet someone?'

'To fall in love,' Chloe said. 'Everybody wants to fall in love.' She put a mug of tea on Teddy's desk. 'What about you, Teddy?'

'I've work to do. I might come along later as a displacement activity.'

We left him still staring moodily at a blank screen.

# 16

# Diana

Henry drove up to London early on the morning of the opening. The gallery owner, Frederick Farry, had telephoned to say he thought the exhibition needed a seasonal touch. Henry had spent three days in the studio and produced six watercolours. They were technically accomplished but I could see his heart wasn't in them.

'I bet they're the only things that sell,' Henry said gloomily as he stacked them in the car. 'We'd better pray this film goes ahead.'

'Did you talk to Clark and Hawkins about the contract?'

'Spoke to a chap there yesterday. He wants a few things clarified. That'll cost a few bob. Still,' he rubbed his hands, 'I must say it's a decent offer. It's nearly enough to meet the estimate.' A sudden blaze of optimism lit his face. For a moment he looked so happy I could have cried.

The schools had broken up for Christmas and we were busiest in the mornings and early afternoons. I decided to close the shop as soon as it got dark and catch a train to Paddington. I hated driving in London.

I was putting on my coat when the telephone rang. I hesitated, torn between a desire not to be late and a worry that the call would be important. Lucy was always at the back of my mind.

'John Finnegan speaking. My sister told me you had some

wines you wanted valued.' I was too surprised, delighted really, to reply straight away. 'Hello? Have I got the right number? Diana Wiseman? John Finnegan speaking. We met at The Lindens.'

I collected myself well enough to thank him for the call, while silently berating myself. You've only met the man once. A smile doesn't mean much. You still don't know if he's married or not. Act your age. For heaven's sake, chill down or whatever it is they say nowadays.

'Are you still interested in having the wines valued?' He sounded brisk.

I was businesslike in reply. 'Yes, absolutely. If it's not too much trouble?'

'Shall we fix a date? Some afternoon when I'm visiting my mother?'

'I ought to tell you, my brother had someone in to value them.'

'Your brother?'

'They're his wines, really. He didn't know they were in the cellar until last week. They'd been there for years. Some of them are forty years old. My father bought them at the end of the war, or just after. They may not be worth much, of course.' I was jabbering like an idiot. 'I don't know much about wine. I mean, I enjoy drinking it, of course, but I don't pretend to be awfully knowledgeable. Henry's the same, I think.'

'What about your husband? Is he a wine lover?'

'No. I mean, he liked wine. But he was more of a whiskey man. When he was alive, that is.'

There was a pause.

'I'm sorry,' said John Finnegan.

'He died eight years ago,' I said. 'Life goes on.'

'Yes. I've found that too.' There was another pause. 'And Henry is your brother?'

'Yes.'

'I looked for you at The Lindens on my last couple of visits.'

'I was frightfully busy last week,' I said. 'And I had to visit my cousin. She's ninety.'

He'll think me a boring person who spends her time visiting ancient relatives, I said to myself. And that's exactly what I am.

'We're at that age,' John Finnegan said.

'Not ninety. Not yet.' I found I was smiling.

He laughed. 'You know what I mean. We're the support troops.' He was suddenly brisk again. 'Do you think your brother still wants me to look at the wines?'

'Absolutely,' I said. 'Henry wants the best price. We have a rough estimate. But I think he would like a second opinion. In fact I know he would like a second opinion.'

'Well, I'm happy to drive over and give you one.' He cleared his throat. 'A second opinion, that is. Good to have a second opinion.'

'Yes. I'd like that too. A second opinion.'

There was a pause. Pull yourself together, Diana, I said to myself. Stop imagining this man is interested in you. But a ripple of excitement ran up my spine.

'I won't get to you before Christmas,' he said. 'This is the busiest time of year for me.'

'Me too,' I said.

'New Year as well.' He paused and cleared his throat again. 'Just after New Year, then? The second of January all right with you? About three o'clock?'

'Splendid.' I hesitated. 'I can offer you tea and Christmas cake. Of course you might have had enough of it by then.'

'I love Christmas cake,' he said. 'Can't get enough of it.'

'I'll see you on the second.'

I was about to say goodbye and hang up when he said quickly, 'Diana?'

'Yes?'

'Merry Christmas.'

'Merry Christmas.' I realised I had been holding my breath. I let it escape. 'Merry Christmas, John.'

# 17

# Louise

Chloe and I were in a taxi crawling over London Bridge, when my mobile rang. I pulled it out of my pocket and saw Michael's number on the display panel.

'My brother. Do you mind if I take this?'

'Go ahead,' said Chloe. 'This traffic is solid. I'm going to chill for a bit.' She slipped a pair of headphones over her ears.

'What's the problem this time, Michael?'

'Are you saying I only phone when there's a problem?'

'If the cap fits.'

'I telephoned you on your birthday. I telephoned you when Maeve was born.'

'How is she?'

'A wee dote. Eight months old tomorrow.' He paused. 'Mum wants me to invite Noreen and Austin to Donegal for Christmas.'

'Do you think they'll come? It's a bit last minute, isn't it? They're usually well organised, those two.'

'Mum wouldn't be asking me if she hadn't spoken to Noreen first. They were going to go skiing but there's no snow. Ho, ho, ho.'

'Are they still thinking about buying a holiday home?'

'As an investment.' Michael practically spat the word in my ear. 'I bet they'll spend the time here scouting about.'

Less time to argue, then. 'What does Siobhan think?'

'Siobhan thinks we should ask them.'

'So what's the problem?'

'No problem. I just thought you'd like to know who all's going to be there.'

Michael chatted on for a bit, relaying snippets of information about his baby daughter, punctuated by fond paternal chuckles. I responded mechanically. I was remembering my sister Noreen's last visit to Donegal.

Siobhan had just inherited the cottage from her grandfather. She and Michael were spending every weekend in Crocknasolas, fixing the roof, redecorating, putting in a new kitchen, converting the byres to bedrooms. Mum had been persuaded to go with them. I flew over to help. Noreen and her husband paid a surprise visit on the Saturday afternoon. It was the first time they had seen Michael and Siobhan since Michael's release from prison and his wedding a few months later.

'It must be at least a year since we've seen you,' Austin said, shaking hands.

'Two years,' said Michael.

'Time flies,' said Austin, looking embarrassed. He was the kind of man who likes a quiet life. Knowing my sister, I suspected she took most of the decisions.

We stood outside remarking on the purple shadows on the mountain, the taste of salt and the smell of turf smoke on the wind. I thought how well the cottage blended into the landscape. The whitewash echoed the clouds drifting above and the white spray on the sea. The slate roof was the same colour as the lane that pointed to the strand. The blue paint on the half-door and the windows was the colour of the sky.

'Like a Paul Henry painting,' I said. 'Nature imitating art.'

'Pity you couldn't put a thatch back on,' said Noreen. 'Nothing nicer than a thatched cottage.'

'Funny how things change,' said Siobhan. 'When people from round here emigrated to America they sent back money for the slates, to slate the roof. Slates were dear. People couldn't afford them. Now they can't afford to thatch.'

'It's still nicer than the horrible bungalows we passed along the road,' said Noreen. 'Bungalow blight.' She shuddered.

'Granda thought so too,' said Siobhan. 'He wouldn't move when Mum and Dad built their bungalow. I was born in this house and I'll die in this house, and there's an end of it, he said. Mum thought a decent kitchen and bathroom and central heating were more important than a view.'

There was an awkward silence. Austin cleared his throat. 'It's a grand view anyway,' he said. 'The mountains behind and the sea below.'

'My Granda used to say a day out of Donegal was a day wasted,' said Siobhan.

We went inside. I saw Noreen take in the hand-dyed rugs on the slate floor, the pale cream wool curtains, the china sparkling in the sunlight on the old pine dresser.

'You've great taste.' She just managed to conceal her surprise.

A turf fire smouldered in the hearth.

'Siobhan's granda kept the fire for a lot of houses around here,' said Michael. 'Every time a family emigrated, they took a clod of smoking turf from their house and brought it to him and he put it on the range here so the fire of their house would never go out. There's a lot of history burning in this kitchen. A lot of pain as well.'

There was another silence.

'Well, everybody seems to be doing well these days, thank God,' said Austin. 'Nobody's emigrating. Not for want or famine anyway. There's a powerful lot of new building round here.'

'Holiday homes,' said Michael. 'They're like a rash.'

'They're empty all winter,' said Siobhan. 'Like ghost villages.'

'Actually,' said Noreen, 'we're thinking of buying one. As an investment. That's why we're here.'

I could have written the row before it started.

'You've a nerve talking in your sniffy way about bungalows when you're going to add to the blight,' said Michael.

'What about you?' said Noreen. 'What's this if it's not a holiday home. Why should we be denied what you've got?'

'This is Siobhan's heritage,' said Michael. 'We come here all year round. Not like the blow-ins from Belfast and Dublin with their Marks and Spencer ready-cooked meals in the boot of their BMWs.'

'We don't have a BMW and I cook a dinner every day. I'd be surprised if you made toast, Michael.'

Noreen looked around for corroboration but Siobhan had slipped outside with Austin. They were examining a black three-legged pot filled with pansies on the windowsill. Siobhan gave me a wee wave and rolled her eyes.

'If you don't live here all the time, it's a holiday home,' Noreen snapped.

'We're going to move here permanently,' Michael said.

'What about Mum?'

And they both looked at me.

Now Michael said, 'One more thing. Would you telephone Noreen and relay the invitation?'

'The invitation is from you and Siobhan, Michael.'

'It's really from Mum,' he said. 'She'll come for Christmas if she gets to see her grandchildren.'

'So this is all a ploy to get Mum to come to Donegal for Christmas?'

'Where else is she going to spend Christmas? Noreen didn't ask her to Dublin.'

I must have heaved a sigh that shook the taxi because Chloe took off her headphones and gave me an anxious look. 'Everything all right, Louise?'

'Fine,' I said. 'Just a change of plans.'

# 18

# Diana

The gallery glittered like a diamond in the dark, but as I hurried towards it I was dismayed to see, through the wide plate-glass window, that Henry's opening was not well-attended. There were, at most, about a dozen people drifting in an expanse of white space. A waiter lolled behind a table laden with bottles and glasses. The optimism that had kept me cheerful on an over-crowded train drained away.

Henry put on a brave smile to greet me. 'We thought it would be a good night for the opening, the week before Christmas, late night shopping, people coming up to town and all that.'

'Early days,' said Frederick Farry. He had big, lugubrious eyes and jowls like a bloodhound. His voice boomed around the near-empty room. 'Early days.' He handed me a glass of wine.

I took a sip and surveyed the company. Henry had joined a cluster of army chums and their wives. Four men in suits had grouped themselves around some kind of abstract steel and glass sculpture. Not by Henry. Apart from a young man in a leather jacket peering at a small landscape, and Ronnie Bolton who was standing in front of my portrait and sending excited hand and eye signals back to me, no one was paying much attention to the paintings.

'I've put a red dot on your portrait, Diana,' muttered Frederick. 'Marvellous piece of work. Not for sale I know, but a red dot encourages the punters. Discouraging to see no red stickers at all, don't you think? People are like sheep. They'll buy if they see other people buying.'

Outside, two taxis grumbled to a halt. Frederick stiffened, scenting new arrivals.

'Excuse me, Diana.' He nodded to the waiter and lifted a tray of glasses from the table.

Susan was first through the door. She looked flushed and triumphant and barely broke her step as she accepted a glass.

'I've just come from my solicitor,' she hissed in my ear. 'Half the pot, plus the house.'

She stepped back and looked around with a glittering smile. 'I feel like celebrating. I've had two glasses of champagne already. Where's Henry? I'm going to buy one of his paintings, I think. As a present to myself.'

Behind her, I saw Louise and Chloe waving at me. I waved back. Susan raised an eyebrow.

'The film people I told you about. They've just arrived,' I said.

'How exciting. You absolutely must introduce me before I circulate.'

I made the introductions and slipped away to speak to Ronnie Bolton.

'Susan's divorce has been settled. Half the pot and the house,' I told him. 'She's in terrific spirits.'

Ronnie gave a low whistle. 'I'm not surprised. She'll be a rich woman now.'

Four more people arrived. Then six. I waved to my cousin Tommy, Daphne's son. The circle of army chums broke up and joined a procession making its way around the gallery. Susan had her hand on Henry's arm and was talking excitedly to him. If Henry married Susan, I thought, all his problems would be over. She could pay for half a dozen roofs.

Then it was as though someone had fired a starting pistol for the party to begin. The room was suddenly full and filled with a noise like turkeys in a shed. Tommy and I had an unsatisfactory conversation yelling at each other.

'We saw your mother on Sunday.'

'What?' He cupped his hand to his deaf ear. 'Mothering Sunday?'

'No. Daphne. Visit. Sunday.'

'Hadn't planned to. We're having her for Christmas.'

I gave up. Tommy gave me a peck on the cheek and moved on.

I was composed now, but I hated standing at parties. Just like Mummy, I thought to myself. She would always find the most comfortable perch in the room. 'I'll just sit here and let everyone come and talk to me,' she would say.

I found a chair near the door to Frederick's office, sat down and pretended to read the catalogue.

'They're not as good as his other stuff, Teddy.' I recognised Louise's lilting voice and accent.

'*Robin on a Five-barred Gate, Pheasant in Snow*. I see what you mean.' A man's voice. Southern English. Deep and fruity. It took on a declamatory tone.

'Stage-coaches, cantering straight out of Merrie England,

In a flurry of whips and fetlocks, sacks and Santas.'

'I can't see a Santa Claus, Teddy.'

'It's a quotation. From a poem by U. A. Fanthorpe. About Christmas cards, but it's really about love.'

Their voices were swallowed by the gabbling crowd as they moved on.

A hand fell on my shoulder. I looked up.

'Peter!' I got to my feet. 'What a marvellous surprise. I thought you weren't coming home until next week.'

'Flying visit. Can't stay. Negotiating a deal in Gresham Street.' He gave me a hug. 'I've taken a break to pop in. Didn't want to miss Dad's opening.' He looked around. 'There's a good crowd here. Lots of jolly attractive women. I bet Dad is . . .' He stopped, mid-sentence. His gaze settled somewhere at the back of the gallery for a moment before he turned his attention back to me. 'Pity I have to go back to work.'

'How long are you staying?'

'Going back lunchtime tomorrow.'

'Does Henry know you're here?'

'I'm just going to find him.'

I had hardly settled back down on my chair when I saw Plum elbowing his way towards me.

'Where's Henry? Got a cheque here for him,' he shouted over the noise. 'I think he'll be pleased. Nice little Christmas present.'

I realised I hadn't told Henry about John Finnegan's telephone call. I jumped up again.

'I'll get Henry for you, Plum.'

'No need. I'll find him.' He began to push his way towards the back of the gallery. I spun on my heel and saw Henry standing near the door, talking to Susan. I squeezed through the crowd to join them.

'Frightful din,' said Henry cheerfully.

'I've just been telling Henry I've bought one of his paintings, as a present to myself,' Susan said. '*Pheasant in Snow*. Charming.'

'So glad you like it,' said Henry.

'How do you pick your subjects?'

It was the kind of question I knew silenced Henry. I put my hand on his arm, smiled apologetically at Susan, and opened my mouth to speak.

Susan persisted. 'How do you decide whom to paint, I mean, Henry?' She tapped him lightly on the arm. She was slightly tipsy. 'Do you ever ask people to sit for you?'

'Sometimes,' Henry said. 'If I see a face that interests me.'

'Does anybody here interest you?' She looked up at him through her dark eyelashes. 'Is there anyone here you'd like to paint?'

'Yes.' His gaze shifted automatically. I saw that he was looking at Louise and Chloe, about ten feet away, talking to each other.

Susan's eyes narrowed.

'The girl with the pink hair? A little young for you, Henry?' She shot him an arch look.

Henry smiled but didn't reply.

'It can't be, surely not,' Susan paused, 'the fil-um person?' She imitated Louise's vowels and intonation. 'When you came back from Ulster you told me you never wanted to hear that accent again.'

'That was because I never heard it from such a good-looking woman,' Henry said.

'Has there been any interest in the portraits?' I asked quickly. 'Any commissions?'

Henry held up crossed fingers in reply.

We fell silent, letting the chatter and laughter wash over us. Susan looked decidedly put out. Henry seemed distracted.

I leaned towards him and murmured, 'I've organised a second opinion.'

'What?'

'The wine,' I said.

'Good idea. I'll get us another glass.'

Susan drifted away. Henry made to take my glass.

'No, Henry. I mean the wine in the cellar.'

Out of the corner of my eye I saw Plum wriggling towards us.

'John Finnegan is going to give us a second opinion,' I said hurriedly.

But suddenly Plum was beside me waving a cheque book and shouting, 'Three thousand pounds sound all right to you, Henry?'

# 19

# Louise

The gallery was in a narrow cobbled street somewhere between Tottenham Court Road and Regent Street. A man in a green velvet jacket and a pink bow tie handed us each a glass of wine. Diana gave us a friendly wave and introduced us to a dark, elegant woman with diamond drop earrings who wanted to know all about the stars of our film, Caroline Cross and William Bowman. We confessed we hadn't met them yet. She made a little moue of disappointment and wandered off.

Chloe and I walked along the line of paintings hanging on the ice-white wall. About half a dozen were well-executed, but otherwise typical boardroom portraits of men in uniform of one kind or another – pin-striped suits, military tunics, medals, red robes and ermine. The English were very fond of badges and uniforms. A hangover from the Empire, I decided.

The other portraits, in oil and collage, were bolder and more alive. I stopped in front of a portrait of an elderly woman. Her body was fragile, her face was strong, her milky eyes were focused on something in the distance beyond the frame and the viewer. She was encircled by a collage of photographs and scraps of velvet and chintz that blended into the armchair that almost enveloped her.

I leaned closer to examine the photographs. A school group of girls in identical summer frocks and blazers. A woman with a young girl on a strand. A family group of three women and two children. A slender girl in some kind of uniform – recognisably a younger version of the sitter.

'My aunt Lucy,' said a voice at my shoulder, making me jump.

'I like it,' I said, turning to face Henry. 'She looks as though she is dreaming about something away back in the past. You've really caught her expression.'

'Thank you. Not for sale, I'm afraid.'

'I couldn't afford it anyway,' I said. 'What I like I can't afford, and what I can afford I don't like.'

'Tell me what you don't like.'

'About what? Life in general?'

He sketched an impatient gesture. 'About my work.'

I hesitated. I didn't want to offend the owner of our principal location. I gripped my glass more tightly.

'I don't like the Christmassy watercolours.'

He was silent, waiting for me to go on. Heat flooded into my face.

'This portrait is full of life. But the watercolours are sentimental. They don't seem to have been painted by the same artist.'

He gave a satisfied nod. 'I agree.'

I couldn't stop myself asking, 'So why did you paint them?'

'To make money,' he said. 'They're all sold.'

'Money isn't everything,' I said.

'That's a sentimental notion if ever I heard one.'

'It doesn't buy happiness.' I groaned inwardly. Another cliché.

He tossed it back with a smile. 'You can do better than that.'

It wasn't the sardonic smile I expected but a warm smile that glinted in his eyes. Dark grey eyes, almost the colour of slate. He held himself in a relaxed, loose-knit way. I shook my head and looked away, suddenly shy and aware of his eyes on me.

More people arrived. The noise level rose. The man in the velvet jacket came over to us. 'Do you mind if I steal the artist for a while?'

Henry touched me lightly on the arm. 'Catch up with you later.'

I had disliked him when we first met. Now, as I watched him move through the crowd, smiling a deprecating smile, shaking hands, I began to see him as attractive, interesting. It was because he was an artist, I decided. Artists were bohemians.

'Frightfully good show, don't you think?'

It was the dark-haired woman with the diamond drop earrings. 'Seen anything that takes your fancy? There are some reasonably priced watercolours.'

'I like the portraits,' I said.

'Henry's terrifically talented. I should have married him instead of that philandering fool I fell for. What a silly girl I was. Still, we all make mistakes.' She smiled brightly. Her glance roamed around the gallery. 'Can you see Henry? I'm too tiny to see over the crowd, I'm afraid.'

'He's by the door,' I said.

'Must have a word with him before I go.' She flitted away.

I felt unsettled and looked around for a friendly face. Chloe was talking to a tall man with a wing of dark hair falling over his forehead. I watched her smiling up at him. Teddy was examining the watercolours on the opposite wall. I picked up a glass of wine from a passing tray and edged through the crowd to join him.

'Maybe they're meant to be ironic,' he said, pointing at a robin on a five-barred gate.

'I think they're meant to be money-makers.'

'Prostituting his art,' Teddy muttered. 'Like me.'

'I like your script.'

'It's not my script,' said Teddy. 'It's a round robin.'

'You write the dialogue,' I said. 'It's sharp.'

'It's not my story any more. It never is with a screenplay. We're the prostitutes of the film industry. Fucked and paid. I should have got used to that by now.'

'Write a novel,' I said.

'There's no money in novels,' he snapped. 'Robins sell. These have all got stickers on them.'

I saw Jacky grinning at us from a few yards away. He had one arm around the narrow shoulders of a spiky youth in a denim jacket smoking a cigarette with an ostentatious tilt of his chin.

'Drama queen,' muttered Teddy. 'Tears before bedtime.'

'Let's join them,' I said.

'Nah. I'm going home, Louise.' Teddy sounded dejected. He raised his hand in a half-wave. 'I need an early start if I'm going to deliver next week.'

I hadn't eaten since midday and wondered if I should go home. I visualised the contents of my fridge. A carton of milk, a morsel of cheese, a bag of salad that was probably past its sell-by date. Like me, I thought with a rush of self-pity. My feet hurt. I wanted to sit down and kick off my high heels. Diana had bagged the only chair and was studying the catalogue. She stood up to greet someone and moved away. I dived into the melee and made for the empty chair. My stomach was clamouring for a hot meal. Chloe surfaced in front of me.

'I've just met an absolute dish. His name's Peter.'

'And?'

'Nothing,' she said gloomily. 'He dashed off to some meeting in the City.'

'At this time?'

'Some deal he's involved in, apparently. They do this alpha male thing of negotiating all night. Dicks on the table. So boring.' She beamed. 'But a perfectly sweet old chap has asked me to dinner. What are you going to do?'

'Go home.' I got to my feet.

And at that exact moment, from somewhere near the door, came a bang, a crash, a shout and the sound of breaking glass.

Chloe and I pushed our way towards the commotion. Henry and Jacky were using paper napkins to mop down Diana and a portly man in a pin-striped suit. Jacky looked stricken. There was no sign of his denim-clad companion.

Teddy was on his haunches fishing a sodden cheque book from a pool of red wine and broken glass. Chloe and I hunkered down to help him.

Diana looked surprisingly serene. Jacky fell to his knees and began dabbing at her skirt with a large white handkerchief.

I had a sense of us grouped like supplicants at the feet of a statue.

'They were having some kind of argument,' murmured Teddy. 'A lot of arm waving. The boy knocked a tray with his elbow. What did I tell you? Tears before bedtime.'

# 20

# Diana

I knew I had an idiotic smile on my face. What was happening to me? Someone had spilled wine over my party skirt and half my brain was thinking I didn't care and was sending up a silent prayer of thanksgiving that Plum had been diverted. The other half was wondering how I would get a red wine stain out of a pale grey taffeta skirt.

The curly-haired designer from the film company was kneeling at my feet, dabbing ineffectually at the stain. He was red-faced with mortification and moaning apologies, interspersed with promises to pay for dry-cleaning or a new skirt. I remembered his name was Jacky.

'I've had this old thing for ages,' I said. 'Absolutely ages. Please don't worry, Jacky.'

'I'm really sorry. What can I do?'

I could see that the party was beginning to break up.

'Get the other casualty into a taxi,' I said. 'He got rather the worst of it, I'm afraid. I'm sure he'll want to go home and change. There's going to be rather a demand for taxis.'

A dark-haired foxy-looking man got to his feet, dangling Plum's cheque book like a dead, wet rat.

Henry said, 'Don't worry about the cheque, Plum. We can sort it out another time.'

Plum was red-faced but gracious. 'No harm done. Could happen to anybody. Spilt plenty of wine myself over the years.'

I swept him out of the gallery just as a taxi swung into the street in response to Jacky's frantic waves from the corner.

'After Christmas, Plum,' I said. 'Time enough after Christmas. Frightfully sorry about your shirt.'

Jacky jogged back, panting. 'Send me the bill for dry-cleaning, please.' He pushed a card into Plum's hand and wrenched open the door of the taxi.

The gallery was emptying on to the cobbles in little eddies of noise and laughter and cheery goodbyes.

Jacky offered me a card as well. He had got his breath back. 'You must send me the bill,' he said. 'Cleaning, replacement, whatever.'

He had such an open, friendly face I found myself saying, 'Actually, you got me out of an awkward spot.'

'Was he going to pounce on you?'

'Absolutely not.' I laughed. 'I'm past the stage of being pounced on, I'm afraid.' But I was secretly flattered.

When I got to Paddington I was humming a tune. It had a jaunty, ragtime beat. I was still trying to place it as I settled into my seat on the train. It came to me when the train slowed down through Slough. 'I'm gonna sit right down and write myself a letter.' It was played at all the parties the year I left school. 'A lot of kisses on the bottom, I'll be glad I got 'em.' All those years ago I had never realised the double entendre. What an innocent I was. I started to laugh.

The drunk in the seat opposite woke up, rolled his head around in an attempt to focus, gave up and slumped forward on his chest, mumbling, 'Someoneshappy.'

John Finnegan was coming to see me after Christmas. I had made sure he would still come by deflecting Plum at the last minute. Ridiculous, really, how a small triumph could transform a day.

# 21

# Louise

The accident signalled the end of the evening. I got my coat and went to find Jacky. He was standing outside.

'Want to go for something to eat?'

Jacky shook his head. 'Nick's in the pub. I'd better go and join him. He's embarrassed. He's young, a bit full of himself. But I can't let him go just like that.' He shrugged. 'Sorry, Louise.'

'Where's Teddy?'

'He went for the tube. Maybe Chloe will be up for a meal.' He gave me a quick hug. 'Enjoy the rest of the evening.' He pulled up the collar of his coat and headed for the yellow lights of the pub on the corner of the street. I set off in the opposite direction, feeling tired, hungry and slightly drunk.

Normally, I liked walking through the West End. When I first came to London, I rented a studio flat near Marylebone High Street and spent winter evenings after work exploring the streets. I sensed an energy contained in the buildings and shops, ready to burst through the walls and windows. I floated through a sea of shoppers bobbing homeward with their parcels attached to them like ballast. I tacked through the chattering crowds flowing out of the theatres and cinemas. I felt invisible and free.

Even after I bought my flat in West Hampstead, I would some-times take a long route home, stopping off at Piccadilly or Bond Street to inhale the optimism in the air, and to relish the guilty, extravagant pleasure of buying exotic ready-made meals in Selfridges Food Hall or Fortnum and Mason.

But tonight I felt isolated and despondent. The Christmas decorations seemed tawdry, the shoppers hunched, the noise from the pubs unmerry.

I looked at my watch. Nearly nine o'clock. Even with late-night opening, those temples of gastronomy would be shut by the time I got there. I was disinclined to shop for my dinner in an over-lit, over-priced late-night supermarket, but my stomach was sending me sharp, nervy reminders that I needed to eat.

I had been wandering without any clear sense of going somewhere. Now I found myself standing outside an Italian restaurant in Goodge Street. Through the window I saw a man and woman rise from a table, still talking intensely to each other as he helped her into her coat. I waited until they emerged, holding hands, before I went inside and was shown to the table they had just vacated.

I ordered tagliatelle in tomato sauce and a glass of red wine. I shrank into myself, in the manner of people eating alone in restaurants. Snatches of conversation swirled around me.

'I nearly died when I saw him . . .'

'He said he had left his wallet at home . . .'

'Nineteen stone and a blonde wig . . .'

'I ended up paying the bill . . .'

My order arrived. I ate efficiently, giving the tagliatelle all my attention, careful not to spill tomato sauce on my white shirt.

'May I join you?'

I looked up, startled. A splodge of sauce landed on my left breast.

Henry said, 'I was on my way to the tube thinking I should eat something. I saw you in the window. Do you mind if I join you? So much nicer to have company, don't you think?'

I swabbed hopelessly at the stain.

'You look like a wounded swan,' Henry said.

I stared up at him.

'Long neck, hair up, white shirt,' he made a vague gesture.

I felt flustered, but managed to say, 'Please sit down.'

He slid on to the seat opposite me, signalled to the waiter and ordered a veal chop and a glass of red wine.

'Where did you learn about art? You seem awfully knowledgeable,' he said when the waiter had gone.

'I went to art college for a year. My parents weren't keen. They wanted me to have a secure job. So I did Economics instead. And ended up in the film industry.' I shook my head at my own foolishness.

'I thought all you film people earned pots of money.'

'Don't be thinking that. Sometimes we don't get paid at all. A lot of the time we work for a share of the profits. Sometimes there are no profits.'

Henry looked surprised.

'It's not that different from being an artist,' I said. 'You do the work, but you might not sell it. Same with us. Sometimes we work for months, even years on a project and we can't get finance for it.'

The waiter brought Henry a glass of wine and darted away.

'Eat, please. Don't wait for me,' Henry said. 'Your pasta will get cold.'

He watched me silently as I twirled my fork as insouciantly as possible, capturing mouthfuls of ribbon. His veal chop arrived as I mopped up the last of the sauce with a heel of bread.

He ate methodically, almost greedily, savouring every bite. When he was halfway through the chop, he laid his knife and fork on the plate and reached for his glass of wine.

'Will this film get made?'

'I hope so.' I tried to smile. 'I'm living on the money from the last film I did. The money I get, back end, from this one will feed and clothe me until the next one comes along.'

'Back end?'

'My percentage of the profits. After the investors have taken theirs, of course. Sometimes there's nothing left for us poor sods who make the films.' I felt the familiar twist of anxiety in my gut. 'Maybe I should give up this business and get a job in a supermarket.' I took a sip of wine.

'So it mightn't get made?' Henry's voice was neutral but his mouth tightened.

'Not every film gets fully financed,' I said. 'But I'm optimistic about this one.'

He reached across the table and touched my hand. 'You've crossed your fingers.'

I almost jumped.

'There's a lot of finger-crossing in this business,' I said unsteadily.

'Hope springs eternal.'

'Now that's a really sentimental notion.'

He laughed, picked up his knife and fork and attacked the veal chop again. He had strong, shapely hands. A minuscule splodge of vermilion paint was lodged under the nail of his index finger. I found myself staring at it.

The waiter cleared my empty glass. 'Another glass of wine, Signora?'

'Make that two, please,' Henry said.

His face was about two feet away from mine. We seemed to be in a bubble of silence. From the blur of faces to my left, as though from far away, came shouts and laughter and the popping of corks.

'Do you still beat your husband?' Henry said softly.

'I haven't got a husband.'

'Haven't got one now, or never had one?'

'I've never been married.'

'How long have you been attached?'

'Is this some kind of interrogation?'

'So. Not attached.'

'In case you didn't notice, I didn't answer the question.'

'I noticed. That's how I know.'

He had a combative smile.

'My turn to ask the questions,' I said. 'What about you? Are you married?'

'Not any more.'

Before I could think what to say next, Henry said quickly, 'I'd like to paint you.'

'I hadn't thought of myself as an artist's model,' I said feebly.

'Don't worry, you can keep your clothes on.'

'I'm not worried.' My face blazed. 'I mean, I didn't think that was what you meant.'

My mobile rang. I pulled it out of my pocket and saw Michael's number on the display panel. Part of me said, leave it. It can wait. You're with an attractive man. He's flirting with you. How long has it been since that happened? Part of me worried that something had happened to Mum. My cheeks cooled.

'Do you mind?' I pointed to the phone. 'I'll go outside to take this. Please excuse me.'

I made my way outside and stood with my back to the window to take the call.

'This had better be important, Michael.'

'Ho, ho. Are you on the pull, Louise?'

'Give over, Michael.'

'What time are you getting in on Monday?'

'I don't know. About three o'clock.'

'You're getting a hire car, aren't you? Siobhan and me were just talking. We could drive to Donegal on Sunday if you're going to be there on Monday. That would give Siobhan a wee bit more time to get things ready. You could take Mum Christmas shopping and drive her down on Christmas Eve. OK?'

I thought about saying I'd planned to go to Dublin and see some friends. I thought how I had done my bit all the years Michael had been in prison. I thought how Michael and Siobhan, and mostly Siobhan, were looking after Mum now. My mind see-sawed between giving in to Michael, or giving out to him about taking me for granted.

'OK, Louise?'

I gave in. 'OK.'

'Oh, and that woman telephoned looking for you again. I said you'd be home for Christmas. Slan! See you in Donegal.'

Henry stood up when I got back to the table. I didn't know if it was a polite gesture or a signal to leave. I sat down. Henry sat down.

'Pudding? Coffee?'

'Coffee keeps me awake.' I silently berated myself for sounding so middle-aged.

The atmosphere seemed flatter. The phone call had broken the flow of our conversation. Henry caught the waiter's eye and mimed signing a bill. I dug in my handbag for my wallet.

'Let me get this,' Henry said.

'No. I didn't . . . You didn't. We didn't set out to do it together.' That sounded wrong. 'Thank you for keeping me company, but,' I added, lamely.

'An unexpected pleasure,' Henry said, with an almost formal bow. 'It's no fun eating on one's own.'

We lapsed into silence. I stared out the window, aware of him studying me. The waiter presented the bill. Henry divided the total and accepted my half in an unembarrassed way. He left a few pound coins as a tip and stood up.

'I'll walk you to the tube. Or perhaps you're going to take a taxi?'

'Tube,' I said. 'It's an expensive taxi ride to West Hampstead.'

A raucous troop of teenagers reeled past me, almost knocking me off my feet. Henry gripped my arm to steady me. I turned to thank him. His face was inches from mine. Suddenly our arms were around each other and he was kissing me, and I was kissing him back, and the blood was singing in my veins and a voice inside me was shouting, Yes, Yes, Yes.

# 22

# Louise

I wakened in the exact position in which I had gone to sleep. Henry's arms were around me. My head rested in the curve of his shoulder. My right arm was stretched across him.

I lay remembering the near-silent journey in the taxi, Henry only letting go of my hand to pay the driver an impossibly large sum of money. I remembered thinking he couldn't be so tight-fisted after all. I remembered him saying, 'I'm fifty-three, I'm divorced, I've no money, a family home I can't afford to keep, and I've wanted to do this since you sat on my sofa and crossed your legs and pushed your hair out of your eyes and gave me that cool smile.'

'It's not a cool smile now,' I told him.

My whole body was a smile.

Henry didn't stir when I lifted one encircling arm, rolled from his grasp and slid out of bed. I unhooked my dressing gown from the back of the door, gently depressed the door handle and slipped across the landing to the bathroom.

Grey light flowed through the frosted glass of the window. I brushed my teeth, pulled a comb through my hair and splashed my face with hot then cold water until my skin tingled. A fragment of verse floated into my mind.

'What is it men in women do require?
The lineaments of Gratified Desire.'

I studied my features with drowsy satisfaction.

Only a week earlier I had told Rebecca I was afraid that parts of me would wither and fall off. 'Atrophied, dessiccated, no longer required,' I had said. 'I've got used to the idea I probably won't have any children. But I don't want to think I'll never make love again.'

'Be like Jacky,' Rebecca had counselled. 'Advertise. It's more efficient than going to parties and drinking too much.'

'Is that what you think I do?'

'It's what a lot of women do, Louise. In between getting divorced and meeting Robert I went to a lot of parties, hoping to meet a prince. I kissed a lot of frogs.'

Now I yawned, stretched, and smiled back into the mirror. Womanhood triumphantly restored.

'I think I've kissed a prince,' I whispered to my delighted reflection.

In the kitchen, I tugged at the blind. It rolled up with a soft snap. I glanced at the clock on the cooker. Ten minutes past eight. I was usually out of the flat by this time, walking up the street, exchanging a greeting with the newsagent who was from Newry and who kept me a copy of Saturday's *Irish Times* and always asked me if I had been home recently.

I foraged for breakfast and found two clementines and an apple in a bowl on top of the fridge, two parsnips, a quarter-litre of milk and the heel of a loaf inside the fridge, an unopened packet of ground coffee in the cupboard and one tea bag in the caddy. A pathetic reminder of my single life.

I filled the kettle at the sink, looking out over damp gardens, black dripping trees, the glistening curve of a railway line beyond the rooftops of a street lower down the hill. I felt slowed down, almost dreamy.

I thought about the tender marvels of the night. We had fitted each other like a hand and a glove. We had fallen asleep with our arms around each other. Henry would ask to see me again. Everything was going to be all right. I would not be punished for my recklessness.

I shivered, suddenly aware of the cold floor under my feet. I sat on the kitchen chair, drew my feet up under me, wrapped the faded blue flannel more tightly around me and prayed I hadn't made a mistake. You've been here before, I said to myself. You have confused neediness with romance. You have wasted days wondering if some man was going to call you after a fling at a post-film party. Rebecca is right. It would make more sense to advertise. But you're here now. Be brave. Be cool.

I went back to the bedroom. Henry had drawn back the curtains and was sitting on the edge of the bed, wearing the white sheet like a toga.

'Hail Caesar,' I said.

'I came, I saw, I conquered,' he beat his fists on his chest and laughed.

'Less of the conqueror, if you don't mind. I'm nobody's slave.'

'And I'm no dictator,' he said softly.

There was a silence. Time seemed to lengthen. I heard a faint swish as a car went by in the street.

'I don't have much in the way of breakfast,' I said.

'I don't have time for breakfast.' He stood up. 'I'm meeting my son.' He looked at his watch. 'Must crack on. I'm supposed to be in Gresham Street at nine o'clock.'

A dull feeling spread through my veins like sludge. A bolter. He couldn't wait to get away.

'Fine,' I said curtly.

He tugged on the sleeve of my dressing gown. 'Don't be like that.'

'Like what?'

'Prickly.'

'Clean towels in the hot press. Help yourself.' A sour taste surged into my throat. I pulled my arm away.

Henry looked puzzled. 'What's wrong?'

'Nothing's wrong. You'd better get a move on if you want to be in the City at nine o'clock.'

'I thought we could travel in together.'

'I'm not going in until later.'

'Aha,' said Henry. He hesitated. 'Maybe we could meet this afternoon. I thought I might pop in to the National Portrait Gallery. Care to come with me?'

'I have meetings all day,' I said stiffly.

'What about lunchtime?'

'Can't leave the office. Sorry. I like the National Portrait Gallery.' My tone was still cool but I managed a smile. 'Maybe another time.' Damn. I could probably get away for an hour if I tried. Better not to seem too keen, I told myself. 'I'll make coffee while you . . . sort yourself out. Whatever. If you have time. Or maybe you'd prefer tea?'

'Coffee is fine.' He cleared his throat. 'I left my stuff at the Chelsea Arts Club. I don't suppose you keep a man's razor, by any chance?'

'I'm not as prepared as you for these encounters.'

'What makes you think I make a habit of this?' He rearranged the sheet around him. 'I've had two brief encounters since my wife left me. Neither of them worked out. Since you askenry sH.'

'I didn't ask.'

'You have a way of not asking that provokes a reply.'

'And you never ask a question that can be answered yes or no.'

He laughed, grasped the belt of my dressing gown and pulled me close to him. He was tall enough to kiss the top of my head. 'You don't miss much.' He rocked me in his arms. 'And since you don't ask, I was a Boy Scout. And you know our motto.'

'I never met any Boy Scouts before,' I said. 'All the Boy Scouts were Protestants where I grew up.' I whisked myself away before he could reply.

I could hear him whistling in the bathroom as I waltzed around the kitchen. Even the kettle seemed in tune when it screeched to a boil.

He came into the kitchen buttoning his shirt, his tie draped around his neck. 'I hate not being able to shave before I face the world.' He ran a finger across the stubble on his jaw and around his mouth.

'Sorry, I'm not set up for male visitors,' I said.

'I'm rather glad about that.'

We stood smiling at each other for a moment. He pulled out a chair and sat down. I carried two mugs of coffee to the table and sat opposite him. I felt self-conscious. The cuffs of my dressing gown were grubby. I hid them in my lap.

'I could make a wee bit of toast if you like.'

'No time. Thank you.' He sipped his coffee, eyeing me all the while.

I found myself saying, idiotically, 'What's a muntjac?'

'It's a small deer. Introduced into this country from China sometime in the mid-nineteenth century. Why do you ask?'

'That day we came to see the house. You told us you'd shot one.'

'Disapprove, do you?'

I shrugged. 'There are hunters in every primitive society.'

'Then there should be plenty in Ulster.'

'Northern Ireland,' I automatically corrected him, while acknowledging the riposte with a tiny smile.

'Ulster, Northern Ireland: what does it matter?'

'Three counties of Ulster are in the Irish Republic.'

'So?'

'So they're not in Northern Ireland.' I sensed the conversation careering off in the wrong direction but couldn't stop myself. 'You can't say Ulster when you mean Northern Ireland.'

'Don't say I've made love to an Irish pedant.'

'I hope I heard that correctly,' I said coldly.

He pushed the mug away and pounded his head with his fists. 'Enough, please. This is too early in the morning.' His arms fell to the table. His fists opened like flowers. 'Give me your hands,' he commanded. 'Look at me.'

He had halted my mad canter towards an argument. I almost laughed out loud with relief. I took my hands from my lap and held them out for him to grasp.

'I want to see you again. May I telephone you?'

'Of course.'

'I'll call you.' He released my hands, stood up and drained the mug of coffee.

I watched from the bedroom window as he sprinted up the street like a boy. At the top, he turned and waved with both arms, like semaphore from ship to passing ship.

# 23

# Louise

I spent most of the day trying not to think about Henry. I persuaded myself that he would wait a few days before contacting me. If he contacted me at all. Men operated on a different timescale, as Rebecca reminded me when I broke my resolve not to mention Henry and told her, over a quick sandwich at a café in Borough market, about bumping into him in the Italian restaurant and about his promise to telephone me. I edited out the bit in between.

Rebecca wasn't fooled. 'You're worried it was a one-night stand,' she said bluntly. 'Nothing you can do about it. He's probably got a thousand things on his mind of which you are only one. Whereas you, although you also have a thousand things on your mind, put him top of the list. It's a boy–girl thing.'

She finished her sandwich and licked her fingers. 'When he calls, don't be too available. Make him think you get asked out all the time. Don't make it too easy for him. Keep him on his toes.'

She turned to take her coat from the back of her chair. She froze for a second then spun back to face me.

'It's him,' she mouthed.

I thought she meant Henry, until I saw that her face was white and her eyes were wide with fear.

I glanced past her to the queue at the counter. Three women with shopping bags, two men in striped aprons and two giggling teenage girls who looked like office workers on their lunch break. The door of the café swung behind them. It banged shut.

Rebecca jumped.

'I don't see anybody,' I said. 'Look around. There's nobody there. Just the usual queue.'

She moved like a mechanical toy, turning back slowly, stiffly.

'Barry is in Belfast, Rebecca. We asked Michael. Remember?'

'I've had this strange feeling a few times.' She shivered. 'I feel I'm being watched. When I look around, I don't see anybody. But this time I saw him out of the corner of my eye.'

'So you didn't get a good look.'

'You think I'm imagining it.'

'He's in Belfast. In the pantomime.'

'It won't have started yet.'

'There'll be rehearsals.'

'He could be here for the weekend.'

There was no convincing her.

'Look,' I said. 'We'll go to the office and I'll look up the Opera House on the Web and find out when the pantomime starts. *Ali Baba and the Forty Thieves.*' I attempted a joke. 'He's probably one of the thieves.'

Rebecca sprang from the table and blundered towards the exit. I picked up the chair she knocked over in her flight, shouted an apology to a waitress clearing tables, and followed Rebecca through the market. I caught up with her about twenty paces from our office building.

'Hold on,' I said. 'Take it easy. There's nobody around.'

I held her hand while I scanned the windows of the warehouses on both sides of the narrow, cobbled street. Chloe waved to me from our office window. I waved back with a big, confident smile, for Rebecca as much as for Chloe. Rebecca didn't let go of my hand until we were inside the building.

'Any calls? Anybody drop in?' I asked Chloe casually when we got upstairs.

'Only one call. A woman wanting to speak to you, Louise. I offered to take a message but she said she'd call again.'

I wheeled my chair to Rebecca's desk. She sat beside me while I tapped 'Pantomime Belfast Ali Baba' into a search engine.

'There you are,' I said quietly, reading from the screen. 'Grand Opera House. Saturday the fifth of December until Saturday the twenty-third of January. It's been running for two weeks.'

'How can we be sure he's in it?'

'Does he still have an agent? I could check Spotlight.' Spotlight is the casting directory used by everybody in the business.

'He's not in it. I've looked.'

'I'll telephone the Opera House and get them to fax me a cast list. Legitimate query from a production company. OK?' Rebecca nodded. 'Robert's back, isn't he? Have you told him about Barry?'

She looked uncomfortable. I guessed what was bothering her.

'You don't want to admit to a mistake, do you? You're embarrassed because you had sex for a few weeks with a man who turned out to be a lunatic. It's not your fault he's a lunatic.' A thought struck me. 'Robert's not the kind of man who wants details of every other man you've slept with, and then gets jealous about them, is he?'

She shook her head.

'Then tell him, Rebecca. If Barry becomes a problem again, you might need some legal advice.'

'Too right,' she said, in a small, miserable voice.

I knew she and Robert were going to Paris for Christmas. I thought about pointing out how unlikely it was that Barry, if he had traced her, would follow her to France, but decided against it. The less Rebecca thought about him, the better. I could see she had calmed down. But she called a minicab to take her to a meeting in the City. She usually walked.

A fax arrived from the Opera House just before she left. I glanced down the cast list and saw K. B. Shaw listed among the thieves. I highlighted the name with a yellow marker pen and handed the list to Rebecca.

'I bet that's him. I bet he's Kevin Barry Shaw.' Kevin Barry was a hero of the Irish war of Independence. It was a popular name in west Belfast. I was rewarded with the first smile I'd seen on Rebecca's face all day.

Jacky made an appearance around four o'clock in the afternoon. He perched on a corner of my desk, swung his foot back and forward and stared morosely at it.

'I hope you had a better night than I had,' he announced. 'Nick left the pub with someone else. I went home on my own and watched a late-night film on the telly.'

Chloe and I made sympathetic noises.

'I'll have to drop a note to Henry and apologise. I didn't see him before I left.' Jacky lifted his head and looked at me. 'Did you see him? Did he look annoyed?'

My heart gave a little leap, but I kept my voice level.

'I don't think he was annoyed at all,' I said. 'I think he had a nice evening. He never mentioned the accident with the tray.'

'You talked to him afterwards?'

'Briefly.' I pretended to glance through papers on my desk. 'He was happy with the way things went.' I hoped the latter, at least, was true.

'Well, I had a terrific time,' Chloe said. 'Chatted up by a mega-fit man, taken to dinner by an absolute sweetie. Ancient but charming.' She giggled. 'He said he just wanted to worship at the fountain of youth.'

Jacky flung his arms wide, like a crooner and sang, 'Is a mixture of gin and vermouth.'

Chloe looked mystified.

'Cole Porter,' Jacky said. '"Two Little Babes in the Wood". What happened to the mega-fit man?' Jacky never missed a trick.

'He had to leave early. But he took my telephone number.' Chloe gave a little shiver of excitement.

'Lucky for some.' Jacky lapsed into gloom again.

'You had three replies to your ad,' I reminded him.

'I'm seeing the second one tomorrow night. He says he's a solicitor.'

'You don't believe him?'

'Last night's little horror said he was an artist. Piss artist, more like.'

'If you want company tonight, I'm free,' I said.

Teddy had turned round to observe our exchange. Something about the set of his shoulders made me suddenly wonder if he had someone to go home to. 'What about you, Teddy?'

He made a face and pointed to the pile of history books on his desk. 'I need to do some more reading. It's becoming a different story.'

'Will there be a hot dinner waiting for you later?' Jacky could freight a question with a world of innuendo.

'I live alone,' said Teddy evenly.

'Where do you live, Teddy?' I asked.

'Hampstead.'

'Home of the intelligentsia,' Jacky murmured in my ear.

'I'm not far away. Drop in on your way home, if you like, Teddy,' I said.

I didn't want to be on my own, waiting for the telephone to ring.

# 24

# Diana

Tomasz dropped his bombshell mid-afternoon, just after we had helped an elderly customer arrange a five-foot Norway spruce diagonally across the interior of her small hatchback. I was thinking as she drove off, branches escaping from the netting and bouncing in the back window like green fingers waving farewell, how odd that I should categorise her as elderly when she could only be, at most, one or two years older than me, and I was secretly preening myself on looking rather good for my age when Tomasz announced he would not be coming back after Christmas. He tried to look apologetic but that toothsome greedy smile broke through the polite pretence.

I hardly needed to ask, 'Anna?'

'We are going to be married.' His grin was positively wolfish. 'I will work with her father. He will open a bakery in Posnan.'

'Congratulations, Tomasz,' I said. 'I hope you will be very happy.'

I was genuinely pleased for him, but a trifle cross about the hoo-ha of hiring a replacement. Then I remembered the chap who had come on his bicycle looking for work. The Lord giveth and the Lord taketh away, I thought.

There could be no doubt about Bill Smith's happiness when he telephoned at about five o'clock and I told him he could start work the following morning and, if everything went well, I could offer him a full-time job after Christmas and the gate lodge to rent, if that suited. He yelped with excitement.

Henry telephoned to say he would be back in time for dinner.

'Had a good time with Peter?' I asked.

'Terrific. Peter's in great spirits.'

Henry sounded wonderfully cheerful. He really should get up to London more often, I said to myself.

He was whistling when he came into the bungalow and he insisted on fetching a bottle of champagne from the cellar on the grounds that he had sold more paintings than he expected.

'How was the Arts Club? Bed comfortable? Sorry I left early,' I said. 'I had an early start this morning.'

'I should go up to London more frequently,' Henry said. 'Where's that stiffie that came in from George and Vanessa? New Year's Eve party at their place.'

It was on the tip of my tongue to remind Henry that only the previous week he had recoiled at the very mention of a party. 'Party? What's to celebrate? More holes in the roof and more dry rot while we hang about waiting for that damned film company to make up its mind. Rather go to bed with a good book.'

I was so thrilled to see him sociable again I merely held out my glass and silently toasted the upturn in Henry's fortunes.

'When is that chap of yours coming to give us a price for the wines?'

'The second of January. It's a Saturday.'

Henry raised his glass and studied the bubbles streaming exuberantly to the surface. 'I think I'll go to George's party.'

I found the invitation among a pile of Christmas cards I was intending to attach to a red velvet ribbon and hang on the wall.

'Bugger. Black tie,' said Henry. 'Why does George have to be so pretentious?'

I knew better than to point out that Jenny had been fright-fully keen on black tie parties in the big house, and that Henry had obediently complied.

'Vanessa likes dressing up,' I said. 'Most women do.'

'You all dress up anyway,' Henry said, 'whatever we chaps wear.' He sounded more amused than querulous.

'You went to lots of formal parties when you were in the army, Henry.'

'Uniform's different.'

'Black tie is just another uniform. Men look good in dinner jackets.'

'I'd better go and hunt for it, I suppose.' He gave a little shrug and an almost sheepish grin.

I smiled at the sound of him pulling out drawers, banging wardrobe doors and whistling.

Daddy had whistled when he felt cheerful. I had a photograph of him in a dinner jacket. Probably the same one Henry was hunting out. It had silk lapels. I remembered stroking them when Daddy picked me up to kiss me goodnight before going out. Wedding anniversary? Hunt ball? Daddy smelled of soap and cigarettes. Mummy was all soft feathers when she kissed me. She smelled of face powder and something sharp and delicious that made me want to inhale it again. When I heard the car growling into the night, I ran upstairs to Mummy's dressing table, lifted the square cut-glass bottle and pressed the tasselled pink bulb to spray a fine mist over my arm. I bent my head to smell my skin. But it wasn't the same at all.

What age was I? Five? It must have been during the war because the house was full. Granny had invited all the relatives living in London to stay at Wooldene for the duration. Daphne told me it was because she didn't want refugees foisted on her and could say with a clear conscience that there was no room at the inn.

'Do you think I could get away with this?' Henry came into the kitchen holding a dinner jacket at arm's length, like a dead animal. A whiff of camphor cut through the cosy smell of the mutton stew in the oven. Paddy woke from his sleep in front of the stove, shook his head, gave a short bark, got out of his basket and padded across the kitchen to sniff a trailing sleeve.

'Falling apart, Paddy. Like its owner.' Henry smiled ruefully.

I took the jacket from him, thinking I hadn't seen him look as well in a long time. A thought occurred to me.

'Taking anyone to the party?' I asked casually.

He hunkered down and scratched Paddy's ears. 'Might do,' he said.

Paddy uttered a soft, delighted moan.

# 25

# Louise

I only ever cooked for friends. On my own in the evenings, I would eat bread and jam or bread and cheese, and munch an apple. Occasionally, I would boil pasta and make a quick sauce by reducing a tin of tomatoes and adding garlic and a splash of balsamic vinegar. I usually had the last two ingredients in the cupboard.

Borough market had closed by the time I issued the invitation to Jacky, so I got off the tube a stop early to brave the Christmas frenzy of the supermarket. Jacky would have been happy to go to a restaurant, but I had a sudden yearning for domesticity.

I queued with my basket at the fish counter – 'try our festive salmon starter' – watching women duck-diving into the freezers while their children ran up and down the aisles, shrieking.

Was that really what I wanted? I asked myself. And a tiny voice deep inside me whispered, Yes.

My small parcel of cod looked miserable in the wire basket. I added a bag of potatoes, a bag of spinach, two beetroots, a packet of mince pies and a bottle of Sancerre and joined another queue for the checkout.

I'm playing wee house, I thought to myself. Cooking for Jacky is like playing wee house with Mona Corrigan and Pauline Downey. We preferred Michael to our dolls. He was a placid baby. Always smiling. Uncomplainingly eating confections of liquorice and banana and God knows what else we dreamed up in our pretend kitchen.

Pauline had a doll's pram. We tried to transfer Michael into it when we were minding him for a few minutes outside the house while Mum went to get her coat. Mrs Kennedy from across the street ran over to us shouting, 'Holy Mother of God, don't drop the baby!'

Mona married a teacher, I remembered. I used to bump into her from time to time before I left Belfast. I lost touch with Pauline when we were burned out of Ardoyne. Her family moved to Strabane. I wondered where she was now.

A nudge on my shoulder told me I was next in the queue. The teenage boy on the checkout wore a red hat and a curly white Santa Claus wig. 'You should be in the queue for six items or less,' he said. 'It would save you time.'

A sudden memory made me smile. Michael, his voice full of suppressed laughter, telling a favourite joke about a farmer driving two stray sheep down a narrow road in Donegal, and blocking the path of a tourist in a fast car.

'The tourist looks up the road and sees the farmer's truck and he says to the farmer, "Why don't you put the sheep in the truck? It would save time." And the farmer looks all puzzled and he says to the tourist. "Sure what's time to a sheep?"'

I was still smiling when I got back to the flat.

Jacky arrived with two bottles of wine. One red, one white, both much better than the wine I had picked up in the supermarket.

'Home cooking. Couldn't beat it with a big stick. Deserves something special,' he said.

I ushered him into the kitchen. He leaned against the worktop, glass of wine in hand, and watched me chopping scallions and folding them into mashed potato.

'As Mammy used to say, that'll put hair on your chest.' He laughed. 'She still hasn't told her sisters I'm gay. Can you believe it? I'm sure they know anyway. I'm nearly fifty, for God's sake.'

'Do you mind going home?' I remembered that Jacky considered his home to be in London, and corrected myself, 'Going back, I mean.'

Jacky shook his head. 'I don't even mind the aunts. They've stopped asking me when I'm going to get married.'

I sprinkled parsley on the beetroot and parsnip soup, ladled it into a bowl, and offered it to Jacky. 'There now. Sit down and get that into you.'

I filled a bowl for myself and carried it to the table. Outside, a car backfired. I jumped and almost spilled my soup.

Jacky said, 'When I first came to London, I used to lift my arms automatically when I went into a shop. I was so used to being searched.'

'You left when things were really bad,' I said. 'Bombs going off every other day.'

'Everybody depressed or cracking sick jokes,' Jacky said. '"Only twenty-four shops to Christmas." That kind of thing.' He took a slug of wine. 'Mostly they were just depressed. You were depressed.'

'I wasn't, was I?' But I knew he was right.

We finished our soup. I stood up and moved to the cooker. 'Michael says the war's over.'

'Well, he would know, I suppose. I must say everybody looked more cheerful the last time I was in Derry.'

I ferried the dishes to the table. Jacky watched the butter melting into a golden puddle on the mashed potato.

'You should be doing all this for a husband and weans,' he said.

I felt a quick sting of tears at the back of my eyes. Jacky had a knack of zooming in to the centre of things.

'I haven't heard you use a real Derry expression like "weans" for ages,' I said.

Jacky looked at me thoughtfully. '*Níl aon tinteán mar do thinteán féin*: there's no fireside like your own fireside. You're a home-bird, Louise.' He helped himself to a spoonful of champ. 'You just haven't found where home is yet.'

I turned back to the cooker, tore off a strip of kitchen roll, dabbed my eyes, blew my nose and sat down again. 'Home is where the heart is.'

'That's another way of putting it.'

'So, where is your heart, Jacky?'

'Here,' he said. 'In England.' He looked abashed. 'I love England.'

'The love that dare not speak its name,' I said.

'Not in the Bogside, anyway.'

When we had stopped laughing, I said, 'I can't imagine loving England.' But almost as the words left my mouth, a picture of Wooldene Hall floated into my head. 'What I mean is,' I amended, 'I can't imagine feeling British. Do you feel British, Jacky?'

He looked affronted. 'Certainly not. I'm a Derry man.'

'So, what do you love about England?'

'Tolerance, order, irony.' Jacky twirled the wine glass in his fingers. 'I think Ireland and England make up missing bits in each other.'

He leaned forward. His voice took on a let-me-tell-you-a-story tone. 'When I was growing up in the Bogside, we ate breakfast, dinner, tea and supper. Mammy cooked dinner in the middle of the day, and I came home from school to eat it. I hardly ever heard the word lunch. Dinner was the decent meal of the day. When I came to England, I began to wonder if the people I met ever had a decent meal. They never ate dinner.'

He paused and lowered his voice for effect. 'Then I realised they were too worried about having it at the wrong time.' He whooped with laughter. 'The English middle classes are para-lysed with social anxiety. Not a bit of wonder they like Ireland. They can relax.'

He was in full flow now, glass in one hand, gesturing with the other.

'They stop worrying about what's U or non-U. Using the right words, doing the right thing. Having dinner at the right time. Keeping up. Nearly everybody in Ireland has an accent. The English can't differentiate, determine the social class. It's liberating for them.'

Jacky paused to gauge my reaction.

'If the English go to Ireland to let their hair down,' I said. 'Why do the Irish come to England?'

'To make money,' he said.

I laughed. 'Eat your meal, Jacky. Whatever it's called.'

We ate in relaxed silence.

'Scrumptious,' Jacky pushed his plate to one side and sat back. 'I'm serious, Louise. You should be doing this for a husband and family.'

'I've left it a bit late for the family,' I said. 'A husband would be nice.'

Jacky softly recited, 'Here in Hampstead I sit late
Nights which no one shares and wait
For the phone to ring or for
Unknown angels at the door.'

'West Hampstead,' I said lightly. 'I live in West Hampstead, Jacky.'

The doorbell rang.

'Bang on cue,' said Jacky. 'An angel at the door.'

It was Teddy.

'This is cosy,' he said when I showed him into the kitchen. He accepted my offer to make him an omelette. He looked relaxed, almost excited. I decided it was probably all right to ask him how close he was to finishing the draft.

'I had to come and tell you. I've turned it around completely,' he announced. 'Chloe came up with the idea of a stalker. That girl will go far.' He paused. 'I've taken it a step further.' He flashed a triumphant smile. 'A female stalker.'

He was bursting to tell us more. Jacky poured him a glass of wine. I stopped whisking the eggs, put the bowl to one side, and listened.

'I had the idea when I was reading about Lettice Knollys,' Teddy began. 'Her mother was a cousin of Queen Elizabeth. Lettice was a lady-in-waiting. When she came to Kenilworth with Elizabeth in 1575 she was having an affair with the Earl of Leicester. She married him secretly three years later. The queen was enraged.'

He had our total attention.

'What if Lettice Knollys had been in love with Leicester for years? She was a lady-in-waiting. She must have met him at court, when he was dancing attendance on the queen, when he was married to Amy. What if Lettice Knollys killed Amy Robsart?'

It was a bold and original idea. Jacky and I applauded.

Teddy looked pleased. 'The screenplay begins with Lettice Knollys telling the story on her deathbed. She's ninety-five. She's had three husbands. Leicester was the middle one. He's the one she's buried beside. That tells you everything.'

'Her one true love,' I said.

Teddy nodded. 'I haven't decided whether it was murder or an accident. Lettice Knollys looked like the queen. They were cousins. Amy lived in the country. She didn't go to court. Lettice goes to Amy, pretending to be the queen. They have some kind of argument. Probably about Leicester. Lettice pushes Amy. Amy falls downstairs and breaks her neck.'

'That's a great story,' Jacky said. 'I love being told a story.'

'We all love a story,' said Teddy. 'We're programmed for narrative. It's how we make sense of our lives. Stories give shape to the randomness of life.'

We can't see our stories while we're living through them, I thought. We can't tell how they're going to turn out. I lit the gas and slid the pan over the ring of flame.

'Stories have been helping people through the night ever since man discovered fire and lived in caves,' said Teddy.

'Let's hope our backers like this one,' I said.

# 26

# Diana

The Saturday before Christmas was mild and bright. Henry played golf for the first time in weeks and came back in terrific spirits, saying he'd shot a net seventy-four and did I want him to do any Christmas shopping. Henry hates shopping. I sent him to the post office with the last half-dozen Christmas cards.

'They'll have to go first class, I'm afraid. We've missed the last day of posting for second class.'

'We're not so hard-up we can't afford a few first class stamps,' Henry said. He sounded so like his old relaxed self I felt like singing.

We were terrifically busy all day in the shop. I was pleased I had hired Bill. He was eager to learn and eager to please. He told me he had been sacked by a Local Authority because he had been convicted of drunk driving and had lost his licence. I got the impression his wife had left him when he lost his job. A casual enquiry after he had demonstrated a remote control Santa for an excited four-year-old boy – 'Do you have children, Bill?' – produced only a shake of the head and a mumbled, 'No'.

I thought about asking him what he planned to do at Christmas but shied away because I feared if he said he had nowhere to go I would feel obliged to offer the gatehouse earlier and invite him to join Henry, Lucy and me for Christmas dinner. So I felt an unchristian sense of relief when I heard him tell Amanda that he was going to spend Christmas with his mother.

I had already invited Father Dobson and his wife to join us. Father Dobson and his wife. The phrase still seemed extraordinary to me even though he had been six months in the parish. Father Dobson had 'come over', as the saying was, from the Anglican Church. I remembered the ripple of excitement that ran around the church six months earlier when Father McIntyre, a strong-minded Glaswegian, read out the Bishop's letter about the appointment of married clergy, all former Anglicans, as curates in the diocese. Father McIntyre had added his own footnote.

'The message is, if you become an Anglican priest and you marry and you then become a Catholic, you can be a priest in the Roman Catholic Church. If you are a Catholic and you have a vocation for the priesthood, you can't marry.' I could hear the suppressed anger in his voice. 'If you can see the logic in that, then you're a better man than me, Gunga Din.'

'That's telling them,' Henry muttered in my ear.

Rupert and Lavinia Dobson had arrived in the parish the following month.

Rupert was a gentle soul. I suspected he was a few years younger than Lavinia who was brisk and competent and played the organ rather better than our previous organist whose eyesight was not good and who had attacked the instrument with more vigour than accuracy.

On Sunday morning, Lavinia beckoned me up to the choir loft after eleven o'clock Mass. Her daughter, Hilary, had just split up with her boyfriend, she said. Could she be invited for Christmas as well?

I liked Lavinia's straightforwardness. So much better than hints and apologies.

'Hilary moved in with this chap,' Lavinia confided. 'We warned her against it but one can't tell young people anything. "Don't be so old-fashioned, Mummy," she said. "Everybody lives together these days. We love each other. We don't need a ceremony to prove it." What can one do? And now she's arrived on the door-step broken-hearted and Rupert is threatening to drive up to London and give this chap a piece of his mind, which is not a bit like Rupert who hardly ever says boo to a goose, but he is frightfully angry and Hilary is having hysterics and saying she'll never speak to him again if he does.'

'I've ordered a twelve-pound turkey,' I said. 'A proper slow-grown turkey needs to weigh at least twelve pounds if it's to taste of anything. One extra won't be a problem.'

'Two extra,' said Lavinia. 'Hilary has a baby.'

Changed times, I said to myself as I drove to visit Lucy that evening. Poor Lucy, sent away, I surmised, to have her illegitimate baby as far from home as possible. Even in the sixties, that supposedly easy decade, to get pregnant without first providing oneself with a husband was considered shocking. Thirty years later, nobody thought anything of it.

It was dark by the time I got to The Lindens. Sunitra was steering a tea trolley across the lobby. I followed her into the fluorescent-lit, shadowless lounge. The lights on the Christmas tree gallantly struggled to twinkle. The television, as usual, was glaring and blaring. Agnes was writing Christmas cards at a table in the corner. She looked up and beckoned me over.

'Lucy's gone to her room. She's still recovering from that cough of hers.'

She completed the address on an envelope, added it to the neat stack on the table, capped her fountain pen and put it to one side.

'I was hoping you'd come in. Lucy said something interesting yesterday.'

I pulled up a chair and sat down beside her, eager to hear.

'Your aunt was asleep in the chair. She woke up with a jump and said "You know where I am, Mother. I'm in Crocknasolas. Where you sent me." So I said, 'Where's that, Lucy?' But she just looked at me as though she didn't know she'd uttered a word. I wrote down what she said. I don't know if I've spelled it right. I showed it to her. "Is that the place, Lucy?" I said. "The place you mentioned just now?" She looked at it but I could tell she couldn't make sense of it. She doesn't even read the newspaper any more, you know.'

Agnes extracted a stamped addressed envelope from the pile on the table. 'I was putting a stamp on this at the time. It was all I had to hand. It's for my nephew. He won't mind.' She turned the envelope over. Across the back she had written in large capital letters C R O C K N A S O L A S. 'It sounds Irish. Maybe the name of a townland.'

'What's a townland?'

'Just a geographical area of land. The size of a farm some-times. All country people in Ireland live in a townland, whatever the post office says. I was born in a townland called Drumsavagh,' said Agnes. 'In County Tyrone. I went back with John and the children about ten years ago. They wanted to see the ancestral home.' She smiled. 'A plain whitewashed farmhouse with a byre. Cousins living in it to this day. A hundred acres of hill-farm. Bigger than when I was growing up. It was a meagre thing then. Number one hundred and four Cookstown Road, according to the post office bureaucracy. But everybody still calls it Drumsavagh.' Her smile died and she looked away. I knew she was seeing beyond the beige sea of carpet and the elderly residents marooned around the television set, to a wilder, far away shore. I suddenly saw the child in her, long-limbed, watchful as a hare.

'Sixty-five years since I left Drumsavagh and it seems to grow closer to me every day. My husband was from the next parish. I met him in Liverpool in 1932. We moved to Hastings when we got married. John was born in 1934.'

She gave a little shake. 'But you don't want to hear all this.'

I protested, but she was resolutely back in the present. Her voice grew brisk. 'So there you are, now. I hope that's some use to you.'

I thanked her and offered to take her Christmas cards to the post.

'The pile grows smaller every year.' She sighed. 'I remember a time when I would be sending maybe a hundred cards or more. I'm sending a dozen this year.'

She handed me the stack. 'All done.'

I looked in on Lucy before I left The Lindens. The light was on, but she was asleep on the bed, still fully clothed and wearing headphones.

I glanced around the room. The escritoire was wedged into a space between the wardrobe and the bed. Four photographs in silver frames stood on a table by the window. I was familiar with them. Granny and Grandpa; Granny and Lucy in Rome; Lucy in her first communion dress; Daddy, Mummy, Lucy, Henry and I – baby and toddler – picnicking on a rug in the orchard. But something must have caught my attention because I tip-toed over to the table and took a closer look at the display. Instead of Granny and Lucy in Saint Peter's Square, there was a photograph of Lucy, aged about twenty I supposed, sitting beside an older woman, in a pony and trap outside a detached, bow-fronted Victorian house with a wrought iron gate and railings and a high wall running along the road. The older woman was holding the pony's reins and had turned to smile at the camera. Lucy was almost in profile, looking straight ahead. I picked up the photograph to examine it more closely. The frame looked to be the same. Lucy must have changed the photograph. Her companion had a broad, smiling face. I guessed she was Nanny O'Rourke.

I couldn't remember how long it had been since I last looked properly at the photographs. Six months? A year? Probably not since Lucy had moved to The Lindens, I decided.

I replaced the photograph and moved to the bed. A faint tinny jangle seeped from the headphones. Lucy's thin chest rose and fell and with each fall her breath escaped in a little puff.

She didn't stir when I kissed her. I slipped quietly out of the room.

# 27

# Louise

I like the drive from Aldergrove airport to west Belfast. The road winds over Black Mountain, and there is a moment when it turns and drops down towards Collin Glen, and the city spreads out below you like a blanket.

A fine rain began to fall as I began the descent and, in the seconds before the wipers swung into action, the lights of the city shimmered and danced in the droplets of water on the windscreen. A fragment of verse drifted into my head.

> 'The bricks they will bleed and the rain it will weep
> And the damp Lagan fog lulls the city to sleep.
> It's to hell with the future and live on the past.
> May the Lord in His Mercy be kind to Belfast.'

I was gripped by a kind of grim but fond nostalgia. After a week, I would be glad to leave again. But for the moment, I was happy to be back.

The city was changing, I said to myself. I sniffed more optimism in the air. On every visit I noticed new restaurants, wine bars, delicatessens, supermarkets, boutiques. I began to think shopping with Mum might even be a pleasure.

I silently noted the landmarks as I passed them in the deepening dark. The brewery, all clatter and lights; the army base, glowering, windowless and covered in barbed wire; the parade of shops with flashing signs, 'Merry Christmas', '*Nollaig Shona Duit*', 'Wishing all our customers a Happy Christmas and Prosperous New Year'.

Mum was asleep in a chair in front of the fire when I let myself into the house in Glanmire Gardens. Builder's Fancy would have been a better name for the road. The front lawns in the cul-de-sac of semi-detached houses were the size of a billiard table. All the gardens were at the back.

The room was as hot and dry as the Sahara. I wasn't surprised Mum had gone to sleep. The fire blazed behind a glass door. I stooped to the hearth and closed the damper. The flames subsided to a flicker. Out of the corner of my eye I saw the *Irish News* slide from Mum's knees to the carpet. A pencil rolled towards me. Mum didn't stir. Michael had told me the new tablets made her sleepy.

I didn't have the heart to waken her. The heat of the room had brought blood to her cheeks. She looked relaxed, curled sideways in the chair, one hand at her mouth as though sucking her thumb.

When I went upstairs and saw the flowers in my room I guessed she had been out to the shops. A good sign. My spirits lifted.

Downstairs, the telephone rang. It stopped after half a dozen trills. Another good sign. On bad days Mum sometimes didn't answer the phone.

She had just put the phone down when I walked into the living room. She gasped and put her hand on her heart.

'Jesus, Mary and Joseph. I didn't hear you come in. You gave me an awful fright, Louise.'

I put my arms around her. 'You were asleep, Mum. I didn't want to waken you.'

'You should have wakened me. I was sitting waiting for you. I thought you'd be here earlier.'

'The plane was late and I had to pick up the car.'

'Lily and Colette are going to call in tonight. That was them on the phone. I've nothing to give them.'

'I can go and get something.'

'If I could get to Sprucefield I could pick up a few other things as well. The shops are open late.'

Mum had never learned to drive. When Dad was alive he did all the driving. When he died, Mum was too distracted to learn. When she felt well enough to face the world she took buses and taxis into the city or out to the shopping centres on the edge of the city.

'The taxi drivers all put their prices up at this time of year,' she said. 'Your Dad never did that to his regular customers.'

'I'll drive you to Sprucefield. If we go now the roads mightn't be too busy.'

I fetched her coat from the hallstand and coaxed her into it before she could change her mind.

'There's a new shopping centre where Supermac used to be,' she said. 'But you won't want to drive all the way over there.'

It was about the same distance.

'Do you want to go there instead?' I was pleased Mum was curious about it. Another good sign.

'I don't mind,' she said. 'Whatever's easier.'

'We'll go to the new place.'

'Maybe it will be too crowded.'

'If it's too crowded, we'll go somewhere else.'

'You won't want to be driving me all round town.'

'I don't mind, Mum. Amn't I here to see you?'

I was so relieved to see Mum in good form, I would have driven her all round Ireland.

'I'm not looking forward to Donegal,' she said, as she settled into the car.

'It was your idea, Mum,' I said, dismayed.

'It was Noreen's idea.'

'Well, I think it's a nice idea, whoever had it.'

'They'll only argue and spoil Christmas for everybody.' The corner of her mouth turned down. 'I don't know why I agreed to go.'

'You're always complaining you don't see enough of your grandchildren,' I said. 'Sure isn't this a great chance to see them?'

'Dara is the only one who'll be there. Fergus is invited to his girlfriend's for Christmas. They live in Wicklow. Her father's an architect.'

'It's nice for Noreen and Austin to get out of the city for while. It'll be nice for you as well.'

Mum lapsed into silence. I glanced sideways and saw her hands were quiet in her lap. She wasn't twisting them or tearing a tissue to pieces, which is what she did when she was agitated. I relaxed and allowed myself the luxury of thinking about Henry.

He had telephoned at lunchtime on Saturday and, without preamble, invited me to a party in London on New Year's Eve. It took me only a instant to consider the idea and say yes.

'Jolly good.' There was a sound like a puff of wind in my ear. I realised Henry had been holding his breath. 'Black tie,' he said. 'Bit of a bore, that. But you girls always like dressing up, don't you?'

My mind was already rifling through my wardrobe. I laughed.

'Nicest sound in the world,' Henry said. 'A woman laughing.'

I wanted to say something witty in reply but felt suddenly shy.

'I'm not very good at this,' Henry said. 'Out of practice, I'm afraid.'

'Me too.' I mentally kicked myself for sounding like someone who hadn't been asked out in a long time.

There was a pause before Henry said in a casual way, 'I might have to go up to London on Monday. Any chance we might meet for a Christmas drink?'

A pleasurable thrill ran through me. I smiled as I said, 'Sorry. I'm flying home on Monday.'

'You sound as though you're looking forward to it.'

What could I possibly say that would sum up the mixture of dread and longing when I thought about Christmas with Mum and Michael and Noreen? I gazed through the window at two pigeons alighting on the roof opposite, hopping from one foot to the other for a moment, before settling down.

'I still have shopping to do,' I said.

'Oh well, mustn't keep you back.'

'No.' That wasn't what I intended at all. 'You're not keeping me back. I'm glad you rang.'

'So am I,' Henry said.

The world outside the window seemed to shift and gain clarity at the same time. The pigeons took off again in a flurry of wings. I felt giddy with hope.

Now, as the car idled at traffic lights, I wondered if Henry would telephone on Christmas Day. I imagined myself walking on the strand near Crocknasolas, talking to Henry on the mobile. I saw, in my mind's eye, the breakers rolling inexorably, magnificently towards the shore. I could almost feel the wind in my face. I realised I was smiling.

'Marian's got engaged,' Mum said, with a sideways glance at me.

The lights changed. I took my foot off the brake. The car slid forward.

'That's nice,' I said neutrally. 'Who's the lucky man?'

'Marian's a year older than you,' Mum said. 'I thought she would never get married. She met him on a walking holiday in Kerry. He has a good job in the bank.'

'In Kerry?'

'If he was from Kerry, sure he'd hardly be taking a holiday in Kerry, would he? He's from Kildare. He works in Belfast. He has a high-up job in the bank.'

I kept my eyes on the road. 'Clearly a paragon.'

'Men don't like sarcasm,' Mum said. 'He's the same age as Marian.' Pause. 'He's been married before.'

'Oh?' I kept my voice neutral.

'He's a Protestant.'

A Protestant from Kildare. Anglo-Irish. Brendan Behan's description of an Anglo-Irish man jumped into my head. 'A Protestant on a horse,' I said out loud.

'I don't know if he has a horse,' Mum said. 'His parents have a hotel.'

I remembered my surprise when Henry announced he was a Catholic. The Catholics I met at Mass in London were from Ireland, or of recent Irish descent. The names I saw in church notices were Irish, Filipino, Spanish, Polish. English Catholics were invisible. I could not have been more surprised had Henry said he was from Mars.

Mum shifted in her seat. 'Still, I'm glad for Marian.' I felt her gaze on me. 'I wish you'd meet somebody, Louise.'

'I like my job. I have a nice flat. I have a nice life.' My response to Mum's frequently expressed hope had become automatic. I swung into the car park and began looking for a space. If Mum was so sanguine about Marian, I said to myself, she might be equally sanguine about Henry, despite her disapproval of divorce. For a heady moment I allowed myself the fantasy of introducing Henry to the family. Marian trumped by a real Englishman. And a Catholic to boot. I almost laughed. Mum triumphant, Noreen silenced, Rosemary pleased. And Michael? What would Michael think?

Stop! I involuntarily stepped on the brake. Don't start imagining things! Behind me, a car hooted impatiently. I saw a space on my right and berthed the car with relief.

'If you don't meet someone soon, I'll have to auction you,' Mum said.

I was so pleased to hear Mum's sly wit again, I didn't mind the reminder of my single state.

# 28

# Louise

The telephone was ringing when we got back to the house. Mum answered it while I put the shopping away.

'Pauline Downey,' Mum said, when I came back into the room. 'Imagine that. She's Pauline Murphy now. She rang for you a couple of times before.'

A warm nostalgia enveloped me. I took the receiver.

'Pauline. I was just thinking about you and your doll's pram the other day, and Mrs Kennedy shouting "Holy Mother of God, don't drop the baby!"'

'I'll get straight to the point.' Pauline sounded embarrassed. 'I wanted to ask you a favour.'

'Ask away.'

'I don't want to do it on the phone, and I'd like you to meet someone. Are you around this evening?'

I guessed Pauline had a son or daughter who was keen to work in the film business and she wanted me to 'put in a wee word' for him or her.

I was rehearsing the advice I usually gave about rewards making up for insecurity, most of the time, and mentally listing the companies I knew were always on the look out for an intern who would work for next to nothing to gain experience, when I walked into the lounge of a hotel in Eglantine Avenue later that evening and saw Pauline's mother rise from a chair to greet me.

I had vivid memories of Mrs Downey dispensing Penguin biscuits and lemonade when we arrived back, pink-faced and panting, from our bike rides. It took a second for me to realise the soft-featured blonde who stood up to greet me was Pauline herself, thirty years older.

'You're the image of your mother,' I said, taking her outstretched hand in mine. 'She'll never be dead while you're alive. How is she? And the rest of the family?'

'Mum's fine. They're all fine.'

We sat down.

'What about you, Pauline? I heard you got married. Have you got a family?'

'Gerry and I will be married twenty-five years next month. We have three daughters. The eldest is twenty-four.' Pauline sounded strangely mechanical. She seemed disinclined to reminisce. Her eyes roamed the near-empty room distractedly. 'It's my mother-in-law I wanted you to meet. Teresa Murphy. She'll be here in a minute.'

'Is she the one who wants the favour?' I smiled to put Pauline at ease. 'Is she looking for a job for someone?'

'She's looking for a body,' Pauline said.

A shock ran through me. I wondered if I had heard her right.

'My brother-in-law was kidnapped by the IRA,' Pauline said in a flat voice. 'They took him out of the house one night. We never saw him again. We never found the body. Not even by the side of the road with a bag over his head.'

'My God, Pauline, I'm sorry.' I moved to put my hand on her arm but she withdrew into the chair. Michael, I said to myself. She thinks Michael has something to do with it. My mouth dried. I tried to swallow. Tried to banish the image of a man kneeling with a gun to the back of his head. Managed to whisper, 'When was this?'

'The twelfth of August, 1981. We were living in Strabane. We think Brendan was taken over the border.'

I was trembling with relief when I said, 'Michael wasn't involved then. We were in Belfast. He was only eighteen. He couldn't have had anything to do with it.'

Pauline turned to look at me at last. 'I know that,' she said. 'But he might know someone. He might put in a word.'

Behind me, a woman's voice said, 'Have you asked her yet?'

I turned and saw a small, plump woman with short grey hair and wary brown eyes.

'It's my son you're talking about.' She took the vacant chair beside Pauline and silently assessed me. I met her gaze as steadily as I could. 'Brendan was my youngest,' she said. 'He was getting ready to go to a dance. The doorbell rang and he shouted up to me, "That's my lift." He went to the door. I was coming down the stairs to say goodbye.' Her eyes clouded for a moment. 'They were holding Brendan's arms behind his back. "We just want to ask him a few questions," they said. They were all wearing masks. I never saw him again.'

She spoke with a quiet dignity. Her sorrow filled the room.

'It's well for you can shed a tear.' Her hands closed into fists. 'I'm long past crying.'

A wave of pity and shame and defensiveness washed over me. 'My brother had nothing to do with this.'

'He might know ones that did,' she said. 'He might know somebody. We just want to know where Brendan is. We just want to give him a decent burial. It's not right to deny someone a decent burial.'

I could only nod in agreement.

Pauline leaned towards me now. 'Will you speak to Michael?'

I nodded again.

Teresa Murphy said, 'Tell your brother our Brendan was no informer. He minded his own business.'

'He was always being stopped by the Brits,' Siobhan said. 'They stopped all the young ones. They lifted Brendan a few times. We were always sick with worry. You know what it's like. We never thought it would be his own side . . .' her voice trailed away.

'I'll be seeing Michael over Christmas,' I said. 'I promise I'll speak to him. But I can't promise he'll be able to do anything.' I made a helpless gesture. 'I wish I could.'

'Michael was a lovely child,' Pauline said. 'He was all smiles.

You'll remind him who I am, won't you? Tell him Brendan was my brother-in-law?'

'Of course I will.'

Teresa Murphy relaxed into the armchair. The atmosphere eased.

'You'll have a drink?' Pauline signalled to a passing waiter.

And suddenly we were chatting about Christmas shopping and how much Belfast had changed. Life in Northern Ireland was full of these sudden lurches, I thought.

A memory flashed into my mind. I saw myself glancing idly out of the kitchen window of a flat, near the university, noticing the dead body of a man at the corner of the street, feeling not shock but a kind of dull acceptance. As though all my sensibility had shut down.

'Probably shoved out of a car,' said the detective who came to interview me. 'You're on a rat run between Sandy Row and the Lower Ormeau road.' He sounded weary and punch drunk. 'I'm not surprised you saw nothing.'

When I looked out of the window again, the body had gone.

I remembered the grim awfulness of the visits to Michael in Long Kesh, the mordant graffiti on the Whiterock road, 'Is there a life before death?'; the roadblocks; the hysterical edge to every social event; the sense of dislocation that came with living in two different worlds at the same time.

I sipped my Guinness and answered Pauline's earnest questions about the film business with a few well-rehearsed anecdotes. To the casual observer, we looked like three friends having a quiet drink together. But I knew we had merely stepped through the invisible wall dividing the world of grief and madness from the world of shopping and small talk and the ordinary decencies of everyday life.

We parted warmly. Pauline and I hugged each other. Teresa shook my hand.

'It's not easy for any of us, is it?' Her grip tightened. 'You'll do your best, Louise, won't you?'

# 29

# Louise

I drove away from the hotel not knowing where I was heading. My mind was filled with a confusion of memories and images that I needed to put into perspective. There was something about being in a moving enclosed space that was oddly comforting. I was aware of houses, shops, the floodlit university, people at bus stops, people going in and out of pubs, the Opera House, the road swinging round and uphill. King Billy prancing on his white horse, pointing his sword at the sky over Clifton Street Orange Hall, Carlisle Circus, the Mater Hospital. I realised I was driving towards Ardoyne. Now Flax Street Mill loomed dark on my right. On my left, the twin towers of Holy Cross Monastery reared into the night sky.

Somewhere behind the houses that fronted the road was the street where I had grown up, played, learned to ride a bicycle. The street we had fled from on an August night in 1969. I know we were terrified, but I couldn't feel the terror any more. Time is a great eraser. The further away, the fainter things become. We feel them less and less until they are like rolls of film stored in our memory.

August the fourteenth, 1969. The police invaded our street and a Protestant mob streamed after them throwing petrol bombs into our houses. I remembered running out of the back door. Dad was carrying Michael under his arm like a big parcel and gripping me by the hand. The air was all black smoke and sparks. The roofs of houses were falling in. I could hear breaking glass, gunfire, engines running, screaming. But we weren't screaming. We were panting with fear and exertion. Mum was in front of us, running, pushing Michael's pram filled with clothes and shoes. We ran to a lorry at the top of the alleyway. I remember Dad and Uncle Sylvester loading a sofa, armchairs, mattresses on to the lorry, Mum heaving suitcases into the boot of Dad's Ford Cortina. I was squashed with the bedclothes on the back seat. Michael and Rosemary sat white-faced in the front of the lorry. Dad gunned the car up the hill. I looked back at Belfast burning.

Noreen was camping in Greece with a group of friends from University College Dublin. We hadn't been able to contact her. Mum was agitated.

'She'll be worried. She'll read about it in the papers.'

'Sure it'll be all Greek to her.' Dad winked at me in the driver's mirror. Even in the midst of terror he could cheer us up with a joke.

I drove up to where the houses were sparse and backed on to shadowy fields. The road twisted back on itself in a horseshoe bend before heading west over the mountain to Aldergrove airport and Lough Neagh. I pulled into the side of the road, parked the car and got out. Pauline and I had often cycled up here on Saturday afternoons when we were schoolgirls. We stood on the pedals, wobbling with exertion, forcing the bikes uphill until one of us would give up and dismount.

Going home had been an exhilarating freewheel down a narrow lane to the Cavehill road and the Waterworks park, followed by a lazy zigzag through terraced streets, past the Primary School and up the Oldpark road. We loved the old metal sign on a redbrick wall: 'Drivers please let down the reins and don't overload up the hill. Donkey Protection Society.'

Sometimes we would leave our bikes in the ditch near where I stood now, to scamper through hazelwoods thick with bluebells and to dangle our feet in the trout stream that flowed through the glen.

Twenty-eight years since I had last stood here, I calculated. It felt like yesterday.

After we were burned out of Ardoyne, we stayed with Uncle Sylvester until Dad found a house to rent on the Springfield road and we moved back to Belfast.

'Out of the frying pan, into the fire,' my father said when the barricades went up near our new temporary home. We moved further into what was by then being referred to as a Catholic ghetto. We hated the word but at least we felt safer. I changed school, lost touch with Pauline, made new friends. We kept our heads down. We tried to get on with our lives.

Below me, Belfast twinkled benignly now. I thought about the jaunty Christmas lights strung like a glittering chain through towns and villages across the North. Peace on Earth, they proclaimed. Fat chance. A bloody litany ran through my brain. Bloody Sunday, Bloody Friday, Claudy, Greysteel, Enniskillen, Omagh. Too many tragedies. I couldn't remember them all. Peace and Goodwill. Fat Chance. No, that wasn't true, there was a slim chance. I had to believe there was a slim chance. And what then? History recorded winners and losers, victims and perpetrators, I thought. Would anybody write about the people who muddled through? The people who reeled around like spinning tops, veering one way then the other, depending on which atrocity touched them last. People, like me, who believed in the ends but couldn't stomach the means? People like me, whose head was filled with the white noise of moral confusion.

# 30

# Diana

On Christmas Eve I closed the shop at lunchtime, brought Amanda, Tomasz and Bill back to the bungalow for a bowl of onion soup and a bacon sandwich, and gave each of them a plum pudding. I handed Tomasz his wedding present – a table-cloth, Ulster linen, easy to carry – and we all wished him a long and happy life with Anna and a safe journey home to Poland.

Amanda was going to spend Christmas with her parents and had offered to drive both Tomasz and Bill to the station in Reading. With the help of Henry, who efficiently rearranged the bags and suitcases in the boot and on the back seat of Amanda's yellow hatchback, they squeezed in cheerfully enough. After a final round of hand-shaking through rolled-down windows, they sailed off down the drive.

Henry and I chose a four-foot Norway spruce from the unsold trees in the yard and Henry carried it into the sitting room in the bungalow while I went over to the Hall to fetch the Christmas baubles and select one or two photograph albums for Lucy to look at. There was a stack of them in the cupboard on the back landing where the Christmas box was stored. When I opened the cupboard door, I tasted dust on my tongue and felt it clogging my skin and coating my hair. I thought about the photograph albums gathering dust in cupboards and drawers and attics all over the world. I thought about memory, and the end of memory. What was in Lucy's mind if not her memories?

Were we made up of memories? Is that what we amounted to in the end, and if so, what was left of us when we had no memory any more?

I opened the album on the top of the pile and turned the pages. The spine creaked and the tissue paper between the pages whispered when I folded it back to look at the photographs under the hard light from the naked bulb on the landing. There is something horribly bleak and miserable about a naked bulb. I made a mental note to replace the lampshade.

The photographs were secured at the corners by neat triangles of white cardboard stuck to the brown paper. I turned the pages. Daddy and Mummy with Daphne and Uncle John on a promenade. The profusion of striped beach umbrellas in the background made me think it was somewhere in France. Le Touquet, perhaps. Or Deauville. I decided it must have been before the war and immediately thought how funny it was that we still said, Before the war, and After the war. Although it was more than fifty years ago and the veterans were all in their seventies and eighties and those of us who grew up during the war were in our sixties. Even Henry, who was born in 1945, talked about Before and After the war. It was in his consciousness, I supposed, because of photography and the cinema. *The Dam Busters, The Cruel Sea, The Colditz Story, Reach For the Sky.* The images were in all our heads. We had seen newsreels from the First World War with its trenches, gas masks and barbed wire. Yet it was as far away from us as Waterloo was from Ypres.

'Do you think the men who fought in the First World War had pictures of Napoleon in their heads?' I asked Henry when I got back to the bungalow with the box of baubles and two photograph albums.

'I have no idea,' Henry said. 'What on earth put that into your head?'

He had one foot on the bottom rung of the stepladder and was disentangling the Christmas lights which were draped around his neck and trailing on the carpet. I explained the sequence of thoughts that had led me to the question.

'I feel connected to everybody who ever lived at Wooldene,'

Henry said. 'Even though we only have photographs from the last hundred years or so.'

'We have the portraits.'

'I feel connected through the house,' Henry said. 'I don't want to be the one who breaks the connection.'

I stooped to pick up the plug of the Christmas lights. 'Let's hope this connection works,' I said lightly.

We spent a happy hour listening to the Festival of Nine Lessons and Carols on the radio and dressing the tree. Henry stood on the stepladder with scissors and a roll of green twine in his hands. Paddy barked excitedly at each glass and silver ball I took from the familiar cardboard box, still bearing the name and address of a department store, long since gone.

'Hard cheese, Paddy. This is a game you can't play.' Henry adjusted the lights while I went back to the kitchen and added a bottle of red wine to the sugar syrup and clove-studded orange I had left heating slowly in a saucepan. Ronnie Bolton had brought the bottle when he came to dinner so it was probably too good a wine to mull, but I think everything tastes better when it's made with good ingredients.

The choir was singing 'While Shepherds Watched Their Flocks by Night'. The smell of hot wine and cloves, cinnamon and orange, combined with the smell of pine from the tree and the logs on the fire drifted satisfyingly through the bungalow. I ladled the hot wine into two glasses and carried them into the sitting room. Henry switched on the tree lights and we stood for a few moments admiring the display.

'This is how Christmas ought to be,' I said. 'The tree decorated on Christmas Eve, not weeks earlier. I hate how Christmas gets more commercial every year.'

'You're part of it, Diana,' Henry reminded me.

I made a face, but had to acknowledge he was right. The shop and Christmas trees made me complicit in the secular hijack of the Nativity.

I sipped my mulled wine and stared into the flames and thought how, when I was growing up, our lives had been ordered by a liturgy that stretched back through centuries and connected us with our ancestors. Holidays were holy days. No one remembered that provenance any more. Now it was all about shopping. Christmas began in November. And when Christmas was over we would be urged to remember Valentine's Day, and then Mother's Day, and then Easter and it would be all pink hearts and flowers and chocolate eggs and fluffy bunnies.

May had been Our Lady's month, I remembered. We had processions at school. White frocks and veils and baskets of rose petals. The edge of Alice Naughton's dress caught fire as she ascended the steps to crown the statue of Our Lady, the Blessed Virgin, on the back lawn. Sister Mary Dominic pulled her off the steps and rolled her on the grass to dowse the flames. Alice was completely unhurt and we said an extra decade of the rosary in thanksgiving. Health and Safety would have banned the deadly combination of tulle and candles. May was all bank holidays and traffic accidents now.

Halloween was All Souls' Day when I was growing up. We went to church and prayed for the dead. Now it was all masks and lanterns and children shouting 'Trick or treat', and where had that come from?

My parents refused to celebrate Bonfire Night. My father said, 'How can I celebrate the death and disembowelling of fellow Catholics, however misguided they were? They only wanted to be treated fairly. They went too far, but I pity them and pray for their salvation.'

Daddy would have absolutely hated the Christmas cards I sold in the shop. Santas and stagecoaches and Victorian England and hardly a Virgin and Child or a kneeling shepherd in sight.

At eleven o'clock Henry and I exchanged presents. I had knitted Henry a blue scarf which he pronounced rather stylish. He gave me a china mug from York Museum. He must have bought it when he went up for a school reunion. It had a picture of a Roman soldier and an inscription in Latin and English. *Persevera Consimilis Militis!* Soldier on!

We turned off the lights on the tree and banked down the fire. Henry hunted out the big torch. I picked up a wreath of ivy and winter jasmine in the porch, and we put on our coats and set out for Midnight Mass.

I love Midnight Mass. Take away the cards and the presents and the Christmas trees and the holly and mistletoe and Santa Claus and all the paraphernalia accumulated over the centuries and Midnight Mass remains the transmitter of the Christmas message of peace on earth and goodwill towards men. And women, I always mentally added when I saw the Christmas banner, thus inscribed, over the crib in the side chapel.

We should really call it a crèche because it is a French crib. St Genevieve's was built in 1835 by a French family who fled the Revolution and settled in Oxfordshire. Two hundred years later, their descendants sold up to a City banker and bought a *manoir* in Brittany and an apartment in Nice. Henry said it was as neat a circle as one could describe in history.

The first parish priest was from Marseilles. He brought traditional Provençal clay figures, Santons, with him as a gift to the parish. Which is why we have Joseph in a black felt hat with a wide brim, Mary in a lace cap and shawl, shepherds in flannel waistcoats with lambs under their arms, a man in blue britches carrying a drum and a monk in a brown habit with a brown-and-white spotty dog.

After Mass, the priest carries a plump pink-faced baby Jesus from the sacristy to the wooden cradle in the crèche and we all sing 'Away in a Manger' which is absolutely one of my favourite carols and I always feel full of peace and hope and good cheer.

Henry's torch made a funnel of light on the path through the walled garden. We paused at the grave of Uncle Edward to lay the wreath and say a prayer, as was our custom. Henry steadied the circle of light on the white cross with its black inscription,

*Edward Louis Wintour*
*Born March 24th 1899*
*Died December 24th 1918*

'Eternal rest grant unto him, O Lord,' we murmured. 'Let perpetual light shine upon him. May he rest in peace. Amen.'

We stood in silence for half a minute. I thought how Daddy and Granny never spoke about Uncle Edward, except in family prayers. Daddy was eleven years old when Uncle Edward shot himself. Lucy must have been about five. She never talked about him either but as long as I could remember she had come to Wooldene at the beginning of April every year to lay spring flowers on his grave. One year I plucked up the courage to ask why flowers were laid in April as well as December. Granny said it was for the feast day of Blessed Edward Oldcorne for whom Uncle Edward had been named.

'Crack on, eh?' Henry now turned the torch towards the gate into the park. I slid back the bolt and the gate swung against the wall and clanged like a bell. The grass was white with frost and a low mist shrouded the woods. I followed the torch beam along the footpath through the park. When we got to the stile, Henry stood for a moment looking back at the Hall.

'Penny for them,' I said.

'It looks in good shape from here. Can't see the holes in the roof.' Henry's sigh made a cloud in the cold air. 'I wonder if this film will really happen. If we'll get the money for the roof. If the old place will ever be home again.'

# 31

# Louise

It rained on Christmas Eve. A sleety rain that pimpled the strand and drove me back to the house and an armchair by the fire. After dark the rain stopped. I went outside to fetch more turf. The wind had cleared the last clouds from the sky. The damp had turned to frost on the slates. A silky layer of ice covered the puddles in the yard. The sky glittered with stars. The moon hung over the hill behind the house. There was salt in the air, and the tarry tang of turf smoke. When I came back in, I suggested walking, instead of driving, to Midnight Mass. 'It's a fine night, and we've been inside most of the day.'

Mum had gone to bed early. Noreen, Austin and Dara had been delayed by heavy traffic on the roads out of Dublin and had just arrived. They were dumb with weariness. Even Dara, who was fifteen and disinclined to go to bed at the same time as his parents, wanted only sleep.

Siobhan decided to stay behind. 'I don't want Maeve to waken and me not there. I prefer going out fresh on Christmas morning anyway,' she said, 'with the sea dancing and the light on the strand.'

Michael dithered, saying he'd like to come with me but it was too far to walk both ways. Siobhan said she would drop us off and we could walk back. It would be my first chance to speak to Michael privately about Pauline Downey's brother-in-law.

I had no idea what I would say to Michael. He had never

talked about his role, rank or status in the IRA. The first time we got to see him after his arrest, Mum cried, 'What in God's name were you doing, Michael?'

Michael put his finger to his lips and shook his head. 'Even the walls have ears.'

He had refused to recognise the court. When he was sentenced, he glanced at me in the gallery, held my gaze for a few seconds and gave a tiny shrug of his shoulders. Mum wasn't in court. From the moment of Michael's arrest she barely left the house, except to visit him in prison.

The weekly visits to Long Kesh, and the preparation for those visits, had been my sentence. Half a dozen telephone calls from Mum the day before the visit. An hour in the car, there and back. The repeated assurances that I would stay for a while with her when I drove her back. The endless waiting. The searches. The dry, stale air in the reception huts.

When we sat across from Michael in the wooden visiting booth, we talked about inconsequential things. Partly because the wardens were listening, partly because neither Mum nor I wanted to know. I learned more about prison conditions from reading *Republican News* than I ever learned from Michael.

Mum spent her visits fretting about Michael's health. He was fair-skinned. In prison, his face and arms became almost translucent. His reddish-brown hair looked dull. He always reassured her, 'I'm one hundred per cent, Mum. Fit as a fiddle.' I remembered him telling us he did a hundred press-ups every day and thirty minutes running on the spot. 'We're having a Best-Looking-POW competition,' he dead-panned. 'The wives and girlfriends are all going to vote.' We never found out if that was a joke.

He talked about his studies and about the exams he was taking. Sometimes he had talked about the birds he tamed. A robin, then a blackbird. He had a way with birds and animals. When we fled Ardoyne and stayed with Uncle Sylvester in the country, Michael, then a soft-hearted seven-year-old, cried when Sylvester said the farm cats were feral and couldn't be brought into the house. He was forever coming back to the farm with injured birds and lame dogs.

Almost the first thing Michael did after his release was to acquire a wire-haired fox terrier he called Scooter. He went everywhere with him. He would have taken Scooter to Midnight Mass if he could, I thought to myself as I cut briskly through the emerging congregation milling around in the dark and set a good pace up the long hill. Cars swished past me, their headlights yellow on the black road. The distant roar of the Atlantic rushed into the silence behind them.

Michael caught up with me halfway up the hill. 'Do you always walk this fast? You're going like a steam engine.'

'I wanted to get away from the crowd. I need to ask you something.'

'Ask away.'

There was no point in prevaricating. 'We used to know a family in Ardoyne. The Downeys. Do you remember them? They were burned out the same time as us. They moved to Strabane.'

'I remember Pauline Downey, she used to come to the house. What about them?'

'She contacted me the other day. Her brother-in-law was taken by the IRA sixteen years ago. They never saw him again. They want to know where his body is. They want to bury him properly.'

Michael didn't break his step. 'Brother-in-law? What's his name?'

'Brendan Murphy.'

'Doesn't mean a thing to me.' Michael's tone was casual. We might have been talking about the weather or the price of drink. 'Are they sure he's dead and not just skipped?'

'The word went round he was an informer.'

'A tout.' Michael's tone changed to contempt.

'A human being,' I said sharply. 'Pauline's brother-in-law. His mother's son.'

Michael stopped. His face was white in the moonlight. 'I'm sorry for Pauline that her brother-in-law was a tout. The lowest of the low.'

Michael started walking again. I pursued him to the brow of the hill.

'If Scooter died, you'd bury him. It's a terrible thing to have no body to bury. How could anyone leave families in limbo like that?'

Michael halted. He turned to face me again. 'Things happened. Bodies were buried and the ones that buried them got shot or arrested or skipped the country. There's men in America or Australia probably know about them.' He looked away and shook his head. 'It's a while ago.'

'It's yesterday to his mother,' I said. 'Can you ask somebody?'

Michael seemed to be contemplating the ghostly sweep of the strand and the black sea beyond.

'Those were bad years,' he said quietly. 'Everybody was jumpy about informers. The leadership changed. The organisation changed. Everybody knew the penalty for informing.'

'Pauline said he was no informer. He was always being lifted by the Brits.'

'That means nothing. The Brits routinely lifted their touts when they wanted information. It was cover.'

There was a burst of laughter behind us. I looked back. The nearest group of walkers was closing on us from about thirty yards away.

'There's things happening anyway,' Michael said. 'All part of what's going on in these peace talks.'

He stood waiting for the group to catch up. A car rumbled past us. Its headlights flickered over the irregular outline of the ruined chapel at the turn of the road. Siobhan had pointed out to me a line of a dozen or so stones, about four inches tall, in a row along the outside wall of the nave. They were believed to be grave markers, she said. The ruins had been used as a grave-yard for those refused burial in consecrated ground. Unbaptised babies, suicides and the unknown dead.

# 32

# Diana

Henry and I drove to The Lindens on Christmas morning to collect Lucy.

'We think she's had another wee stroke,' Morag had said when I telephoned to talk about keeping Lucy overnight. 'She might get a wee bit disorientated if she wakes up somewhere she's not used to.'

'But I can take her home for the day, do you think?' I hated the idea of Lucy having to spend all Christmas Day in The Lindens with a tired, listing tree, roaring television, forced jollity and hideous paper hats.

'Och, she'll be fine with you for a few hours,' Morag said. 'She likes to get out. It will do her good.'

I carried the Zimmer and Lucy's handbag and Henry carried Lucy from the car to our sitting room. 'Much easier than a wheel-chair. You're as light as a feather, Lucy,' he said.

I remembered how easily John Finnegan had lifted Lucy. Now she had the same pleased, slightly puzzled expression on her face. She looked too small for the armchair.

'I'll fetch a pillow,' Henry said, 'make you more comfortable.'

'Thank you. You're so kind.' It occurred to me that Lucy wasn't sure who Henry was. He didn't visit her as often as I did and, by his own admission, they didn't talk much.

Lucy steadied herself on the Zimmer while I helped her out of her coat.

'That's a nice brooch, dear,' she said.

'A twenty-fifth wedding anniversary present from Geoffrey.'

'Geoffrey,' Lucy repeated. 'Is he well?'

'Geoffrey's dead, Lucy. He died eight years ago.'

She looked bewildered. I wished I had told a lie.

'I'm so sorry, dear,' she said. 'So many things to remember.' Her eyes grew watery. 'It's not easy being old.' She blinked and smiled bravely. 'I like your brooch.'

'Thank you. It's pretty isn't it?'

'Where did you get it?'

'Geoffrey gave it to me. For our wedding anniversary.'

'That's nice. And how is Geoffrey?'

'Oh, same as ever,' I said breezily.

Henry returned with a pillow and we eased Lucy into the armchair. I placed the photograph albums on a side table beside her. 'We really must go through these some time,' I said. 'I don't know who some of the people are. Would you like to have a look?'

I watched her out of the corner of my eye as I attended to the fire. She turned the pages with more obedience than interest as though she didn't know any of the faces in the photographs.

When I got to my feet after putting more coal on the fire and replacing the fireguard, Lucy was asleep. Through the window I saw Rupert and Lavinia Dobson advancing up the front path, preceded by a tall thin girl, whom I took to be Hilary, pushing a pram laden with all the paraphernalia which accompanies babies these days. When Catherine was a baby, I'm sure we travelled with only a bottle, a nappy and a shawl. Hilary wore high-heeled black platform shoes, like little hooves, and was as skinny as a giraffe. Lavinia was carrying the baby, in a blue shawl and blue knitted hat, as proudly as a flag. Rupert was carrying a pot of pink hyacinths.

I adore babies. For years after Catherine was born, I never quite gave up the hope of having at least one more child. I absolutely loved becoming a granny and when Carl's job took Catherine and the children back to California I felt the loss like a blow to the heart. I always kept an up-to-date photograph of

Freddy and Grizelda in my handbag and I looked forward to July not just because the gardens at Wooldene were positively opulent in summer, but because Catherine would come with the children and stay for at least three weeks.

I love the fuss that attends babies. We greeted the Dobsons in a flurry of introductions and hand-shaking and cheek-kissing and exchanging of Christmas greetings and transferring of baby and pram and hyacinths. Henry carried the baby paraphernalia to the spare bedroom, followed by Hilary with baby Oscar, who was pleasingly round and plump and demanding to be fed.

Lucy wakened when I ushered Rupert and Lavinia into the sitting room. Better not confuse her with too many explanations, I thought. Rupert wasn't wearing a clerical collar. I introduced them simply as Rupert and Lavinia Dobson.

Rupert corrected me, with emphasis – 'Father Rupert' – as he took Lucy's outstretched hand. 'I'm the new curate. Diana has taken pity on us since we're fairly new to the parish.'

Lucy gave him a bright smile. 'Lovely to meet you, Father.' She seemed suddenly alert and I wondered if she found it easier to deal with new people than with people she suspected she had seen before but could not place. 'And how do you like this part of the world?' Another of Lucy's devices, I realised, was to use general phrases and descriptions instead of the proper names she couldn't remember.

Rupert and Lavinia launched into a duet of appreciation of rolling hills, splendid views, marvellously welcoming community, frightfully interesting history, wonderfully mild winter because of course they had come south after eight years in Northumbria, which they couldn't bear to call North Tyne and Wear or whatever ghastly name the bureaucracy had bestowed on that area which was lovely really, and they'd liked being near the sea, but the North-East was hideously cold and they were Southerners at heart really what with Rupert being a Surrey boy and Lavinia having grown up in Hove, and so they felt immediately at home in Oxfordshire, and had Lucy always lived in this part of the world?

Lucy hesitated. 'Diana makes me very comfortable and at home here.'

I was relieved she had remembered my name. 'Lucy was born here,' I smiled at her. 'Not here in the bungalow, of course, because this wasn't built until the sixties, but at the Hall.'

Rupert and Lavinia said how wonderful to grow up in such a beautiful place and might they see around the Hall sometime when it was convenient and was it true that a Hollywood producer wanted to use the Hall for a costume drama about Sir Walter Raleigh?

'A remake of *Kenilworth*, actually,' I said.

'Sir Walter Scott.' Lucy brightened. 'Amy Robsart dead at the bottom of the stairs with a broken neck.'

Memory is an extraordinary thing. Lucy promptly recited the entire plot of *Kenilworth*. Henry came into the room in time to join in a discussion about Sir Walter Scott and historical novels and the mysterious death of Amy Robsart. I retreated to the kitchen to sprinkle salt and a few sprigs of rosemary on the potatoes before sliding them into the oven to join the turkey.

Hilary came into the kitchen and asked if I needed help. 'I've settled Oscar. He'll sleep for a while now, with any luck.'

She looked tired. I marvelled to myself that anyone so pale and thin could have produced such a round, rosy baby.

She read my thoughts. 'I'm not anorexic or anything. I've always been thin. Oscar is a total surprise to me too.' She paused. Her mouth trembled. 'A total surprise to Jeremy as well.'

I handed her a glass of sherry and waited for her to continue.

'He was going to take six months off work. We were going to go travelling. We had everything planned.'

Except Oscar, I said to myself. Except a wedding. Why did young people not get married any more?

'He's a lovely baby,' I said. 'It's nice to have a baby in the house again.'

'I wish Jeremy thought that,' she said.

It was always the way, I reflected. Half the world terribly wanting babies and the other half not wanting them. There never seemed to be a fit between the two. I thought again about Lucy and how her life might have turned out if she had been born sixty years later and whether we would ever find out what had happened all those years ago and did it really matter since her store of memories seemed to be shrinking like a pool of water in the sun.

Lucy lived in the moment and was comfortable in the present tense. I would have to make the moment as jolly as possible.

'You don't look like your brother,' she said to Lavinia, who had clearly been fooled by Lucy's ability to cover up her difficulties because she launched into an explanation of how Rupert had been an Anglican vicar and had come over to Rome complete with wife, daughter and baby grandson. I braced myself for Lucy's reaction but she simply said, 'How interesting,' which I realised was another device for coping with anything she couldn't understand.

I began to relax and was pleased to see Lucy eat a little of everything, drink two small glasses of wine, and join in the conversation at table, which was mostly about food and how Brussels sprouts in a plastic bag in the supermarket did not have one tenth the flavour of the sprouts I had picked that morning, and was it true that sprouts needed frost, and wasn't the weather surprisingly mild except for the overnight frosts?

'Just as well for the sprouts,' said Lucy, which made everybody laugh.

Rupert rather portentously asked if the ladies were going to leave the gentlemen to the port, adding, 'I don't suppose it matters which way we pass it since there are only the two of us, Henry.'

Hilary and Lavinia bristled.

'Good Lord, no,' said Henry. 'We don't go in for that old-fashioned nonsense. Ladies first in this house.' I was able to leave Lavinia and Hilary at the table while I guided Lucy into the sitting room because I wanted to leaf through the photograph albums with her before it was time for me to drive her back to The Lindens.

I placed an album on Lucy's knee and knelt beside her to turn the pages. A group photograph from Mummy and Daddy's wedding took up all of the first page. My eye went from left to right across three rows of relatives on the lawn in front of the Hall.

'That's you, Lucy.' I pointed to the prettiest of the blonde beaming bridesmaids.

Lucy stared at her younger self.

I pointed to a man I was pretty sure was Daphne's husband, Theo. 'Who is that, Lucy?'

I sensed Lucy grow agitated. I put my hand on her arm. 'What is it, Lucy? What's the matter?'

'I know these people are connected to me,' she said in a near-whimper, 'but I don't know who they are.'

'Shall I help you, Lucy?'

She nodded.

I began incanting the names slowly, evenly, like a prayer. Lucy's mind was like this photograph album, I thought. There was no room for new photographs and some unseen hand was tearing out the pages.

By the time I reached Catherine's christening, Lucy had fallen asleep. Into the silence that followed came the sound of Oscar crying. I heard Hilary hurry down the corridor towards him. I glanced at the clock and saw that I would have to drive Lucy back to The Lindens within the hour. I called everyone into the sitting room and went to make the tea and cut the Christmas cake.

When I wheeled the tea trolley out of the kitchen, Hilary was carrying Oscar along the corridor, wrapped in his lacy blue blanket and snuggled into her shoulder.

I followed them into the sitting room. It was the first time Lucy and the baby would be in a room together and I wondered how she would react. My fear that Oscar would trigger unhappy memories was tempered by hope that he would trigger any memories at all.

At first Lucy seemed bewildered by the sudden appearance of a baby. Then she leaned forward and put her arms out.

'Would you like to hold him?' Hilary asked. 'He's usually fine with strangers.'

She settled Oscar into Lucy's arms and stood back, beaming with pride. Rupert and Lavinia made admiring noises. Oscar lay in Lucy's lap and gazed up at her.

'Good baby,' Lucy said. 'Good baby.' She studied his face.

I held my breath and exchanged a glance with Henry.

Rupert said something about wishing he had a camera and what a lovely picture they presented, the old and the young. Lavinia hovered, like an eagle guarding its nest.

'He's not my baby.' Lucy's voice had a note of alarm.

Oscar began to cry. Lavinia swooped on him and bore him to the sofa with little soothing noises.

Lucy looked distressed.

'Christmas cake, anyone?' Henry slid a slice of cake on to a plate and handed it to Lucy with a smile. It did the trick.

'Thank you, dear,' said Lucy. 'I'm rather fond of cake.'

Lavinia and Hilary took turns holding Oscar while they drank tea. Rupert talked at length about his preference for good old English tea over coffee, and how tea never kept him awake at night even though it had as much caffeine, or more, than coffee. Henry helped Lucy to her feet so I could begin the slow process of taking her to the lavatory before we set out for The Lindens.

The Dobsons were gone when I got back. I slumped into a chair and heaved a great sigh.

Henry poured me a glass of whiskey.

'It may not be as bad for Lucy as you think,' he said. 'Willem de Kooning painted while he had dementia. The paintings were lighter, more joyful than his earlier work. He saw everything fresh again, I think. Like a baby. Forever in the now.'

# 33

# Louise

Sometimes I wish I could stay in the present. Make time stop. I felt like that when we were eating our Christmas dinner in Donegal. We seemed like a happy family again. Rosemary and Seamus telephoned from Boston. Mum got to speak to her American grandchildren. Noreen congratulated Siobhan on the turkey. Michael and Austin talked about fishing. Dara told me about a recent triumph on the football field. Maeve sat in her high chair and contentedly fed herself with mashed potato and gravy. Mum said Maeve had Titian curls.

'You never told me I had Titian hair,' Michael said in mock indignation.

'Girls are Titian,' Mum said. 'Boys have red hair.' She laughed.

We were a happy family when we were small. My earliest memories are of Noreen leading me by the hand to Mister Softy and buying me an ice cream. The money was provided by Mum or Dad, of course. But to me, Noreen was the provider of treats.

Rosemary, who was only two years younger than me, sometimes played with me and the other ten- and eleven-year-olds who had started at the big school. Michael followed us around contentedly.

Mum and Dad were, well, Mum and Dad. Constant as the stars. Even when we became too old to believe in Santa Claus, we kept family traditions like Christmas stockings and going into Mum and Dad's room to open the presents which were stacked at the bottom of their bed instead of under the tree in the front room.

I was touched when I wakened on Christmas morning in Crocknasolas to find a bulging knitted sock hanging from the end of my bed. The bulges were an apple, a clementine and a bar of Tiffin chocolate. Michael and Siobhan had made a Christmas stocking for Mum, Noreen and Austin, and Dara as well.

'I'm far too old for that sort of thing,' huffed Mum. Michael winked at me. We could tell Mum was pleased. Noreen was all smiles.

The happy family feeling lingered after we got up from the table that evening. We sat around making little contented noises and taking turns to entertain Maeve. After about an hour, Michael hoisted Maeve from Mum's knee.

'Bath time, young lady.' Maeve chuckled and waved at us over Michael's shoulder as he carried her off.

Siobhan wouldn't let Mum help to clear up. She shooed her back to the sitting room and settled her on the sofa to watch *It's a Wonderful Life* on television.

Noreen and I cleared the table and loaded the dishwasher. Through the open door I saw Michael, Austin and Dara arrange themselves around a table near the window to play cards. The bright sound of the television drifted into the kitchen. Siobhan said, 'That film's on every year, but I've nearly forgotten the words.' We all laughed. I wanted the moment to last for ever.

When we went back into the sitting room, Mum was engrossed in the film. Michael, Austin and Dara were intent on their card game. Michael and Austin were drinking whiskey. Dara had a bottle of Guinness at his elbow. Noreen brought him a glass.

'You go easy, now,' she said. 'Guinness and wine don't mix and you've had a couple of glasses already.'

Siobhan uncorked another bottle of wine. We sat watching the film, half-dozing, for a while. Mum fell asleep.

The film ended. I switched off the television. Mum woke up, wished everybody goodnight and went to her room. Siobhan announced she was going to bed too. 'Michael?'

'When I finish this game,' Michael said.

Noreen wandered over to the card players. 'What are you playing?'

Dara said, 'Long Kesh.'

Noreen stiffened. Austin put his hand out in a gesture of appeasement.

'I hope you're not filling Dara's head with a lot of nonsense,' snapped Noreen.

I remembered her at Michael's wedding, the colour high in her cheeks, leading the conversations as far away from Belfast and Ireland and politics as possible. Dara and Fergus had found out that Michael was in the IRA. His release had been part of the British Government's response to the IRA ceasefire and had been in all the papers. Noreen spent the wedding steering them away from Michael and towards Marian and Auntie Colette, and Mum's cousin Lily and her son who had gone to university in Manchester.

Dara had asked me if it was true his Grandad had been in the British Army and Michael had been in the IRA. 'Mum never tells us anything,' he complained.

'She wants to keep you out of politics,' I said.

And Dara had replied, with all the solemnity of a fifteen-year-old, 'Sure life is politics, Louise.'

Now he glowed with enthusiasm. 'It's a great game, Mum. It's a kind of whist that any number can play. The IRA internees made it up.' It was the wrong thing to say.

'I'm not interested.' Noreen's cheeks were flushed.

Michael started chanting in a low voice,

'The Queen is out in Africa

Dancing with a Black

She put in jail a few years back.'

He punched the air. '*Tiocfaidh ár lá.*'

'Interesting thing about irregular verbs in Irish,' Austin began in a carefully bright voice.

'Mouthing slogans. That's all you're good for, Michael.' Noreen's face was blazing now. 'That and blowing up people.'

'Future tense.' Austin tried again. 'Our day will come. *Ár lá.*

181

Our day. Like *Ár nAthair atá ar neamh*. Our Father who art in heaven. The second . . .'

Noreen and Michael ignored him.

'I learned Irish in prison,' said Michael. 'We had more than grammar on our minds.'

'Blood and mayhem,' hissed Noreen.

'Independence. An end to colonialism. There's dignity in independence.'

'Dignity?' Noreen's voice rose. 'Defiling the name of Ireland, more like. Terrorising your own community. Killing civilians. Innocent civilians.'

'Mum,' Dara got to his feet, 'does that mean killing soldiers is all right?'

'You stay out of this, Dara.'

'It's Christmas,' said Austin. 'Can we please not fight at Christmas?'

'Tell that to the IRA,' said Noreen.

'There was always a ceasefire at Christmas,' I said.

'You stay out of this too,' said Noreen. 'Miss sit-on-the-fence. You never condemn anything.'

'There were terrible things done by all sides,' I said.

Austin patted me on the shoulder. 'True enough,' he said. 'True enough. Can we all agree on that and go to bed now? Nothing is simple.'

'It's very simple, Austin,' said Noreen. 'Killing is wrong.'

'Would you kill to defend Dara?' asked Michael.

'I'd kill to defend Mum.' Dara swayed. His voice was slurred.

'I'd rather you didn't,' snapped Noreen. 'And you shouldn't be drinking whiskey. You're too young.'

'You should be in bed,' said Austin. 'Go to bed, that's a good man.'

'You're poisoning the young. Poisoning everything. Poisoning democracy,' Noreen's voice was rising.

'The Brits poisoned democracy,' Michael was bellowing. 'The Unionists poisoned democracy. They threatened violence and the Brits caved in. Ireland voted for independence and got partition.' He paused to haul air into his lungs. 'Violence is the only thing that works.'

'All power comes from the barrel of a gun.' Dara's eyes glittered. His spots stood out like purple blisters on his face.

'You see? Filling their heads with nonsense.'

'Actually, that was Mao Tse-tung,' said Austin.

Noreen didn't even glance at him. 'Another monster. Look how many people he killed. Millions.'

'I don't think there's a comparison,' I said.

'Shut up, Louise. Things would have got better in the North.'

Michael shouted, 'What planet are you living on, Noreen? Planet South Dublin with your fancy friends and your formals and your blind eyes? Why can't you see the repression, the injustice?'

'You only made things worse. Free education did more for Catholics than the IRA ever did.'

'Bollocks.' Michael was trembling. 'Why do you think all those people took to the streets in the Civil Rights Movement? They'd passed their eleven-plus. They all had degrees, for fuck's sake, and they still couldn't get jobs. They couldn't get houses. Dad fought for the Brits and couldn't get a council house. Second-class citizens in our own country. That's what we were. Do you not remember?'

'Sure what do you remember? You were a child when this all started.'

'I wasn't a child when ten men died on hunger strike,' said Michael. 'I wasn't a child when the Brits wrecked our house and humiliated Dad. I wasn't a child when they shot a fifteen-year-old from our school, sitting on his own front wall.'

'What about all the people blown up by the IRA? Violence breeds violence, Michael.'

'It's the only thing the Brits respond to,' said Michael. 'Peaceful demonstration never changed anything. The Brits shot peaceful demonstrators on Bloody Sunday.'

'The IRA has bloodier hands. What about Enniskillen. What about Omagh?'

'We weren't responsible. Omagh was the Real IRA.'

'And what are you?' Noreen's voice soared. 'The unreal IRA? Listen to yourself. You're unreal, Michael. That's what you are. Unreal. Catch yourself on.'

Michael yelled at her, 'I'm proud of the IRA.'

'I'm proud of being Irish,' Noreen shouted back. 'I'm ashamed of the IRA.'

'Are you ashamed of me?' Michael took a step towards Noreen.

Austin moved to step between them. Balls of barbed wire rolled around my stomach. I felt sick. I heard a retching sound. For a second I thought it had come from me. Then I saw Dara, green-faced, stumble towards the door. I sprinted after him, overtook him, got the door open in time for the stream of vomit to arc over the doorstep and land in the darkness of the yard.

I guided Dara towards the drain at the side of the house. I held his hair off his face as he shuddered and vomited again. Through the window I saw Mum and Siobhan in the sitting room. Siobhan had Maeve in her arms. Mum was crying. Siobhan, stony-faced, flicked her head in a silent gesture of dismissal. Michael, then Austin, then Noreen filed past her, faces averted, and disappeared down the corridor.

# 34

# Diana

Ronnie Bolton, his brother and sister-in-law David and Anthea Barnes, who were staying with him, and Susan Reynolds came over to Wooldene on Boxing Day for a bit of rough shooting. I gave them all a late lunch of Christmas leftovers. I hadn't enough soup so I sweated some leeks, added a chopped green chilli, vegetable stock and a splash of white wine, brought it to the boil, tipped in a packet of frozen peas and whizzed the lot in the food processor. Everyone pronounced it delicious. Susan and Anthea asked for the recipe.

They had arrived back almost as wet as the dogs because they'd been caught in a heavy shower and had tramped through dripping woods. I distributed towels and served lunch on trays in front of a roaring fire in the sitting room. I left them all enjoying brandy and mince pies and said I was off to visit Lucy.

Henry offered to go instead.

'You do too much,' Susan said. 'Give yourself a rest. You had Lucy all day yesterday.'

David said he hoped he would have someone like me to visit him when he was decrepit and shoved into a nursing home. Anthea was piqued. She asked David if he supposed she *was* going to shove him into a nursing home. David said of course not, but Susan came out with me to the car and whispered that Ronnie and she thought Anthea was just the type to abandon poor old David if he got difficult, and did I want her to come with me to visit Lucy?

I felt obliged to confess to Susan that my motives were less than saintly because there was a rather lovely man who sometimes visited his mother at The Lindens. I hoped I might bump into him, I said, because I had taken a silly fancy to him, ridiculous really at our age.

Susan smiled her dry, enigmatic smile. 'Speak for yourself, Diana. I have a lot of life left in me.' She closed one eye and tapped the side of her nose with a meticulously manicured finger.

'Got your eye on someone, Susan?'

I wondered if it was Henry. But Susan just laughed and kissed me on the cheek and promised she wouldn't say anything to anyone if I promised to do the same. We both said, 'Cross my heart and hope to die,' very quickly and giggled like schoolgirls.

I found myself smiling all the way to The Lindens. The sky was filled with the phosphorescent light that comes after rain. The grass seemed luminous and the bare branches of the trees were etched against the sky. Oxfordshire is glorious in summer, I know, but winter has its own beauty. I can see past the trees to the houses and gardens, ponds and streams that are hidden when I sail past them in summer.

It was cold and damp and growing dark. I sat with Lucy in the lounge. We drank tea and played Gin Rummy. Morag had said it was good for Lucy's short-term memory.

Lucy was intent and concentrated when she looked at her cards. I loved the triumph in her face when she completed a set and made a final discard.

'Did you enjoy yesterday, Lucy?'

'Yes, dear. Every day is much the same here, but everyone is very pleasant, I have to say.' Lucy added a king of diamonds to the ten, knave and queen, discarded the three of diamonds, and tapped the table. 'How's that!'

'You win, Lucy.' I tried again. 'Did you enjoy meeting the Dobsons yesterday?'

'Oh, yes, dear. Very nice.'

'Rupert and Lavinia Dobson,' I said, 'and their daughter Hilary and the baby.'

'Baby,' she repeated.

'Lucy, do you remember telling me about a baby?'

Lucy's mind was like an old wireless set with loose connections. Sometimes the wires touched and the light came on and music played, but one didn't know exactly which knob one had pushed or pulled to produce the effect. Sometimes the light went out and there was no sound at all, and sometimes the set seemed tuned to another station entirely.

A hunted look came into Lucy's eyes. She shrank away from me. 'Edward's mine,' she said. 'I'm keeping him.'

'Of course,' I said. 'It's all right, Lucy. Just tell me where Edward is.'

Now there was a mulish set to her mouth. 'I'm doing it. I don't care what you say.'

I did not know where Lucy was in that moment. She was not in the bland, beige lounge of The Lindens. She was somewhere far away where I could not reach her. I picked up the cards, shuffled them and started to deal another round of Rummy. Lucy did not pick up her cards. I pushed the card table to one side, pulled my chair forward and laid my hands on Lucy's tiny fists. They trembled like frightened wrens under my palms.

'It's all right, Lucy. Tell me what's wrong. What is troubling you?'

I felt her fingers uncurl. She slowly looked around her. The only other occupants of the lounge, two floppy men in wheelchairs, were asleep in front of the flickering television. I turned my head so that my ear was close to Lucy's mouth.

She whispered, 'I want to be buried with my baby.'

I barely had time to absorb the shock of Lucy's words, much less think of a reply, when I heard the door of the lounge open.

'Tell me where, Lucy,' I said quickly. 'Where?'

But she had lost the connection. 'What, dear?'

John Finnegan was coming across the room towards us. My head was a jumble of thoughts. I wanted to continue the conversation with Lucy. I wanted to speak to John Finnegan. I was surprised that Agnes was not with him. I was aware that Lucy was readying herself to greet him. I was aware of his quick smile. I wondered if he could see all the confusion in my face.

'My mother has gone straight to her room,' he said. 'I came in to say hello to Lucy.' But he was looking at me.

He bent down to shake Lucy's hand. 'You were gone when I collected my mother yesterday. I hope you had a pleasant day.'

'Very pleasant, thank you,' Lucy nodded. 'So nice of you to come and see me.'

John Finnegan straightened and offered me his hand. 'Hello, Diana. Did you have a good Christmas?'

'Yes, thank you. Lucy spent the day with us.' I turned to smile at her.

'Nice to see you and,' she faltered, rallied, 'both of you. I won't keep you.' She gave a polite nod of dismissal, sank back into the chair and closed her eyes.

I stood up feeling dismayed and close to tears.

'Let me walk you to your car.' John Finnegan put his hand on my arm and warmth flooded into me like an electric current.

When we got to the lobby, he asked if I had a coat. I shook my head. 'I left it in the car.'

He took off his overcoat and draped it around my shoulders. I fought an overwhelming urge to lean back against him.

'She forgot who I was, just now, I think.' I could hear a faint tremor in my voice as we walked across the car park towards my battered hatchback, parked under a cold blue light.

'It's probably worse for you than it is for her,' he said.

'That's what Henry says.' I attempted a shaky laugh.

'She's good at covering up.' John smiled. 'It's those nice convent manners.'

'How do you know she went to convent school?'

'She reminisces with my mother,' he said.

I had almost forgotten my own manners. 'How is your mother? Did you have a good Christmas?'

'Sharp as a tack, and yes we all had a lovely time.'

I fumbled in my cardigan pocket for the car keys.

'Here, give them to me.' He unlocked the door and held it open for me. 'Get in, Diana, or you'll catch cold.'

I shrugged off his coat as gracefully as I could. 'Thank you.'

He took his coat and handed me my keys. I got into the car and wound down the window to thank him again.

'Happy New Year,' I added.

'Are you doing anything special for New Year?'

'Staying at home.' I immediately scolded myself for sounding sad. 'I'm invited to a party in London. I haven't quite decided whether to go or not.'

Come on, Diana, I said to myself, ask him about his own plans for New Year. But before I could speak, he was turning away.

'Have a safe journey home,' he said over his shoulder.

'You too,' I called out.

He got into a dark blue or grey Mercedes saloon and waited until I drove past him before following me out of the car park and setting off in the opposite direction.

On the way home, Lucy's whispered request ran round and round my brain. 'I want to be buried with my baby.' I had always assumed Lucy would be buried in the family vault. I had asked to see her will when she had given me enduring power of attorney. I didn't recall any instructions about where she wished to be buried. I could not be sure that the baby had ever existed. Might it only have existed in Lucy's demented imagination? What would be the right thing to do?

The smell of burning toast greeted me when I opened the kitchen door.

'Cheese on toast,' said Henry. 'I was feeling a bit peckish. Want some?' He pushed a plate across the table towards me.

I was too preoccupied to think about eating.

'Lucy was talking about the baby again. She wants to be buried with him.'

'Good Lord.' Henry swallowed. 'Where?'

'In Ireland, I suppose. I always assumed she would be buried in the family vault. What do you think we should do?'

'We have to get her to talk about it, I suppose.'

'She's like a light bulb going on and off, Henry. Sometimes she's there and sometimes she's not. What do I do if she never mentions the baby again?'

Henry folded his arms and rocked back and forward. 'Why is Lucy suddenly talking about this now? What has put the idea into her head? If it was important to her, you'd think she would have mentioned it before.'

'I have no idea,' I said unhappily.

'Is she capable of knowing her own wishes?'

We considered these questions silently for a few minutes.

'I've thought about trying to trace Nanny O'Rourke,' I said. 'But she's probably dead by now.'

'Or over a hundred. I've just done the arithmetic,' said Henry gloomily. 'I suppose we could try looking for her relatives. But I haven't the foggiest where to begin.'

'We could look in Lucy's suitcase,' I said.

# 35

# Louise

We were all subdued at breakfast on Boxing Day. Maeve, who on Christmas Day had gurgled, hummed, chortled and banged her spoon on her plate, was discomfited by the tense atmosphere that lingered after the arguments of the previous night. She cried, struggled and threw morsels of bread and apple on the floor.

Siobhan set dishes of sausages, bacon, scrambled eggs, toast and grilled tomatoes and a steaming pot of tea on the long pine table in the kitchen, keeping up a stream of bright chatter all the while. Austin offered some comments about the weather. The rest of us hardly spoke except for murmured requests for salt or pepper or butter. Dara was still in bed.

After breakfast, Noreen and Austin announced they were going to drive through the Gap of Mamore and walk on Leenan strand. Michael muttered something about taking a detour to see some newly built holiday cottages. I couldn't breathe until I realised they either hadn't heard him or had chosen to ignore the barb.

Siobhan and Michael set off with Mum and Maeve to visit relatives of Siobhan who lived about five miles away. Scooter bounded into the space behind the back seat. They offered to squeeze me in too, but I preferred to stay by the fire and read my book. I hoped, too, that Henry might telephone.

Around noon, Dara came downstairs, mumbled a greeting

and sloped into the kitchen. I heard him clattering around and smelled toast burning. When he emerged, his face was still the grey-green colour of the sea. I suggested we go for a walk.

He slouched along the strand, head down, hands in the pockets of his jeans. 'I feel awful about last night,' he said, 'being sick in front of you and all.'

'Never worry, Dara. I've seen it all before.'

'I can't stand all the arguments. I get all churned up.'

'Me too.'

'Mum and Dad never told us about Uncle Michael. That he was in prison, you know. Fergus and me found out by accident one time Auntie Rosemary rang up and Mum wasn't there. She was raging with her. We would have found out anyway. It was in the papers when he got out.'

'She just wanted to protect you,' I said.

'Mum's always worrying,' he said. 'Am I doing my homework? Am I doing my piano practice? I'm watching too much tele-vision. I'm eating too many crisps.'

'She only wants the best for you.'

He picked up a stone and hurled it into the dancing advancing waves. 'I don't know why she's bothered. It's all old stuff to us. Like it's real history, you know. Old stuff.'

He has no memory of bombs and hunger strikes, I thought. It had been the same for me, when I was his age. The Second World War had been history to me. I knew about it from films and television. Steve McQueen in a prisoner of war camp. Frank Sinatra on a train pretending to be German. Comedies on television about the French Resistance and the British Home Guard. Dad slapped his leg and roared with laughter at them.

'But you were a real soldier,' I said.

'If you didn't laugh, you'd cry,' he replied.

He never talked about what he'd done and seen in the war. At least not to us children.

The light was fading from the sky when we got back to the house. I helped Siobhan assemble a meal of cold cuts from the turkey and the ham. Through the kitchen window I saw Austin and Noreen drive back into the yard. Noreen went into the house. Austin stood by the car, refolding a map like a sheet. I saw Michael cross the yard to speak to him. They looked like stick men. Then I saw their bodies soften and expand. They shook hands. Austin clapped Michael on the back. I relaxed.

Siobhan had seen them too. Her hands tightened on the edge of the sink, and loosened again.

'I wish I could stay longer,' I said to her. 'It would be nice for Mum as well.'

'Your Mum's staying on,' Siobhan said. 'She decided on the way back from Auntie Joan's. Joan is on her own too. They're going to the sales in Derry tomorrow. They both dote on Maeve.'

I felt a rush of relief. 'That's great.' I sat down, the drying cloth still in my hand.

'I think we can get your Mum to come down here more often,' Siobhan said. 'She might even move here with us permanently. We're working on her.' She laughed. 'We've got as far as her saying we'd have to promise to bury her with your Dad. "I've nothing against Donegal," she says, "but it's Milltown Cemetery with Jimmy for me."'

Michael came into the kitchen in time to hear this last statement.

'Bury me in Donegal,' he said. 'When I was in the blocks, I didn't dream about going home to Glanmire Gardens. I dreamed of Donegal. I dreamed of the big strand with breakers and white spray on black rocks and the mountains towering over it all. We all had a place in our heads we went to when we wanted a bit of peace. Packy Lennon told me he used to imagine he was in Morelli's in Portstewart buying an ice cream. Imagine! See me? When the warders were getting on my wick, I'd just close my eyes and think of Donegal.'

'It wasn't me he fell in love with,' Siobhan said. 'It was this place.'

Michael stood behind Siobhan's chair and wrapped his arms around her shoulders. She leaned back against him.

'This house has a great sense of itself,' Michael said. 'It's because your grandfather and his grandfather before that lived here.'

'And it was a poor place then, and their children left here and went away to England and America because the land was stony and there was no work.' Siobhan twisted her neck to look up at him. 'Don't get too sentimental, Michael.'

'Do you not think everybody has a perfect landscape in their head? And maybe they don't know it until they see it? That's what I was like when I came here first. I just knew it was the place for me.'

There came, unbidden, into my mind an image of sunlight glinting on the windows of a brick and flint house and lighting the sides of the valley in which it sat, untroubled and serene.

'Put the kettle on, Michael.' Siobhan unfolded his arms from around her neck. 'I want to hear all the news from Louise before she goes back to Belfast.'

Michael dropped a kiss on her head and moved to obey her.

Siobhan put her arms on the table and leaned towards me. 'What about you, Louise? How's it going?'

'Waiting for the green light, as ever,' I said.

'Dare I ask, is there a man in your life?'

I must have hesitated too long, or given some faint signal to Siobhan, because a smile spread from her eyes to her mouth. 'Ah, go on. Tell me about him.'

She was an easy person to confide in.

'He's an artist,' I said.

'An artist? Isn't that wonderful.'

'I've only just met him.'

'But you're seeing him again?'

I nodded.

'And you know he's the man for you. I can tell,' Siobhan said. 'You have a light in your eye.'

'He's English.'

'Sure nobody's perfect. My granda used to say, everybody's Irish in the sight of God. Did you hear that, Michael?'

'Hear what?'

'Louise is in love.'

'Be sure and keep him on his toes,' said Michael. 'Like Siobhan does with me.' He settled the teapot on the table.

'It might come to nothing,' I said. 'Don't say anything to Mum. I don't want the third degree.'

'He's an Englishman,' said Siobhan.

'As long as he isn't in the army,' said Michael.

Noreen stopped me on the stairs when I was taking my suitcase to the car. I suspected she had been coming to look for me.

'I'm sorry, Louise. But these things need to be said sometimes. I haven't changed my views. Michael has his views and he has paid the price for them. We don't need to go through it all again.'

'There'd be no harm letting Dara talk to him,' I said.

'I don't want Dara thinking Michael is some kind of hero,' Noreen said. 'I want him to go to college and get a good job and be happy and not get mixed up in politics.'

'The war's over, Noreen. Michael is history to Dara,' I said. 'Living history. Let him hear Michael's side of the story. He gets the other side from you.'

Noreen made a small sound like a sniff. I moved to continue down the stairs. Noreen put her hand on my arm to stop me and said in a rush, 'Don't think I don't appreciate how much you did for Mum all that time.'

'Michael's doing it now,' I said.

'If Mum moved here, I could do more. We wouldn't be far away in the holiday home. We'd be here most of the summer.' There was a pleading look in Noreen's eyes. 'Try to persuade her, Louise.'

She means it, I thought. Noreen really wants to do more for Mum. My spirits lifted.

'She might come round to the idea,' I said. 'Give her time.'

We hadn't hugged each other properly in a long time. I felt real warmth beneath the awkwardness.

They all came out to the yard and stood blinking in the headlights and waving goodbye to me as I reversed and swung round before bumping slowly down the lane. I could hardly see for tears.

# 36

# Louise

I had hoped Henry would telephone while I was still in Donegal, indulge my romantic notions by talking to me while I roamed along the strand with the wind in my hair. Too late for that now, but I placed the mobile beside me on the passenger seat in case he called me during the journey.

The phone chirruped as I was coming off the motorway on the outskirts of Belfast. I grabbed it with my left hand, glanced quickly at the screen and saw it was Henry's number.

'Hold on, please. I'm driving.' I steered with one hand towards the car park of a pub just off the roundabout. 'Won't be a minute.'

I parked under the cold glare of a security light. Flashing yellow-and-white reindeers pulled a red and white Santa Claus and his sledge across the roof of the pub. I felt I was in the middle of some lurid wonderland. I imagined Henry in his kitchen, in the warm glow of the stove and the lamp on the dresser.

'I'm in my studio,' Henry said. 'Bloody cold.'

'You've been painting?'

'Just nipped out to fetch something for Diana. Something she wants to sort out.'

There was a pause. A car pulled into the space beside me and two men loped towards the entrance of the pub.

'Did you have a nice Christmas?' I asked.

'Yes, thank you. And you?'

I thought about saying half the day had been spent arguing. 'Very nice, thank you,' I said. 'I was in Donegal.'

'Never been to Donegal.' Henry paused. 'Funny, we were talking about Donegal the other day. Someone my aunt knew went to live there.'

'Whereabouts?'

'No idea,' Henry said. 'It was a long time ago. When my aunt knew someone there, I mean.'

There was another pause.

'The party's at eight.' Henry cleared his throat. 'I thought, if you were free that is, bank holiday and all that, I might come up early and we could do something together.'

I thought of rumpled sheets and rain outside the window. I wished I had a fireplace in my bedroom. 'We could go to the National Portrait Gallery, or the Tate,' I said.

'I wasn't really thinking about art, Louise.'

Santa Claus seemed suddenly softer, more refulgent. The door of the pub opened and a burst of applause escaped. From inside came the opening bars of a waltz played on the accordion. I wondered what I should wear to the party.

'I might stay up on New Year's Day. If that's all right with you?'

'Yes,' I said. 'Oh yes, Henry.'

I sat in the car for a few moments after Henry rang off. The door of the pub swung open and a group of men came bounding out. Their shouts reverberated around the car park.

'Bout ye!'

'Happy New Year!'

They swaggered towards the road, heads down, hands in pockets, elbows extended, shoulders hunched. One man seemed detached from the group. He was taller and wore a raincoat. His hair was slickly black under the security lights. I rolled down the car window.

'Barry!' I cried. 'Hello! Barry!'

He turned and stared for a moment before walking back

towards me. I hadn't meant to call out to him and hadn't prepared what to say.

'How's the panto? I heard you were one of the forty thieves.' I could have bitten my tongue off. 'Good to know you're working. In the theatre, I mean.' My voice trailed away.

Barry's face was like a mask. He didn't speak.

'Ali Baba. The Opera House. Someone mentioned it to me. That you were in it.'

'I didn't think you were interested in me, Louise.'

'I'm not. I mean. Your name just came up and somebody said you were in the pantomime.'

'Just came up casual, like?' He was enjoying my discomfiture.

'I think it was Michael said something. He asked someone.' I clung to the half-truth like a drowning woman to a branch. 'Because I was thinking of taking my mother to the pantomime. Only there isn't time,' I added in a rush. 'I have to get back to London.'

'No contest then,' Barry said. 'Will you be seeing your friend in London?'

My first thought was Henry. My heart gave a little jump.

'Your friend the producer,' said Barry. 'The producer of lies. The perjurer.'

A young man sprinted up the steps of the pub and held the door open for his girlfriend. Barry glanced at them. A smile played around his mouth.

'Are you coming or going, Louise? Are you stopping for a drink?' The pub door banged shut. 'Don't worry. I'm not offering to buy you one,' Barry said.

I was unnerved by his ability to read my mind. 'No,' I said. 'I mean, yes. Join me. Yes.'

'You're as big a liar as your friend,' Barry said. He turned on his heel. 'Watch out. She'll set you up too. She'll walk all over you if you're not careful.'

'Happy New Year,' I called out to his retreating back.

His arm shot out. Two fingers pointed at the night sky.

But at least I had established that Barry was in Belfast.

I wanted to telephone straight away and put Rebecca's mind at rest. Then I remembered she had gone to Paris with Robert. It would be an awkward conversation to have on a mobile phone if she was having a romantic dinner in Paris. The good news would have to wait.

# 37

# Diana

Henry and I sat for at least five minutes looking at the small brown leather suitcase with Lucy's initials A L W, for Agnes Lucy Wintour, embossed in faded gold letters on the lid.

'Do you really think we should do this? Have we a moral obligation to carry out Lucy's wish? She might have imagined the entire thing. Who knows what's going on in her head at the moment,' I said unhappily.

'If we go through her things we might find out if it's true or not,' Henry said.

'Even if it's true, do you think we need to act on it?'

Henry thought for a few minutes. 'If you went to Father Dobson or Clark and Hawkins for advice and they all said we didn't need to take account of Lucy's wishes because she isn't fully compos mentis, would you be happy with that?'

I hesitated. 'I would still feel duty-bound to try, I think.'

'Then we have to go through Lucy's things.'

I undid the leather straps and clicked open the suitcase. The lid fell back on the kitchen table to reveal a silver box, a tin box with a picture of the Houses of Parliament on the lid, a wooden box with ivory inlay, a fat foolscap envelope and a missal with a mother of pearl cover inlaid with silver filigree.

I opened the missal and read the inscription aloud. 'To Lucy on the glorious occasion of her First Holy Communion, from Papa. June 1921.'

The silver box was lined with worn blue velvet. Inside nestled a sapphire and diamond ring, a ruby and pearl brooch and a three-strand pearl necklace.

The tin box contained a Victorian penny-pamphlet biography of Blessed Edward Oldcorne, some newspaper cuttings, four black-and-white photographs and a bundle of letters.

The pamphlet had belonged to Granny. It was signed in her maiden name in a rounded, childish hand. I picked out a photograph of Lucy, aged about forty I supposed, in a fur jacket and jaunty hat. She was standing beside a handsome big-boned man wearing a Fedora and holding a racecard and a pair of binoculars. He and Lucy looked excitedly happy. The other photographs featured the same man alone with Lucy on the deck of a ship and in a group at some kind of formal dinner.

I passed them one by one to Henry.

'I'm glad Lucy had some love in her life,' he said.

The letters had date stamps from the fifties. I put them to one side. 'These are too private, Henry.'

The wooden box held a photograph of a fine-boned blond man with a moustache and soft dark eyes, an envelope addressed to Lucy and a blue knitted baby's bonnet no bigger than the palm of my hand. I dug in my pocket for a handkerchief to blow my nose and passed the photograph to Henry.

'Good Lord. Polish cavalry, I'd say.' Henry turned it over. 'Must be Polish. It's all words with consonants and no vowels, except for "All my love, Antoni. January 1939."'

The envelope held a Mass card, black edged with a black crucifix on the front. *Mass will be said for the repose of the soul of Antoni Kazanowski.* A woman's handwriting, I guessed. There was a note inside the card, in the same handwriting.

*Dear Lucy,*
*I am more sorry than I can say. It is hard to discern God's purpose sometimes. I pray that your sorrow will ease and you will know happiness again. There will always be a welcome for you here from Donal and me.*

I showed the note to Henry. 'Daphne was right. Lucy went to Donegal to have her baby.'

He sat back in his chair and scratched his chin. 'We have to find out where this place is. Find out if Peggy Brady is still alive or has any relatives alive who might remember Lucy.'

'It was nearly sixty years ago, Henry. Are we absolutely insane to even think of doing this?'

'Is there anything to say where Lucy's son is buried? There must be something.'

'Nothing,' I said. 'Unless it's in one of the foolscap envelopes.'

We opened an envelope with 'Certificates' written on it in Lucy's handwriting and found share certificates, Lucy's birth certificate, three out-of-date passports and pedigree certificates for all of Lucy's cats.

'This is hopeless.' Henry put his head in his hands.

'I'll take another look at Lucy's will,' I said.

That afternoon, I drove to the family solicitors in Oxford. Richard Hawkins showed me into a private office, all imitation Sheraton furniture, regency stripes and imitation prints of the colleges on the walls.

'I'll pop back in a few minutes and see if there's anything you need explained, or clarified,' he said.

The document was as straightforward as I remembered. Lucy had left no instructions about her funeral. It was pretty much as I had told Henry. Richard put his bald head around the door.

'Any questions?'

'My aunt has dementia, Richard,' I said. 'Last week she expressed a wish to be buried with a child we think was born in 1940 when she was unmarried. We never knew about this child's existence until last week. We think he was born in Ireland, in County Donegal, but we don't know exactly where. There is nothing in my aunt's will to indicate where she wishes to be buried. There is space in the family vault. Do you think we have an obligation to see if it's possible to find this grave in

Ireland and arrange for Lucy to be buried there when the time comes?'

'That's a jolly tricky question.' Richard pursed his lips and gazed out the window. 'There is no clear direction in the will. There is also the question of your aunt's state of mind. All in all, I don't think anyone would blame you if you felt it was too difficult a task to fulfil.'

'Thank you, Richard.' I shook his hand and gave him back the will. 'That's very helpful.'

Henry was right, I thought. In my heart I felt we should at least try to find the grave of Lucy's son.

# 38

# Diana

On Wednesday morning we began getting the gate lodge ready for Bill. He wasn't moving in until the end of the following week. I wasn't reopening until after Epiphany but paint takes longer to dry in winter and, as Henry said, better to get on with it as early as possible. He planned to stay up in London after George and Vanessa's New Year party, and would be leaving after lunch.

The washing machine in the lodge was too small to take more than a couple of cushion covers. We piled all the curtains and loose covers into Henry's car, took them to the bungalow to be washed and drove back with six tins of pale cream emulsion.

Henry spent the rest of the morning painting the gate lodge while I drove one of our elderly neighbours to the station and saw her safely on to the train to Brighton where she was going to spend the New Year with her nephew. I made an onion tart when I got back and served it with cold turkey and an endive salad.

'Absolutely the last of the turkey, Henry. No more turkey until next Christmas, I promise.'

'When this film gets the go-ahead, I'll take you to a smart restaurant to celebrate,' Henry said. 'Lobster, champagne and sinful puddings.'

I was delighted that Henry was going to spend a few days in London. It was another sign of his improving spirits. 'You worry too much about Henry,' Susan had said to me on Boxing Day.

'Oh, well,' I had replied vaguely, 'older sister and all that. He has no one else really to worry about him apart from Peter, and he's in Brussels and about to marry the wrong woman, Henry thinks.'

'Like father, like son,' Susan had said drily. 'But really, Diana, don't you want someone to come along and worry about you, the way you worry about Henry and Lucy?' That was when she had offered to come with me to visit Lucy and I had felt obliged to tell her about John Finnegan. I hadn't told her that I still sometimes thought of Henry as the nine-year-old I had gone to meet off the train at King's Cross after Daddy died. Henry in short trousers, cap and blazer, white-faced, trying to be brave and not cry.

'I might drop in on Freddy at the gallery,' Henry was saying nonchalantly. 'See if he's sold any more paintings.'

Something in his voice caught my attention and I looked sharply at him. He had a look of eager longing. I was suddenly reminded of a schoolboy bursting into the house, face blazing with excitement, to announce that he had built a snowman, or found a robin's nest. He's met someone, I thought.

'The thing is, I'm taking Louise O'Neill to the party.' Henry looked almost embarrassed.

A pang of envy passed through me like a shadow through sunshine. I felt happy for him and was acutely reminded, at the same time, of my own need. So when John Finnegan telephoned, shortly after Henry left for London, to tell me, apologetically, that he could not after all come to assess the wine cellar on Saturday, but might he come later that afternoon instead? I was so irritated and depressed by this second reminder that I was a single, older woman, alone at New Year, I would have snapped at him had he not disarmed me by adding, 'I wouldn't ask at such short notice, except you said the other evening that you might be at home today. But perhaps you've decided to go to that party after all?'

He said he would be at Wooldene within the hour, and yes, I had already given him directions.

*　　*　　*

I took off the paint-spattered dungarees and ancient grey jumper I had worn while redecorating the gatehouse and inspected myself in the long mirror on the wardrobe.

'Item, two lips indifferent red; item, two grey eyes, with lids to them; item, one neck, one chin, and so forth.' Where did that come from? *Twelfth Night*? How did that quotation begin? 'I will give out divers schedules of my beauty: it shall be inventoried, and every particle and utensil labelled to my will.' That was it. I began my inventory: pleasingly long and still shapely legs, with a red splodge and spidery red and purple lines running along the muscles above the knee I had twisted ten years earlier tripping awkwardly over a length of hosepipe. I couldn't kneel to get to my feet and lay on the crazy paving, staring at the swifts swooping and diving through the sky, until Geoffrey came home and took me to hospital. Two pale circles, the size of sixpences in old money, between my left breast and my collarbone, where I had been spattered by hot oil from a frying pan and two round crusts had formed and I hadn't been able to wear low-necked frocks all summer. I put my hand on the spots of pinker skin that had grown beneath the scabs. They were hardly noticeable now. The white diagonal ridge of my appendix scar. All these little scars, like mementoes, on my body.

I pushed my hair back from my forehead. Item, two lips needing lipstick; item, two blue eyes; item, blonde hair, greying at the roots; item, one waist, thickening.

I sat down at the dressing table to apply the much-needed lipstick.

# 39

# Diana

John Finnegan whistled when he saw the first stack of cases. '1945 Bordeaux?'

One of the cases had been opened. He lifted out a bottle and studied the label. 'I've never seen one of these. It was a legendary vintage.'

He put the bottle back as though laying a baby in its cot.

'Henry was told he might get as much as two thousand pounds,' I said.

John Finnegan looked surprised. 'I wouldn't put that much on it,' he said. 'Of course, your friend might know a private collector who'd be willing to pay that. But to be honest, I wouldn't go that high. Even for a bottle of 1945 Lafite.'

It took me few moments to take in what he'd said.

'A bottle?' I said faintly. 'Did you say a bottle?'

I must have gone white because he put the bottle back in the case and took my arm. 'You're trembling. You look pale. Do you want to get some fresh air?'

'Did you say it wouldn't fetch two thousand pounds a bottle?'

'Afraid not.' His voice was suddenly harsher. 'Sorry to disappoint you. I think your friend was optimistic. Five- to six-hundred at most, in my opinion.' He took his hand abruptly from my arm.

'I think I need to sit down.' But there was nowhere to sit.

I put my hand on the cellar wall to steady myself. It felt cold and slightly damp. 'Henry's friend said the whole lot, all the wines, everything you see here, was worth about two thousand pounds.'

John Finnegan stared at me. 'Everything here?'

I nodded.

'Then he's either a fool or a crook.' He shook his head in disbelief. 'The Bordeaux alone is worth twenty thousand pounds at least. I haven't even looked at the rest.' He looked at me more kindly now. 'I thought you were being greedy but you were shocked at how much it was, not how little?'

'Yes.'

'I can see why you needed to sit down.'

His smile was so sympathetic I found myself telling him all about Henry and the roof and our fear that the Hall would have to be sold and although Henry and I would be all right and we'd find somewhere to live we'd feel it was a betrayal of all the generations who'd lived here and loved it like we did. It all poured out of me in an unstoppable stream.

'And then this film company came and said they'd like to use the house for filming. We thought it would provide some of the money for the roof but now it looks as though it might not happen.' I stopped, feeling suddenly stupid. 'Plenty of people have worse problems. You probably have worries of your own and here am I banging on about a house.'

'If I had grown up somewhere like this, I'd feel that way too, Diana.'

He touched my arm and smiled reassuringly. 'Now. Let's see what else is here.'

It took us almost an hour to go through all the boxes, checking that there were no breakages. I handed each bottle to John who took notes. I returned each bottle carefully to its case. We took a break every ten minutes or so and exchanged little snippets about our lives. He was a widower. His wife had died six years earlier. He lived in west London. He had two grown-up married sons, a French daughter-in-law, an Irish daughter-in-law and six grandchildren. One of his sons was going to take over the business. The other was an actor. 'It's all he ever wanted to do. He seems to get parts. Nothing big, but he's always in something, thank God. He's what they call a character actor.'

I told him about Catherine and Carl and my grandchildren in California and how I missed them and how at first I hadn't known what to do with myself when Geoffrey died.

'I paid off all the Lloyd's debts and went back to work as a secretary, but the world had moved on. Nobody wanted impeccable shorthand any more. I wasn't much good with computers. When Jenny did a bunk, Henry suggested I come back here which meant I could rent out the house in Amersham. I've always liked gardening and I began selling vegetables and herbs and the business sort of took off.'

'You sound surprised,' John said.

'I never imagined myself running a business, even a modest one.'

'It just takes common sense, intelligence and a willingness to work hard. You have all those qualities,' John said. I felt absurdly pleased at the compliment. 'Good looks and charm help as well.' He smiled and handed me the last bottle. 'I'm not surprised you run a successful business.'

Blood raced to my cheeks. I turned away to stow the bottle in its case. Good Lord, he's flirting with me, I thought to myself in astonishment.

'We're done here.' He leafed through his notebook. 'I'll check all the prices and get back to you, but at a rough guess you've got about fifty thousand pounds' worth here.' He looked up. 'Will you have dinner with me tonight, Diana?'

I don't know which was the greater shock, hearing the value of the wines or the unexpected invitation. I had the sudden feeling I could fly.

He glanced at his watch. 'It's five o'clock. I took the precaution of booking a table. New Year's Eve and all that. It's booked for eight.'

'You're very sure of yourself,' I said faintly.

210

'It's not myself I need to be sure of.' John looked me directly in the eye. 'You like me, don't you?'

I swallowed. 'I'm not used to this, John. I'm out of practice.'

'It's like riding a bicycle,' he said.

# 40

# Louise

The days dragged when I got back to London. I went to the office each morning intending to organise the paperwork and set up a filing system for *Kenilworth*. We were still aiming for pre-production at the end of January. Rebecca, in a brief telephone call from Paris, had told me she was optimistic. She loved Teddy's new script.

London was a strange mixture of frenzy and calm. The West End was noisy with shoppers chasing bargains in the sales. The streets around our office were quiet. The market was closed. The coffee shops and sandwich bars were silent. I had a sense of time suspended. Of being in some kind of limbo between Christmas and New Year.

I was imposing my own sense of suspension on the environment, I told myself as I stared out of the window at the empty street below. I shook myself and tried to concentrate on lists, dates and calculations. But my mind kept veering delightedly backwards and anxiously forwards, and always to Henry.

I made a few telephone calls to check that provisional bookings for crew, equipment and vehicles were still in place. Hardly anyone I called was at work. I left a lot of messages. I went through the revised script and rewrote the budget for each character in line with Teddy's changes.

In the afternoons, I braved the winter sales. On the third afternoon in a minuscule boutique near Bond Street I pounced on a mid-calf length halter-neck frock in pleated silk marked fifty per cent off. It was a perfect fit. The colour shimmered between purple and pink. At half-price, I could just afford it. I queued at the till, delighted with myself. 'It's already been marked down,' said the gaunt and ageless assistant at the till. 'This is the sale price on the ticket.' I froze in the act of handing over my credit card. A picture of Henry in a dinner jacket floated into my head. He was coming towards me, smiling. I was wearing the pink dress.

From far away I heard the assistant say, 'A dress like this is an investment.'

I allowed her to take the card from my hand.

Henry telephoned to confirm he was coming to London the day before the party. 'I thought we could have dinner at the Chelsea Arts Club. I usually stay there when I come up. Pick you up about half-past seven?'

I was too shy to ask him to stay at the flat. Besides, I liked the fact that he didn't presume. Take it easy, I said to myself. You hardly know him. But inside I was humming with anticipation. I bought a man's razor, just in case. I ignored the doomy voice that whispered, Don't count your chickens . . .

I was trying on shoes with the pleated silk dress when Henry rang the doorbell at about six o'clock. I answered the door wearing a high-heeled silver sandal on one foot and a black suede wedge on the other.

'I dropped off my bags and came straight here,' Henry said apologetically. 'There was almost no traffic. I couldn't wait to see you.'

He produced a bouquet of pink and white roses and carnations with the flourish of a conjuror. 'You should have had these after, you know, the gallery and all that. Didn't seem much point in sending flowers when you were about to go away.'

'Thank you.' I buried my face in the flowers. The carnations smelled of incense.

I took a bottle of champagne from the fridge and two flutes from the kitchen cupboard.

'Very grand,' said Henry with a teasing smile.

I lifted a blue vase from a cupboard and filled it at the sink. 'My friend Jacky McQuitty told me you should always keep a bottle of champagne in the fridge. To celebrate your joys, or drown your sorrows, or just because you feel like having a drink.'

'And which is this?' Henry began easing the cork from the bottle.

I placed the vase of flowers on the table and picked up my glass. 'I hope it's about celebrating joy.'

Foaming liquid escaped from the bottle and cascaded into my glass.

'Fountains of joy,' said Henry. 'Fountains of joy.'

He put down the bottle. He took a step towards me.

I learned two things that evening. Champagne goes with everything, even baked beans on toast. And pleated silk doesn't crease.

When I woke up the following morning, Henry wasn't beside me. I sat up with a sense of panic and switched on the bedside light. Something on the wall, about six feet beyond the foot of the bed, glowed in response.

I padded across the room, gasped and clapped my hands in delight. An oil painting of a blazing coal fire in a black grate stood against the wall. It concealed the white-painted rectangle of hardboard which in turn concealed the empty space where a fireplace had been before the house was converted into flats.

I sat on the carpet and held out my hands to the painting. It seemed three-dimensional. The flames jumped out at me. I am warming my hands on love, I thought to myself.

From the landing came the sound of whistling. The bedroom door opened. Henry reversed into the room carrying a tray with two mugs of tea and a plate of toast.

'You're a mind-reader,' I said.

'It wasn't hard to guess that you'd like breakfast.'

'I meant this.' I propped myself up on my hands and pushed my bare toes towards the fire. 'It's the most amazing and imaginative thing anyone has ever given me. Thank you.'

'Oh, it didn't take me long to knock that up.'

I could see the care with which he had articulated the gleaming metal curve of the grate. I noted the shading and perspective that gave the fire prominence and depth, the use of texture to make the flames appear to lick the illusory chimney.

'That took you days, Henry,' I gently contradicted.

We sat on the floor with our backs against the bottom of the bed and ate toast dripping with butter.

'You have transformed this room,' I said. He has transformed my life, I thought.

I asked Henry if he had made a new year's resolution.

'Only to see more of you.' He smiled. 'What is your resolution?'

'Oh, the usual one. To be good.' I leaned my head on his shoulder. 'I haven't made a great start. Are you a practising Catholic, Henry?'

'At this moment I'm a frightfully relaxed Catholic.' He kissed the top of my head. 'My family have been Catholics for ever. We claim to be distant relatives of a Catholic martyr. It's part of my DNA. It's just a bit difficult to live up to.'

'I thought all Englishmen were Protestants,' I said. 'And posh Englishmen were Protestants on a horse.'

'I haven't got a horse,' Henry said. 'Not any more. I had a pony when I was little.'

'You see? A posh English Catholic. You're exotic to me, Henry.'

'I'm still pretty exotic to the English,' Henry said. I looked at him in surprise. 'We're a small, exclusive club, we recusants. We stick together, even now. I spent my childhood holidays being trailed around various relatives and family connections. Most of them a lot grander than us. My mother was reduced to boasting that we got our cooks from Arundel.'

I didn't understand the reference. 'Arundel?'

'Arundel Castle. The Dukes of Norfolk. England's leading Catholic family. They used to import their servants from Ireland, so they'd be Catholics.'

'We're just the servant class to you,' I said, suddenly stung. 'You look down on the Irish. You even call your bloody dog Paddy.'

Henry was icy. 'I love my dog.'

'It's not an equal relationship.' I stood up, filled with a kind of angry pride. 'I'll be nobody's servant. You'll not look down on me, Henry Wintour.'

'You'll not look down on me either,' Henry smiled up at me. He pulled me down beside him. 'Don't be prickly, Louise. This is an equal relationship. Let's have a different conversation.'

We lay in the glow of the painted fire. He asked about my work. I described to him a little of the frenzy of film-making. I told him about call sheets, sign-out forms, production reports.

'Stop.' He put his hands over his ears. 'I'm exhausted already.' He faked a hangdog expression. 'You won't have any time for me when you're at Wooldene.'

'From time to time I'll need a little rest and recreation.'

'Or the other way around.' He reached for me and held me until we had collapsed under the weight of our happiness.

'It will be spring when − if − we start filming,' I said dreamily.

Henry softly recited, 'Nothing is so beautiful as spring, When weeds, in wheels, shoot long and lovely and lush.'

I imagined us at Wooldene walking hand in hand through the great park beyond the formal garden. The trees would be green. We would lie in the sun-dappled grass. No, I thought. It would be night, because I would have been working all day. We would lie on a rug and look at the stars through the trees.

In the bathroom, Henry's razor lay on a shelf. He had folded his towel neatly over the rail. He had wiped the basin clean of the soapy speckled scum that was the usual detritus of men shaving. I felt as light as air and filled with silent laughter.

After breakfast we walked on Hampstead Heath. The trees were starkly, mysteriously red and brown against the evening sky. They reminded me of the trees at Wooldene, and my first glimpse of the Hall. It occurred to me that the loveliest Irish landscapes had no tall trees. In the west there were only low trees and bushes. Ash, rowans and gorse, the occasional grim plantation of pines, stiff against the soft contours of the land. England, by contrast, was abundant with tall trees. English painting was full of them. I told Henry I had first seen him leaning against a tree.

'I was reminded of a Gainsborough. *Mr and Mrs Andrews.*'

'We must go and look at it,' Henry said.

We drove to the National Gallery.

'When Diana and I were small,' Henry said as we climbed the marble steps to the second floor, 'my father took us to art galleries in the school holidays. He used to ration us to a painting each. That way he said we would really look at them. Not just give them a strolling glance.'

We made our way to the room that housed *Mr and Mrs Andrews*. The painting was smaller than I remembered. About four feet wide by two feet high. Mr Andrews stood languidly beneath an oak tree, shotgun under one elbow, the other elbow on the green wrought-iron bench on which Mrs Andrews posed, straight backed. Tiny crossed feet in pink brocade shoes peeped out from underneath the hooped skirt of her glistening blue silk frock. She looked both complacent and calculating. Mr Andrews' slightly pop-eyes had a vacant stare. You could tell he had never lifted a spade in his life. The dog gazed adoringly up at him. The entire scene was quietly imperious and unmistakeably English.

'Well? Why did you think of this when you saw me?' Henry hissed.

'It was the way you commanded the landscape,' I whispered back. 'Like a landlord. Master of all you surveyed.'

We stood admiring the painting. The rolling acres of the Andrews' estate spread out behind them like a green and gold carpet. Henry remarked how the curve of the bench echoed the curve of the cornfields; the pointed toes of Mrs Andrews' shoes rhymed with the feet of the bench.

I had a vision of Henry and me in the Uffizi, the Louvre, the Prado, rationing ourselves to one or two paintings a visit. Henry drawing my attention to details, talking about technique.

'Is this one of the paintings your father took you to see?'

He shook his head. 'No. I remember all of them.' He paused. 'Not very many, I'm afraid. He died when I was nine.'

I squeezed his hand in sympathy.

'Silly accident,' Henry said quietly. 'We were still farming the estate then. We were short a ploughman. Daddy was driving a tractor. It overturned and fell on him.' I sensed, rather than heard, his sigh. 'He wanted to be an artist. My grandmother disapproved. She told him he would almost certainly be poor, and probably a failure. She expected him to do his duty, like his ancestors. Wintours served in the Peninsular war, the Crimea, South Africa, India and the Western Front, you know.'

I imagined ranks of ancestors lined up behind Henry. Sons and daughters of the Empire. Admonishing him for being an artist, not a soldier.

The air was still. I could hear echoing whispers, distant foot-falls on marble floors. I could hear Henry breathing.

We floated down the staircase to the lobby. We skipped down the stone steps to Trafalgar Square. We stood at a pedestrian crossing, smiling at each other, waiting for the green light.

'I don't want to leave you, but my things are at the Arts Club.'

'Don't leave them there tonight, Henry,' I said.

# 41

# Louise

We walked up the steps of the tall Georgian terrace house with the Christmas wreath on the door and lights blazing in the ground-floor windows. Henry held my hand. He relinquished it only to let me shake hands with the host and hostess who greeted us in the wide, high-ceilinged hallway.

'George is my second cousin, Vanessa was at school with Diana,' said Henry.

He led me into a large drawing room. There was a log fire at one end and a big bay window at the other. About fifty guests stood around in clusters. Henry guided me around the clusters, introducing me. 'Louise works for a film company. They're hoping to use the Hall as a location.'

The only person who was younger than me was a thin blond boy, who moved smilingly through the company, topping up glasses from a bottle wrapped in a white napkin. Henry said he was the grandson of a cousin.

Almost everybody seemed to be related to Henry by blood or marriage. I felt suddenly on display. I clutched Henry's hand more tightly.

He whispered in my ear, 'You look ravishing.'

I knew I looked, and sounded, different from the other women in the room. Almost all of them wore floor-length dark velvet skirts with long-sleeved jersey tops. The remainder wore dark velvet trousers and ruffled shirts. They drawled. In my high heels

I was taller than most of them. I felt like a flamingo in a herd of similarly camouflaged animals. A foxglove pretending to be a daisy.

The parties I went to in Belfast usually gravitated towards the kitchen and almost always involved at least singing, if not an ad hoc céilí band. There were always groups of people arguing on the stairs. There was usually as much drink as food.

Film parties in Dublin and London were raucous and unpredictable. You never knew what you would find when you walked into a room. A huddle of giggling girls snorting coke, or three people in a bed. Or both. There might be food. There might not. There was always champagne.

This party was less noisy and more decorous. I exchanged small talk about the film business, the weather, how it was much easier to drive in London during the school holidays. Silly to think I could ever feel at home among people like this, I thought as I nodded and smiled. Henry seemed at home. Head to one side, listening, making the same noises. He caught my eye and winked. I felt a fluttering in my stomach.

After a time I escaped to a downstairs cloakroom. I was re-applying lipstick, when I overheard a conversation in the corridor outside.

'She knows how to spend money. That frock must have cost a fortune.'

'The last thing Henry needs is a spendthrift. Do you think she has money, Hetty?'

'Not old money, with that accent.'

My heart began to pound. I splashed cold water on my cheeks to cool them.

Another voice, a man's voice, this time said, 'Is this a queue?'

I prepared to exit, head high. I reached for the door handle.

'What do you think of Henry's inamorata, Cosmo?'

I froze.

Cosmo, whoever he was, made a kind of honking noise.

'Well at least we know where you keep your brain. Come on, Bunty. I'm dying for a pee. There's another loo upstairs.'

I counted to five. Opened the door. A portly man with bulging eyes and a tiny mouth stood outside. He reddened. I gave him my sweetest smile and went to find Henry.

'I'm glad you like my dress, Henry. I bought it in a sale. Half-price.'

'Half-price, whole-price, I don't care. You look magnificent in it.'

A buffet was laid out in the equally high-ceilinged room across the hall. Cold beef, salmon, game pie, salads. Lemon tart, chocolate mousse. Cheddar and Stilton. An assortment of small tables had been set up in various corners of both rooms. Henry steered me to a quiet table in a dining-room alcove. I felt happy and slightly tipsy.

We were joined by Vanessa and her brother-in-law, Tommy, who was, inevitably, Henry's second cousin.

'So nice to see a new face,' boomed Tommy. 'What part of Ireland are you from?'

'Belfast.' That usually silenced people.

'Never been to Belfast,' said Tommy. 'I've been to West Cork. Some friends of ours have a house there.'

'Do you mean the Thompsons? Rather a nice house I believe,' said Vanessa. 'Georgian. They had to do a lot of work on it. So sad, Ireland. All those lovely Georgian houses gone to rack and ruin, torn down, burned.' Her voice trailed away.

'All those abbeys and castles,' I said, 'looted, reduced to rubble, gilded ceilings pulled down, statues smashed by Cromwell.' I felt my colour rise.

Henry patted my arm. 'Don't get on your high horse with us, Louise. You can't blame us Catholics for Cromwell. We fought against him too.'

'Not one of us,' said Vanessa, drily.

I wasn't sure if she meant me or Cromwell.

'Shall we get some pudding, darling?' Tommy rose with a smile.

Henry put his arm around my shoulder and kissed my cheek. 'I wish we could slip away,' he said. 'But we can't really leave before midnight.'

Music started up. Beatles tunes from the sixties. The young

blond grandson who'd been on drinks duty came up and asked me to dance.

'I've never met anybody in films,' he said. 'Any chance I could be an extra in this film you're making at Wooldene?'

I told him to telephone Telekinetic in a few weeks, when I might know if the film was going ahead or not. 'Are you an actor?'

'I'm a lieutenant in the army, actually. Just back from a tour in Ulster.'

I almost flinched. I felt light-headed. As though I was about to lurch again from ordinary life into a kind of insanity. Except this wasn't really ordinary life, I thought. I didn't belong in this world of drawing rooms and dinner jackets and conversations about school fees.

'Are you all right? You look a bit green.'

'A bit too much to drink,' I said. 'I'll sit down if you don't mind.'

Then Henry was at my side looking concerned. 'I'm not one of you, Henry,' I said. 'My father was a taxi driver. My mother was a hairdresser. I'm from a different world.'

'Don't you like my world?'

'The Daisy in me likes it,' I said. I found myself telling him the story of my baptism.

Henry laughed. He slapped his leg. He seized my face in both hands and kissed me. I felt curious eyes on us. I didn't care. Everything was all right again.

Henry went to fetch a glass of water for both of us.

I sat listening to the conversations humming around me. A man with side-swept hair and a fruity voice was talking to the blond lieutenant. 'Henry and I ran a laundry together. Jolly interesting. Very useful while it lasted.'

So Henry had run a laundry, he hadn't mentioned that. But we hadn't talked much about our work. I remembered Jacky, in one of his riffs on the English, declaiming, 'English toffs and aspiring toffs, even more so, turn up their noses at trade.' Strange. Diana, clearly a toff, ran a shop. I gave up. I was less interested than Jacky in English social codes. I just liked the idea of Henry doing something ordinary. It made him more lovable, somehow.

A woman to my left was complaining, 'Cosmo can't be satisfied with making something simple. He leaves pots and pans all over the kitchen. I have to sit there saying it's wonderful, darling. Aren't you clever, darling? Gritting my teeth because I know there'll be hours of washing-up to do.'

They're not so grand, I said to myself. They do their own washing-up. They complain about their men. A phrase came into my mind. 'The Colonel's Lady an' Judy O'Grady are sisters under their skins.' Rudyard Kipling? My maternal grandmother was an O'Grady.

A space cleared. I looked across the room at the wide bay window, a polished oval table, and a wide silver bowl of pink and white huge-petalled roses. Another line of poetry came into my head.

'World is crazier and more of it than we think.'

I stood up and walked to the window. I bent to smell the roses. They were made of silk.

There was no sign of Henry. I assumed he was in the kitchen looking for water. I made my way towards the stairs down to the basement. Voices drifted up from the stairwell.

'Surprised to see you with a bogwoman. Fucks like a rabbit, I suppose that's it.'

I froze.

'You were a shit at school, Thompson.' Henry's voice was level, languid even. 'You were a shit in the army. You're still a shit. If it wasn't cruelty to animals, I'd knock your rabbit teeth down your throat.'

I moved away quickly and stood trembling in the hall. An imperious voice summoned everyone to the drawing room.

Big Ben sounded a sonorous bong.

A chorus of voices cried, 'One!'

Bong.

'Wait for me.' The man with the bulging eyes and the small mouth rushed past me across the hall.

Bong.

'Three!'
Bong.
'Four!' The chorus grew louder.
Bong.
Henry came towards me holding out a glass of water.
'The bell was silent in the air
Holding its inverted poise –
Between the clang and clang a flower,
A brazen calyx of no noise.'
Bong.
'Ten.'
Henry was smiling.
Bong.
'Eleven.'
He handed me the glass of water.
Bong.
'I'm falling in love with you,' he said.

# 42

# Louise

The next hour was like a dream. I danced on air. I drank champagne. I smiled at everybody. Mostly I smiled at Henry.

He had booked a taxi to take us back to the flat. We were about to get into it when Henry realised he had forgotten his overnight bag. He ran back into the house. I waited on the pavement.

You are intoxicated, Louise O'Neill, I said to myself. You are drunk on Henry Wintour. I waltzed happily under a streetlight.

A man in a waxed jacket and tweed cap emerged from the house. He paused at the bottom of the steps and smiled.

'Saw you dancing with young George at the party. Would have cut in myself for a bop only Henry was too quick for me.' He doffed his cap. 'Hector Hargreaves.'

I remembered the side-swept hair and fruity voice. I stopped dancing. I shook his outstretched hand. 'Louise O'Neill. Did I overhear you say you used to run a laundry with Henry?'

'He told you that story, did he?' Hector sucked in air and blew out a breath. 'Dangerous times.' He shook his head.

I wondered what was dangerous about running a laundry. Hot steam? Hot irons?

Hector folded his arms and began reminiscing. 'Oh, yes. Thank the Lord we had a few laughs along the way. Did Henry tell you about the time we sent out the wrong trousers? Arrested some poor chap who was nearly shitting himself with fright.

Hauled him off with the trousers round his ankles.' Hector snorted with laughter. 'All sorted out eventually. Chap was probably up to no good anyway. We had a good laugh about it.'

My mind was racing to keep up with what Hector was saying and make sense of it. 'When was this?'

'Oh, must be,' Hector gazed thoughtfully at the ground, 'now when was I in Belfast? Ten, eleven, maybe twelve years. Ten years ago, anyway.' He looked up, snorted with laughter again and slapped his hand on his thigh. 'Good wheeze. While it lasted.'

I felt as though I was rising through the air, looking down on myself listening to Hector.

'Henry's idea. Set up a cut-price laundry in terrorist heartland. Run forensics on the clothes. Brilliant.'

Now some kind of clawed creature was scrabbling around inside me. Bile gushed into my throat. I stared at Hector, unable to speak.

'Shame we got rumbled.'

I heard a high-pitched voice. My voice. 'How did that happen?'

'The terrorists used to pay visits to chaps who'd been lifted by us. Interrogate them. Check they didn't say the wrong thing. Shoot them if they did. Poor buggers got done over twice. They found out about the wrong trousers. Seems one of their top thugs got a wrong pair as well. Put two and two together. Pity. We'd been dying to get our hands on this chap. Got some gibbering taxi driver instead. Henry was furious. Until he saw the funny side. Laughed like a drain.' Hector's guffaws bounced off the concrete and ricocheted around the street.

'What happened to the laundry?' That high pitched voice again.

'Folded.' Hector sniggered. 'No pun intended.'

Waves of rage and hysteria billowed through me. I wanted to hit him. Blood rushed to my head. I felt dizzy. I was dimly aware of Hector looking at me curiously. Of the taxi engine rumbling.

'Must dash. Catch you another time.' Hector backed away from me. Raised his hand in farewell. 'Say night night to Henry for me.' He turned and hurried away.

I wanted to run but my feet were like lead. Henry was walking towards me. His smile died when he got close enough to see my face under the streetlight.

'Louise? What's wrong? Your face is the colour of concrete.'

Hot tears stung my eyes. 'You were in the army. You were in Belfast.'

'What's brought this up?'

My voice came jerkily. 'Hector told me about the laundry.'

Henry looked blank.

Anger drove the words out of me. 'My father. My brother. Our house wrecked. You laughed about it. My father had a heart attack because of you. My brother joined the IRA. He spent years in prison. My mother went out of her mind.'

'What?' Henry looked astonished. He took a step towards me. He tried to take my arm. I batted him away like a wasp.

'I thought you were different.' I was trembling. 'But you're the same as all the others. You think of us as inferior. You joke about us.' I could barely see. 'You didn't tell me you were in the army.'

Henry's face was white in the light. His eyes were like black stones. 'You didn't tell me your brother was a terrorist.'

'He's not a terrorist.'

'Don't give me that freedom-fighter nonsense.'

'It's not nonsense. You were bloody occupiers.'

'We came to stop you killing each other.'

'Bollocks. How many Unionists did you kill? You took sides. You colluded.' I think I was shouting.

Everything seemed crazily askew. Words spilled out of me. 'You don't understand. You won't understand. You'll never understand.'

'You're making an exhibition of yourself.' Henry wrenched open the taxi door. 'Get in.'

'No.' I turned my back on him and ran, stumbling, towards what looked like a main road. My heels clattered on the pavement. I heard no footsteps following me.

The taxi caught up with me at the end of the street. The window rolled down. The taxi driver waved what looked like a twenty-pound note at me.

'Your boyfriend's given me the fare. Hop in.'

I looked back down the street. There was no sign of Henry.

'Don't be stupid, love. Get in,' said the taxi driver. 'A lot of couples fight on New Year's Eve. It's the drink that does it. You'll make it up in the morning.'

'I don't think so,' I said.

# 43

# Diana

Henry returned from London in an absolutely foul mood. He stomped through the kitchen and disappeared down the corridor before I could say anything. He reappeared about ten minutes later. He looked composed, but there was an angry glint in his eyes.

Asking about the party was not a good idea, I decided. Nor was it the moment to tell Henry about my dinner with John Finnegan and the startling suggestion he had made between the cheese course and the pudding.

John had begun by saying he liked to eat dinner like the French. 'Finish the wine with the cheese, and then have dessert. Makes more sense.'

'Me too,' I agreed.

'You like France, Diana?'

'Absolutely. Most English people like France, don't you think? We certainly like to buy houses there.'

'Do you have a house in France?'

'Good Lord, no. I just about manage to keep a house in England.'

'But you'd like a house in France.'

'Golly, yes,' I said.

'I like France too,' he said. 'I've spent a lot of time there over the years, because of the business. I'd like to spend more time there when I retire.' His smile held a hint of something I couldn't quite decipher. 'I'm going to retire next month.'

Just my luck, I thought. I meet a man I like – I didn't dare allow myself anything stronger than liking – and he hops off across the channel like a frog.

'You have a house in France?' I said brightly.

'I'm planning to buy one this year.' He toyed with a spoon.

'Whereabouts?'

'Wherever you like,' he said.

I thought I hadn't heard him correctly. 'What?'

'I'll buy it wherever you like,' he repeated.

My heart started thumping.

'I'll be sixty-five in April.' John reached across the table and grasped my hand. 'I don't know what age you are, Diana. But whatever it is, you can't know how much time is left to you. I don't know either. None of us do. I only know I want to make the most of the time that's left. And I want to spend that time with you.'

His statement was both a surprise and not a surprise. I looked wonderingly at our entwined fingers.

'I don't know you very well,' I said.

'Sometimes you have to take a chance.'

I felt lightheaded. My heart was now thumping so terrifically hard I was sure he could hear it. I wondered if I was dreaming.

'I've been a widower for six years.' His voice hoarsened. 'Six lonely years. I want someone to share my life with again. I want someone to share adventures with. I want someone to laugh with.' His voice softened. 'I want someone to hold.' He looked almost shy. 'What do you say, Diana?'

'You don't look sixty-five,' I said.

He laughed. 'You look like a schoolgirl.'

'I feel like a schoolgirl.'

'You make me feel so young. Isn't that what the song says? But we're not young any more.' He released my fingers and picked up the wine glass. He studied the play of light on the ruby liquid. '*Carpe diem.*'

'I have Lucy to think about,' I said.

'It will be a gradual move,' he said. 'Just long weekends and holidays at first. I have my mother to think about as well. She wants to stay where she is. I can visit her on weekdays when I'm retired.'

'I have a business too, you know.' I spoke more sharply than I intended.

'We can get someone to run it.'

I noted the 'we'. High-handed, I said to myself. The thought was curiously pleasurable but I didn't want him to think he could have everything his own way.

'I like running the business,' I said. 'I'm good at it. I built it up from very little.'

'We can get someone to run it on the weekends we're away.'

'What about Henry and the Hall? What if this film doesn't get made?'

'The wine in the cellar will pay for the roof.'

'Nearly,' I conceded. The thought jumped into my head: Henry is in love. The very word filled me with an extraordinary feeling of joy.

'You see? You're thinking about it,' John said.


I had been thinking about little else until Henry's return from London. When he reappeared in the kitchen, I went on stirring the risotto and merely said, 'Would you like some good news, Henry?'

'That would make a change.' He sounded more depressed than angry.

'John Finnegan came yesterday to value the wines in the cellar.' I paused for effect. 'They're worth about fifty thousand pounds.' I turned to see Henry's reaction.

He looked stunned.

'I couldn't believe it either,' I said. 'But it's true. Fifty thousand.'

Henry shouted, 'Hallelujah!' and danced on the spot like a Cossack. Paddy barked.

Henry fell back on the sofa. Paddy scrambled up beside him.

'Did you hear that, Paddy? Fifty thousand pounds, fifty bloody thousand pounds.'

'The 1945 Mouton Rothschild alone is worth hundreds of pounds a bottle. Thousands of pounds a case.'

'You're absolutely sure about this?'

'John said it was a legendary vintage. The bottles are all genuine. Apparently fakes turn up from time to time. But we found original receipts in the boxes. John telephoned just now. He's checked the prices of all the wines.'

I didn't add that he had asked me to go house-hunting in France with him in April.

'Finnegan's Fine Wines will buy the lot from you for fifty thousand, near enough,' I said. 'Or you can send them to auction. Up to you, really, John says.'

'The Lord giveth, and the Lord taketh away,' said Henry slowly. 'What would you rather have, Diana? Love or money?'

'Nice to have both,' I said lightly. 'But since I seem to get by on not much money, I'd choose love.' I hesitated, unsure of Henry's mood. 'What about you, Henry?'

He shook his head. 'I haven't been given the choice.' He turned his head away and began to stroke Paddy.

I tested the rice. Still chalky. I added more stock and went on stirring.

Henry got to his feet. 'Plum,' he said harshly.

'John says he's either a fool or a knave.'

'We'll soon see.' Henry marched to the telephone. He thumbed through the address book. He stabbed the telephone keys.

'Plum?' Pause. 'Happy New Year to you too.' Henry sounded almost affable. 'About those wines, Plum. What did you think they were worth?' Pause. 'Yes, I thought I remembered correctly. The thing is, since they're not worth all that much, really, when you think about it, I thought we'd just drink them. Diana I got stuck in over Christmas. Jolly nice Mouton what-not. Scoffed the lot.'

A faint squawking sound came from the telephone. Henry had a look of grim enjoyment on his face. 'Another thousand? Without the Mouton whatsit? Why didn't you offer that before, Plum? Trying to diddle me?'

More agonised squawking issued from the telephone. 'I don't

think so, Plum,' said Henry. 'Goodbye.' Henry replaced the receiver. 'Creep.'

He was lost in thought all through supper. He hardly spoke except to mutter the occasional appreciative word. I waited until we had cleared the table before announcing, 'Henry, I think we should go to Donegal.'

# 44

# Louise

I was angry. I was heartsick. I was numb.

I was angry because Henry hadn't told me he had been in the army. Had served in Northern Ireland. Had spied on us. Had supervised the ransacking of our house. Had laughed about it.

I was angry because I had allowed myself to hope.

I was heartsick because hope had died in me.

I was numb because I wanted to talk to Henry and I didn't want to talk to him. I wanted to see him and I never wanted to see him again. I was a cloud-burst of grief and confusion. I wanted time to run backwards.

I kept asking myself what would have happened if I'd never met Hector with his snorting laugh and ridiculous hair. What if Henry had mentioned casually that he had been in the army? I would have asked him if he had been in Northern Ireland. He would have said yes. I would have hesitated, chosen my words carefully, and told him about Michael. And then what?

Would Henry have commiserated?

I didn't want commiseration.

Would Henry have asked me how I felt about Michael?

I would have found it hard to put my ricocheting thoughts into sentences, disentangle the emotions, knotted inside me, since the day of Michael's arrest. Anger because I thought he had thrown away his future; disappointment because he hadn't confided in me; relief that he hadn't confided in me; pride because he was prepared to risk his life for his principles; shame because of the terrible things with which he was associated.

Would Henry have understood?

No point in wondering. It was too late now.

I put a twenty-pound note in an envelope and posted it to Henry. I couldn't bring myself to write a note. What was there to say? I turned the painted fire to the wall. Empty canvas stared back at me. The weekend seemed to last a year.

It was a relief to go into the office on Monday and exchange small talk with Chloe. She had spent New Year in Scotland.

'The usual Hogmanay ball,' she said. 'Tartan sashes, kilts, hairy knees and nobody remotely fanciable. Not like the handsome son of the handsome Henry.' She sighed.

My heart turned over. I felt dizzy.

'Are you all right, Louise? You look tired.' The note of concern in her voice brought me close to tears.

'I'm fine, thank you,' I said. 'I didn't have any breakfast. I probably need something to eat.'

Rebecca whirled into the office a few minutes later. She looked tired. I remembered I needed to reassure her about Barry Shaw. I felt I could talk to her about Henry as well. She had been with me in Belfast. She would understand how I felt. She would commiserate. Help me sort myself out.

'On second thoughts, Chloe,' I said, 'Would you mind getting me coffee and a croissant, and some painkillers, please?'

When she'd gone, I told Rebecca I had seen Barry in Belfast. 'He's in the pantomime. I spoke to him.'

For a moment I thought Rebecca was going to faint. She put two hands on her desk to steady herself. 'I thought I was going mad. I thought I saw him last night. I thought I saw him at a bus stop this morning.'

'Well you can stop worrying,' I said. 'I saw him in Belfast. I spoke to him about the pantomime. It's on for another two weeks at least.'

Rebecca blew all the air out of her lungs and collapsed in her chair like a balloon. 'I thought he'd caught up with me.'

'It was your imagination,' I said gently. 'He's not after you. Put him out of your mind.'

'I was frightened of what he might do. You know what he was like.'

I silently recalled Barry's obsession, his creepiness.

'He's not after you,' I repeated. 'He's in Belfast. Playing a thief in a pantomime.' I laughed. 'You couldn't make it up.'

Rebecca wasn't listening. 'I can't ever let him find me. He'll want revenge.'

'Revenge?' I was suddenly enraged. Barry's malign shadow still falls on us like a curse, I thought. 'Don't be a victim, Rebecca,' I said. 'Don't let him win. If anybody should want revenge, it's you.'

A strange smile came over Rebecca's face. 'I've had my revenge,' she said. 'The bastard went to jail because I set him up.'

At first I couldn't take in what she'd said. I stared at her. She was holding out her foot, seeming to admire the shine on one patent leather high-heeled shoe. She re-crossed her legs and studied the other shoe.

'I set him up,' she said. 'I framed him, like they say in the movies.' She glanced up. 'Don't look so horrified, Louise. You're gasping like a goldfish.'

I felt unreal. As though the conversation was being held by two different people, and I was watching from somewhere in the ceiling.

'I told Barry I needed the money to pay a debt,' Rebecca was saying calmly. 'I knew he didn't have any money to lend me. I gave him the necklace and earrings to take to the pawnbrokers. I told him I was too embarrassed to go myself. I told the police he'd stolen them. Simple.' She was glitteringly defiant. 'Take what you want and pay for it. That's always been my belief. I acted on it.'

She stood up, suddenly pugnacious. 'What was I supposed to do? Run away? Give up my job? My good job? I was only a month into my contract. That bastard wasn't going to ruin my life. I knew the police would believe me and not that toe-rag.'

I found my voice. 'It's perjury, Rebecca. It's a crime.'

236

'So is planting bombs and shooting soldiers. You seem to take that in your stride, Louise.'

I wanted to cry out that this wasn't the same. This was a different kind of wrong. But all the muddled emotions inside me rose into my throat and choked me. I had no reply. I couldn't explain why I was so shocked by her confession.

'We all make moral compromises,' Rebecca said stonily. 'You make yours. I make mine.' She exhaled long and hard. 'Now I know why Catholics believe in confession. I feel surprisingly better for having told you.'

She took my arm. I tried not to flinch.

'You mean you haven't told Robert?'

'He'd want me to tell the police. Confess to perjury.'

'And you think I won't tell you the same thing.'

'Robert sees black and white. You see grey.'

'He's a lawyer. All lawyers see grey,' I said.

'I'll tell Robert in my own time,' she said. 'I hadn't bothered mentioning that creep to him. I'd managed to forget about him. Until I thought I saw him again.' She shuddered.

'Well, you were mistaken about that at least,' I said quietly.

Rebecca dropped my arm. A determined look came into her eyes. 'I'm going to get this film made, Louise. That's all that matters now. I'll think about telling Robert. When the film's made.' She met my gaze squarely. 'I'll think about it.' Her expression changed to wariness. 'You're not going to tell anybody, are you?'

'No,' I said. An old childhood expression came to me. 'I won't tell on you.'

Rebecca sat down abruptly. 'Right. Back to work. We have a film to make.' She lifted the telephone and tapped in a number.

The door opened. Chloe backed in, balancing three cardboard cups of coffee, a bag of croissants and a box of aspirin, like a plate-spinner in a circus. I hurried to help her.

When I glanced back at Rebecca, she looked her old, businesslike self, smiling persuasively as she spoke into the telephone.

My head was throbbing. I took two aspirins and went back to revising the budget in line with Teddy's revised script. The words swam on the page. The clattering and shouting in the market got louder. The room got stuffier.

I didn't feel like company so I went out early for lunch. Instead of heading for the café in the market, I changed course and walked towards the Southbank and a café that was usually quiet before one o'clock.

I was surprised to see Teddy and Jacky at a table in the corner. They looked equally startled to see me. I hesitated. Teddy stood up and insisted on buying me a coffee. I sat down beside Jacky.

'I thought nobody I knew would see us here. The coffee's awful. The tea's worse.' Jacky scrutinised my face. 'You look terrible, Louise.'

He seemed so happy I didn't want to spoil his mood by spilling out my misery and confusion. And even if I could talk about Henry, I had to keep Rebecca's confession to myself.

'I drank too much at New Year,' I said. That was probably true.

The three of us walked back to the office together. Jacky linked arms with me on one side, Teddy on the other. They were almost skipping. I couldn't help feeling the chill wind of exclusion.

We found Rebecca all sparkling eyes and windmill arms.

'I've just been on a conference call with the Americans. They love your screenplay, Teddy. They might give us more money if we get the right actress for Lettice.'

She mentioned the name of an actress who had been nominated for an Oscar in a 'best-supporting' role.

'She's just finishing a film for Miramax. She's starting another film in July. She might be able to fit us in. Her agent has seen the script. Robert and I are going to Los Angeles to see if we can nail down a deal.'

I could feel the adrenalin surge around the room like an electric current.

'Her agent says she won't do it without a guaranteed release clause,' Rebecca said. 'If we have to look for somebody else we might have to delay production. Can we do it in time, Louise?'

I bent my head to the budgets, the schedules and the revised script. Rebecca was leaving for the airport in two hours. There wouldn't be time to agonise. There was hardly time to think. Thank God for work, I said to myself.

Rebecca had put on her coat and was drumming her fingers on her handbag when I finished my calculations and called out, 'We can do it. Start pre-production at the end of January. Start shooting interiors mid-April. Shoot exteriors end of May. Finish shooting beginning of June.'

A thought wormed its way from the back of my mind. I wanted the production delayed. I didn't want to be at Wooldene, working with Rebecca, avoiding Henry at every turn. I could find Rebecca another line producer and find myself another job.

I stamped on the worm. The film business combined insecurity with a culture of brief liaisons. None of us in the business could afford to let our emotions interfere with our jobs. Henry would probably stay out of my way. I would finish this production and then find another job.

Rebecca paused in the doorway. 'Keep your fingers crossed, everybody. I'll phone as soon as I know the answer.' Her voice drifted up the stairs before the door swung closed again. 'You can relax until then. Have fun.'

Teddy and Jacky drifted out behind her. Chloe announced she was going to a party later on. 'Some old friends from Edinburgh. Want to come?'

I pictured rooms crowded with bright, energetic young graduates, dancing vigorously, eyeing each other up. I felt instantly weary and over-conscious of my forty-one years.

'I'm partied out,' I said. 'Thanks all the same.'

I stayed at my desk in the empty, darkening office, listlessly rearranging files. I began sketching a floor plan for the pre-production office, which we had agreed would be in the kitchen and servants' quarters of the Hall. Visions of Henry flinging open doors to show us the housekeeper's parlour, the pantries and sculleries, 'plenty of space here, I'd say, for all your desks and what-not,' swarmed into my brain. I batted them away.

Michael telephoned. 'You'll be pleased to know Mum's decided to spend her weekends in Donegal for a while, to see how she

239

likes it. She came up to Belfast with me yesterday to collect some things. I started teaching again today. I'll take her back down again with me at the weekend. Isn't that great?'

'Terrific, Michael.'

'Donegal's magic for the spirits. She gets on great with Joan.'

'I could do with my spirits being lifted.' The words were out before I could stop them.

'Are you feeling a bit down? Why's that?'

I lied and said I was in a sort of limbo waiting for the green light for the production. Things always went a bit flat then.

'Why don't you go back to Crocknasolas for a while? Charge your batteries. Siobhan's on her own with Maeve. She'd love the company.'

'She might want to be on her own. She had a full house at Christmas.'

Five minutes after I finished my conversation with Michael, the telephone rang again. I heard Siobhan's soft voice in my ear. 'You didn't stay long enough at Christmas, Louise. Come on over and stay until you're ready to start work on the film.'

I muttered something about the cost of the flight.

'You won't be spending money here. I've enough food to feed an army. The scenery's free.'

I hesitated.

'Bring your friend, if you like.'

'I'll be coming on my own,' I said.

# 45

## Diana

Henry and I flew into Belfast City airport the Tuesday after New Year and picked up a hire car. Henry knew how to get to the motorway which would take us north and west out of the city. He concentrated on driving and didn't say much, apart from muttering that the road system had changed and that everything looked a lot better, even in the dark. Five minutes from the airport, he took a wrong turning and we found ourselves facing a wall, the headlights illuminating two giant red hands and the slogan 'IRISH OUT'.

'I thought they were all Irish,' I said.

Henry reversed smartly. 'To us English they're all Irish of one persuasion or another. If only it were that simple.' He swung the car around. 'The Catholics want to be Irish and the Protestants want to be British.' The headlights picked up another mural. A black-clad man in a balaclava with a rifle and a grenade, a soldier in battle fatigues, an armed policeman on a blood-red background. 'ULSTER'S DEFENDERS'.

'Are we safe here, Henry?'

'Belfast people, Catholic and Protestant, are kind to strangers. It's each other they can't stand.' Henry's laugh had no humour in it. '"Oh stranger from England, why stand so aghast?"' he declaimed. '"May the Lord in His Mercy be kind to Belfast." I had that quoted to me by a nun in West Belfast,' he said. 'We arrested five schoolgirls during a riot and brought them back to the school. Hard to say who got the bigger scolding, the girls for going on the demonstration or us for arresting them.'

A cloud shifted and the near-full moon lit what looked like something from a film about the war. Gun towers, barbed wire fences, grey concrete walls.

Henry answered my unspoken question. 'Police station. They were all heavily fortified. I was in a good few of them.' He was silent for a moment. 'I don't really want to think about it,' he said. 'Do you mind if we listen to the radio, or talk about something else?'

'I wonder when we'll hear from the film company,' I said.

'I don't care if we never hear from them,' Henry said savagely.

So, he had been rebuffed. My sisterly heart went out to him. I felt a rush of anger against Louise. I thought about asking Henry if he wanted to talk about it, but a quick glance at the set of his chin was enough to tell me that now was not the time. I switched on the radio, hunted for a signal and found a station broadcasting orchestral music. Henry gave me a quick grateful smile. I reclined my seat, closed my eyes and allowed myself to dream about John Finnegan and a house in France. Normandy perhaps. Or the Loire. A house with blue shutters, yellow sunflowers in the garden and purple grapes on the wall. From time to time I opened my eyes and saw dark hills flying past the rain-spattered window.

Just after eight o'clock, Henry, who had been silent for most of the journey, said, 'Not long now. We've crossed the border.'

I hadn't noticed. There had been no customs hut or check-point to mark where the United Kingdom ended and the Irish Republic began. Only the weather had changed. Thin, wispy snowflakes now drifted whitely through the beam from the head-lights and melted invisibly into the black road. When we reached our hotel in a small market town, we ran with our bags across the car park to the back entrance of the hotel.

'Go on into the dining room, if you want dinner,' said the white-haired, pink-cheeked receptionist. 'Seamus will take your bags up to your room.'

The dining room was half-empty. A three-foot Christmas tree

and a large poinsettia sat listlessly on a mahogany sideboard. The menu was unexciting, featured variations on a turkey theme and did not hold out much promise. But our steaks were juicy, lean and tender and cooked exactly as we had ordered. The Brussels sprouts weren't overcooked. The potatoes were floury and full of flavour.

When we got up from the table, Henry looked positively cheerful. I felt optimistic. Though that might have been the result of half a bottle of wine and a greedy portion of trifle which had been absolutely saturated with sherry.

After dinner, we took a stroll around the square on which the roads into the town converged. It wasn't like an English town, and yet it seemed more familiar than foreign to me. I realised that the shops with their wide wooden-framed windows and proprietors' names above the doors reminded me of the English towns of my childhood, before corporate brands colonised the streets.

Three skate-boarders, in jeans and anoraks, circled and spun around a statue in the centre. The sleety rain had stopped. The paving glistened damply. Parked cars glinted like mosaic under the street lamps. Red, green and white Christmas lights, strung between the lamps, swung in a salty wind. Henry and I turned into the wind and walked down to a bridge over a black river rushing towards the sea.

'I wonder if Lucy came here,' I said.

'Probably. It's the nearest town to the address on the letter.'

'Can you imagine her standing here?'

Henry's reply was a long, drawn out 'yes'.

He stared at his feet. It occurred to me he was thinking about someone else entirely.

The following morning we breakfasted early and handsomely on bacon, eggs, sausage, tomato, fried potato cake and a giant pot of tea. Henry said it was an Ulster fry. Two other guests, a plump woman, about my age I guessed, and a younger blonde who could have been her daughter, followed us into the dining room. They sat near a window silently contemplating the morning mist drifting over the river. They looked tired. The receptionist came into the dining room, glanced around, and hurried to their table. Her face had lost its pink complexion and was all pale concern. She clasped the older woman's hand and spoke quietly to her.

Two men in blue uniforms came into the dining room. The receptionist beckoned to them.

'Police,' Henry whispered. 'Garda.'

I thought for a moment we were going to witness an arrest, but the police shook hands with the women and looked worried.

The waitress brought two pots of tea and two racks of toast to their table. She stood poised to take their breakfast order. The older woman shook her head. One of the policemen said, 'It could be a long day, Mrs Murphy. Would you not eat something? It'll be another half-hour before we get started.'

The younger woman said, 'The guard is right, Teresa. We should at least have a bowl of porridge. You could manage a bowl of porridge, couldn't you?'

The waitress took that to be an order and scurried away.

I realised Henry and I were being rather rude in staring at them. I indicated to Henry that we should be on our way.

We headed along the coast under a grey sky. I thought the landscape washed out, as though colour had seeped from it, until my eye adjusted and I began to see the subtle differences between the blue-grey of the low mountains, the pearly grey of the clouds, the silvery grey of the sea and the grey-green winter fields dotted with black boulders. We turned a corner. The sky cleared suddenly. The sun splashed purple and green and blue and gold on the mountains. The sea dazzled. White clouds danced across the sky, violet shadows swept across the fields. Everything was utterly, stunningly transformed.

This was only my second visit to Ireland. I remembered a brief trip in the fifties when 'the season' included a hunt ball in a draughty hotel in Dublin. Mummy had only just managed to scrape together enough cash to send me. It was not long after Daddy died. The task of finding me a husband had assumed even greater urgency, I supposed. It had rained for three days. I caught a cold, not a husband. I never saw the countryside.

Henry was equally taken with the scenery. He turned the car

into a gateway. We got out and stood holding the doors against the buffeting wind from the sea, watching cloud shadows scudding across a crescent of white sand. A formation of lapwings banked and whistled over the intervening patchwork of small, stony fields. A curlew cried, 'cooo-leee'.

My attention was distracted by a flurry of activity on the edge of my vision. I turned to look. On a side road, about a quarter of a mile away near what looked like the ruins of a castle or church, white figures clambered out of a white van. As I watched, two white cars with blue and yellow markings flew past us. They turned into the side road and parked behind the van. The van moved forward. Now I could see a line of dark figures across a field, heads nodding and rising methodically, like crows pulling worms. I realised they were digging.

When we passed the field a few minutes later, I noticed a group of men in white boiler suits and the two women we had seen at breakfast standing watching the diggers. Plastic sheeting flapped in the wind.

'Must be a murder investigation,' said Henry.

A mile or so further on, we spotted a white-painted Victorian house with bow-windows and railings on the right-hand side of the road.

'That's it. That's the house,' I cried.

As we drew up opposite, we saw, to our dismay, a large sign over the door. Youth Hostel. It looked shut for the winter. We knocked on the door. No reply.

'It's definitely the right house.' The wall was crumbling in places, the wrought iron gate was missing, but the house was otherwise exactly the same as the house in the photograph. 'I wonder how long it's been a hostel.'

'Years,' said Henry gloomily.

'We could ask in the village,' I said.

The girls behind the counter in the mini-supermarket flicked their ponytails, giggled at Henry's question and said they didn't know anything about the hostel and were only helping out for the day. The boy in the garage shook his head and said his parents might know but they were away at a wedding.

'You've picked a bad day to be asking,' said the barman in the otherwise empty pub. He had fierce black eyebrows but a friendly smile. 'Near everyone's away at a wedding. I don't know the bride or groom. I'm only a blow-in.'

Henry ordered two coffees. 'How long have you lived here?'

'A year,' said the barman. 'Take the weight off your legs. I'll bring the coffees over to you.'

The smell of freshly brewed coffee filled the bar. The barman noted my surprise. 'We get a lot of French and Italian tourists,' he said. 'They're wild fussy about their coffee.' He seemed inclined to chat.

'Weddings is big in Donegal. Keeps all the hotels busy. There's not much else to do in the winter. There's more goes on in the summer.'

He carried two steaming cups to our table. 'I thought when you walked in you were something to do with that business up the road. They were digging all day yesterday. They put up lights and went on digging after dark. We had them in near closing time. I had to put on another barrel.'

'We drove past them,' I said. 'What are they looking for?'

'The body of some poor buggers shot by the IRA.' He made a quick sign of the cross. 'God rest them. Informers, they say.' His sigh seemed to encompass all the troubles of the world.

Henry drained his coffee and stood up abruptly. 'I think we should get going.' He glanced at the tab, dug in his wallet, handed the barman a note. 'Thanks for the coffee. Keep the change.'

'What was all that about?' I demanded when we got into the car. 'I hardly had time to finish my coffee.'

Henry stared straight ahead. He made no attempt to start the car.

'I used to run informers,' he said. 'I can't help wondering if any of the poor buggers they're looking for was one of mine.' He made a helpless gesture.

I didn't know what to say.

'They were mostly pathetic,' he said. 'One or two were tired and just wanted a ticket out. They were the ones with real information to sell. The others were people whose little weaknesses we

246

could expose.' He leaned back and closed his eyes. 'Adulterers: we threatened to tell their wives. Homosexuals: we threatened to tell their wives or their parents. Petty criminals: we could get charges dropped.'

I found my voice. 'What happened to them?'

'The big fish, the supergrasses, got out. We set up new identities for them. The little fish went on swimming. Some of them survived. One or two got shot. One or two got out before they got shot. One or two simply disappeared.'

'Do you think this,' I hesitated, 'person they're looking for is one of them?'

'God knows,' said Henry. He opened his eyes. 'We went in to help, dammit.' He sat up. He thumped the wheel. 'We went to stop them killing each other. We had the best intentions.' He was silent for a moment. 'It became a very dirty war. Mistakes were made.' His voice faded. 'I was glad when I left. I don't want to talk about it any more, Diana.' He heaved a sigh that shook the car. He turned the key in the ignition. 'Let's get out of here.'

He looked straight ahead when we passed the site of the excavations the second time. My quick glance took in the addition of a mechanical digger. Its great yellow claw hovered over the ground. The two women had gone.

# 46

# Diana

The Registry of Births, Marriages and Deaths was housed in a long Victorian building on a hill above the sprawl of Letterkenny.

'Fastest growing town in Europe,' said the registrar, with a hint of pride. She had a friendly face and a confiding manner. We gave her Lucy's name, the address on the letter, the year of the birth and the name Anton Kazanowski.

'We're quiet today,' she said, 'come back in an hour's time.'

We drove to a hotel on the outskirts of the town, ordered soup and sandwiches and sat beside a window overlooking a sea lough. Henry found a newspaper to hide behind. I sat thinking about John Finnegan and whether, as he had confidently predicted, we would rub along happily together. 'We're both too old to play games,' he had said. 'We're free. We can go away together and find out if we're as well suited as I think we are.' He had touched my hand and I had felt heat flooding through my veins.

I think I sighed, for Henry lowered the newspaper and said, 'I'm sorry I haven't been great company, Diana. I've been a bit preoccupied.'

'I've got a lot to think about too,' I said.

'How's that man of yours? The wine chap.'

'He's very well,' I said.

'Glad to hear it. Thanks to him, I'll have cash to fix the roof.'

'Mummy wouldn't have entirely approved of him,' I said.

'Mummy was a frightful snob,' said Henry. 'I loved her dearly, but she was a snob.' He paused. 'Finnegan. Sounds Irish.'

'His parents were Irish.'

'Catholic?'

'Yes.'

'Widower?'

'Yes.'

'He's free to marry you,' said Henry, drily. 'That at least would have made Mummy happy.'

'I hardly know him,' I protested.

Henry raised a knowing eyebrow and went back to reading the newspaper.

My eyes followed the white flash of a gull along the shoreline to where a mechanical digger crawled through the grey breezeblock maze of a building site. The digger stopped, scooped black earth into its yellow claw, swung round and crawled out of sight again. I thought of the white faces I had seen in the back of the police car. I remembered how Lucy had clung to my hands when she told me that she wanted to be buried with her baby. I wondered how we would arrange it, when the time came, always providing of course that we found the baby's grave.

'No luck,' said the registrar, with a sympathetic shake of her head. 'I took a look at two or three years either side as well. If there was a birth to anyone of that name it wasn't registered. I looked to see if an infant death was registered in that name, although I didn't think anyone would register a death without registering the birth.' She saw our disappointment and added, 'I wouldn't lose heart. We do a lot of searches for Americans looking for their ancestors. Sometimes a birth isn't registered.' She paused. 'But all baptisms are registered.' She smiled. 'I looked up the parish for that address and I took the liberty of ringing the parish priest for you. Father Buckley. He'll have a look for you. He says you can call with him any time tomorrow.' She handed us the sheet of foolscap on which she had scribbled the address, telephone number and directions. 'All the best.'

# 47

# Louise

'Come straight down to Crocknasolas,' Siobhan had said. 'Don't stop off to see your mum. Michael is taking her to see *Titanic*. You sound as if you need a bit of time to yourself.'

Her voice was warm and sympathetic. I almost blurted out my misery about Henry, my worry about Rebecca's unwanted confession, my sense of being adrift on a sea of confusion. But I was shy of confiding in Siobhan. Although she was a good ten years younger than me, she seemed so confident in marriage and motherhood. I felt emotionally inept.

The light was fading from the sky when I set out from Aldergrove airport to drive to Donegal. I was accustomed to driving east over the mountain and when I reached the roundabout where I would normally swing left to go to Belfast, I had to drive round it twice to find the road to the motorway that would take me north and west instead.

I flicked on the indicator and felt an almost imperceptible lightening of my spirits. I was steering away from my troubles. I felt cocooned. When the rain started – a light spattering on the windscreen, then a downpour, then a torrent – I pushed all thoughts of Henry, Rebecca, Barry Shaw, Mum and Michael out of my mind and concentrated on the slippery road ahead.

On the Glenshane Pass through the Sperrin mountains, I stopped for a cup of coffee at a roadside pub. Apart from two elderly men on bar stools, nursing pints of Guinness, I was the only customer.

'Terrible night,' said the barman. He had one eye on the weather map displayed on the television screen at the back of the empty lounge. 'Not much better tomorrow, by the looks of it.'

I carried my coffee to a table near the television as the spinning globe that announced the *Northern Ireland News* flashed on the screen. I warmed my hands on the cup and was about to raise it to my lips when I heard the newsreader say, 'Police in the Irish Republic will resume their search at first light for the remains of victims abducted and murdered by the IRA in the seventies and eighties.'

I put the cup down and stared at pictures of a reporter in a raincoat, wet hair plastered to his head. Behind him, a line of Gardai in pale blue boiler suits were digging in a bog. They trod on their spades, rhythmically, like line dancers, flinging black earth to one side. The shot changed. I almost started out of my seat when I recognised Pauline and Teresa Murphy getting into a car and being driven away. The reporter said relatives had been visiting the sites of the excavations. Next came shots of men in white boiler suits shutting the back door of a white van. The reporter's voice-over said after more than a day excavating at this site in Donegal, Gardai and pathologists had taken away what were believed to be human remains.

You have little enough to worry you, Louise O'Neill, I said to myself. What are your troubles compared to Teresa Murphy, or any of the other poor souls who can't bury their dead? I whispered a prayer. Please God, let Teresa Murphy's long wait be over.

My coffee was cold and tasted of nothing. Sadness settled on me. I got back into the car and resumed my journey in the still-torrential rain.

Siobhan took one look at me and immediately prescribed a plate of scrambled eggs, a walk to the pub, a hot whiskey and bed. In that order. She asked about my journey. She chatted about Maeve. Gradually, I began to relax.

I thought I wasn't hungry until the scrambled eggs were set down in front of me. The prescribed walk to the pub near the strand loosened my limbs, stiffened by hours in the car. Perhaps it was the sea air, perhaps it was the music and the easy banter swirling around Mulligans', perhaps it was the hot whiskey, but when I walked back up to the house I knew Siobhan's prediction, 'You'll sleep without rocking,' was both welcome and accurate.

I wakened to the smell of bacon frying. The room was filled with light. I looked at my watch. It was after ten o'clock. I pulled a jumper over my nightdress and hunted the smell down the corridor to the kitchen. Siobhan was on the telephone. She mouthed a greeting and pointed to the range cooker. I opened the oven door and took out a dish of grilled bacon and tomatoes and two plates. She pointed to the kettle and teapot. I made the tea.

Siobhan replaced the receiver. 'Michael and your mum are coming down on Friday night. How long can you stay?'

'Depends on when I hear from Rebecca,' I said. 'If she gets the green light it will be all go straight away.'

Siobhan divided the *Irish Times* between us.

'I've put Maeve down for a sleep. We'll have a bit of peace to read the paper.'

We made bacon sandwiches and turned our chairs to warm our feet cosily on the oven door. The telephone rang. I hardly noticed Siobhan get up to answer it. My attention had been caught by a box at the bottom of the front page of the newspaper.

### Breaking news

Pathologist says remains found in Inishowen those of stillborn infants. Search concluded, say Gardai. Excavations begun at new site in Monaghan.

The cloud of sadness descended again.

Siobhan topped up my mug of tea. 'You haven't been in great form.' Her observation held the hint of a question.

'Nothing seems right at the moment.' I hesitated. The impulse to confide fought another deeper need to nurse my wounds before revealing them. I settled on a half-truth. 'I know the women waiting for the results of these . . .' I waved my hand wordlessly at the newspaper. 'I was at school with Pauline Downey.'

'I know,' said Siobhan. 'Michael told me.'

Of course, I said to myself. They're married: they open their hearts to each other. Michael will tell Siobhan things he would not tell another living soul. He is her lover and her best friend. It hit me, like a thump on my own heart, that I was mourning the loss of both in Henry.

'Michael was sorry he couldn't help your friend. He doesn't know where any of these bodies are buried. In case you were thinking,' Siobhan said quietly. 'He would say if he knew.'

'I wasn't thinking that.' Her statement startled me out of my misery. I had never talked to Siobhan about Michael's involvement in the IRA. 'I just thought maybe he could ask somebody. Brendan Murphy disappeared in 1981. I know Michael wasn't involved then.'

'Yes, he was,' said Siobhan. 'He joined the queue the week Bobby Sands died. May 1981. He told me. It was the hunger strike that made him join. The fact that all those men were prepared to die.'

I stared at her.

'But Michael was always in Belfast,' Siobhan said. 'He wouldn't have known about goings on in Strabane.'

I felt as though the inside of my head was full of fudge and information was fighting to get through.

'I thought Michael joined because our house was wrecked. Because he was arrested. Because Dad was arrested. Because Dad never got over it. Because it caused his heart attack.'

'Michael always said it was the hunger strike that did it.' Siobhan paused. 'He told me your dad accepted it, his becoming a volunteer. He didn't like it, but he accepted it. He just made him promise there would be no guns in the house.'

I looked at her in astonishment. 'Dad knew?'

'Oh, aye. Your dad told Michael all he would get at the end would be a Republican funeral. A pair of black gloves and a beret on his coffin. Or if he was lucky, he would end up in jail.'

'Did Mum know?'

She shook her head. 'Your dad said the fewer knew the better.' She leaned across and squeezed my hand. 'That's all in the past, thank God. Michael's out of it now. He's done his bit. He has a new life. You don't have to worry about him any more. Your mum doesn't have to worry about him.'

I was still trying to take in what Siobhan had just told me when I went to get dressed. I moved like a sleepwalker. I heard a whimper from Maeve as I passed her room. The door was open. She was standing up in her cot. She held out her arms to me. 'Lala.' It had been Michael's name for me as well when he was a baby and Pauline and I had wheeled him in his pram around Ardoyne.

I hoisted Maeve over the bars of the cot. She chuckled and laid her head on my shoulder and wrapped herself around me. Her red curls tickled my cheek. She smelled of soap and talcum powder. I clung to her innocent softness.

'It will all be over when you're grown up,' I whispered. It was a prayer as well as a promise.

# 48

# Diana

Father Buckley was a tall, thick-haired bear of a man. His clerical collar was just visible under a cable-knit jumper. He greeted us warmly and ushered us into the front sitting room of the detached grey-stone house beside the chapel. A turf fire burned in the grate. A grandfather clock ticked beside a wide mahogany bookcase. A set of golf clubs leaned against a wall. On a table in the bay window piles of books and papers had been swept aside to make room for a thick, cloth-backed ledger.

'Sit down. Make yourselves comfortable. You'll take a cup of tea?'

We sat down on a sofa by the fire. Father Buckley lifted the ledger from the desk and placed it on a low table in front of us. 'That was a very interesting story you told me,' he said. 'This is the parish for that address all right. You have a look now, while I make the tea.' He hurried out of the room.

Henry slid the red silk marker through the pages and opened the ledger. The left-hand page began with an entry for December 1938. The last entry on the right-hand page was December 1940. We ran our eyes down the entries in between. No Wintour, or Lucy, or any name at the address on the letter sprang out at us. Henry put his finger on each entry in turn and we scanned the pages slowly. The date of birth was inscribed first, then the date of baptism, then the baby's name, then the parents' names. Every child recorded had two parents. No parent was called either Lucy or Wintour.

'I give up.' Henry sank back into the sofa. 'We've done our best, Diana.'

Father Buckley pushed a tea trolley into the room. 'Did you find what you were looking for?'

I shook my head.

Father Buckley tutted in commiseration. 'Could this child have been born somewhere else? Letterkenny hospital, maybe?'

'I'd expect the birth to be registered if the child was born in hospital.' I glanced at the entries again. 'The baptism is nearly always only a day or two after the birth,' I observed.

'Neo-natal mortality was higher then,' Father Buckley said. 'They wouldn't take the risk of the baby dying before it was baptised. It wouldn't have got a Christian burial.'

'The doctrine of limbo,' said Henry.

A memory flashed into my head. I put my hand on Henry's arm. 'Lucy talked about limbo.'

'Not so much a doctrine, more of a theological hypothesis.' Father Buckley settled into an armchair. 'It's not in the new catechism. There'd be no difficulty these days giving Christian burial to an infant that hadn't been baptised. We even have a special service for them.'

'What about sixty years ago?' I said. 'What happened to un-baptised babies then?'

Father Buckley looked uncomfortable. 'I believe they were buried in special places. Sometimes outside the walls of a grave-yard or near holy wells, or monuments to Saints, or in early Christian ruins, places like that.'

It took me a moment to absorb this. 'Like the ruins we saw being dug up yesterday?'

'Down the road? A sad business and no mistake,' said Father Buckley heavily. He shook his head and sighed. 'That poor woman spent all day yesterday trailing from one site to another in the hope of finding her dead son.'

We sat in silence for a moment.

'I'd better pour this tea before it gets cold,' Father Buckley said. His chubby hands were surprisingly delicate with the china teapot. He indicated the milk jug, sugar bowl and plate of chocolate biscuits on the trolley. 'Help yourselves.' He sat back. 'I've been thinking,' he began. 'There'd be people in the parish might remember this Doctor Brady and his wife.' He paused. 'It's a pity Seamus Cassidy is dead. He knew every stick and stone in the parish and the seed, breed and generation of everybody for miles around.' He thought for a moment. 'His granddaughter and her husband are fixing up the old place now. Will I give them a ring?'

Henry shrugged. 'Worth a try. Thank you, Father.'

Father Buckley set down his cup and saucer, got up and went out into the hall. I heard the low rumble of his voice. I imagined he was relating the story of the two eccentric English people who had pitched up in the parish on a wild goose chase.

He came back in again. 'Siobhan is going to ring back.' He had almost a bounce in his step. Clearly our visit had enlivened his day. 'She'll make a few calls. She'll find you somebody who remembers Doctor Brady and his wife.' He settled into the armchair again. 'More tea?'

The telephone rang. Father Buckley put down the teapot and hurried back to the hallway.

He reappeared a few minutes later. 'Siobhan's mother's cousin grew up near that house. He's moved now, to live with his sister.' He sat down again. 'Siobhan is going to ring him. All we have to do is wait.' He gave a satisfied smile.

The hands of the clock stood at half-past ten.

Henry gestured to the golf clubs and asked Father Buckley if he played much in the winter. This prompted a discourse on the relative merits of different courses.

I gazed out at the bungalows and cottages dotted over the landscape, as though a giant hand had scattered them, higgledy piggledy. Blue smoke spiralled from every chimney. I imagined our story being relayed from house to house across the parish in the modern equivalent of smoke signals. I watched the hands of the clock creep towards eleven o'clock. Father Buckley put more turf on the fire.

The clock struck eleven. The telephone rang. Father Buckley hastened into the hallway again. 'You're on,' he called out to us.

Henry and I got to our feet. Father Buckley came back into the room, beaming. 'Doctor Brady retired in the fifties and went to live in Galway. He must be dead by now. But your man used to work for him. He's up near Ballyliffen now. He's a great fiddle player. The house is hard to find. Siobhan was thinking of taking a run over there anyway. She's on her way to you now. She'll drive ahead of you and show you the road.'

'That's a frightful amount of trouble for her,' Henry said. 'If she would just give us the directions, I'm sure we'd find our way.'

'You can debate that with her,' Father Buckley said genially, 'when you see her.'

# 49

## Louise

I drove to Malin Head and parked the car below the low hill known as Bamba's Crown. I wanted the wind to blow through me and take all my troubles away. I got my wish. A near-gale whistled in from the Atlantic and wafted white streaks of foam across the darkening sea.

I tucked my gloveless hands under my armpits, put my head down and walked up to the old Lloyd's signal station. I thought about the messages relayed from here around the world. Fingers tapping out Morse code. Unseen ships answering.

I remembered my father taking us all here when we were small. What age was I? Nine, ten? Michael was a baby. We were on holiday in a caravan park at Portstewart. Dad drove us in the taxi to a ferry across Lough Foyle. I had never been on a ferry before. I was bursting with excitement. I remembered Dad telling me about sunken ships and U-boats torpedoed in the Atlantic. 'Only a few miles from here, imagine.' I didn't want to imagine all those people trapped and drowned. I had run back down the hill to Mum and Michael.

It started to rain. We ate sardine sandwiches and drank lemonade in the car. We all laughed when Dad said Malin was the sunniest spot in Ireland. 'Honestly. It's true. I'm not making it up.' He didn't wink, so I knew it was true.

Still hard to believe, I thought now, with the horizon a black line under a grey sky and the salt-wind scalding my ears, drowning the sound of the sea.

There had been a big IRA arms find at Malin Head. When? Ten years ago? More? Had Michael known about it? Or was he in prison by then? I tried to imagine him telling Dad he was in the IRA. Where, when had he told him? In front of the television, over a bottle of stout? In the taxi, when Dad picked him up from town, when there were no buses and it was too dangerous to walk? I imagined my father saying, 'You can't eat a flag and you can't eat a gun,' putting his head in his hands.

What would Dad have thought of Henry? No point in wondering.

A ray of sunlight broke through a bank of cloud and lit the shore. The stones on Ballyhillion beach glittered amber, gold, purple, green and silver. I suddenly felt I was standing in a vast, windy cathedral. I felt insignificant. A speck in time. It was a curiously calming thought.

The cottage was empty when I got back. I made myself a cup of tea, carried it into the sitting room and switched on the television.

Teresa Murphy's face filled the screen.

'I've waited seventeen years to get back the body of my son and give him the dignity of a Christian burial,' she told a reporter. Her voice was strong. She didn't falter. I felt ashamed of my quick, cheap tears. I said a silent prayer and switched off the television.

When I remembered my tea, it was cold.

Mum telephoned. 'Did you see the news? Did you see Pauline? And poor Mrs Murphy.' Her sigh travelled down the wires to me. 'Thank God for a small mercy.'

'Sad to be thanking God because a body's been found,' I said. 'But at least it ends their misery.'

'The misery never ends,' said Mum. It sounded like a rebuke.

'I know, Mum. I'm sorry. I just meant . . .'

'I know what you meant. It's all right.'

We were both silent for a moment.

'I still miss your dad,' Mum said. 'I still think, If only I'd made

260

him give up smoking. Sitting in that taxi all day, smoking. I should have made him walk more. He never got enough exercise.'

'Being arrested didn't help,' I said.

'He'd been complaining about indigestion for weeks,' Mum said. 'I should have made him go to the doctor. I blame myself.'

'I blame that raid,' I said, 'the shock.'

'I don't think it made any difference,' Mum said. 'Your dad was philosophical about it. Things were never black and white to him. Not like Michael.' She paused. 'Is that why Pauline wanted to see you?'

I didn't pretend not to understand. 'She wanted me to speak to Michael. She thought he might know something. I asked him. He said there were things happening. Negotiations. He didn't know anything about Brendan Murphy.'

'I'm glad about that,' Mum said.

'You don't have to worry about Michael any more,' I said.

'I never stop worrying about you all. I worry you'll never settle down, Louise. That you won't be happy like your dad and I were happy.'

I made myself smile into the receiver so that I wouldn't sound sad. 'I'm happy, Mum. You don't have to worry about me either.' I put down the receiver and burst into tears.

The telephone rang again. 'Louise?' It was Mum. 'I was thinking you sounded a wee bit upset just now,' she said. 'Is everything all right?'

I blew my nose. 'I've got a bit of a cold. I'm fine, Mum. Just worried about whether this film's going to get made or not.'

'You were always a worrier,' she said.

I had to smile through my tears. 'Isn't that the pot calling the kettle black? I thought you were the worrier.'

'I worry less than I used to,' she said unexpectedly. 'Maybe it was being down in Donegal with you all. Seeing the new generation. Dara and Maeve. And Michael looking so settled. I feel better than I have for a long time.'

'What about—' I stopped myself. There was a new tone in Mum's voice. I didn't want to remind her about the arguments at Christmas.

'The arguments?' Mum was too quick for me. 'Sure you all made up in the end. There are arguments in every family. Just because you disagree with someone doesn't mean you don't care about them. I never agreed with what Michael did, but that doesn't mean I don't love him.'

I couldn't remember how long it had been since Mum and I had talked like this. Not since Michael was arrested and Dad died and Mum got depressed and everything bad seemed to come at once. Maybe it was easier to talk connected only by a telephone cord.

'I love him too,' I said.

'Michael did what he thought was right,' Mum said. 'Even if other people think he was wrong.'

'Like Noreen,' I said.

'Noreen's another one who does what she thinks is right.'

There was a pause. I closed my eyes and imagined Mum sitting in her chair by the fire. She seemed to be sitting straighter. Her voice was stronger. We have changed positions, I thought. I am the child again. I gripped the cord.

'Sometimes it's hard to know what's right,' I said.

'Follow your heart and you'll find your home.'

It sounded like a quotation. I was diverted. 'Who said that?'

'Your dad said it to me before we were married. When I was hesitating. Your grandfather didn't like him, you know. He didn't want a son-in-law who'd been in the British army.'

I never knew my grandfather. He died before I was born. He was smiling in the photograph that stood on Mum's mantelpiece. I tried to imagine him stern.

'He came round in the end,' Mum said. 'Just like your dad said he would, if I stood my ground.' There was a pause. Then Mum said, 'You have to live your own life, Louise.'

# 50

# Diana

Siobhan was a friendly blonde with a musical voice. We never got her second name.

'It's no trouble at all to me,' she said. 'No trouble at all. He's Mammy's cousin. I was going to take my daughter over to visit him anyway. He's on his own for a few days. I'll do his shopping while you talk to him.'

She was right about the house being hard to find. We turned off the main road and drove through a landscape of meagre farms and patchwork fields. Small cottages nestled low to the ground. I thought it strange that they faced away from the sea, until I realised they were turning their backs on the wild Atlantic winds.

We followed a series of unsigned, twisting narrow lanes to a whitewashed cottage above a small stony beach. I could taste the spit of sea-spray in the wind. The door opened. A thin elderly man with grey hair cut close to his head, leaning on two sticks, stood in the doorway.

'Johnny Joe Friel,' said Siobhan.

She exchanged a greeting with him, in what I assumed was Gaelic. She introduced us in English.

'I'll take your shopping list, then I'll be off,' she said.

Johnny Joe steadied himself at a dresser just inside the door. He uncapped a bottle of whiskey and poured three glasses. He added a splash of water from a jug to each glass. 'You'll take a wee dram to keep out the cold.'

The room was as hot as a furnace. The windows were double-glazed. The sea sucked silently on the pebbles fifty yards beyond the glass. Seagulls mewed soundlessly above the waves.

Johnny Joe waved a stick at the sofa on one side of the peat fire. 'Sit down. Sit down.' He manoeuvred himself into a chair opposite us. He hauled one leg on to a stool. He put out his hand to take the glass of whiskey I passed to him and sat at a slight list to the room, like a boat drawn up on the beach.

'Lucy Wintour,' he said. 'I always thought it was an inappropriate kind of name for a girl who looked like summer itself.' His eyes had an unfocused look, as though he was seeing back into his skull-like head. 'And how would you be related to her?'

'She's our aunt,' I said.

'She must be a good age by now.'

'Eighty-six. Nearly eighty-seven.'

'Boys oh boy.' He stirred. 'She was a fine-looking girl. I remember her sitting in a field of daisies in a blue frock with daisies on it. Full of the joys of spring.' He took a sip of whiskey. 'And how is she now?'

'Her memory isn't great,' I said carefully. 'We were hoping you could help us. Do you remember a baby?'

Johnny Joe gripped his glass and stared out the window. I could see his jaw working.

'She asked me to make her a cradle,' he said. 'I ended up making her a coffin. A blue coffin.'

Henry was going to say something. I stopped him. I sensed Johnny Joe was just beginning a story.

'She came over to Doctor Brady's. It must have been,' he stared into his whiskey, 'oh, summer of 1939 or forty. I can't remember if the war had started. There was a lot of talk about it anyway. She was a lovely-looking girl. Dark hair. Dark eyes. I was working around the house. She used to talk to me about this and that. Just oul chat. She wore a wedding ring. But I never heard tell of a husband. When I got to know her a wee bit, she told me she wasn't married. Mrs Brady made her wear the ring so she wouldn't give scandal. Then one day she asked me if I would make a cradle for the baby. "I want him to have something that

264

I've given him," she said. "And how do you know it's a him?" I
knew her well enough to joke a bit with her. "He kicks like
Stanley Matthews," she said.'

He stopped, stared out of the window again. I dared to prompt.

'Do you remember the baby being born?'

'Oh, aye. There was an awful fuss. The baby was early. I was
cutting the grass in the orchard. Mrs Brady came running out
to me and said the doctor was on a call up the mountain and
I was to take the bicycle in the yard and go after him.'

I pictured him, a bony seventeen-year-old, cycling up a stony
track, head down, jacket flapping in the wind.

'Then you see, the couple that were coming up from Galway
to take the baby weren't able to come up. They were away at
some do or other in Cork. You couldn't travel around as fast in
those days. Lucy was nursing the baby until they came. They
were going to take it back to Galway and have a big christening
there.' He heaved a great sigh. 'I was in and out of the house. I
would see her crying. I felt powerful sorry for her.' He was silent
for a moment.

Neither Henry nor I moved. We hardly breathed.

'The baby died,' he said. 'A cot death. I came in one morning
and everyone was distraught. He hadn't been baptised, you see.
Mrs Brady was berating herself for putting it off to please the
couple from Galway. "Sure he could have had two baptisms,"
she said. "And what harm would that have been?" Then there
was a whole fuss about where they were going to bury the baby.
Lucy came to me and she said, "Johnny Joe, would you make
that cradle into a coffin?"

'I took the rockers off the cradle. I made a lid. I painted it
pale blue. I painted a black cross on the lid. Lucy said she was
taking it back with her to England. She wouldn't hear no to
that. It was no use the doctor talking to her, or Mrs Brady.
"That's what I'm doing," she said. "You won't stop me. I don't
want him to be on his own."'

Henry dug in his pocket for his handkerchief and mopped
his face. I could feel sweat trickling down between my shoulder
blades.

'Mrs Brady wanted to go back to England with her. Lucy wanted to be alone. She said Mrs Brady could go with her as far as the Liverpool boat. They put the coffin in a big canvas bag. The doctor drove them to the station in Strabane. "You'll not say a word of this to man or beast, Johnny Joe," he said to me. Nor have I. Until today.'

For a few moments, the only sound in the room was the peaceful ticking of a clock.

Henry broke the silence. 'Thank you.' He turned to me. 'Mystery solved.'

Johnny Joe said something in Gaelic with a great air of solemnity, like a judge pronouncing a verdict.

We waited for the translation.

'Time is a great storyteller,' said Johnny Joe.


On the way back to the hotel, we switched on the car radio. 'In the last half-hour,' said the newsreader, 'Gardai digging at a site in County Monaghan have found the remains of Brendan Murphy who disappeared in August 1981 after being taken from his home by masked men.' She paused for a moment. 'Digging continues at eight other sites near the border.'

I thought of the men in blue boiler suits; the mechanical digger clawing at the ground; the two women we had seen in the hotel. 'May he rest in peace,' I said.

'Amen,' said Henry. He made the sign of the cross. 'At least we now know where Lucy's baby is buried,' I said.

# 51

# Louise

I sat for a long while staring into the fire, letting my thoughts drift like the smoke up the chimney. I remembered Jacky saying, '*Níl aon tinteán mar do thinteán féin.*' There's no fireside like your own fireside. Michael was fond of that proverb too. Home is where the hearth is. Henry standing in front of the huge hearth at Wooldene. Big enough to roast a hundred rabbits. He had been flirting with me and I hadn't realised until later. So many things I hadn't realised. Michael already in the IRA. Mum blaming herself for Dad's death. I blamed Henry, but it wasn't his fault. Not his fault he was born in England. Not my fault I was born in Northern Ireland. Chance. I hadn't been dealt such a bad hand compared to other people. I didn't have a son shot as an informer. I hadn't had my legs blown off. I had a job, friends, family. I was an independent woman. I made my own way in the world. There was dignity in independence. Who said that? Michael. Talking about politics. Dara. 'Sure life is politics, Louise.' Out of the mouths of babes and sucklings. Henry would have smiled. Why had Henry joined the army? If Michael had been English would he have joined the army? Why did men want to be soldiers? Dad. Wanting to become more of a man. Was that what Henry thought? Henry in uniform. Unimaginable. Fleck of paint under his nail. Beautiful hands. Gentle hands. We were right for each other. Complete. And I had driven him away. Pride had not let me run after him. No, not pride. Self-protection. He might have rebuffed me. Then where would I be? And where am I now? In limbo. Waiting. A spark of hope. Better not to hope. Cold. I mustn't let the fire go out.

The telephone rang and interrupted my thoughts. A jubilant Rebecca shouted in my ear. 'It's a done deal. Crack open the champagne. We go into pre-production on Monday.'

She was unstoppably exuberant. 'I'm on my way to the airport. In a limo. I'm totally exhausted. The negotiations went on half the night. The agent threw a complete tantrum and nearly walked out. I didn't think it would happen until the last minute. I got to bed at five in the morning. I've had hardly any sleep. I'm getting by on adrenalin. I can't believe it's happening at last.' I heard the faint chink of glass on glass. 'Isn't it fantastic? Everybody loves the script.'

I didn't need to say anything. Rebecca burbled on.

'I'll take the weekend off. I'll start on Monday with a hang-over, but who cares?'

I imagined her in the back of a taxi gliding through a sunlit Los Angeles, drinking champagne.

'We'll start pre-production in London. When can we move into Wooldene? What does the contract say?' She didn't wait for an answer. 'Whatever it says, see if we can do it sooner. Wait a minute.' I heard laughter and more clinking. 'I feel as if I'm flying already. Have a great weekend, bye.'

Things move fast in the film business when you get the green light. Get the worst task out of the way first, I told myself. I telephoned Chloe. 'Could you ring Wooldene, please, Chloe? Tell them we'd like to move our office there at the end of next week.'

Mission accomplished. I had avoided speaking to Henry. Somehow, it didn't feel like success.

Chloe was almost delirious. 'Omigod. I can't believe it's really happening.' I pictured her jumping up and down, waving to her flatmates. 'I wish I had somebody here to celebrate with me.'

'Me too,' I said. 'I'm on my own here, as well.'

I telephoned Jacky and told him the good news. He whooped with joy. I heard him call out, 'It's greenlit, Teddy. Open another bottle.'

My adrenalin was flowing again. I changed my flight back to London, made some cashflow projections on the back of a Christmas card. When Siobhan returned carrying Maeve in her arms, the lights were on, the table was laid, lamb chops were roasting in the oven and I was mashing potatoes.

'Good news. It's all going ahead,' I called out.

Siobhan reached out to include me in her embrace. The three of us – Siobhan, Maeve and me – waltzed around the kitchen, squealing with delight.

Michael telephoned while Siobhan was putting Maeve to bed. I told him I had seen Teresa Murphy interviewed on television.

'She has a body to bury, at last. A good deed after a bad deed,' I said.

'There was a war on,' Michael said. 'These things happen. I'm glad for Pauline's sake.'

There was a silence. 'I've just been told the film's going ahead. I'm going straight back tomorrow morning.'

'Brilliant. I'm sorry you'll be gone when I drive down with Mum. She's in good form. I took her to the pantomime at the Opera House. First time in yonks that I've seen her having a good laugh. She's nearly herself again.'

'I was thinking the same,' I said.

'Before I forget, strange thing: remember your man, Barry Shaw? He wasn't in the pantomime.'

'Are you sure? He was only one of the thieves.'

'He wasn't even an extra. I looked in the programme. Every man and his dog was listed, including the man who played the triangle, and he only hit it twice.'

'Wasn't there a K. B. Shaw?'

'I don't remember.' A pause. 'I still didn't see anybody who looked like your man. Well, I just thought you'd want to know.'

The information unsettled me. The following morning, while I waited at the airport for my flight, I rang the Opera House. I said I was trying to contact an actor I thought was appearing in the pantomime. 'Shaw. K. B. Shaw?'

'Kieran Shaw? A wee blond chap with a moustache? They'll all be in later. Do you want to leave a wee message?'

'No message.'

I felt uneasy all through the flight to London. I told myself I was being silly. I resolved not to say anything to Rebecca. It was unlikely Barry Shaw was in London. But when my taxi pulled away from Paddington, I found myself looking back to see if another taxi was following. This is ridiculous, I told myself. I looked at my watch. Michael would be finished teaching. I might catch him at Mum's before they set out for Donegal.

I telephoned Michael as soon as I got to the flat.

'Why are you so worried about where this eejit is?' he demanded.

For a moment I felt overwhelmed by the need to tell him how Rebecca had lied in court to send Barry Shaw to prison. That knowledge weighed on me. I would have liked to share the burden and the fear. I could imagine the extent of Barry's rage at the injustice. I didn't want to think about what he might do in revenge. But I could not betray a confidence.

'Rebecca is frightened he's stalking her again. She thought she saw him over here. This kind of worry is the last thing she needs going into a production.'

'She's probably imagined it.'

'Even so. I'd like a big favour. Would you ever find out his mother's address, or telephone number, and ask her where he is?'

'What am I supposed to say? Why am I supposed to be looking for him?'

'Tell her anything. Tell her I'm looking for him in connection with the film. There's a grain of truth in that.'

'We're about to get into the car. I won't be able to do much before Monday.'

I had to be satisfied with that. I would be vigilant around the office. We should be leaving for Wooldene at the end of the week. Rebecca would be based there, safely out of the way, for the next few months.

I opened the curtains in the bedroom and lay in bed looking at the night sky. The sky had cleared. I could see the moon. Was it waxing or waning? There had been a full moon at New Year;

I was watching a waning moon. I remembered something I had read in the newspaper that morning, there would be another full moon in January. It was unusual to have two full moons in a single month. It was the origin of the expression, 'once in a blue moon'.

# 52

## Diana

I was so excited and relieved when Chloe telephoned, I could have waltzed around the kitchen.

'Three bedrooms? I can do that straight away. What else should I do?'

'If you could clear the rooms we are going to use for offices, that would be a great help, thank you,' said Chloe. 'And if you have any old tennis balls, you could cut them in half for us, please. We put them under the legs of furniture we're going to move.'

Henry came into the kitchen. I gave him the thumbs up.

'We probably have a box full of worn tennis balls somewhere,' I said to Chloe.

Henry raised an eyebrow. I put my hand over the mouth-piece. 'Telekinetic. The film. It's got the go-ahead. They're arriving next Friday.'

A range of expressions passed over Henry's face. Delight, relief, puzzlement. 'What have tennis balls got to do with it?'

'Tell you later.' I spoke into the telephone again. 'Hello? Chloe? I was just telling Henry the good news. We look forward to seeing you at Wooldene. Bye.' I replaced the receiver. 'We ought to put out the red carpet.'

'We ought to put buckets under the leaks in the roof,' Henry said.

★   ★   ★

Susan drove over with Paddy. 'He had a wonderful time chasing ducks.' She added, with only the hint of a blush, that Ronnie Bolton had invited her to spend a week with him on Antigua. Ronnie is one of the sweetest-tempered men I know. I thought he would be frightfully good for Susan.

'He's a good match for you,' I said.

'Nice to have someone to grow old with.' She glanced at me, speculatively, from under her lashes. 'What about you? What about this man you said you rather fancied?'

My heart swelled. 'We've been to dinner twice,' I confided. 'He telephones every other day.'

Susan laughed and hugged me. For a moment I felt we were schoolgirls again, swapping notes about the boys we had met in the holidays.

I collected Bill from the station in Reading the next morning. I assumed he had travelled up from the West Country. He had spent Christmas and New Year with his mother, he said. I had planned to set him digging the vacant beds in the vegetable garden, planting the greenhouse tomatoes, and cleaning the tools, but I thought most of these tasks could wait.

'You've arrived at absolutely the right time,' I told him. 'I'm going to need help to get the Hall ready for the film company. Frightfully exciting, don't you think?'

Bill seemed thrilled by this second-hand association with fame. 'Anything I can do, Mrs Wiseman.' He was almost bouncing in his seat. 'Glad to lend a hand.'

Henry, Bill and I moved all Henry's easels, canvases and painting paraphernalia from the barn to an empty storehouse at the back of the stableyard. We cleared out all the cupboards and drawers in the back kitchens of the Hall. These were to become the production offices, I explained to Bill. I switched on the storage heaters. I got three bedrooms ready in the west wing.

Henry and I tidied the grave in the walled garden in preparation for the consecration ceremony. Daphne couldn't come but said she would be with us in spirit. Peter said he would fly over from Brussels and stay with us for the rest of the week.

'He could do with a break,' Henry said. 'He's considering a job offer in London. I gather Christine isn't keen.'

I drove to The Lindens, shortly after breakfast time on Tuesday morning. I brought my mink. Geoffrey gave it to me for my fortieth birthday. It's one of the few valuables I hung on to. There isn't a big second-hand price for mink. I hadn't been wearing it because I absolutely hated being shouted at in the street. I couldn't help thinking that if I went to France I could wear it as much as I liked in the winter and nobody would yell 'murderer' or throw paint at me.

I wrapped Lucy into it. Not just for extra warmth, but for a sense of occasion. Lucy sensed it. She knew something important was happening. I placed a bunch of snowdrops in her lap. She held my hand tightly while Henry steered the wheelchair down the path through the walled garden to the grave. Father Dobson and Peter were waiting for us. The morning was cold but bright. The bark of the yew tree looked almost purple. The scarlet berries glistened with frost.

It was a simple ceremony. Father Dobson sprinkled holy water on the grave. 'O God, whose blessed Son was laid in a sepulchre in the garden: Bless, we pray, this grave, and grant that those whose bodies are buried here may dwell with Christ in paradise, and may come to your heavenly kingdom; through your Son Jesus Christ our Lord.'

Lucy's voice sang out clearly, 'Amen.'

Henry, Peter, Father Dobson and I stood, heads bowed in silence, for a few moments. I glanced at Lucy. She looked calm, not at all bewildered. She leaned forward and scattered the snowdrops on the grave. She rested back with a sigh. 'Thank you, Mummy. It was the right thing to take him home.'

We had lunch in the bungalow. Lucy had no memory of having been there before. 'This is nice,' she said, looking around.

Paddy jumped up on her knee. Lucy fondled his ears. He settled into her lap and looked up at her with soft, soulful eyes. 'What a lovely dog,' she said to me. 'Is he yours, dear?'

She had no idea who Peter was but tried to conceal it by

seizing on the fact that he lived in Brussels. 'And what is the weather like in Brussels?' she asked him, at regular intervals. 'Oh, much the same as here,' he answered patiently, every time.

Father Dobson attempted a conversation about the Christmas Day we had spent together but Lucy was embedded in a more distant past. 'Nicky's in France,' she announced, with the air of someone who has just solved a mystery. 'That's why he's not here. He's fighting Hitler.'

'Should we bring her over to the Hall?' Henry asked quietly.

I thought not. Wherever Lucy thought she was, one thing was clear. She was serene. She showed no distress, no discontent.

Henry and I drove her back to The Lindens. John had told me he was visiting his mother that afternoon, so I was slightly on edge when Henry and I followed Lucy, on her Zimmer, into the lounge. I terribly wanted John and Henry to like each other.

John stood up, his hand extended, a broad smile on his face when he saw our little procession. Henry was profuse in his thanks about the wine. He and John slipped into easy conversation. Lucy dozed in her chair. Agnes and I eyed each other. I wondered if John had told her about his interest in me.

Lucy woke with a start. She sat up in her chair and gave every impression of following a discussion about the wine regions of France. She put out her arm, tugged on my sleeve and said in a loud whisper, 'Which one of them is your husband?'

Agnes clapped her hands and laughed.

John said, 'I need your advice about something, Diana. Could I have a quick word? It will only take a moment.'

He steered me out of the room and along the corridor, away from the glass door of the lounge. I could hear a faint grumbling from the kitchen, the hum of an air-conditioner, the muffled blare of a television on the other side of the wall.

'I hadn't intended to propose to you in the corridor of a care home,' John said. 'Maybe it's a portent of things to come. I want us to be together in our old age. Diana, will you marry me?'

I had my back to the wall. What could I do but surrender?

# 53

## Louise

The days running up to our move to Wooldene were a frenzy of meetings and telephone calls. Every day I got up from my desk at hourly intervals, walked to the window and scanned the street. I never noticed anyone loitering. I became more and more certain that the Barry sightings had been the product of stress and a guilty conscience. The closer we got to our departure for Wooldene, the more relaxed I became about Barry.

But the more anxious I became about Henry. I wasn't ready to face him. I wanted to avoid him, for the first few weeks at Wooldene at least. By that time I thought I might feel calmer. Ready to be dignified and cool. Ready to apologise, even, for shouting at him. Night after night I had rehearsed such an exchange until my brain got tired and insisted on sleep.

In my imaginings, Henry and I would bump into each other in the garden or on the lane leading to the barn. I would speak first. I would say something like, 'I'm sorry things turned out the way they did. I'm sorry I shouted at you in such an un-dignified way. We must agree to differ. I realise we may bump into each other again over the course of the production. When we do so, I hope we can greet each other in a calm and friendly way.'

Henry would be stiff, but gentlemanly. Gentlemanly. That was another word I never heard used and had only read in books, but it was the word that came to mind when I tried to picture our exchange. In the worst of my imaginings, Henry would nod curtly, and walk on.

Chloe made and received all the calls from Wooldene. 'We're going up on Friday morning. Diana is giving us lunch,' she said. 'I accepted for all of us. I hope that's OK.'

I pretended to Chloe that I couldn't leave London until late on Friday. I was driving a hired van loaded with files, equipment and Jacky's design folders. I suggested that instead of coming in the van with me, Chloe should drive down with Rebecca. I would leave after seven on Friday evening, to avoid the traffic. 'Enjoy the lunch,' I said to Chloe. 'I bet Diana's a terrific cook.'

I wasn't clear of London until nearly nine o'clock. An accident on the North Circular road slowed traffic to a crawl. I was on the motorway, thinking I would at least get there by half-past ten, when my mobile rang. There wasn't a service station before my exit, so I waited until I came off the motorway before parking by the side of the road to look at the screen and see who had called me. I recognised Michael's mobile number immediately and called him back.

'I'm on the Stewartstown road,' he said. 'It's taken me all week to find her. The things I do for you. You owe me a pint at the very least for this.'

'Barry Shaw's mother,' I said.

'She'd moved house twice. I just said I was trying to get hold of him. Here's me, "Would you have a telephone number for him, Mrs Shaw?" Here's her, "He's in England." Here's me, "Would you have a telephone number in England for him?" Here's her, "It's expensive phoning him on his mobile." I eventually got his mobile number out of her.'

'Hold on.' I switched on the interior light in the van. I rummaged in my bag for a pen.

'It won't do you any good. There's no signal where he is, apparently.'

'She must have some way of contacting him.'

'She has. He has a number at work, for emergencies. I had to drag that out of her too.'

'You're a star, Michael.'

He dictated the number. I wrote it down on the back of the big production notebook I carried with me everywhere. Michael rang off. I replaced the notebook on the seat beside me and resumed my journey.

I had driven for about a mile when a sudden memory caused me to brake violently and steer the van to the side of the road. I grabbed the notebook. I didn't need to switch on the light. I could read, in the light from the dashboard, a telephone code I recognised. It was the telephone code for Wooldene.

I felt clammy. My mouth dried. I leafed back through the book but my fingers wouldn't work properly. Eventually I found the list of numbers for the production. Henry Wintour, Wooldene. It was almost the same number. Only the last digit was different. Barry Shaw was somewhere in the area. I was rigid with shock. I dialled Barry's number, not really knowing what I would say.

I didn't have to say anything.

'You have reached the shop at Wooldene Hall Herb Farm and Garden Centre.' I recognised Diana's unmistakably patrician tones. 'I am sorry we are not available to take your call. Please leave your name and number after the tone. We will return your call as soon as possible.'

I think I stopped breathing. Cars flashed past on the road. I started to shake. I sat on my hands to calm them before I put them back on the wheel. I thought of dialling 999. But what would I say? Henry. Bugger pride, I had to telephone Henry. I dialled the number. It rang for what seemed like ages.

'Henry Wintour speaking. Please leave a message for me or Diana after the tone.' It was so like Henry I nearly laughed in the midst of my fear.

I stumbled through a message. 'I think you have a madman working for you. His name is Barry Shaw. He has been stalking Rebecca. I think she's in danger. I'm on my way to Wooldene now.' I thought for a second before adding, 'This is not a joke.'

I wrenched the van into gear and headed into the night.

# 54

# Diana

On Friday evening Henry hosted a dinner to introduce John to our friends and family and celebrate what I felt both thrilled and embarrassed to call my 'engagement'.

'It makes me sound like a twenty-year-old,' I said to Susan and Vanessa as we powdered our noses in the plush and pleated splendour of the ladies' cloakroom at the Savoy.

'If Ronnie pops the question, I shall take enormous delight in talking about "my engagement" and flashing my ring without a trace of embarrassment,' said Susan. 'And you should do the same.'

I spread my hands and held them out for scrutiny. 'These are so cracked and worn from gardening, I don't want to draw attention to them by wearing diamonds. I told John I only want a plain gold band.'

'I don't think anyone will be looking at your hands,' said Vanessa. 'Your face is glowing with happiness. You might not pass for twenty, but you certainly don't look your age. Whatever it is.'

'I think it's called, "a certain age",' said Susan.

I laughed. 'I'm sixty-two,' I said. 'And I've never felt better.'

Henry proposed a champagne toast to John and me. I could see diners at the other tables looking curiously at us. John held my hand under the table. I knew I was pink with pleasure.

I let John field all the questions. When and where were we getting married? Were we going to have a reception? A honeymoon? Where were we going to live? How had our children received the news?

We were going to be married quietly in Paris at Easter. We would spend our honeymoon house-hunting in the Loire. We would have a grand party at Wooldene when the filming was over. Our children, despite their surprise at the suddenness of the announcement, had all declared they were pleased.

Catherine had said, 'Thank God. I was so worried about you, Mummy, getting old in England and me so far away. Now you have someone to look after you.'

'I'm not quite in my dotage,' I had said tartly. 'I hope you're happy for me, too.'

'I looked him up on the Internet,' she said. 'In case, you know . . .'

'In case he was some kind of fraud and I was some kind of fool?'

'No,' she said, meaning yes. 'He's got quite a big business. Carl and I were rather impressed.'

Carl had seized the telephone to wish me good luck and remind me that his eighty-year-old mother was now married for the third time, having buried two husbands, and seemed very happy in a retirement community near Santa Monica. I had thanked him and said I rather hoped this marriage would see me out.

Vanessa produced a camera and began to take photographs. I slipped out to the ladies' cloakroom to put on some lipstick. On the way back to the dining room, I caught sight of a television weather forecast. The symbol for snow was unmistakable. I stepped into the bar to hear what the forecaster was saying.

'Snow spreading from the north-east will reach high ground by midnight. The snow will gradually become heavier and cover most of the eastern counties before morning.'

A few inches of snow made the roads into our valley icy and treacherous. More than a few inches and Wooldene would be cut off. We wouldn't be able to stay up in London, as we had planned. Henry and I would have to drive back after dinner, I decided.

The party was wonderfully jolly. I didn't want to spoil it with a bad weather report. I silently nominated myself driver and restricted myself to half a glass of the rather fine burgundy which Henry had made John choose, 'Because you're the expert and I'm jolly glad about that.' Henry didn't know exactly how much John was going to pay him for the wines in the cellar but had been told it would be at least fifty thousand pounds.

John and Henry argued quietly over which of them should pay the bill. John gave in gracefully. I suspected he would add whatever outrageously large sum the dinner had cost to the cheque he would write out to Henry for Daddy's wines.

I thought myself the luckiest woman in the world.

Peter decided to come with us. He and Henry were relaxed and glowing on the way home.

'Clever old thing,' Henry said, when the first swirling snowflakes settled on the windscreen. 'Good for you, Diana. We'd have been stuck as soon as we got off the motorway.'

The snow was falling heavily as we approached the neighbour's house where we had left Paddy. Henry sat up, suddenly alert. 'Good Lord. Don't stop. This is rear-wheel drive. We mightn't get away again. We can walk over and get Paddy in the morning.'

Visibility was about fifteen feet. The snow billowed towards us. I drove into an infinity of white.

# 55

## Louise

The snow fell slowly at first, the snowflakes drifting languidly through the beam of the headlights. About two miles from Wooldene they began to fall faster, more purposefully. By the time I turned into the driveway, snow had outlined the black branches of the trees. They loomed towards me like skeletons.

Some instinct made me stop where the road turned right to run along the garden wall. I switched off the engine and the headlights. Total darkness. From somewhere in the woods I heard a harsh triple bark, followed by a scream, like an injured cat. I jumped. Calm down, I said to myself. It's only a fox. I felt around until I found the glove compartment. A tiny light came on when I opened it. I took out a torch. The beam was thin, and barely penetrated the blackness of my surroundings.

I opened the driver's door and stepped, ankle deep, into the snow. The door slid shut with a clunk. I waited, heart pounding, until my eyes adjusted to the darkness. I plodded to the wall and followed the needle of light along it. The door in the wall was open. I stepped through it and directed the torch along the path to the house. It occurred to me, in a pulse-quickening moment, that while I could not see the house, someone looking out from it would see the torch beam moving through the garden. I said a prayer and tramped on.

Snowflakes tumbled through a panel of light. I guessed the source to be a room at the side of the house. I moved towards it.

The light was coming from a gap in the curtains of a wide, mullioned window. I moved to the edge of the light and found myself backing into a hedge. My jeans clung wetly to my legs, my jacket was soaking, my feet were freezing. I shivered with cold as well as fear. I looked through a veil of snow into what I recognised as the room Diana had called the winter parlour. I could see the edges of the heavy brocade curtains, the oak table, half-covered in some kind of carpet or tapestry, candles burning in a silver candlestick.

As I watched, a man approached the window. I backed further into the hedge. He looked straight at me. It was Barry. I almost cried out. He lifted a bottle of vodka to his lips, took a slug, wiped his mouth with the back of his other hand, bent down. When he straightened again I saw he had the bottom edge of a curtain in one hand and was pouring the rest of the vodka over the brocade. He dropped the curtain and disappeared from view for a moment. He reappeared with a second bottle. He unscrewed the cap and poured the contents over the tapestry on the table. His actions seemed utterly insane and incomprehensible to me until he fished something square and white from his pocket and placed it on the tapestry. I thought it was a bar of soap. Then I realised it was a firelighter.

I thought my brain would seize up as I tried to remember the layout of the back kitchens. Come on Louise. Visualise. Yes. At least one corridor led to an outside door. Barry had his back to me. I ducked down and scuttled past the window, along the side of the house, round to the back. Light shone from an open door. The passageway was brightly lit. I tried to move quietly. I was breathing so heavily I thought Barry might hear me. Left or right? Left seemed to lead through a kitchen. To the right, doors opened off a corridor. I was suddenly aware of thumping and muffled shouts. There was a door with a key in the lock about twenty feet away, at the end of the corridor. I sprinted towards it. I turned the key, pulled open the door. Rebecca and Chloe tumbled out and almost knocked me down.

Rebecca was hysterical. 'He's here. He was stalking me. I knew it was him all along. He's a maniac.' She was sobbing, gasping for breath. 'He locked us in. I thought we would suffocate. God knows what he was going to do.'

'He's going to burn down the house,' I said. 'Quick. We have to get out of here.'

I turned to run. Barry Shaw blocked the end of the corridor. He had a gun in his hand.

# 56

# Diana

I drove Henry's old estate car like a hearse and hoped that no small animal would cross my path. I didn't dare brake as we coasted down the valley. I steered into the bend before the entrance to Wooldene and said a silent prayer of thanks as the car rolled under the archway.

'Well done, Diana,' said Henry.

At which point, a dog fox streaked through the headlights. I braked. We skidded slowly, unstoppably, into the ditch.

'Buggeration,' said Henry.

I sat in exhausted silence. Henry poked around in the glove compartment until he found a torch.

'Shanks' pony from here, I think.' Peter tried to get my door open, but he sank knee-deep into the snow. He must have gone over on his ankle. I heard him cry out in pain. Henry helped him out of the ditch. I crawled out on the passenger side. Peter was limping. Henry and I linked arms with him. We set out slowly for the bungalow.

At the turn of the driveway, Henry's torch picked out a red van.

'At least Louise got here safely,' I said. 'She was coming down after the others.'

Henry made a sort of harrumphing noise.

Peter said, 'If it snows like this all night, they'll have to dig themselves out in the morning.'

We had reached the back door of the bungalow. The spade was in a bucket of sand.

'Oh, good,' I said. 'Bill has cleaned the tools.'

I had let the stove go out. The kitchen was cold. I made Peter lie down on the sofa with his leg elevated. I improvised an icepack with a tea-towel and a bag of frozen peas.

'A whiskey would warm us all up,' I said. 'A hot toddy.'

'You certainly deserve one,' said Henry. 'You got us back in one piece. It was a bit hairy going down the hill. We were nearly in the ditch once or twice.'

'Third time lucky,' said Peter.

It was probably relief that made me laugh. 'Sorry about your ankle, Peter. But I'm awfully glad you decided to come back with us.'

'Fancied a bit of shooting?' said Henry.

'I thought I might bag something.' Peter smiled. A rather raffish smile, I thought.

Henry took a bottle of whiskey from the cupboard.

'Before you have a whiskey, Henry,' I said, 'while you still have your coat on, would you be an angel and take a spade over to the Hall? Please?'

I decided to make up a bed for Peter in the spare room before Henry came back. I had my arms full of blankets and sheets when I noticed the message light winking on the answering machine. Lucy was always at the back of my mind so I heaved the bedclothes on to one arm and pressed the playback button. Louise's frightened voice filled the hallway.

I couldn't take in what she was saying at first.

Then Peter was behind me shouting, 'Where's the key to the gun cabinet?'

# 57

# Louise

Rebecca's mouth opened in a voiceless scream. She grabbed my arm to steady herself. Chloe leaned against the wall, gasping for breath. My heart drummed in my ears. I wanted to run but I made myself stay still. A small voice inside me said, Stay calm, keep him talking. Make yourself smile. Keep your voice light. Be smooth. Be rational.

I said in as steady a voice as I could muster, 'Please put the gun down, Barry.'

'Fuck off.' He gestured with the gun. 'Get the fuck back into the storeroom. All of you.'

Rebecca uttered a low moan and gripped my arm more tightly.

Chloe said jerkily, 'This is some kind of sick joke, but it's not funny. It's horrible. Whose idea was it?'

'Not Jacky. Not Teddy. Not those mincing creeps,' said Barry. 'Blame your boss. Go on, tell her, Rebecca. Tell Chloe why I'm here.'

He knows all our names, I thought. He's showing off. He wants us to know he's been watching us for ages.

'If you set fire to the house,' I said, 'the owners will hear the smoke alarms and come running.'

'There's nobody around,' Barry said. 'They've all gone up to London. They're staying overnight. When they come back, they'll find this place burned to the ground. And you know what? You'll be blamed.' He laughed unpleasantly. 'Rowdy women, drinking vodka, knocking over candles. Tut tut. You ran away from the flames. Only you ran the wrong way. You thought the door of the storeroom was the back door.'

I was dumb with fright.

Rebecca's voice was a croak. 'I'll give you money. Compensation.'

'You stupid cow,' he hissed. 'Do you think money would satisfy me?'

'I'll telephone the police,' Rebecca said quickly. 'Now. On my mobile. I'll tell them what I did. That I set you up. That I lied in court. You can listen to me do it.'

Barry shrugged. 'There's no signal here.'

'We can use the landline.'

'I cut the landline.' He was gloating now.

I managed to speak. 'There's a telephone in the bungalow.'

Rebecca dropped my arm and put her hands up in surrender. 'I'll tell the whole world,' she said. 'Only don't hurt Louise and Chloe.'

'Then you wouldn't get blamed,' Barry said. 'I want you to get blamed for something you didn't do. Spend years in prison. Innocent. Like me. Convicted on the word of a liar. It burns you up, you know. The injustice. The unfairness.'

'This isn't justice,' I said. 'This is revenge.'

'It's both,' said Barry. 'That's the beauty of it.' He looked elated.

I risked a step forward.

'I'll shoot you, Louise.' Barry gripped the gun with both hands. He giggled. 'And then I'll burn the place down.'

My brain was racing. Say something. Anything. Not anything. Something to make him human.

'What would your mother say, Barry? She wouldn't want you to do this?'

'Fuck you! Keep my mother out of this.'

Wrong! Wrong! my brain screamed at me.

I heard Chloe's voice. Light and remarkably steady. 'If you shoot Louise, the police will know there was someone else here. Someone else to blame.'

I sensed a flicker of hesitation.

'You've worked this out terrifically well.' Chloe sounded breathlessly admiring. 'It would be a shame to spoil it.' Barry looked at her as though seeing her properly for the first time. I glanced at her. She was smiling at him.

I held my breath.

Rebecca said, 'Have your revenge on me, Barry. Shoot me. But leave Louise and Chloe out of it.'

He shook his head. 'Too late. They'd spoil the story.' But there was a hint of regret in his voice.

Chloe spoke again. 'You're awfully clever, you know. It's a great plot. It would make a great movie. You could act in it. You could be a star.'

Barry smiled. He drew himself up. His chest swelled. He swept a theatrical bow.

Rebecca sprang at him like a tiger. The gun came up. And at that exact moment, I heard a roar and a shining blade scythed through the air and caught Barry on the shoulder. The gun went off with a deafening bang. A bullet ricocheted off the ceiling. Rebecca screamed. Henry roared again and swung the spade. It hit Barry around the midriff this time. I heard his ribs crack. He fell like a stone. Henry stood over him like a gladiator.

I was vaguely conscious of Diana with a shotgun in her hands. Peter reaching for Chloe. Rebecca sliding slowly to the floor, blood staining the sleeve of her cream silk shirt. Henry saying, 'If he moves, shoot him, Diana.'

# 58

# Louise

Henry took command. He examined Rebecca's arm and pronounced, correctly as it turned out, that the bullet had smashed her upper arm bone and she was in shock. He decided, also correctly, that the spade had dislocated Barry's shoulder, had cracked one or two ribs, but had caused no life-threatening damage. He sent Peter to the bungalow to dial 999. He asked Chloe to elevate Rebecca's arm. He took over the shotgun and asked Diana to fetch bedclothes to keep Rebecca and Barry warm while we waited for the ambulance. He directed me to make hot sweet tea. He paid me no special attention. I was simply another soldier in his troop.

The police arrived. 'We'll take charge of the weapons now, Sir.' The armed response team swarmed over the Hall. The paramedics loaded Rebecca and Barry on to stretchers. A detective took statements from all of us. I sensed Henry glancing at me from time to time. Once, I looked directly back at him, but I couldn't read his expression.

The police searched the building in case Barry had hidden incendiary devices. They thought it unlikely since his modus operandi seemed to be firelighters, vodka and the curtains, but it was better to be safe. Chloe and I certainly should not sleep there, they said.

By that time it was five o'clock in the morning, and we were past sleep. Diana ushered us back to the bungalow for breakfast;

grilled sausages and bacon, scrambled eggs and toast. Henry looked up from his plate occasionally to smile genially at the table in general. There was no special smile for me. My feet were cold from tramping through the snow. I was tired. Chloe and Peter were bright-eyed, questioning me, trying to impose a narrative on the jumbled events of the night. They wanted the backstory.

I told them how Barry had stalked Rebecca in Belfast. How she had told me he was stalking her again and I thought she had imagined it. How my brother had discovered – can it only have been a few hours previously? – that Barry wasn't in Belfast. How I had realised Barry was at Wooldene.

Henry was watching me, listening intently. I didn't dare look directly at him.

'I didn't know she'd set him up. Not until a few weeks ago. She told me just before Christmas,' I said. 'I didn't know how to react.'

Diana said gently, 'That's a big burden to carry. How awful for you, Louise.'

'Hard to know what to do if a friend dumps something like that on you,' said Peter.

Chloe said, 'I wouldn't have known what to do, or say.' Her head was resting on Peter's shoulder. She smiled at me.

I felt suddenly exhausted, but curiously lighter too. Almost light-headed.

'You knew what to say to Barry. You were amazing, Chloe,' I said. 'You took exactly the right line with him.'

'I could tell he was vain,' she said. 'He plucked his eyebrows.'

'Well done.' Another wave of tiredness hit me.

'You kept him talking, Louise. Gave me time to think.'

'You saved us, Chloe.'

'Rebecca saved us,' she said. 'It was brave of her to jump on him like that. She could have been killed.'

'We could all have been killed.' I started to shake.

The next thing I knew, my feet were resting on a hot water bottle and Henry was tucking me into bed. I seemed to be wearing striped pyjamas that were several sizes too big for me. Men's pyjamas. I tried to lift my head from the pillow. Tried to say, 'We need to talk, Henry.' But I was drifting, sliding into deep, dreamless sleep.

When I made my way to the kitchen, sometime in the early afternoon, Diana was sweeping the floor. Chloe and Peter were sitting at the table, drinking coffee. The spaniel was slumbering in his basket by the fire. Henry was at the sink, washing up. The fevered atmosphere of the night had dissipated. Everything seemed incongruously normal. I wondered if I had imagined Henry tucking me into bed. But I hadn't imagined the pyjamas, now draped over a chair in what was obviously Henry's bedroom.

There was a chorus of good mornings, laughingly changed into good afternoons.

Henry turned to greet me. 'Did you find everything you need? Clean towel and so on?'

'Yes, thank you. And thank you for giving up your bed,' I said awkwardly.

There was a pause.

'I ought to ring the hospital,' I said. 'Find out about Rebecca.'

'She's fine,' said Chloe. 'I rang this morning. She was a bit sleepy after the anaesthetic. She wanted to get back to work.'

I was filled with a sad fondness. 'That's Rebecca. She won't let anything or anyone defeat her.'

Diana put aside the brush and asked Peter and Chloe to come with her to the Hall to help take down the curtains. 'They stink of alcohol. I want to take them to the cleaners before it starts snowing again. Henry will get you something to eat, Louise.'

When they had gone, Henry and I stood looking at each other for what seemed like ages. The words I had rehearsed – sorry, agree to differ, the production, would have to meet, calm and friendly – floated around my brain but refused to form themselves into a sentence.

'That night, after the party,' I began, 'I shouldn't have shouted at you. I'm sorry. I was drunk. I would have said things differently sober.'

'You're sober now,' said Henry. 'Say what you like.'

I told him about Dad's heart attack, Mum's depression, Michael's arrest. It flowed out of me in a calm steady stream.

'I'm sorry about your father,' Henry said gently.

'Thank you.' I felt peaceful and tired at the same time.

'Do you remember the raid on our house?' I asked. 'Were you one of the soldiers?'

Henry shook his head. 'I just oversaw operations. Handled the intelligence, made decisions. Made mistakes.' His voice was steady. He met my gaze directly. 'It was a very dirty war.'

'I know,' I said.

'I did what I thought was right.'

'So did my brother.'

'Yes,' said Henry. He paused. 'Maybe I'll meet him under better circumstances some day.'

The room seemed brighter. As though a cloud had moved to let the sunlight in.

'It's getting better now, isn't it? All that,' Henry hesitated, searched for the right word, settled on a sweeping gesture, 'stuff. Being sorted out. Things changing. There's hope, isn't there?' He took a step towards me. His face was full of yearning. 'Is there hope for me as well?'

I held out my arms in response. We rediscovered the magic of touch. We talked to each other that afternoon as the hand talks to the glove.

It was dusk when we walked through the gate into the garden and stood for a moment looking at the Hall. A fresh fall of snow had covered the footprints along the paths and across the front garden. It was as though everything had been smoothed over, made new again. Lights blazed from every window. The house seemed to be alive, beckoning to us. I tugged at Henry's hand.

'Come on,' I said. 'There's a film to make.'

# 59

# Louise

Henry and I were married in a civil ceremony as soon as the film was completed. Father Dobson gave us a blessing but Henry still felt he had excluded himself from the club. Diana said, in her kind way, 'They wrote the rules when girls married at fourteen and were dead at forty. Mrs Price at Beech Farm has just buried her third husband. She was married to each of them for twenty-five years. I was married to Geoffrey for twenty-five years. I hope I will be married to John for longer. I hope you will have a very long life with Henry.'

Rebecca took a day out from post-production to go to court. She was given a two-year suspended sentence for perjury. Robert defended her. They married as soon as *Kenilworth* was released. It was a minor success. I haven't seen Rebecca since the premiere. She and Robert moved to New York. We exchange Christmas cards.

Barry Shaw was sectioned under the Mental Health Act. He was transferred to Carstairs Hospital in South Lanarkshire, and then to a secure unit in Purdysburn in County Antrim, to make it easier for his mother to visit him.

Diana and John bought a house in France. They didn't use it much while Diana's aunt Lucy and John's mother were still alive. Lucy died in 1999. John's mother died a year later. Diana and John began spending their winters in Nice and their summers in England. They are probably strolling along the Promenade des Anglais about now.

Mum moved to Donegal with Michael and Siobhan. Noreen and Austin bought a holiday home about ten miles away. 'Not as ugly as most of them,' Michael conceded. I think he is secretly glad. Mum is happier because she sees more of her grandchildren and because I am settled at last.

Mum was disappointed I couldn't be married in church. But she likes Henry. 'Your dad would have liked him too,' she said. Noreen and Rosemary are a little in awe of him.

For a couple of years, Henry and Michael moved warily around each other, like boxers in a ring. Then one winter, Michael took Henry rough-shooting near Ballybofey. I don't know what they said to each other as they tramped over the hills but there was a definite thaw. They've been easier in each other's company since then. There's some kind of irony in that.

When our twins, Conor and Harry, were born, I left the film industry and took over Diana's business. 'Why not?' I said to Henry. 'I'm an accountant, after all.' I do a good line in organic boxes, home delivered.

Chloe and Peter live in California, not far from Peter's cousin, Catherine, and her family. He and Chloe formed a production company. They successfully pitched a film to Hollywood about a female pyromaniac who targets men who reject her.

Jacky and Teddy have defied all predictions and stayed together. They came to see us at Christmas. We talked about *Kenilworth* and how it had changed all our lives. We marvelled at the changes in Northern Ireland.

'We shouldn't be surprised,' Jacky said. 'The unfinished business, the big quarrel, was always between England and Ireland. As soon as the two governments talked to each other like equals, made an agreement, the secondary quarrel was bound to be resolved one way or another.'

'Hindsight is a great gift, Jacky,' I said.

Later that night, when Jacky and Teddy had gone back to London and the twins were in bed, Henry and I settled down in front of the fire in the winter parlour.

'When you were talking politics to Jacky, I was trying to remember something that old boy, Siobhan's cousin, said to Diana and me about time and stories,' said Henry. 'I think it's an old Irish saying. He said it in Gaelic as well.'

'*Is maith an scéalai an aimsir,*' I said. 'Time is a great storyteller.'

Wooldene Hall
15 January, 2008

| | | | | | | | | | |
|---|---|---|---|---|---|---|---|---|---|
| 1 | 21 | 41 | 61 | 81 | 101 | 121 | 141 | 161 | 181 |
| 2 | 22 | 42 | 62 | 82 | 102 | 122 | 142 | 162 | 182 |
| 3 | 23 | 43 | 63 | 83 | 103 | 123 | 143 | 163 | 183 |
| 4 | 24 | 44 | 64 | 84 | 104 | 124 | 144 | 164 | 184 |
| 5 | 25 | 45 | 65 | 85 | 105 | 125 | 145 | 165 | 185 |
| 6 | 26 | 46 | 66 | 86 | 106 | 126 | 146 | 166 | 186 |
| 7 | 27 | 47 | 67 | 87 | 107 | 127 | 147 | 167 | 187 |
| 8 | 28 | 48 | 68 | 88 | 108 | 128 | 148 | 168 | 188 |
| 9 | 29 | 49 | 69 | 89 | 109 | 129 | 149 | 169 | 189 |
| 10 | 30 | 50 | 70 | 90 | 110 | 130 | 150 | 170 | 190 |
| 11 | 31 | 51 | 71 | 91 | 111 | 131 | 151 | 171 | 191 |
| 12 | 32 | 52 | 72 | 92 | 112 | 132 | 152 | 172 | 192 |
| 13 | 33 | 53 | 73 | 93 | 113 | 133 | 153 | 173 | 193 |
| 14 | 34 | 54 | 74 | 94 | 114 | 134 | 154 | 174 | 194 |
| 15 | 35 | 55 | 75 | 95 | 115 | 135 | 155 | 175 | 195 |
| 16 | 36 | 56 | 76 | 96 | 116 | 136 | 156 | 176 | 196 |
| 17 | 37 | 57 | 77 | 97 | 117 | 137 | 157 | 177 | 197 |
| 18 | 38 | 58 | 78 | 98 | 118 | 138 | 158 | 178 | 198 |
| 19 | 39 | 59 | 79 | 99 | 119 | 139 | 159 | 179 | 199 |
| 20 | 40 | 60 | 80 | 100 | 120 | 140 | 160 | 180 | 200 |

| | | | | | | | | | |
|---|---|---|---|---|---|---|---|---|---|
| 201 | 216 | 231 | 246 | 261 | 276 | 291 | 306 | 321 | 336 |
| 202 | 217 | 232 | 247 | 262 | 277 | 292 | 307 | 322 | 337 |
| 203 | 218 | 233 | 248 | 263 | 278 | 293 | 308 | 323 | 338 |
| 204 | 219 | 234 | 249 | 264 | 279 | 294 | 309 | 324 | 339 |
| 205 | 220 | 235 | 250 | 265 | 280 | 295 | 310 | 325 | 340 |
| 206 | 221 | 236 | 251 | 266 | 281 | 296 | 311 | 326 | 341 |
| 207 | 222 | 237 | 252 | 267 | 282 | 297 | 312 | 327 | 342 |
| 208 | 223 | 238 | 253 | 268 | 283 | 298 | 313 | 328 | 343 |
| 209 | 224 | 239 | 254 | 269 | 284 | 299 | 314 | 329 | 344 |
| 210 | 225 | 240 | 255 | 270 | 285 | 300 | 315 | 330 | 345 |
| 211 | 226 | 241 | 256 | 271 | 286 | 301 | 316 | 331 | 346 |
| 212 | 227 | 242 | 257 | 272 | 287 | 302 | 317 | 332 | 347 |
| 213 | 228 | 243 | 258 | 273 | 288 | 303 | 318 | 333 | 348 |
| 214 | 229 | 244 | 259 | 274 | 289 | 304 | 319 | 334 | 349 |
| 215 | 230 | 245 | 260 | 275 | 290 | 305 | 320 | 335 | 350 |